SWEET BETRAYAL

LAUREN WILDE

ZEBRA BOOKS
KENSINGTON PUBLISHING CORP.

To my brother, James, with Love

ZEBRA BOOKS

are published by

Kensington Publishing Corp.
475 Park Avenue South
New York, NY 10016

First printing: February, 1990

Printed in the United States of America

A BARGAIN SEALED

"I want to become your mistress," Anita said calmly.

Adam knew that it was insanity, that he should refuse, but his mind was no longer in control. In a voice ragged with desire, he asked, "When would our alliance begin? This minute?"

A victorious flicker appeared in Anita's dark eyes and then vanished. "If you wish."

Slowly, Adam stepped forward and cupped the back of her head, his mouth descending on hers in an endless demanding kiss as he molded her soft body to his hard length.

As he plundered her sweetness, his lips against hers, a shiver of delight ran through Anita. She had never expected the desire he would awaken in her with his sensuous caresses on her back, her hips, his warm mouth playing and coaxing over hers . . . she had never believed him capable of such gentleness — of such passion. She had made a terrible mistake.

Anita opened her mouth to tell Adam she wanted out of their arrangement, but with his touch he was robbing her mind of that thought . . . and all others. . . .

HISTORICAL ROMANCES BY VICTORIA THOMPSON

BOLD TEXAS EMBRACE (2835, $4.50)

Art teacher Catherine Eaton could hardly believe how stubborn Sam Connors was! Even though the rancher's young stepbrother was an exceptionally talented painter, Sam forbade Catherine to instruct him, fearing that art would make a sissy out of him. Spunky and determined, the blond schoolmarm confronted the muleheaded cowboy . . . only to find that he was as handsome as he was hard-headed and as desirable as he was dictatorial. Before long she had nearly forgotten what she'd come for, as Sam's brash, breathless embrace drove from her mind all thought of anything save wanting him . . .

TEXAS BLONDE (2183, $3.95)

When dashing Josh Logan resuced her from death by exposure, petite Felicity Morrow realized she'd never survive rugged frontier life without a man by her side. And when she gazed at the Texas rancher's lean hard frame and strong rippling muscles, the determined beauty decided he was the one for her. To reach her goal, feisty Felicity pretended to be meek and mild: the only kind of gal Josh proclaimed he'd wed. But after she'd won his hand, the blue-eyed temptress swore she'd quit playing his game — and still win his heart!

ANGEL HEART (2426, $3.95)

Ever since Angelica's father died, Harlan Snyder had been angling to get his hands on her ranch, the Diamond R. And now, just when she had an important government contract to fulfill, she couldn't find a single cowhand to hire on — all because of Snyder's threats. It was only a matter of time before she lost the ranch. . . . That is, until the legendary gunfighter Kid Collins turned up on her doorstep, badly wounded. Angelica assessed his firmly muscled physique and stared into his startling blue eyes. Beneath all that blood and dirt he was the handsomest man she had ever seen, and the one person who could help her beat Snyder at his own game — if the price were not too high. . . .

Available wherever paperbacks are sold, or order direct from the Publisher. Send cover price plus 50¢ per copy for mailing and handling to Zebra Books, Dept. 2889, 475 Park Avenue South, New York, N.Y. 10016. Residents of New York, New Jersey and Pennsylvania must include sales tax. DO NOT SEND CASH.

Prologue

The town of Reynosa, Mexico, baked in the searing summer sun. Heat waves radiated from the parched ground and the flat roofs of the small adobe buildings scattered along the muddy, sluggish water of the Rio Grande. Not a breath of air stirred, nor man or animal. Only a solitary horned toad found the energy to flick its tongue out to catch an ant scurrying across the dusty main street.

Suddenly, a band of riders came down on the town, their horses' hooves thundering and shaking the ground. Torn from their lethargy, the Mexican inhabitants who had been lazily dozing in the sun dove for the cover of their homes, bolting the doors behind them, and the town dogs barked furiously, while the small American garrison of soldiers stationed in the town hurried here and there to fortify themselves for what they thought was a Mexican attack.

Once inside the town, the riders slowed their

horses and trotted down the main street, looking surly and mean-eyed, their reins jingling and the leather of their worn saddles creaking. Every man was armed to the teeth, a pistol strapped on each hip, a saber hanging from the front of his saddle, a huge Patterson Colt in a saddle holster on each side of his mount, a short rifle in yet another scabbard, a Bowie knife strapped to his boot, and a tomahawk hanging from his belt—an awesome arsenal of weapons. Yes, these were fighting men, but not the Mexicans that the Americans had been expecting. They were General Zachary Taylor's best fighters, his elite scouts and advance troops. But they wore no uniforms, for they were Texas Rangers in the service of the Federal government.

The Rangers had just spent ten grueling days deep behind the enemy's lines and had traveled no less than two hundred and fifty miles over some of Mexico's most rugged, most arid terrain, not once taking off their coats, boots, or spurs. Their clothes were stained and mud-splattered, ripped in some places where they had tangled with the thick, thorny mesquite brush, and every man who didn't normally wear a beard was sporting a ten-day growth of bristles on his lower face. They looked like hell and smelled to high heaven.

The lieutenant in charge of the American garrison rushed out into the street and intercepted the man at the head of the horsemen, saying, "Why didn't you warn us who you were, Captain McCulloch? We've been expecting an attack from General Canales. We could have shot you, riding in so sudden like that."

McCulloch's dark, weathered face was a mask,

showing no emotion, but the captain's hat was pushed back on his forehead—a sure sign that McCulloch was in a foul mood, as each and every Texan present knew. The Rangers held their breaths, feeling a little sorry for the fresh-mouthed, green lieutenant who didn't know any better than to tangle with their captain.

A silence hovered ominously over the motley group of Rangers; even the town dogs sensed the danger and stopped their yapping, cowering with their tails between their legs. Mexican spectators who had curiously emerged from their houses ducked back into them and again barred their doors. Looking up into McCulloch's dark, piercing eyes, the lieutenant's hair rose on his nape and sweat popped out on his forehead.

Then McCulloch sidestepped his horse and, without a word to the officer, rode on, his company of Rangers following, their horses' hooves beating a steady clip-clop on the packed dirt.

As they passed, one soldier whispered to another standing beside him, "So that's the famous Texas Rangers. You sure could have fooled me. They look like a bunch of wild outlaws."

"I heard the Mexicans call them *los Diablos Tejanos,* the Texas Devils," the second soldier whispered back.

The first soldier took a closer look at one of the Rangers riding by. Dressed entirely in black, his lips set in a thin, angry line across his deeply tanned face and his green eyes glittering with fury, he looked even more dangerous than the others. The soldier could feel the Texan's animal savagery coming from him in powerful waves. A shiver ran over the soldier before he whispered to his companion, "Yeah, I see what the Mexicans mean. That one does look like the devil himself."

Chapter 1

"Well, I guess our boys will show these Meskin bastards a thing or two today. We'll teach those greasers not to mess with us Rangers."

Adam Prescott glanced over at the huge man who had made the boast and was standing next to him beside the dusty main street that ran through the sun-baked town of Reynosa. With his massive body, his thick shaggy hair and bushy beard and eyebrows, Buck Jones did look rather like a bear, something that the other Texas Rangers had often said about his friend, but Adam had never noticed before. The coal-black eyes sitting amid all that ginger-colored hair only enhanced the resemblance, as did the glowering expression on Buck's face, or what you could see of it, that is. At six-foot-two, Adam matched his friend's height but came nowhere close to equaling Buck's breadth. Except for his exceptionally broad shoulders, Adam was slim built, all sinewy muscle over a long frame. The only man Adam had every seen that was bigger than Buck was the Ranger giant, Big Foot Wallace.

"Yes," Adam responded a little tardily, "if our boys win these races today, maybe these bastards here in Reynosa will stop taunting us with threats that General Canales is going to attack us some night and slit our throats."

At the mention of General Canales, the "Chaparral Fox," Buck's big body stiffened. The general was a totally unprincipled officer of the Mexican Army who led a group of irregulars who spent the better part of their time robbing and murdering along the Texas border, nothing but common bandits who hid under the guise of soldiers. It was Canales and his band of cutthroats that had raided Adam's ranch and caused the death of his wife, Canales who had been one of Adam's brother's jailers when his brother had been taken hostage by a Mexican military force that had invaded the Texas republic four years before.

Buck slashed a glance at Adam and saw his friend's eyes blazing like green fire, his lips set in a thin, angry line, the scar on his forehead, which disappeared in his thick raven hair, a jagged white line against his deeply tanned face. Buck could feel the hatred coming from the tall, rugged Ranger in powerful waves. Buck didn't blame Adam for his strong feelings. He had lost a brother at the Goliad massacre himself. Almost everyone in the new state of Texas had lost a friend or relative in the fight for independence from Mexico or during the long, bloody ten years that Texas had walked alone, denied annexation by the very country that had encouraged her revolt. Too poor to afford a standing army, Texas had turned to the only men she had for protection, the Texas Rangers. Strictly volunteers, rarely numbering over a hundred men at one time, the Rangers were the only thing that stood between the Comanches to the west and the Mexicans to the south, both nations committed to the destruction of the newly founded republic. Thanks to the new five-shot Patterson Colts, the Rangers were finally getting the upper hand over the Indians, but the Mexicans were an entirely different matter. They raided across the border with impunity, sometimes under the Mexican flag, sometimes not, murdering, looting, raping, plundering. Pitted against the superior Mexican Army that was considered to be one of the best in the world, always grossly outnumbered, the best the Rangers could do was skirmish with the Mexicans. Never able to hit back at their enemies in force, the Texans' frustration fed their anger. Thirsting for a revenge that had never been completely satisfied, their rage welled deep within them, a hatred that was ready to erupt. Buck was one of them. Adam was one of them. And now that the United States had declared war on Mexico, they could finally strike back. Yes, they had an old score to settle with the Mexicans. Not just Canales, but every damn Mexican in Mexico.

"We ain't afraid of Canales and his cutthroats," Buck threw back. "Hell, we were out there looking for him in that desert for over a week, but the wily old fox slipped away from us. We'd love nothing better than to have him come riding in here."

Adam recalled the long, futile search for their old enemy, feeling frustration boiling up along with his seething hatred for the general and his bloodthirsty bandits. General Taylor had sent Ben McCulloch and his company of Rangers to scout the Linares Road as a possible route to Monterrey, the next American objective to conquering northern Mexico. The Rangers could have told Taylor that the route was too rugged and arid for his big army to transverse in the scorching summer heat, but they didn't bother. The Texans had heard rumors that Canales and his band were recruiting in the area and saw no reason why they couldn't conduct a little unfinished state business while performing their role as Taylor's elite scouts. As soon as they had confirmed that the water holes to Linares were dry, they had searched the area for the Chaparral Fox. For two days, they had gone without water under the searing sun, their throats parched, their lips cracked, so dehydrated that they could no longer perspire. They were almost mad with thirst before they finally found a water hole. And then, perversely, a thunderstorm had swept through the area that night and wiped out Canales's trail. The Rangers had rode into Reynosa two days later, seething with anger, and since their arrival, had been taunted by the Mexican population with threats of Canales. God, how he wished that bastard *would* show his face! Adam would give anything to get his hands on the Chaparral Fox.

"Looks like they're forming the race at the other end of town," Buck said, squinting his eyes as he gazed into the bright morning sunlight. "Let's mosey down there and watch."

"We're not interested in the beginning of the race," Adam answered, "just the end. Let's walk to the finish line. We can get a better view there in the wide open."

The two men walked through the crowd of Mexicans gathering for the race outside their adobe buildings, the pistols strapped on each hip slapping ominously against their thighs. The Mexicans scurried out of the path of the dangerous-looking, mean-eyed pair, one looking like a huge lumbering bear and the other, in his dark clothing, like a sleek, green-eyed panther stalking his prey. It wasn't until they had passed that the Mexicans shot surly looks at the two towering Rangers' backs, muttering contemptuously but always carefully under their breaths, *"Diablos Tejanos!"*

"What's this holiday the greasers are celebrating today?" Buck asked Adam.

"San Juan's Day. But I understand this isn't going to be an ordinary horse race. The object is to get a chicken from one point to the other without your opponents snatching it from you. Whoever crosses the finish line with the chicken is the winner."

The two Rangers came to an abrupt halt, their path barred by four rough-looking Mexicans glaring at them insolently with their black eyes. Adam and Buck recognized the four as some of the Mexicans who had been particularly insulting and bothersome and glared back. It became a silent contest of wills, the seconds ticking by into minutes. Then Adam and Buck reached out simultaneously and roughly shoved the men out of their way.

Buck and Adam continued their walk without once glancing over their shoulders, both knowing that their unconcern for protecting their backs was the ultimate insult to the Mexicans who had just challenged them. As they walked down the side of the

13

dusty street, Buck spied three soldiers standing in front of a cantina across from them. Seeing the looks of shocked disapproval on the trio's faces, Buck said in a disgusted voice, "Well, I guess they'll go running to their commanding officer now and tell him that we Rangers have been mistreating the innocent civilians in Reynosa again." Buck snorted, saying, "Hell, there ain't no innocent civilians in Reynosa. If they ain't riding with the bandits raiding Texas, they're selling their plunder, especially the hides from stolen Texas cattle. Noel told me he saw a whole stack of hides with his brand on them in one of the stores here. Saw a couple of yours, too. Christ, the whole town ain't nothing but a nest of thieving cutthroats!"

"The Americans don't understand the Mexicans. They don't know they're like the Indians, that the only thing they respect is strength," Adam answered, his voice tinged with bitterness. "Nor do they hate the Mexicans like we do. Their emotions aren't involved in this war, like ours and the Mexicans' are. The soldiers in the regular army came down here to fight because they were ordered to by a government lusting for land, and the volunteers came for glory and excitement."

"Lusting for the land?" Buck asked in an outraged voice. "Are you talking about that territory between the Nueces River and the Rio Grande? Hell, that land belongs to the United States, just like it has to Texas for ten years now. I was at San Jacinto when Santa Anna agreed with Houston to set the border between us and Mexico at the Rio Grande. And if you don't believe me, you just ask McCulloch. Ben was there, too. He was in charge of the Twin Sisters,

14

those cannons the people of Cincinnati sent us."

"Yes, I know, but Mexico never recognized Texas's independence. Santa Anna fell from power shortly thereafter and the Mexican government refused to honor his agreement with Houston. Santa Anna himself later repudiated the treaty. He claimed the entire Treaty of Velasco was invalid, since he signed it under duress, that Houston's men were threatening to kill him if he didn't."

"You're goddamned right we were threatening to kill him!" Buck said angrily. "And if it hadn't been for Houston, we would have strung him up right then and there. That dirty bastard had it coming for what he did at the Alamo and Goliad. Why, he ain't nothing but a cold-blooded murderer, giving the men at the Alamo no quarter, then massacring the prisoners of war at Goliad."

"I agree heartily. You know how strongly I feel about Santa Anna. But the point is Mexico never recognized Texas as a free republic. As far as they're concerned, Texas is still a part of Mexico, albeit a rebellious state, but still a Mexican state. And that state's southern boundary has always been the Nueces River. Besides, when I said lusting after the land, I wasn't referring to the disputed territory. President Polk has his eyes on much more than that. He wants California and the New Mexico Territory, too. That's what this war is really about, and not Texas's annexation, or its disputed boundary."

Buck frowned. He vaguely remembered Adam telling him that the United States had tried to buy California and the New Mexico Territory for twenty-five million dollars. God almighty! He hadn't known there was that much money in the whole world! And the Mexican government was downright stupid to refuse the offer. Hell, their government was almost as broke as the Texas government, and they'd probably lose California and New Mexico anyway. Both were on the verge of revolting, at least, according to Adam.

Buck shot Adam an admiring glance from beneath his shaggy eyebrows. He hadn't known a thing about national and international politics until he had met Adam eight years before. Raised in the western hills of Georgia, he had been poorly educated, wise in frontier ways, but otherwise a simple man. But Adam had come from a well-to-do South Carolina family and had received an excellent education, had even studied law and passed the bar. Buck had never fully understood what "passing the bar" entailed, but he had a deep respect for Adam's education, almost to the point of reverence, and was still amazed that such an intelligent man like Adam would choose an ignorant old cuss like him for a friend. But that's what they were, Buck thought proudly, neighboring ranchers in Texas and best friends.

The two Rangers left the adobe-lined street and strolled into an open area that was studded with cactus and low mesquite brush, then weaved their way through the mixed crowd of Mexicans and American soldiers that were waiting for the races to begin. In the distance, the Rio Grande looked like a glittering silver ribbon winding its way through the brown countryside.

As they passed by another group of soldiers, Adam saw one eyeing Buck's coonskin cap with

16

obvious distaste. The moth-eaten fur blended in with Buck's hair and made his big head appear even larger, and the other Rangers frequently teased Buck about the unusually long, ringed tail, saying that Buck looked like he had a pigtail hanging down his back. Buck had worn the cap at the Battle of San Jacinto and considered it his talisman, and he never went on Ranger business without his lucky hat, even sleeping in it at night if he feared an attack. Adam himself had been taken aback by the filthy-smelling thing the first time he had seen it, but guessing the soldier was thinking the same thing made him feel defensive in his friend's behalf. He shot the man a murderous look over his shoulder that made the poor soldier's face pale and his knees quake.

"Did you see the way that soldier sneered at us when we walked past him?" Buck asked, having no idea that it was his cap the soldier had been eyeing. "That's what I mean. It ain't just the way they criticize us for how we treat the Meskins. Seems like no matter what we do, Taylor's army looks down on us Rangers. You remember when we arrived in Matamoros and had to camp beside the Rio Grande? The Army didn't bother to give us tents or camp utensils. We had to make huts out of palm leaves to keep off the scorching sun and heavy rains, and then they had the audacity to say our camp looked like a Hottentot village. I know we Rangers have always provided our own weapons and ammunition, and we ain't never had no uniforms or pay, but it does seem like the Army could have given us tents like the other volunteers."

"From what I've heard, those tents are so moth-eaten they leak like sieves, and I wouldn't wear one of those wool uniforms, even if they gave me one. They must be hotter than hell."

"Yeah, seems pretty stupid to send an army to fight in Mexico in wool uniforms, but still it seems like they could have given us something to protect us from the elements. We'd still be out in the open if we hadn't found that old deserted gin house here in Reynosa, and the soldiers are still criticizing us, saying we live like a bunch of savages."

"They say that because we shelter our horses inside the gin house, too, that we take more pains with their appearance and well-being than our own."

"Well, hell yes, we take care of our mounts," Buck spat. "The condition of a man's horse can make the difference between life and death."

"They're not used to living on the frontier like we are. They've never seen a horde of Indians or Mexican bandits coming down on them. They can't understand our preoccupation with our mounts, or our weapons."

"Well then, they're just plain stupid! Every Ranger knows the rule for survival is first take care of your mount, then your weapons, and last the man. Those fool greenhorns don't know nothing!"

"No, they don't know a damn thing about survival," Adam agreed. "But what in the hell do you care what they think of us?"

"Well, it just seems like they could show us a little more respect. In Texas, when a group of Rangers ride in, the whole town comes out and greets them. Ain't nothing too good for us Rangers. But ever since we came down here, we've been treated like dirt. Hell, we've been doing all the work while they've been sitting on their asses. We've been the ones out scouting, taking Mexican villages and capturing herds of cattle to feed them, or at least Hays's company of Rangers has. I'm getting damn tired of being treated like I'm the scum of the earth. If they'd been out scouting for weeks at a time under that hot sun with no water to even drink, much less bathe in, they wouldn't look so hot themselves. And yet, they're always saying how dirty and unkempt we are."

"The hell with what they think!" Adam spat. "We didn't come down here to win any beauty contest. We came down here to kill Mexicans!"

"Yeah, but still . . . " Buck's voice trailed off.

Adam shook his head in exasperation. Personally, he didn't give a damn what the men in Taylor's army thought of him. Most of them were nothing but Yankees anyway. But Buck, despite his size and rough exterior, was a sensitive man at heart. He wanted to be liked and respected by his new fellow countrymen. In truth, most of the Rangers resented the Americans' contemptuous attitude. They were accustomed to being treated with admiration by the Texans they so valiantly defended, people who put more stock in a man's deeds than his appearance. No, the Americans couldn't begin to understand how the Texans thought or what they felt.

Adam glanced across at Buck. The giant's expression was darkly brooding. "Cheer up," Adam said, hoping to ease his friend's hurt. "By the time this war is over, we'll teach both the Americans and the Mexicans to have more respect for us."

"Yeah," Buck answered, his face lighting up with

expectation. "We'll show 'em what we Texans are made of. Starting today! Our boys will win every damn chicken race. Ain't a greaser in Mexico that can outride a Ranger."

"Which of our boys is riding in the first race?" Adam asked.

"Clinton DeWitt."

Adam nodded in satisfaction at the Rangers' first choice to pit his riding skills against the Mexicans, then came to a stop and gazed down the two-mile course where the race would take place, saying, "This looks like a good spot to watch." Adam squinted, peering into the distance, then said, "If I'm not mistaken, that's DeWitt mounting up right now."

As the Ranger mounted at the starting line and accepted the chicken, the whole populace of Reynosa jeered him. Undaunted, DeWitt spurred his horse and set out at a breakneck speed down the dusty, rutted street, flying past the adobe buildings that lined both sides, followed by a band of screaming Mexican horsemen. Adam and Buck yelled encouragement as DeWitt came barreling down the road, dodging his opponents that darted out from the sides of the street right and left, then pulling ahead of them. Just as the Ranger and his horse burst into the open, a finely mounted Mexican suddenly flew at him from behind the last house and seized the chicken from the surprised Ranger. A deafening cheer came from the Mexicans all around.

"Dammit!" Buck spat. "If that ain't just like a sneaky greaser. What in the hell was he doing hiding behind that house? Why wasn't he with the others, like he was supposed to be?"

20

"You didn't expect them to play fair, did you?" Adam answered in a tight voice. "Besides, DeWitt isn't beaten yet. Look!"

Adam and Buck watched breathlessly as DeWitt spurred his horse and tore after the Mexican with the chicken. Soon the Ranger had brought his mount up to the Mexican's so that their horses were racing side by side. Standing in his stirrups, DeWitt reached across, grabbed the Mexican by the neck, and threw the startled man to the ground, catching the chicken in the other hand as the Mexican fell. Then DeWitt raced his horse across the goal line, holding the limp chicken above his head and giving a triumphant yell.

Stunned by the unexpected defeat at their own game, a silence fell over the crowd of Mexicans watching the race. Adam and Buck grinned smugly.

"Un Tejano muy bravo," a female voice said from behind Adam and Buck.

The words were not meant as a compliment. They were dripping with sarcasm. Adam whirled angrily, expecting to see one of the street women who enjoyed taunting the Rangers, since the voice had had a throaty, seductive quality about it. What he saw took him by surprise. A young woman, hardly more than a slip of a girl, stood defiantly before him, as well dressed in her dark-blue riding outfit as any of the young ladies he had known in South Carolina. But there the resemblance to a dainty southern belle ended. No southern woman of quality had skin the color of golden honey, cheeks flushed like sun-kissed peaches, lips the color of rich red wine, hair so black that it shone with a bluish luster. Hers was an exotic beauty that didn't subtly tease and tantalize but hit a man's senses squarely, stunning Adam and taking his breath away.

Before Adam could recover, a distinguished, silver-haired man stepped up to the girl. Adam gave the man a quick appraising glance, noting his stately bearing and his black charro suit, the tight pants and short jacket elaborately decorated with silver threads.

"Anita!" the man whispered in an urgent, frightened voice. Taking the girl by the elbow, he tried to pull her back from the two dangerous-looking men towering over her.

Anita jerked her arm away, her flashing black eyes locked on Adam's rugged face, saying, "No, Grandfather! I am not afraid of these *Diablos Tejanos*. They may intimidate others, but they do not frighten me. They are nothing but little boys who play childish games, hiding behind their big guns."

Adam's green eyes narrowed menacingly at both the girl's words and her contemptuous stare. When the girl didn't cower under his murderous gaze, a look that usually made even the bravest of men tremble in fear, but stood her ground boldly, a muscle twitched angrily in his jaw.

"May I remind you, señorita," Adam said in a voice throbbing with barely suppressed fury, "that the childish game is your own, and that our man won— without his gun!"

Her coal-black eyes clashed with Adam's green, glaring ones. "Only because he had a superior horse, señor, and *not* because of the man. That is the way it is with you *Tejanos*. Because you are physically bigger, your guns better, your horses swifter, you think you are superior to us. You use your advantages over the weak like a club. You are nothing but weak-minded, cowardly bullies."

Seeing Adam turn stiff with outrage, Anita's grandfather drew in a sharp breath, his face drained of all color. Terrified that the furious Texan might hurt his granddaughter, he quickly stepped between the two. "Forgive my granddaughter, señor. She is young and impetuous. She does not realize what she is saying."

Anita stepped from behind her grandfather, her dark eyes flashing dangerously, but before she could open her mouth to retort, the old man hissed, *"Silencio!"* Then, taking her arm, he quickly and firmly led her away.

"Who in the hell do you suppose they are?" Buck asked in astonishment as he and Adam watched the two thread their way through the crush of Mexicans standing beside the road and craning their necks to see the starting line where the next race was forming.

Adam forced his rage down. "Well, they're certainly not peons. They're dressed too well and their English is too good," he answered, his eyes still glued on the couple. "I'd guess he's one of the local rancheros."

"One of those wealthy Mexican aristocrats?"

"An aristocrat, yes. He's Spanish to the bone, and they both have that haughty bearing of the Mexican upper class. But wealthy? No, I'd say their fortunes have seen better days. Their clothing, while undoubtedly expensive at one time, was a little threadbare in places."

Buck looked at the couple thoughtfully as they crossed the street to two horses tied to a hitching rail

23

at the side of one of the adobe buildings. The old man held the girl's arm firmly, as if he were afraid she might bolt, his face no longer pale but highly colored as he angrily admonished his granddaughter. The girl appeared to be paying absolutely no attention to him, her head held proudly, her small chin thrust out defiantly, her dark eyes glittering and staring straight ahead.

Buck felt a strong admiration for the girl's spirit, then chuckled. "God, she's a fiery little thing. Imagine her standing up to you like that, spitting out like a little kitten. And stubborn, too. I bet that old man has his hands full with her. And look at the way she walks. Like a queen!"

Adam had thought the girl was more like a fierce lioness than a spitting kitten, but what Buck had said about her carriage was true. The young woman's walk was regal, except for the graceful sway of her hips, a motion that was strangely at odds with the rest of her stiff demeanor, and therefore, disturbingly seductive. Adam felt a stirring in his loins, the arousal stunning him with its suddenness and intensity.

Mesmerized, Adam stared at the girl as her grandfather bent and cupped his hands to help her mount her ornate, silver-studded sidesaddle. Anita swung into the saddle with one smooth, incredibly graceful movement, hooking her knee over the pommel and picking up her reins. The spirited stallion beneath her pranced restlessly, and, totally unperturbed, she bent forward and soothed the powerful, impatient animal by stroking its sleek neck, waiting for her grandfather to mount his horse.

Then, as her grandfather turned his horse and galloped off into the countryside, Anita straightened in her saddle, haughtily turned her head, and deliberately met Adam's gaze, her dark eyes full of contempt.

Adam felt that scornful look like a slap in the face. His anger rose like a monstrous wave inside him. As Anita skillfully galloped her horse off after her grandfather's, he spat, "Proud, insolent little bitch! Someone needs to bring her down a peg or two!"

Buck's bushy eyebrows rose at Adam's strong words until they blended in with the fur on his coonskin cap. He had watched the silent confrontation between the two and recognized it for what it was. The fiery Mexican girl had thrown down her contempt like a challenge, and Adam had picked up the gauntlet. But Buck wasn't quite sure what the battle lines of this contest would be, if it had continued. Would it be Texan against Mexican, or an even more ancient struggle—the ageless battle between male and female?

The sound of galloping hooves and the Mexicans' wild yells all around him tore Buck from his thoughts, and he turned to see another Ranger barreling down the narrow street with a band of howling, furious Mexicans behind him. The races continued all day, the Texans beating the Mexicans in every contest, until the Mexicans were forced to admit that there were *no mas gallenas* in Reynosa.

At the announcement, Buck chuckled and said, "You're damned right there ain't any more chickens left. I guess we showed these greasers who's the better horsemen."

Adam didn't respond. As the two Rangers walked back to the gin house where they were quartered, Adam took no satisfaction in hearing the surly Mexicans admit defeat. That pleasure had been ruined by the arrogant Mexican girl. His emotions were in a turmoil as he wondered if his frustration stemmed from being cheated of the opportunity to strike back at her, or a niggling feeling deep down inside him that told him the girl had not been totally unjustified in her contempt — for the Texans *had* won because of their superior mounts, and not their skill.

Chapter 2

The days that passed seemed an eternity to Adam and Buck as they waited in Reynosa for General Taylor's lagging army to catch up. Both men were accustomed to activity and needed outlets for their energy.

"Damn," Buck grumbled one day when he and Adam were sitting beneath the shade of a squatty mesquite tree. "I wish the hell something would happen. I came down here to fight greasers and I ain't seen hide nor hair of the Meskin Army. I wish we'd come down here with Walker's company of Rangers. At least they got to see some of the fighting. They got to take part in the battles at Resaca de la Palma and Palo Alto."

"Those were just skirmishes compared to what's coming up," Adam answered. "Monterrey is going to be the big battle. Besides, Taylor hadn't even called for volunteers when those battles took place. Walker and his company weren't even official Ranger representatives."

"Hell, I don't care if they were official or not,"

Buck tossed back. "They still got to see some fighting." He gazed off, a puzzled expression on his face. "I wonder how in the hell Walker pulled that off? Some of the boys in that Ranger company the governor sent down to Corpus Christi when Taylor and his army landed there said Taylor refused their services as scouts. Told them if they wanted to go along, they'd have to herd cattle. Then Walker showed up after Taylor reached the Rio Grande, and his whole company got signed on as scouts."

"You heard Walker's explanation when we asked him about it in Matamoros. Sam said Taylor had decided his dragoons weren't up to the job of keeping his communication lines open in that rugged, mesquite brush country between Fort Brown and Point Isabel. Sam just happened to show up at the right time and place."

"Yeah, as usual," Buck answered bitterly. "Walker has an uncanny way of always being in the thick of the fight and always being there first."

Adam laughed. "Look at it this way. Instead of envying Sam and his company, we should be grateful to them. Because of the excellent job they did, they cleared the way for the rest of us Rangers getting in on this war."

That was true, Buck admitted silently. Now Jack Hays, Sam Walker, Ben McCulloch, John Pierce, Robert Gillespie—all the great Ranger captains and their companies were together in one regiment. Buck completely discounted the East Texas regiment of Rangers. As far as he was concerned, they were as much tenderfoots as Taylor's soldiers. It was the West Texas Rangers who were the real frontiersmen, experienced in fighting both Indians and Mexicans.

"Besides, I'd rather serve under McCulloch any day," Adam added.

Buck knew why Adam preferred McCulloch to Walker. Like him, Ben McCulloch was well educated, had even left his service as state representative to fight in this war. McCulloch's group of Rangers had more lawyers, doctors, surveyors, legislators and newspaper editors in it than all the other Ranger companies combined, and Buck knew Adam felt more comfortable with them. Buck didn't mind. There were enough farmers, ranchers, shopkeepers and blacksmiths to keep him company, and McCulloch's company was the best mounted, armed, equipped, and disciplined outfit in the Ranger service. Besides, despite their differences, the men had one thing in common—their hatred of Mexicans. And that was a powerful cohesive.

A week later, Adam and Buck had just returned to Reynosa after a successful campaign against marauding Lipans that McCulloch had sent them on and had barely bedded down for the night when they were awakened by John McMullen, one of Ben's lieutenants.

"I know you boys are tired," McMullen whispered to keep from waking the other men. "But I figured you wouldn't want to miss out on this, particularly you, Adam."

Adam raised up on one elbow and shook his head to clear it, asking in a groggy voice, "What is it?"

"I overheard some greasers talking in a cantina this

afternoon. Seems one of the rancheros is having a *fandango* tonight and Canales is supposed to be attending."

Instantly, Adam was wide awake, the adrenaline flowing through his veins.

"Thought I'd take some of the men and just mosey over to that dance and have a look," McMullen continued. "You boys want to come along?"

The question was totally unnecessary. Both Adam and Buck were already jerking on their boots, their eyes glittering with anticipation.

Silently, they crept around the sleeping men, for McMullen had explained that he wanted to keep this patrol small, thinking that the smaller it was the less likely the Mexicans would notice their departure from town. Above all, McMullen didn't want someone beating them to the ranch and warning Canales.

After the Rangers had saddled their horses, they led them from the dilapidated gin house and a good distance away from the town before they mounted and rode toward the ranch. A sliver of a moon hung in the dark sky, surrounded by glittering stars, and somewhere in the brush-studded prairie, a coyote howled mournfully.

Coming over the rise of a hill that overlooked the hacienda, they looked down, seeing the dancing lights of the swaying lanterns in the patio where the *fandango* was taking place and hearing the faint strains of guitar music that floated in the air.

"We'll leave our horses here and go the rest of the way on foot," McMullen said, swinging down from his mount. "Spread out and surround the place."

At a half crouch, the men fanned out, moving

30

steadily toward the hacienda, racing from one clump of mesquite brush to the next. When they reached the high walls surrounding the ranch house, they hugged them, staying hidden in the shadows and waiting for McMullen's signal, hearing the laughter and spirited music behind the walls as the Mexicans enjoyed themselves, totally unaware of the dangerous men about to pounce on them.

Adam stood beside one of the gates that led to the patio, his back to the wall, his gun drawn, his muscles tense with expectation. When McMullen gave the signal by making a slashing motion with his arm, Adam spun around, kicked the wooden gate open, and stepped onto the patio.

As McMullen boldly walked into the dance with several Rangers at his heels, the women screamed and the men bolted for the exits, then came to abrupt halts at finding them all blocked by a cold-eyed Texan, his gun drawn and pointed menacingly at them.

Ignoring the frightened, trembling Mexicans standing before him, Adam scanned the dimly lit patio for Canales. Men still scurried here and there, trying to find an escape, and women ran helter-skelter across the cobblestones and around the tingling fountain, shrieking in terror. The sight of a solitary figure standing in the shadows of an arch that led to the house caught Adam's attention. He knew by the white mantilla draped over her head and the white dress that clung to her curves that it was a woman. But why was she standing so still? Adam wondered. Was she frozen with fear, so terrified that she couldn't even move?

But there was something about that woman's regal stance that struck a familiar cord in Adam, and, suddenly, he knew who she was and why she wasn't screaming and running like the other women. That one didn't know the meaning of fear. But he'd teach her. By God, he'd *make* her cower!

Slamming his gun into his holster, Adam pushed aside the Mexican before him and angrily strode across the patio. Seeing the tall *Tejano* with the strange glittering green eyes coming toward them, the Mexicans scurried away, breathing a sigh of relief when the man passed without even giving them a glance, the heels of his boots beating a staccato on the cobblestones, a sound as ominous as the ticking of a clock marking the last seconds of a man's life.

Curious to see who the unfortunate man was that this *Tejano* was stalking with such murderous intent, they glanced at the shadowy figure in the distance, then, seeing that it was a girl, sucked in their breaths, wondering why she didn't flee while she still had the chance.

But the Mexicans didn't know Anita. She was fearless. She would never turn and run from anything, or anyone, much less this arrogant *Tejano* approaching her. No, it was not fear that Anita felt but outrage at the *Tejanos*'s rudeness, their overbearing manner, their use of fear as a weapon against her people . . . Her small body shook with rage.

As Adam came to a stop before Anita, his big body towering over her small one, he saw her tremble and smirked with smug satisfaction.

"You filthy pigs!" Anita spat.

Adam's head snapped back at the angry words. He

looked down into a pair of flashing, black eyes. The little señorita wasn't one bit cowed. The smile on his face turned to a dark scowl "Watch your tongue!" Adam demanded. "I've had about all of the insults I intend to take from you."

"It is you who are the insulting ones!" Anita retorted. "Breaking into a private party and frightening everyone half out of their wits. What did you expect to find here, that you come bursting through the doors with your guns drawn? The entire Mexican Army?"

"No, Canales and his murdering bandits," Adam answered, then glanced about him, the girl's question having reminded him of his reason for being here.

"The Chaparral Fox?" Then Anita scoffed, saying, "You have been sent on a wild goose chase, señor. Canales is not here. Nor are any of his men."

Had he been mistaken, or had he seen the girl's nose wrinkle in distaste at Canales's name from the corner of his eye, Adam wondered. Then, turning his attention back to the girl and seeing her eyes glittering with mockery, he asked in a scathing voice, "And I should take your word for it? A Mexican's?"

Anita bristled at the way the tall, dark *Tejano* had said "Mexican," as if she were the scum of the earth. She glared at him, impotent with rage.

Several Rangers coming from inside the house passed them, and Adam knew by the angry looks on their faces that they had not found Canales. The sly fox had slipped away from them again.

After hearing the Rangers' report, McMullen scowled, then turned to the frightened Mexicans. "We were just passing by and heard the music.

Thought we'd drop in for a little visit, but since you don't seem very neighborly, we'll just be on our way."

"How about a song before we leave, Lieutenant?" one of the Rangers asked. "These greasers can sure coax some pretty sounds from those guitars of theirs."

McMullen nodded curtly to the musicians to play. Nervously, the Mexicans picked up their guitars and began to strum them. As the soft sounds drifted in the air, several of the Texans boldly took Mexican women in their arms and began to dance. Too terrified to object, the women danced woodenly, while the Mexican men glared resentfully at the Rangers but made no move to stop them.

Adam stepped forward and slipped his arm around Anita's small waist. Furious, the girl whirled away from him and stepped deeper into the shadows, hissing, "Keep your hands off me, you filthy pig! Do you think I would dance with the likes of you?"

As her dark eyes swept scornfully over him, Adam became acutely conscious of the seven-day growth of beard on his face, of his dirty, rumpled clothing, of the odor of man sweat and horse sweat about him. After a week of trailing and fighting Lipans, he had been too exhausted even to bathe or shave when he and Buck had rode in. The realization that he *did* look and smell like a filthy pig did nothing to soothe his anger. Instead it fired it. He wanted to throttle her; he wanted to kiss her.

The last came as a shock to Adam, but it was true nonetheless. Her exotic beauty, her intoxicating scent, her fiery defiance attacked his senses and, already aroused with anger, his lust surged to the surface. For a brief moment, he waged a silent battle with himself, his animal instincts struggling with his principles. Why not take her? he thought in a twisted rationalization, punish and humiliate her while he satisfied his lust at the same time. Did she deserve any better than his wife had been given? And wasn't that the rules of war between their peoples? An eye for an eye, a tooth for a tooth?

He sprang with lightning swiftness and slammed Anita's small body against the adobe wall behind her, taking satisfaction in hearing the breath rush from her lungs at the impact. Holding her there by her shoulders, his fingers biting into the soft flesh, he glared down at her, his voice a low growl as he said, "I can do worse than ask you for a dance. I can force you to submit to me completely. Right here! Right now! And your cowardly countrymen wouldn't do a damn thing to stop me."

So that there would be no doubt in her mind of his intent, Adam ground his hips against hers, pressing the rigid proof of his arousal against her loins. Anita's heart hammered wildly in her chest, but her fierce pride would not allow her to show fear. She glared at him, her defiance only goading him more.

As Adam's head descended, Anita twisted hers to the side to avoid his lips. With an angry snarl, Adam crushed her to him with one powerful arm, yanked the fragile mantilla away with his free hand, and cupped the back of her head, forcing it around and holding it firmly as his mouth crashed down on hers, his teeth grinding against her soft lips before his tongue plunged into her mouth, ravishing and plundering.

Anita went stiff with outrage at this violation to her body. Her instincts told her to fight this animal who was forcing such intimacies on her, but she wouldn't give the arrogant *Tejano* the satisfaction of struggling against his superior strength. Instead, she stood perfectly still, enduring the wild thrusts of his tongue and his teeth cutting her lips.

Perhaps it was her failure to show her fear by struggling against him; perhaps, deep down, he had hoped for an answering response; perhaps Adam simply was incapable of rape. He ended the brutal kiss abruptly and drew back, staring down at Anita with a puzzled expression on his face. Then, seeing her lips were bruised and bleeding, he frowned, feeling shame creep over him.

Releasing her, Adam stepped back, and had Anita not done what she did next, he might have found the decency to apologize. But Anita didn't want an apology. She wanted to humiliate him as much as he had humiliated her. Looking Adam directly in the eye, she wiped her bruised mouth with the back of her hand, her facial expression one of utter revulsion. Then she spat at his feet, turned, and walked haughtily away.

Adam felt her contempt like the lash of a whip, and the anger in him that had died down to a smoldering ember flared anew. He stared at her stiff back as she walked proudly away, clenching his fists at his side, a muscle twitching in his jaw, fighting back the urge to go after her and finish what he had started.

"Adam?" Buck asked, lumbering into the shadows of the arch. "What are you doing over here in the dark? I've been looking all over for you. We're leaving."

When Adam didn't answer, but continued staring at the doorway where Anita had disappeared, Buck frowned, then asked, "Didn't you hear me? We're pulling out. Canales ain't here."

Buck turned and walked away. Adam had completely forgotten about his old enemy. He had been much too occupied with his new adversary. He looked around him, seeing that the dancing had stopped and the Rangers were walking to the exits, deliberately putting their backs to the Mexicans, as if daring them to use their knives. Adam shot a heated glance at the doorway where Anita disappeared, then turned and followed his friends.

The Mexicans watched as the hated *Tejanos* departed as swiftly and silently as they had appeared, noting that all had deep scowls on their faces. But it was the tall, dark-haired Ranger with his feline walk and his angry, glittering eyes that made a cold shiver run up their spines. There had been murder in the *Tejano*'s strange green eyes, and he had looked like the devil himself.

Chapter 3

In July, General Taylor moved his army to Camargo, two hundred fifty miles upstream from Matamoros. Adam and Buck were in the patrol that acted as rear guard of the half of the American army that made the hot, arduous trip overland and arrived at the city after most of the troops had already settled down in their new camp.

The two men reined in on the crest of a ridge that overlooked the city and gazed down at it. Then Buck shook his shaggy head in disgust and said, "Damnation! Taylor must have rocks in his head to pick this place as his starting point to attack Monterrey. There couldn't be a worse pesthole in Mexico."

Adam nodded in silent agreement. Camargo sat in a sunburned bowl of rocks, without a tree in sight, and he knew from his previous forays with the Rangers into Mexico that the temperatures in the daytime rose well over a hundred degrees and it was sweltering at night, too, the rocks holding the daytime heat. It was a huge oven where water was scarce and dust infiltrated everything, and the place was infested with snakes, tarantulas, scorpions, and hordes of ants.

"Well, let's hope we don't have to stay here long," Adam commented. "And thank God we're finally here, even if it is a pesthole. I'm tired of eating this army's dust. What was the name of that cantina that McCulloch told us to meet us at?"

"*Los Toro*. He said we couldn't miss it, that it was the only one on the waterfront."

"Well, let's find our camp, stable our horses, and get over there. I could use a drink."

Thirty minutes later, Adam and Buck strolled down the waterfront, then paused, watching the American troops who made up the other half of Taylor's army disembarking from a dozen steamers floating in the muddy river.

"There ain't nothing in the world that would get me to step foot on one of those steamers," Buck said. "Did you hear what happened the other day? One of the steamer's boilers burst and killed almost every man on the boat. Those things ain't nothing but death traps."

Adam didn't like the idea of traveling on a troop steamer any more than Buck, but not because of the danger of a boiler exploding. The men were crowded in so tightly that they could hardly turn around, and Adam was a man who didn't like to be hemmed in. He needed space around him, and the more the better. That was one of the reasons he had left his law practice. He couldn't stand sitting around in a small office or a musty courtroom all day. It seemed as if the walls were closing in on him, smothering him.

Buck warily eyed the hot cinders shooting from the smokestack of one steamer. "Come on. Let's get away from here before another one of those fool things blows up," he said.

The two men shouldered their way through the crush of soldiers on the river landing, sidestepping lumbering wagons piled high with supplies. Amongst the crowd, Buck spied several American soldiers with their arms thrown around the shoulders or waists of Mexican girls, the couples oblivious to anything but each other. He grinned. "Looks like there's as much fraternizing going on with the little señoritas here as there was in Matamoros."

"I hope not," Adam replied in a hard voice. "Those soldiers are crazy to get themselves involved with a Mexican woman. They're just as treacherous as the men."

Buck scowled at Adam's words. He hated Mexicans, too, but that strong feeling had never been directed to the women of that country, since they weren't the ones who waged war, who killed and maimed. Women the world over were just bystanders to war, having no say in the matter, and too often, if they happened to be on the losing side, the victims, considered part of the spoils by the victors.

For some time, Buck had been deeply concerned over his friend. Adam certainly wasn't the same man Buck had known years ago. While Buck had been content to make a comfortable living from his ranch for his wife and four sons, Adam had been fired with ambition, envisioning a cattle empire like some of the high-class Mexicans who had abandoned the land north of the Nueces after the revolution. Adam had deserted his law practice in San Antonio and thrown all of his considerable energies into his ranch, amazing Buck with his determination and industry, and after two years, Adam had the most impressive ranch in the area. Then Adam had gone to South Carolina, married his childhood sweetheart, and brought back his beautiful young wife. But after his wife's death, Adam was never the same. His interest in his ranch and his dream seemed to have died with her. Adam neglected the ranch, spending most of his time riding with Rangers, particularly if their quarry was Mexicans. Buck knew that Adam had more reason than most to hate the Mexicans, but what worried Buck was that Adam's whole life seemed to revolve around his desire for revenge, while the other Texans, like himself, could continue some semblance of a normal life.

Martha, Buck's wife, thought Adam needed a wife and family to take his mind from the disastrous events that had taken place and to give Adam a reason for living again, other than his intense hatred. But Adam had shown no more interest in the young ladies in the area, who had cast inviting looks at the handsome, young rancher, than he had his ranch. The closest he'd seen Adam come to showing any spark of interest in a woman was the day of the races at Reynosa, and despite the fact that Adam and the girl named Anita had hurled angry words at each other, Buck had sensed something come alive in Adam. It was a shame that they had never seen the girl again, Buck thought. Mexican or not, she might just be what Adam needed.

Buck tore his mind from his musings and glanced across at Adam. The young Ranger was staring ahead, looking, as he so often did, dark and brooding. Buck fervently hoped that Adam would find the means to purge his soul in Mexico and attain some peace of mind. There was more to living than revenge.

Adam and Buck stepped inside the dim interior of the cantina and stood, relishing the cool shade after the blistering sun. Then, seeing two of the Rangers in their company, they weaved their way through the crowded tables in the smoke-filled room to where their friends sat and joined them.

"Where's Ben?" Adam asked, looking around the cantina. "He told us this morning he'd meet us here."

"Taylor sent word he wanted to see him before we left camp," a Ranger named Pete answered. "He said he'd join us here after he got through at headquarters."

A chubby Mexican bartender waddled over to the Rangers' table, carrying a tray with five glasses on it. As he sat the glasses on the table, Buck spat. "Dammit, don't tell me Taylor has prohibited the sale of whiskey and hard liquor here, too!"

"Yep, he sure has," Clint, another Ranger, answered. "We're back to drinking a mixture of wine and cordials, just like in Matamoros."

"You reckon they're as potent as those back in Matamoros?" Buck asked speculatively.

"We'll know if we can't walk out of here," Adam replied dryly.

Pete laughed. "Yeah, I gotta hand it to those bartenders back in Matamoros. Taylor sure underestimated their ingenuity when they came up with that drink they called Old Rough and Ready. It only took one of those to send you out into the street reeling drunk."

At that minute, McCulloch walked in, and although his face revealed no emotion, the Texans at the table knew that Ben was as mad as a hornet. His hat was pushed back on his head.

As soon as McCulloch was seated, Adam asked, "What's happening now?"

"It seems General Taylor heard about our Fourth of July celebration down in Reynosa and isn't too happy about it," McCulloch replied in a terse voice.

Buck and Adam had been out on patrol that day and had not participated in the festivities, but they had heard about it from the other Rangers. The Texans had decided to celebrate their new national holiday with a barbeque of Mexican pigs and chickens that they had "accidentally" shot while firing salutes in honor of the day.

"Well, what was Taylor's complaint?" Clint asked.

"Taylor said he heard it was a drunken brawl," Ben answered in a flat voice.

"Ah, hell, we only had two horse buckets of watered-down whiskey," Clint objected. "He just said that 'cause he's a teetotaler."

"And that we were trying to terrorize the citizens by shooting up the town," McCulloch added.

"We *didn't* shoot up the town. We shot us some meat!" Pete said angrily. "And, dammit, Taylor better not tell us we ain't got the right to a few Mexican pigs and chickens, not after those murdering cattle thieves have been robbing us blind for years."

"That's something else he complained about," McCulloch continued, pushing his hat back another inch on his head. "Us seeking out our old enemies.

43

He heard about those cattle rustlers we caught red-handed and hung. He said this isn't Texas and we're not down here to chase down Mexican outlaws or settle old scores, and, even if we were, we certainly didn't have the right to act as judge and jury."

A deep scowl came over the Texans' faces. In Texas, the Rangers were much more than frontier soldiers. They were the only law-enforcement force that the republic and new state had, and they had been given extraordinary powers. Their duties included not only apprehending the criminal, but acting as judge, jury — and executioner.

"Anything else?" Adam asked tightly.

"Yes. He wanted to know why Hays and Walkers' companies haven't brought in more prisoners of war, and said he certainly hoped we'd do better."

The Rangers made no comment. It was the Mexican Army themselves who had set up the rules of war regarding prisoners between the two, but unlike the Mexicans, who accepted the white flag of surrender and then massacred their prisoners, the Texans didn't even bother to take them. The Rangers gave the Mexican soldier only two options: he could either run like hell for his life, or die with his weapon in his hand.

"I hope to hell you told him why we Rangers don't take prisoners!" Buck spat.

"I didn't bother," McCulloch answered in a taut voice. "I told him I could ill afford the luxury of taking prisoners who would hamper our activities while ranging behind enemy lines, that we would be lucky to get back with our own lives, much less having to worry about a bunch of Mexican prisoners, and not to expect us to bring back any more than the other Rangers."

McCulloch looked around at the resentful expressions on the men's faces. "If it will make you feel any better, Taylor did commend us on the job we did reconnoitering the Linares route. He may not like our tactics, but he admits our company has the best scouts in the regiment. In fact, he's got another job for us. He wants us to figure out which route would be the best for his army to take to Monterrey, the China route, or the Mier route. I told him we'd investigate the China route first."

"The China route?" Adam asked in surprise. "Hell, why bother? We know that route is as rugged and arid as the Linares route."

"Well, Adam, in view of the general's criticism, I think we owe it to him to give both routes a thorough reconnaissance," McCulloch answered in smooth voice. "Maybe we can redeem ourselves in his eyes." A slight smile played over McCulloch's thin lips. "Besides, I've heard that Colonel Seguin and his irregulars operate out of China."

Every Ranger at the table suddenly snapped to attention. Juan Seguin was a former Texas patriot who had switched sides after the revolution and was considered a traitor in Texas. Next to General Canales, Seguin was the second most wanted man on the Rangers' list. The men shot sharp glances at their captain.

His face totally devoid of expression, McCulloch reached for the brim of his hat and jerked it low on his forehead. Every man at the table breathed a sigh of relief, knowing that nothing had changed. They would continue to fight the war against the Mexicans as they saw fit, despite Taylor's criticism. And if they happened to run across some outlaws whom they recognized, or old political enemies while they were in Mexico, they'd continue to disperse their quick, lethal justice, too. It would just save them the trip, the time, and the trouble later on.

A few days later, McCulloch's men moved out of Camargo for China. The mission turned out to be another big disappointment for the Rangers, for Seguin and his men had fled before they reached the town. And to the intense frustration of Adam, Buck, and the other Rangers, the same remained true during the following weeks. As Taylor slowly and methodically moved his army deeper and deeper into Mexico toward Monterrey, the only Mexicans the Rangers captured were spies who told of a massive Mexican force that was gathering at Monterrey. The only Mexican soldiers the Texans even got a brief glimpse of were the cavalrymen they flushed out of the dense brush that covered the area they were passing through, but they ran after brief skirmishes that only served to heighten the Rangers' frustration and sharpen their appetite for some real action. By the time they did reach Monterrey, Adam, Buck, and the others were more than primed for the long-awaited confrontation between them and their old enemies. To the last man, they were chomping at the bit.

Chapter 4

Adam and Buck were part of the American advance column that reached Monterrey first, and when the old fortress town came into view, they reined in their horses and gazed at it. Monterrey sat in a wide valley between the majestic Sierra Madres among corn fields and lush pasture where cattle grazed. But Adam didn't take the time to enjoy the beautiful, peaceful scene that the mountain valley presented. He hadn't come to enjoy the scenery but to fight Mexicans. He turned his full attention to the massive black fort that guarded the city and was surrounded by a moat and high walls. A frown creased his forehead as he wondered why Taylor hadn't brought along his heavy siege guns. Obviously his light artillery couldn't begin to breech those walls, and it would be suicide for his troops to try to storm them.

Still frowning Adam turned in his saddle and gazed to the east, seeing at least one fort in that direction, then swung around and looked to the west at the two large, steep hills that flanked the city. The Mexican spies they had captured hadn't lied, he thought grimly. Monterrey was well fortified and bristling with forts and gun batteries. The city was almost an impregnable stronghold.

At that moment Ben McCulloch rode up to Adam and Buck and said, "Adam, you and Buck do some scouting to the west. But stay away from Federación and Independencia. We already know those steep hills are fortified. What Taylor wants to know is what's behind them."

Adam and Buck rode out, giving the two big hills a wide berth, then swung southwest behind them, finding only a lush grassland where a few cattle grazed indolently in the September sun. They came across a hacienda and approached it cautiously, with guns drawn. Riding through the open wooden gate that sat between the high walls, they found the courtyard completely deserted, except for a goat that was tied in one corner. The goat looked up, its long gray beard dragging the ground, then dropped its head to continue grazing on a patch of grass around it.

A quick search of the ranch house told them it had been abandoned, the unmade beds and uneaten food on the table a testimony to the occupants' quick flight.

"Where do you suppose they went?" Buck asked, helping himself to a stack of cold tortillas sitting on the table.

"I imagine to Monterrey, behind the protection of the walls."

They walked back out into the courtyard, mounted, and rode away, still heading west. Cresting a hill, they looked down on yet another hacienda. From their vantage point, they could see the courtyard was deserted, not a soul in sight.

"Looks to me like the Meskins pulled out of there, too," Buck commented. "Think it's even worth the trouble of searching it?"

"No, probably not. But there's a well down there, and my canteen is empty. Let's go down and fill up. We've got a hot ride back to camp."

They galloped down the hill to the hacienda. This time the heavy wooden gate was closed. Adam dismounted and swung it open, the rusty hinges squeaking in protest, then walked in, leading his horse behind him. Quickly glancing around the courtyard, he saw that it was completely empty, its only occupants a few chickens scratching in the dirt off to one side.

Buck dismounted, and the two men walked over to the well that sat in one corner of the courtyard. After quenching their thirst and filling their canteens, Adam filled a bucket sitting nearby and watered the horses.

Buck eyed the chickens thoughtfully. "Some chicken stew would be mighty tasty tonight."

"Help yourself," Adam answered with a shrug, then watched with amusement as Buck chased one hapless chicken around the courtyard. With his massive size, Buck wasn't very agile, and the squawking, flapping chicken continued to elude him. Finally trapping it in one corner, Buck bent to pick it up.

"If you lay one hand on that chicken, I will kill you, you thieving *Tejano*."

Adam stiffened. He didn't even have to turn to know who had spoken those angry words. He recognized that deep, throaty female voice, the seductive tones throbbing in the air and bringing an answering throb to his loins.

Slowly, Adam turned and saw Anita standing in the doorway, dressed in a low-cut *camisa* and ankle-length skirt and looking even more exotic and beautiful than he remembered. Only briefly did he wonder why she was dressed in peasant clothing. His emotions took precedence over everything. A fleeting burst of joy ran through him, a feeling which Adam firmly told himself was happiness at finding his old adversary, and not the woman. Then, realizing that she was holding a gun, he scowled, for the weapon was pointed directly at him and not at the chicken thief.

Buck had whirled around at Anita's voice and now stood staring at her in astonishment. "What are doing *you* doing here?"

"I'm the one who should be asking that question!" Anita snapped, her black eyes flashing. "It is you who are trespassing. But then, I don't need to ask. I know why you're here. To plunder the abandoned *ranchos,* like the thieves you are."

Adam's eyes flared at the insult. Buck stepped forward, saying hotly, "That ain't true! We were just doing some scouting and stopped in for some water."

"Then you deny that you were going to steal my chicken, *Tejano*?"

An embarrassed flush rose on Buck's face. "Oh, hell, it's just a scrawny little chicken."

"But it is *my* scrawny little chicken," Anita reminded him.

While Buck and Anita sparred, Adam had been inching closer to the girl. Suddenly realizing his close proximity, Anita centered the muzzle of the gun on

Adam's broad chest. "Don't come any closer! I will not hesitate to kill you."

Adam came to a dead halt, seeing the deadly glitter in her dark eyes. Frustration rose in him. It was humiliating to be held at bay by a wisp of a girl holding an ancient musket. Ancient musket? Adam gave the gun a closer look. The barrel and trigger mechanism were badly rusted. He doubted that the gun would even fire.

"I wouldn't shoot that thing if I were you," he drawled lazily. "It's so rusted it will probably explode in your face."

Anita shot a quick glance down at the gun. It was a mistake, for with lightning speed, Adam lunged forward and jerked the musket from her hands. Looking down at the gun in disgust and ignoring the outraged girl, he said, "Christ! This thing is so old, it's an antique. It must date back to Cortez."

Anita was seething, most of her anger aimed at herself for having allowed the *Tejano* to distract her. Now she had only her fierce Mexican pride left to defend her. "Perhaps it does date back that far. My grandfather claims Cortez as one of his ancestors."

Adam looked up and, seeing the dark, fearless eyes and proud stance, didn't doubt Anita's claim for one second. And the other ancestor? he wondered, his eyes roaming over the honey-colored skin, skin that was much too dark to be pure Castilian. An Aztec princess, perhaps?

Anita was very aware of Adam's scrutiny, a look that seemed to be stripping her to the bone. She straightened to her full height, somehow managing to look imposing despite her diminutive size. "Get out

51

of my home," she ordered in a haughty voice.

Adam scoffed. "Haven't you forgotten something? I've disarmed you."

"I don't need to be armed. Unlike you, I don't need to hide behind a gun. And I'm not afraid of you, *Tejano*. Now get out!"

The way Anita said *Tejano* grated on Adam's nerves. Angrily, he caught her arm and pulled her forward. "Not until I've gotten some questions answered. What are you doing here in Monterrey?"

Raising her chin defiantly, Anita glared at him, stubbornly refusing to answer.

Shaking her, Adam thundered, "Dammit! Answer me!"

"I told you," Anita answered, still glaring her defiance. "This is my home."

"Then what were you doing in Reynosa?" Adam asked. Then, as a sudden thought occurred to him, his eyes narrowed dangerously and his hand tightened on her arm. "Were you spying for General Ampudia? Nosing around the border to find out how many men Taylor had so you could come back here and tell him?"

"General Ampudia?" Anita spat in disgust. "Even if I were spying, do you think I would tell that insane sadist anything?"

Anita's answer took Adam aback. He knew the Mexicans in and around Monterrey were terrified of Ampudia because of the commanding officer's cruelty to his own people, but he had never expected to find one so openly contemptuous of the general. "Then what were you doing there?"

"It's none of your business, but my grandfather

and I went to Reynosa to pick up some cattle."

Again Adam's eyes narrowed suspiciously. "Stolen Texas cattle?"

"No. We would not want your miserable, skinny longhorns. My grandfather raises prime beef, the best in Mexico. We went to Reynosa to pick up two bulls we were having shipped from Spain. Breeding bulls to improve our stock."

"I didn't see any cattle when we rode up," Buck remarked.

Anita shot him a heated look. "No, you did not. Do you think we're foolish enough to leave them grazing in the open where your army can steal them? They are hidden in the hills, where you can never find them."

While Anita was talking, Adam was searching the interior of the house behind her with his eyes. "Where is everyone else?"

"Gone. To Monterrey."

"And you're here all by yourself?" Buck asked in a shocked voice.

"No, my grandfather is here."

"Where?" Adam asked.

"Upstairs."

As Adam pushed past her, Anita caught his arm. "No! Do not disturb him. He's ill."

"Ill? With what?" Adam asked.

"His heart. He had an attack shortly after we returned from Reynosa."

Adam glanced over her shoulder at the top of the stairs, then back at Anita. He didn't trust her. She'd be crazy to stay in a deserted hacienda with the entire American army within riding distance with no one to protect her but an ailing old man. No, there must be another reason why she didn't want them to go upstairs. Was she hiding Mexican soldiers?

Adam whirled, saying over his shoulder while he drew his gun, "Come on, Buck. Let's have a look upstairs."

Adam rushed up the stairs with Buck fast on his heels. Anita followed angrily.

When he reached the landing, Adam motioned for Buck to take one side of the long hallway, while he took the other. The doors were all open, and Adam quickly ascertained that the bedrooms were all empty. Then, at the end of the hall, he found one door closed. Backing away from the door, he prepared to kick it in.

Anita jumped before him, hissing, "You fool! Do you want to kill my grandfather, frightening him like that?"

Before Adam could reply, Anita turned and opened the door, swinging it wide open so that Adam could see into the entire room. Adam stepped forward and glanced around before his eyes came to rest on the old man sleeping in the big bed. Anita's grandfather lay on his back with his hands folded over his chest. For a moment, Adam thought he was dead because his face was so thin and his color so pasty, except for his lips, which had a bluish cast to them. Then, seeing his chest slowly rising and falling, Adam frowned.

Anita pushed Adam back into the hall and closed the door firmly behind her. "Are you satisfied now?" she asked angrily.

Buck had walked up when Adam was preparing to

kick the door in. From the hallway, he had seen the elderly Mexican and had been shocked at how ill he looked. He swept his coonskin cap off and said, "Sorry, señorita. I guess we owe you an apology."

Anita's dark eyebrows arched in surprise. But before she could answer, Buck continued. "Is that why you're here all alone? Did all the servants and ranchhands run off and leave you? Wouldn't nobody stay and help you get your grandfather into Monterrey?"

"I wouldn't take my grandfather to Monterrey, a city that is about to be attacked. I told you, he is ill. He needs peace and quiet. Besides, even if he was well, we would not leave. This is our home. We would never abandon it, as the other *rancheros* have done."

"Your grandfather needs to be under the care of a doctor," Adam pointed out. "Perhaps one of the American doctors would have a look at him."

"And do what? Bleed him like the Mexican doctors wanted to do?" Anita flared out. "No, I am better at healing than they are."

"But, you're just a girl," Buck objected.

"*Sí*, I am young," Anita admitted. "But I have the gift for healing. Everyone for miles around comes to me when they are ill. Since I was hardly more than a child, I've treated our *vaqueros* and their families."

"Yeah, and a lot of good it did you," Adam commented with a sneer. "They showed their appreciation by running off and leaving you."

"They were afraid," Anita pointed out calmly.

"Yeah, typical cowardly Mexicans!" Adam threw back.

Furious, Anita drew herself up to her full height.

"Get out! Get out, you damned *Tejanos!* Get out of my house, and get out of Mexico," she shouted angrily.

"No, not yet," Adam replied in a low, menacing tone of voice. "Not until we've taken care of some unfinished business between us."

The two glared at each other murderously, both refusing to give ground, and Buck felt like he was standing between two lions about to pounce. What's more, he wasn't sure which would tear the other apart.

Buck stepped forward and took Adam's arm in a firm grasp. "Come on, Adam. Let's go. Taylor is waiting for our report."

With Buck using his massive body to shove him, there wasn't much Adam could do but turn and walk down the steps. But how it galled him to leave without settling up with that little spitfire. Again, he regretted not having followed through with his threat that night at the *fandango.*

As they rode away from the hacienda, Buck asked, "What did you have to go and make that crack about cowardly Meskins for? It just got her all riled up again."

Adam didn't answer, because he didn't know the answer. For some reason or another, the thought of everyone running off and leaving Anita had angered him. When she had so calmly replied that they had left because they were afraid, as if that were a reasonable explanation, it had angered him even more. Then the insult had just slipped out, an automatic reaction. From then on, everything went downhill.

Damn! What was wrong with him? Adam wondered. He could see getting upset if someone deserted an Anglo woman and left her unprotected, but Anita was a Mexican, one of the enemy. Why in the hell should he care what happened to her? And even more puzzling, why hadn't he been able to forget her? Since that night in Reynosa, the memory of her had teased him from the corners of his mind. Was it because she had aroused his lust, as yet unsatisfied, or was it because she refused to show fear, to cower, something that he would tolerate from no Mexican? Whichever, she disturbed him deeply. No one had ever been able to arouse his emotions as she had. She seemed to bring out the worst in him. Yes, she spelled trouble with a capital T—and he hoped to hell he never laid eyes on her again!

Anita stood at the window in her grandfather's room and watched as the two Rangers rode away over the rolling grassland towards Monterrey, her eyes locked on the tall, dark-haired Texan. When she had first realized it was he standing in her courtyard, a strange thrill had run through her. Anita was puzzled by her reaction. Long ago, she had locked herself away from the world in a tight vacuum, suppressing her emotions and letting no one penetrate her protective shield and touch her feelings. Then why had she been actually excited to see him of all men? He was her hated enemy, a savage who had come to her country to kill and maim her people. And yet, deep down, a tingle of electrical excitement remained in knowing that he was here in Monterrey.

Chapter 5

A light drizzle was falling when Adam awoke the next morning, and there was a chill in the air. He sat up, ran his hand through his dark hair, and gazed across the fire, seeing several Mexican prisoners huddled together, the firelight casting eerie shadows over them and their fierce-looking, bearded captors.

"Where did you pick them up?" Adam asked the Rangers.

"Sneaking through the area between the black fort and those big hills," one of the Texans answered. "Figured they were taking messages to the men entrenched up there."

Buck stirred, then sat up. "What time is it?"

"Around five, I'd guess," Adam answered, picking up one of his Colts and breaking it down.

"You gonna clean it again?" Buck asked. "Hell, you cleaned all your guns last night."

"I just want to be sure they're in perfect working order. This is one day I don't want any foul-ups."

Buck picked up his coonskin cap and shook it. Dust flew everywhere. Then, holding it up closer, he scowled darkly. "Dammit, look at that! Something's been gnawing on its tail."

Adam wondered how Buck could tell. The tail had always looked a little chewed up. "It was probably a field mouse from those corn fields over there."

"Well, dammit, if it's got corn to eat, why did it have to chew on my hat?" Buck grumbled, slamming the cap on his head.

As Adam concentrated on oiling his gun, Buck asked, "You heard who we've been assigned to today?"

"All of the Rangers have been assigned to General Worth's division." Adam's green eyes glittered with satisfaction. "And the Rangers will go in first."

"Hell, we always go in first," Buck responded. "Didn't you know that? We've got to go in and flush those greasers out like a bunch of quail, so the soldiers will know who to shoot at." Buck paused, then asked, "General Worth? Ain't he that ruddy-faced Kentuckian we rode with before?"

"Yes."

"Well, I guess if we've got to have a big-shot officer tagging along, Worth is just as good as any."

"Perhaps better. I heard General Worth has been unhappy because he's still a brevet brigadier, that he vowed he'd earn either a grade or a grave at Monterrey."

A wide grin spread across Buck's face. "I see your point. If he's bucking for a promotion, he'll get the lead out, and we'll see some real action for a change."

* * *

That afternoon Worth's column pulled out, a third of Taylor's army, two thousand strong, of which half were Rangers. Leading the way, the Texans turned west, guided by a frightened Mexican prisoner who was coerced to tell the truth with a rope around his neck. They trotted down the Marin road through sun-washed corn fields, the stalks withered and dry. Behind them, the troops marched at double time, four abreast, their eyes bright with anticipation.

"What's the battle plan?" Buck asked Adam as they rode along. "Or does Taylor even have one?" he added sarcastically, still smarting under the general's low opinion of the Rangers.

"He does. According to Ben, we're to make a wide sweep around Federation and Independence hills, find the Saltillo road, block it, cutting off the Mexican supplies, and then attack from the west, while the rest of Taylor's army marches between the Citadel and La Terenia and attack from the northeast. Catch the city in a nutcracker, so to speak."

"Sounds like a good plan to me," Buck admitted grudgingly.

Shortly before sunset, Worth's column was six miles from Taylor's army and almost within reach of the Saltillo road. Before them, a spur of a hill extended from the right and pushed the road to the left, directly under the gun batteries on Independence Hill. General Worth, with forty of McCulloch's Rangers, dismounted and ascended the hill to view the fortifications, the Rangers each carrying one of his Paterson Colts for added protection. On their way back down the hill, some dismounted Mexican dragoons, hidden in a nearby corn field, suddenly attacked, their guns rattling as they fired.

Adam, walking just behind General Worth, saw a movement amongst the dried cornstalks from the corner of his eye just seconds before the Mexicans' fire burst from the field. "Look out, General!" he yelled, pushing Worth down before he dove for the ground, his Colt spitting bullets.

It was over within minutes, the Mexicans mowed down by the Rangers' scathing fire. The shots were still echoing through the surrounding hills when Adam stood and helped Worth to his feet. "Sorry I knocked you down, General. But I didn't know if you had seen them."

"I didn't," Worth admitted in a dazed voice, looking at the corn field in amazement. Half of the field had been completely leveled, while the rest of the stalks were broken and dangling at crazy angles.

Regaining his composure, Worth turned to Adam, saying, "Thank you, young man. You saved my life. I'm indebted to you."

Before Adam could answer, McCulloch rushed up. "Are you all right, General?"

"Yes, thanks to this young man here," Worth answered.

McCulloch smiled. "This is my good friend, Adam Prescott, General. He's one of my best men."

Worth smiled at Adam and replied, "I can well believe that, Ben. I've never seen anyone move as fast as this man did." The general's gaze quickly swept the area around him, littered with dead Mexicans. "Or fire with such deadly expertise," he added.

Adam bent and picked up the general's hat, handing it to him. The officer accepted it, placed it on his graying head, and gave Adam a silent nod of thanks before turning and walking back down the hill.

When they reached the bottom of the rise where their horses and the rest of the company were waiting, Buck asked Adam, "What happened up there?"

"Some Mexican cavalry were hidden in a corn field and tried to ambush us."

"Anyone killed or wounded?"

"Nope." A slight smile played over Adam's lips. "Only Mexicans. And there aren't any wounded. Just dead ones."

"Hell, you might know I'd be stuck down here holding the horses and couldn't get in on the action," Buck complained.

"Cheer up. You'll see plenty of action tomorrow," Adam replied, trying to console his friend.

"Yeah, but tomorrow ain't Sunday," Buck answered bitterly.

"What's that got to do with it?"

"Well, the Alamo fell on a Sunday, and I was kinda hoping we could beat the tar out of these Meskins on the same day."

"I'm afraid it's going to take more than one day to take this city, Buck," Adam answered in an ominous tone of voice.

Chapter 6

Adam's prediction that it would take more than one day to win a victory at Monterrey proved true. The next day, Worth's army, with the Rangers always in the lead, fought their way to the Saltillo road. Then, leaving their horses behind, the Texans crossed the Santa Catrina River through a furious artillery barrage and, with Worth's troops fast on their heels, stormed up Federation Hill to take Fort Soldado.

It wasn't until after their victory that they discovered that Taylor's army had taken a tremendous beating on the other side of the city and been forced to retreat. But Adam, Buck, and the rest of the Rangers were determined that they wouldn't be cheated of their long-awaited revenge and swore that they would take Monterrey even if they had to do it by themselves.

The next day, before the sun had even risen and in a driving rain, they and Worth's troops climbed the steep end of Independence Hill that the Mexicans had thought unapproachable and swarmed over the top in a surprise attack that sent the Mexican garrison there fleeing for the heavily fortified Bishop's Castle at the other end of the hill. Then, leaving the Americans behind, the Texans raced down the hill to take the castle in a fierce, bloody battle that shocked the American troops with its savageness and sent the remaining Mexican garrison in full flight to the city below to get away from the terrifying *los Diablos Tejanos*.

The third day, Worth's army, again led by the bold, fearless Rangers, attacked the city of Monterrey itself, slowly taking the city, not block by block, but house by house, firing at the Mexicans who were shooting at them from the flat rooftops and loopholes of the houses, until the enemy brought up their cannons and positioned them on the roofs, bringing both Taylor's and Worth's armies to an immediate standstill.

It was then that Adam and Buck, trapped in a captured Mexican house with several artillerymen, came up with an ingenious idea. Discovering that the stone wall that separated the house from the next was soft enough to pick a hole in, they set to work with picks and knives until they had a hole in the wall large enough to throw a shell with a short fuse through. Tossing the shell into the next house, Adam and the others dove to the floor, the tremendous explosion shaking the ground and crumbling the wall as pieces of adobe flew everywhere. Then Buck and Adam leaped up, scrambled over the rubble, and rushed up the stairs, their guns spitting death to the surprised Mexicans on the rooftop.

From then on, the Rangers and Worth's troops tunneled their way through Monterrey, totally abandoning the streets and fighting grimly on even after Taylor had withdrawn from his side of the city and left the Mexicans to concentrate their full efforts on Worth's men.

It was the fourth day, when Adam, Buck, and several other Rangers were firing from the roof of the post office they had taken the night before, that another Ranger arrived on the scene and announced Taylor had ordered them to withdraw so that Taylor's artillery could shell the city before the main attack began.

Adam looked at the stunned men standing around him. Like him, their faces were blackened with smoke from blasting their way though the houses and their clothing was caked with mud from scaling Independence Hill in the rain. Several of the men had sustained minor wounds that further stained their tattered clothing with blood, and all of them were hot, thirsty, and bone-weary. A sudden fury filled Adam, and he cried out at the newcomer angrily, "Shell the city! Dammit, why didn't Taylor do that yesterday? Now he wants us to pull back? Give up what we won with blood and guts? Hell, no!"

"I know how you feel," the bearer of the shocking news answered. "The Ranger captains feel the same way and sent back word to Taylor that we've carried the lower part of the city by ourselves, and we ain't budging. Worth ordered his regulars to fall back and bring the wounded out with them. I came to warn you that you'd better prepare yourselves. In about five minutes, all hell is going to break loose."

It did. Within minutes of the courier's departure, the bombardment commenced with the Texans still in the target area. Crouched on the dirt-packed floor of the post office they had captured, with their arms folded over their heads to protect them, Adam, Buck, and their brother Rangers muttered curses as the shells shrieked overhead, then dropped with a heart-stopping explosion that brought the ceilings and walls crashing down all around them. The barrage seemed to last a lifetime, and when it finally ended, the Texans crawled from the rubble, coughing from the dust and smoke but, miraculously, unharmed except for a few bruises and scratches.

"That goddamned Taylor!" Buck exploded, shaking the dust from his coonskin cap. "If I could get my hands on him right now, I'll kill him with my bare hands!"

Shortly thereafter, the Texans received another message from Taylor, via Worth. This time, they were told to hold their positions and suspend advance until a staff conference could be held and a plan of action agreed upon. Again, the Texans could only shake their heads in disgust, wondering why Taylor was doing all the things today that he should have done yesterday, and only after they had all but captured the city single-handedly.

The order to advance never came. Instead, news arrived that the Mexicans requested a parley. Thoroughly disgusted, the Texans sat in the rubble and awaited news of the truce.

"What in the hell does Taylor want to talk armistice for?" one Ranger asked angrily "We've almost got them licked. Give us a few more hours, and they'd be surrendering unconditionally."

"Surrender, hell!" Buck spat. "Why don't he just

let us finish them off, once and for all?"

"According to Worth, Taylor wants to avoid that final bloody spasm in the Grand Plaza," McCulloch, who had joined the small group, explained, his voice heavy with bitterness.

"Well, it wouldn't be his troops taking the Grand Plaza," Adam pointed out angrily. "We're the ones sitting right on top of it. Hell, his troops withdrew yesterday. Since we're the ones who would be doing it, why doesn't he ask us what we want?"

A silence fell over the Rangers, each man embittered by what he considered Taylor's refusal to let the Rangers have the unmitigated victory for which they had fought so fiercely.

Finally, Adam rose, saying to Buck, "I saw a water barrel a street back yesterday. I'm going back to get a drink of water and fill my canteen. If the barrel hasn't been blown to pieces, that is."

Distracted with his morose thoughts, Buck nodded his head, and Adam strolled off down the street, picking his way through the crumbled walls that all but blocked the narrow street in some places. Finding the barrel still intact, Adam bent and dipped his hand into the murky water, pushing the scum on the top aside. He heard the sharp crack of the snipers' musket before he felt the ball slam into his leg midway between his knee and groin. The impact of the shot spun him around, and Adam grabbed the water barrel to steady himself, while his other hand flew for the gun strapped to his hip.

Pulling it from his gunbelt, Adam quickly scanned the rooftops, then, spying the fleeing sniper, aimed and fired. The Mexican arched and cried out as the bullet hit him squarely in the back, then tumbled from the rooftop to the street below.

Buck, McCulloch, and several of the other Rangers came tearing down the street with their guns drawn. Seeing Adam, who had slumped to the ground beside the barrel, Buck ran over to him, while the other men quickly searched the area for more snipers.

Crouching beside Adam, Buck looked at his friend's leg, seeing the blood pouring from between Adam's fingers as he clutched the wound. Taking his Bowie knife, Buck quickly cut Adam's pants leg and ripped it open, then pushed Adam's hand away. "Let me have a look."

The gaping hole was already black and blue around the ragged edges, and the wound was bleeding freely, too freely to suit Buck. He glanced around and, spying a piece of white material under the rubble, yanked it out, seeing that it was a pair of the loose pants that the peons wore. Tearing it in two, he bundled up half of it and pressed it against the wound, then bound it tightly with the other half, seeing Adam stiffen with pain as he tightened it.

"I'm sorry, Adam," Buck said, his voice husky with compassion, "but it's gotta be done. You're bleeding like a stuck pig."

"I know," Adam muttered between clenched teeth. "But, Buck, I think it broke my bone. I've taken balls before, but they've never hurt like this."

"Is the ball still in there?"

"Yes. I can feel the damn thing."

"Then maybe it's just resting against the bone," Buck suggested hopefully.

"No, I distinctly felt something snap."

McCulloch rushed up and asked Buck. "How bad is it?"

"Pretty bad, I'm afraid. The ball is still in there, and he's bleeding like a stuck pig. Besides that, he thinks the bone is broken."

McCulloch could see that the wound was bleeding badly. The makeshift bandage that Buck had applied was already soaked with blood. "Let's get him over to that house that's still standing and see if we can get the ball out."

Buck and Ben helped Adam stand. When he put his weight on the injured leg, Adam's face drained of all color and beads of sweat popped out on his forehead from the piercing pain that shot up his leg. He sucked in his breath sharply to keep from crying out.

"Hell, he can't walk," Buck said, "not even with us helping him." Bending, he said, "Lean over my shoulder, Adam. I'll carry you."

"I'm too heavy," Adam objected weakly.

"Goddamn, you stubborn cuss!" Buck spat, his voice overly gruff with concern for his friend. "Will you do what I tell you to do? Or do I have to knock you out?"

Adam was in no position to argue. An alarming weakness was engulfing him and a shadowy curtain coming down over his eyes. Without will or volition, he slumped forward over Buck's broad shoulder, and the giant lifted him with a grunt that came more from satisfaction than effort.

The walk to the house seemed an eternity to both men. Every time Buck took a step and jarred the injured leg, Adam tensed with pain, and Buck felt him stiffen and knew that his friend was suffering. By the time Buck laid Adam down on the earthen floor inside the dim house, both men were covered with a fine sheen of cold sweat, and Buck's shirtfront was soaked with Adam's blood.

A lamp was found and quickly lit; another Ranger produced a bottle of tequila that he had found in the rubble. Two-thirds of the fiery liquor went down Adam, the other third was poured into the gaping hole in his leg after he passed out. McCulloch tried to pry the ball out with the tip of his knife first, then Buck, then another Ranger. At each probe, Adam's body jerked, and the men winced.

"Dammit, I've seen stubborn balls before, but this beats them all," Buck said in utter frustration.

"It's lodged beside the bone someway or another," McCulloch replied, grim-lipped. "I'm afraid we're only pushing it deeper. We'll have to take him to the army hospital in the morning and see what the doctors can do."

"How are we gonna get him clear across the city?" Buck asked. "I can't carry him *that* far."

"I'll have the boys look around for some transportation tonight," Ben answered, then seeing the worried look on Buck's face, added, "Stop worrying, Buck. We'll find something."

True to his word, McCulloch did manage to find something — a small Mexican cart and a mangy burro to pull it. He had also sent back to the main camp for Buck's and several of the other Ranger's horses.

Adam was carried to the small cart and placed in it as gently as the men could manage. Buck looked down at his friend, thinking that Adam looked awful, then blurted, "You look like hell, Adam."

"You'd look like hell, too, if you had the hangover I've got," Adam threw back in a weak voice. "My head is pounding something awful from that damn tequila."

It wasn't Adam's bloodshot eyes that Buck had been referring to, but the unusual brightness in Adam's eyes and the deep flush on his face, both testimony of his feverish state. Buck had taken a quick look beneath the bandage that morning. What he had seen had alarmed him. The wound had turned red and angry looking, and Adam's entire leg was swollen to twice its normal size. Even more alarming, were the mean red streaks that ran from the wound to Adam's groin. Buck knew the import of those streaks. Infection had already set in.

Buck climbed to the top of the cart and sat down on the seat, picking up the reins to the burro. If the circumstances had been different, the other Rangers might have laughed. The shaggy giant looked ridiculous sitting on the little cart, rather like a big bear, a humorous oddity that one might see in a circus.

After Buck's horse was tied to the back of the cart, four of Adam's friends mounted and pulled up around the cart to act as a vanguard, for although the armistice had become official that morning, the Texans didn't trust the Mexicans not to attack the two lone Rangers.

Before the cart rolled away, McCulloch said to Adam, "I'd go along, too, except I have to pull my company out this morning. Buck can stay with you as long as necessary and will keep me informed on your condition."

"Thanks, Ben, for all you did," Adam said between dry, cracked lips.

"No thanks are necessary," Ben replied. "I'm just sorry I couldn't get that damn ball out and save you this trip."

The strange procession moved out, two keen-eyed Rangers before the cart and two behind it. For a while, the going was rough. Almost every street was partially blocked with rubble, some entirely, and every jarring bounce of the cart sent a stabbing pain through Adam's leg. Once out of the battle zone, they made better time, the little Mexican burro gamely pulling the cart over the cobbled streets, enticed by an ear of corn that one of the Rangers in front had tied to his horse's tail.

When they reached that part of Monterrey where the civilians had not been evacuated prior to the battle, the Mexicans stood in front of their houses and stared at the Texans with hostile eyes. The Rangers scanned the rooftops above them, alert for any sign of an ambush, one hand on their reins, the other resting on the butt of their guns.

It was midmorning by the time they reached the other side of the city, and there, their progress was slowed to almost a standstill. The streets were crowded with wagons taking Taylor's wounded that had been gathered up that morning to the field hospital. Several times, they were forced to stop while the medics carried the injured men from the houses where they had been taken by their comrades-in-arms, and once when the medics spied a hand in the rubble and dug down into it, finding, miraculously, that the buried American soldier was still alive.

The sun was blazing down on them when Buck finally brought the cart to rest in front of one of the huge hospital tents. Climbing down from his perch, he caught the arm of a passing orderly. "I've got a wounded man here."

"Take him inside," the orderly answered, starting to walk away.

"Wait a minute," Buck objected. "We could use a litter."

"There aren't any left," the orderly answered wearily. "Unless you want to wait until one of these wagons are unloaded."

Buck glanced down at Adam lying cramped in the space the small cart offered him. His eyes were dulled with pain, and the flush on his face was even deeper in the hot sun. "I'll carry him in myself."

The orderly nodded, then said, "Put him on an empty cot—if you can find one. As soon as the doctor is free, he'll have a look at him."

As the orderly rushed away, the Rangers around the cart dismounted and helped Buck get Adam over his shoulder and into the tent. Spying an empty cot in one corner, Buck walked over to it and placed Adam on it, the other Rangers following. Then the five men looked about them in shock.

The Texans had seen more than their share of gruesome things on the frontier, from Indian atrocities to Mexican massacres, but they weren't so hardened that they weren't affected by what lay before them. They had never seen so much suffering by so many in so small a space. The tent was crammed full with wounded lying on small cots with bloody bandages on every conceivable part of the body. Many writhed in agony, while the semiconscious babbled in delirium, and still others begged pitifully for water, or something to ease the pain. The tent was unbearably hot, the heat intensifying the rank odors: the brassy smell of fresh blood, the sour smell of vomit, the pungent order of disinfectant, the musky smell of sweat, the sickening stench of putrefaction. Flies swarmed over everything—the bloody bandages, the men, both dead and alive, the urinals, the water containers. It was a living hell, a hell conceived by man and born of the insanity of war.

Buck glanced down at Adam and breathed a silent sigh of relief that he hadn't noticed the horrors around him. Adam's eyes were closed as yet another wave of excruciating pain washed over him. Deliberately, Buck placed his big body between Adam and the rest of the misery in the tent.

An orderly walked up, brusquely saying to the Rangers, "You men move on. We hardly have room here for the wounded, much less visitors."

As the orderly walked away, the Rangers shuffled their feet, hating to leave their friend here and yet knowing that there was nothing more they could do for him.

"You're going to stay, aren't you, Buck?" one Ranger asked the giant.

Buck would sooner leave Adam alone in hell than this place. "You're damn right I'm staying! Just let them try and push me out."

The Rangers didn't doubt Buck's words for one minute. With his bulk and fierce determination, it would take Taylor's entire army to evict him.

"Well, I guess we'd better be going," another

Ranger said. "We *are* just getting in the way."

Adam opened his eyes and muttered, "Thanks, boys."

"Thanks ain't necessary," a lanky Texan answered. "You'd do the same for any of us."

"And when you get better, I'll see if I can't dig up another bottle of tequila for you," another said.

Adam's head was still pounding from the liquor he'd consumed the day before. He managed a weak smile. "Thanks, Emil, but I think I'd just as soon skip that."

After the Rangers had left, Buck sat beside Adam and patiently waited for a doctor to come and examine him. But no doctor came. Had Buck not seen how frantically busy the medical staff was, he might have gotten irritated at the delay, but the activity of the staff was just as feverish as the men they treated, and Buck knew that they were doing the best they could under impossible conditions.

As the afternoon wore on, more wounded were crowded in, the newly arrived simply laid on the bare ground. Time and again, Buck watched as the wounded were carried on bloodstained litters from the main tent to the smaller one next door, and he knew from the screams coming from that tent that the surgeons were busy with their probes and saws. Sometimes the men came back with fresh bandages or swathed stumps that had once been limbs, and sometimes they didn't come back at all, their empty cots quickly occupied with newly arrived injured. One instance was etched in Buck's mind, a mental image that he would carry to his grave. A young soldier had awakened and discovered that his right arm was missing. The look of total horror on the youth's face would haunt Buck for the rest of his life.

Darkness fell, and the lamps were lit, casting eerie shadows and making the scene inside the tent even more ghoulish as the dead, stiff-limbed, and pastyfaced were removed. Finally, a doctor appeared beside Adam's cot, and Buck could have cried with relief. He knew that his friend's condition had worsened since morning. All afternoon, Adam had been alternating between periods of acute alertness punctuated with intense pain and periods of incoherent delirium.

The doctor looked at the giant sitting beside the cot with a mixture of surprise and irritation. Usually the wounded were brought in by medics, and not by friends, and if the latter were true, their comrades-in-arms quickly left, if not asked to do so by the orderlies, then by their own volition. No one in their right mind wanted to stay in this hellhole unless absolutely necessary. Besides, why had the giant's commanding officer allowed him to stay? Then, realizing that the huge bear of a man was one of those Rangers he heard so much about, the doctor understood. The Texans' officers had no more regard for army rules than their undisciplined men.

Sighing in a mixture of exhaustion and contempt, the doctor crouched and removed the filthy bandage over Adam's leg. Buck almost gagged when the covering was removed. The stench from the draining pus was overpowering. Seeing the look of horror on the giant's face, the doctor shook his head in exasperation. What had the Texan expected? Of course the wound was infected. He had seen wounded brought in with their clothing dusty and splattered with mud, but these two looked like they had been wallowing in it, like two pigs. And didn't they ever shave?

The doctor had no way of knowing the ordeals the Rangers had been through during the past five days, nor had he heard that it was they who had given Taylor his victory at Monterrey. The doctor had been too busy with his own ordeal, and even if he had known, he would have scoffed at the word "victory." There was nothing victorious about the misery and suffering and death he had seen. For the army, the battle was over. For him and the rest of the medical staff, it was just beginning.

Wearily placing the bandage back over the wound, the doctor rose and said, "I'm afraid we'll have to amputate. Immediately!"

"Amputate?" Buck gasped in shock.

Suddenly, Adam was awake and alert. "No! I won't let you cut off my leg!" He turned his head to his friend, his eyes imploring. "Don't let them do it, Buck."

"Is that really necessary, Doc?" Buck asked. "Can't you just remove the ball and set the bone?"

Dammit, the doctor thought angrily. Did the giant think he enjoyed cutting off someone's limb, that he was some kind of sadistic ghoul who cut for the fun of it? To amputate a limb both sickened and angered him. If only there were some way to fight the infection without maiming a man for life. But if there was, the doctor didn't know the treatment. The only known cure for sepsis as bad as this was severing the limb, and even that might not help.

Angry and frustrated at his own inability to heal

without maiming, the doctor's words were harsher than he meant them to be. "I have no time to argue with you! That wound is dangerously septic, and unless the leg is removed, this man will die. For all I know, gangrene may have already set in." The doctor turned, saying over his shoulder, "I'll send some orderlies for him as soon as one of the operating tables is available."

Adam clutched Buck's arm, his grip surprisingly strong for a man as ill as he was. "Don't let them do it, Buck. For God's sake, get me out of here!"

Buck hesitated. He didn't know what to do. He knew Adam's leg was dangerously infected, but was it really so bad that gangrene had already set in? And if he took Adam away, where would he take him? The Rangers had already tried to remove the ball and failed. And a Mexican doctor, even if he could find one that he trusted, would probably want to amputate, too.

"I'd rather be dead than lose my leg, Buck. Get me out of here. At least let me die in one piece."

Buck didn't doubt Adam's words. His friend had lost interest in life ever since his wife had been killed. Only his thirst for revenge kept him going. Without his leg, Adam couldn't ride. His search for revenge would be over. Then he might completely give up, become just an empty shell going through the motions of living and hating Buck every second of it. But neither could Buck let his friend die, not without trying to save his life. If only Martha was here, Buck thought. She'd know what to do. Women had a way with the sick, an uncanny sense of what needed to be done.

Suddenly, Buck's head snapped up, and a gleam came into his dark eyes. Raising his bulky body from the ground, he said, "I'll be right back, Adam. Just let me check to see if that cart and mangy burro are still out there."

When the surgical orderlies came for Adam, they found an empty cot. Reporting it to the doctor, the officer rushed to the scene to find both his patient and the shaggy giant had disappeared. For a brief moment, his anger surged, then abated to be replaced with an inkling of respect. The Rangers were fiercely independent men, a breed unto themselves, guarding their right to make their own choices in death as well as life. The doctor fervently hoped somehow, someway, by some miracle, that the young Texan would survive.

Chapter 7

It was almost midnight by the time Buck drove the little Mexican cart through the hacienda gate and into the courtyard, the burro's and his horse's hooves clattering loudly on the cobblestones in the night stillness. As Buck stepped down from the cart, he knew that those inside the house had heard the noises. A light suddenly appeared in a upstairs window, and a few moments later, a second appeared in a downstairs one.

Just as Buck was about to knock on the massive, heavily scrolled door, it swung open, bathing him in bright light. Blinking against the sudden glare, Buck saw Anita standing in the doorway, dressed in a nightgown and shawl, with the same rusty musket held before her.

"You!" Anita gasped in surprise. Then her dark eyes narrowed "What are you doing here *Tejano?*"

"My friend is badly wounded. He got shot in the leg. The army doctor wanted to amputate, but Adam made me promise that I wouldn't let them. I brought him to you."

"Me? Why me?"

"Because I don't want him to die, and you said you had the healing gift." To Buck's ears, his reasons seemed lame. He had been a fool to think that this girl—a Mexican—would help him. "Look, I'll pay you anything," he said in a desperate rush of words. "Just name your price."

Anita drew herself up to her full height, saying stiffly, "I do not take money for healing others."

For a moment, Buck considered forcing the girl at gunpoint, then decided against it. No, he couldn't force her to use her skill, nor could he demand it. Perhaps another would do so out of fear, but this one didn't know the meaning of the word. No, to save Adam's life, she would have to be willing, and as critically ill as Adam was, it would take all of her skill and knowledge.

Knowing he had gambled and lost, Buck turned and walked heavily back to the cart. Seeing the look of anguish in his eyes before he turned, and the defeated slump of his shoulders as Buck walked away, something tore at Anita's heart. She remembered the giant's concern for her safety the day he and his arrogant friend had stumbled across her home, and the big man's embarrassment when she had caught him red-handed, stealing one of her chickens. Before she realized it, the words were out. "Do you give up so easily, *Tejano?* You disappoint me. I thought you were all such fierce fighters. Is your friend's life not worth fighting for?"

Buck turned, a puzzled frown on his face, not knowing how to answer and wondering if the girl was taunting him.

Anita turned. "Maria, take this." She shoved the gun into the hands of the startled woman who had been cowering to the side of the door.

Anita picked up a candlestick lying on a table in the foyer, and as she stepped through the door, the old woman caught her arm and cried in terror, *"No, patrona! Es uno de los Diablos Tejano!"*

Making an exasperated sound and jerking her arm away, Anita walked from the hacienda to the back of the cart. Holding the candlestick high, she gazed down at the man revealed in the flickering light. Unconscious and sprawled like a limp rag doll some child had cast aside, he didn't look at all like the arrogant *Tejano* whom she remembered. That man had been bursting with vitality, a perfect physical specimen of manhood at its prime, almost overpowering her with his masculinity and virility. This man was on the brink of death, a pasty pallor showing through the deep flush on his face, his breath coming in shallow gasps. A shiver ran through Adam as yet another chill raked his body. Seeing it, Anita noticed that Adam wasn't even covered with a blanket. Then her eyes fell on the bloody bandage on his thigh. A stench rose from it, and Anita recognized that smell only too well.

Seeing Anita's small nose wrinkle and aware of the stench himself, Buck muttered, "The doctor said gangrene may have already set in."

"No. I can tell you without even looking at the wound that it is not gangrenous. I have seen gangrene before, and it has a very distinctive odor to it. Once you have smelled it, you never forget it. But your friend is very ill."

Tears shimmered in Buck's eyes. "I know. He's gonna die," he choked out.

Again something tugged at Anita's heart, and she frowned. Why should she feel compassion for these two? They were *Tejanos*. That very day they had subjected her people to a humiliating defeat. And yet she couldn't turn them away. Because they were killers, she would not let them make her one, too. *Madre de Dios,* then she would be as low as they.

She stepped back and said in a hard, decisive voice, "Bring him into the house."

Buck's head snapped up from where he had let it hang in defeat. "You mean, you'll treat him?" he asked in surprised disbelief.

"Isn't that why you brought him here?" Anita asked in a brittle voice, then turned and walked back to the hacienda.

Quickly, Buck drew Adam's limp body over his shoulder and followed, afraid if he hesitated in the least, Anita would change her mind.

When they walked into the house, Anita said to the old woman, "Heat water and bring it to the west bedroom, Maria. And bring me my medicine kit immediately."

"No, *patrona,*" the frightened woman said, "do not do this. General Ampudia said anyone giving comfort to the enemy would be shot. We will all be killed. Everyone on the *rancho!*"

"Do not mention that coward's name to me!" Anita flared out, her black eyes flashing. Then, seeing the terrified expression on the old woman's face, she said more calmly, "No, Maria. Ampudia no longer holds any power in Monterrey. Today he is a prisoner himself, and tomorrow he will be gone for good. Now, do as I say."

Deciding that she would rather face Ampudia's wrath than the small girl's standing before her, the woman rushed away to do her mistress's bidding, crossing herself and muttering prayers as she went.

Anita led Buck up the stairs and turned in the hallway in the opposite direction from which her grandfather's bedroom lay. Buck glanced at the closed door at the end of the hallway as he stepped onto the landing, wondering if Anita was putting so much distance between the two men because she was afraid Adam would disturb her grandfather, or because she did not want the old man to know that she was giving comfort to the enemy.

When they reached the bedroom, Anita placed the candlestick down on a nearby table and quickly turned down the covers. Buck gently laid Adam on the bed, straightening his limp legs before he rose. Then, Anita did something that shocked Buck speechless. She started stripping Adam's clothes from him.

Looking over her shoulder, Anita snapped, "Don't just stand there! Help me. He's deadweight."

"Can't . . . can't that wait till later?" Buck stammered.

"What good would it do to clean his wound if he is still wearing filthy clothing?"

It sounded reasonable to Buck. "All right, ma 'am. If you'll just step out in the hall, I'll do it."

Anita whirled. "Step out?"

"Yes, ma'am. It don't seem fitting for a young girl like you—"

"Dios! Do you think I have never seen a naked man? I told you everyone brings their sick to me. That includes men."

Buck still didn't think it was proper. If Anita had been older, or married, he could accept it, but she was just a young girl and, undoubtedly, still an innocent where men were concerned.

"Do you think you *Tejanos* are made any differently from Mexican men? That you are bigger, or better built?" Anita asked in a scathing voice.

Buck winced at her candid question, then answered, "No, ma 'am. But in Texas, young ladies just don't do that kinda thing."

Buck looked so uncomfortable that Anita had to laugh.

"Nor do they in Mexico, *Tejano,*" Anita admitted in a voice that surprised Buck with its softness. "But I am not like the others. I am a healer, and there are times when modesty must be set aside for more important matters. Now, please, help me."

Buck blushed beet red as he helped Anita strip Adam, then squirmed when she insisted that he be bathed before she would attend to his wound. But as Anita worked swiftly and efficiently, paying Adam's male body no more attention than if she were bathing her own, Buck began to feel his embarrassment slipping away as he saw the wisdom of her words. Modesty could be a serious encumbrance when a life was at stake.

When the bath was over and the linens changed to fresh ones, Anita covered Adam with a sheet, exposing only his injured leg. Then she removed the bandage, tossing it into a wastebasket on the floor.

The wound looked even worse than it had at the hospital, and Buck was amazed that the Mexican girl didn't faint at the sight of it. His own stomach was rolling dangerously.

Anita knelt beside the bed and felt around the wound. "Is the ball still in there?"

"Yes. We tried to remove it, but we couldn't get it out. And the doctor wouldn't even try. He was just gonna cut it off."

Anita shook her head in disgust at Buck's last words. "It has to come out."

"I know," Buck answered glumly.

Buck watched while Anita scrubbed the wound with soap and water so vigorously that he wondered why her hands had any skin left on them. Picking up a long probe that she had boiled in a pot of water earlier, she worked gingerly and carefully, probing here, there, then another spot, the expression on her face one of intense concentration.

Then she smiled. "Ah, there it is. It worked its way behind the bone."

"Can you get it out?" Buck asked anxiously, peering over her shoulder.

"If I can work it up an inch or two, I can get it with my fingers."

Buck was horrified at the thought of putting a finger into that bloody, putrid wound. A probe or a knife perhaps, but a bare finger? But a minute later, Anita sat aside the probe and did just that, and Buck's stomach lurched.

Adam moaned, and his leg jerked. "Perhaps you should hold him down," Anita suggested. "This might hurt enough to bring him back to consciousness."

Buck was glad to have something to do to take his mind off the gruesome thing Anita was doing. He bent over the bed and held Adam's shoulders firmly. As Anita probed deeper with her fingers, Adam cried out and arched his back, bringing cold sweat to Buck's forehead.

"I got it!" Anita cried.

Buck turned and saw the bloody ball lying in her hand. It seemed impossible that something that small and harmless-looking could cause so much hell. But Buck knew that the battle for Adam's life was far from over.

"First, I will wash out the wound with saltwater, and then I will apply a poultice to draw out the infection."

"Saltwater?" Buck asked with a deep scowl. "Ain't you got any tequila?"

"Liquor only burns the tissue, adding further injury," Anita replied. "A mild solution of saltwater works much better. I don't know why, but it reduces the swelling and seems to soothe the tissue."

"Where did you learn that?" Buck asked in amazement.

"When I was visiting relatives in Tampico, I noticed when we bathed in the gulf that a festering sore improved after being in the salty water. Perhaps it washes out the infection."

Buck nodded. He had noticed the same thing but had never thought to apply it to treating a wound. "Adam said he felt the bone snap. Do you think it's broken?"

"*Sí.* The ball was right up against it. The bone was

probably what stopped it. But hopefully it is a clean break. I didn't feel any jagged edges."

Again, Anita worked with a swiftness and efficiency that amazed Buck. First, with his help, she put an oilskin sheet on the bed and flushed the wound with so much warm saltwater that Buck feared she would drown Adam in the process. After removing the oilskin and changing the linens again, she placed a poultice of herbs over the wound, bandaged it, then applied a splint to Adam's leg. By the time she was finished, the sun was rising.

Anita arose from where she had knelt beside the bed, pushed her long black braid back over her shoulder, and placed a hand on Adam's forehead. It was burning hot. "And now, we must fight the fever."

And fight they did. By this time, Adam's body temperature was dangerously high, and he was wild with delirium. It took all of Buck's considerable strength to keep him in bed while Anita sponged his body with cool water.

For the second time, Buck blushed with embarrassment, but not because of Adam's nudity. Fighting them to rise from the bed, Adam was letting go with a steady stream of vile curses and obscenities that were unfit for any woman's ears—or any man's, for that matter. In a brief lull in the battle, Buck took the opportunity to apologize on behalf of his friend. "Please forgive Adam's foul language, ma'am. He don't know what he's saying."

Anita shrugged and replied calmly, "There is nothing your friend could say that would shock me. I have treated delirious men before and heard every possible obscenity and vile word there is. The only difference is the language. Your friend curses in English, and they in Spanish."

Anita finally managed to get a herbal tea down Adam, almost getting her hand bitten in the process. Apparently the tea had a sedative effect, for Adam was soon in a deep sleep. Buck took satisfaction in noting that Adam's breathing was deep and regular and that his coloring was more normal.

"How long will this last?" Buck asked

"Hopefully for several hours."

Buck heard the weariness in Anita's voice, but that was the only thing that betrayed her exhaustion. Her carriage, her very being, was just as regal as ever. He was amazed at her strength of will and her cool efficiency. During the long night, and the even longer day, not once had she hesitated or given in to her fatigue. And she was bound to be bone-tired. He was, and he was a man with the strength and stamina of an ox.

Suddenly realizing that Anita was still in her nightgown, Buck averted his eyes, "I'll stay with him now, ma'am."

"Sí, I think the crisis is over. I will send Maria up with something for you to eat and water with which to freshen up. If you need me during the night, my room is the second door down, on the right."

Anita walked to the door and opened it.

"Ma'am?"

Anita turned.

Buck looked her directly in the eyes. "Thank you."

"De nada, Tejano."

Buck winced at the last word. There was always a hint of contempt in it when Anita said it. Did she still consider him her enemy? Buck didn't, not after all they had gone through together over the past twenty hours. No, for that time, they had worked as allies, fighting a common, more ancient enemy— death.

"Ma'am, would you do me one more favor? Would you call me Buck?"

Over the past day and night, an inkling of respect had crept into Anita for the giant. There was a nobility about his fierce loyalty to his friend that surpassed her contempt for men of his kind. And not once had he returned her contempt—as his arrogant friend had. No, if anything, he had been humble, treating her with the same respect he would have afforded one of his Anglo women. He had even thanked her, not out of simple politeness, but with the sincerity of true gratitude.

Anita laughed, a low, husky sound that had the same quality as the throaty tone of her voice, something that fascinated Buck. "*Sí,* I shall call you Buck. On one condition."

"What's that?"

"That you call me Anita and not ma'am. *Dios!* It makes me feel so old, as if I were ancient."

Buck nodded in silent agreement, and Anita smiled and stepped from the room, closing the door quietly behind her.

Buck frowned, wondering why he'd ever called her ma'am. It was usually a term of respect that he reserved for a much older woman. In Texas, he would have called a girl her age by her name, and he had known her name all along.

Slumping in an easy chair by the bed, he pondered

over this puzzle for a long while before he understood. Despite her youth, there was a maturity about Anita that far surpassed her age. She was one of those rare people who were born with a wisdom as old as time itself.

The first thing Adam became aware of when he awoke the next morning was the smell of freshly laundered sheets. With his eyes still closed, he inhaled deeply, thinking that Beth must have just changed the linens. Then he remembered. Beth was dead, murdered in the most vile manner man could devise, and he had not slept in a bed in months.

His eyes flew open, and he sat up. A pain tore through his leg and pierced his groin, causing him to suck in his breath sharply and collapse weakly on his elbows. When the wave of pain had passed, he stared down at his bandaged and splinted leg in a brief moment of confusion. Shaking his head to clear it, he looked around him.

Nothing in the room was familiar, not the heavy, dark furniture, or the grilled sconces on the walls. Realizing that the room was bathed in sunlight, he turned his head and gazed out the window, seeing the mauve and purple mountains in the distance, their peaks partially obscured by white, wispy clouds. Suddenly, he knew where he was.

The door opened and Buck stepped into the room. "What am I doing here?" Adam demanded in an angry voice.

Buck was surprised to see Adam awake and alert, but not surprised by his anger. That he had expected to face, but not this soon. Closing the door behind him, he said, "I brought you here."

"Dammit, I know that! But why here? To *her* home?"

"Because I didn't know where else to take you," Buck replied reasonably. "It wouldn't have done any good to take you back to the Rangers. There wasn't nothing any of us could do. I remembered Anita saying she had a healing gift, so I brought you here."

"I hope to hell you paid her well!"

Nope. She wouldn't take no money. She's too proud. And I wouldn't mention it, either, if I were you. It will only get her all riled up."

"Dammit, Buck, of all the people to make me beholden to, why did you have to pick *her?*"

"You *ain't* beholden! I am. I'm the one who asked. And she was the only one I could think of."

"She's a goddamned Mexican!"

"She's a healer! And you still got your leg, in case you ain't noticed — and your life!"

It was a point Adam could hardly argue with. "All right, so the ball is out. Now, let's get out of here."

"Are you crazy? The ball might be out, but you're a long way from being healed. Your leg is broken. It will be months before you can ride again. And if you think I'm gonna drive you all the way back to Texas in that miserable Mexican cart, you're loco!"

What about the Rangers' camp? You can at least take me there."

"There ain't gonna be any Rangers' camp in a couple of weeks. The Rangers are going home. Our enlistment has expired, and Taylor ain't asking for reenlistment."

Adam was shocked. "Then it's over? Mexico surrendered?"

"Hell, no, Mexico didn't surrender. Taylor may think they're going to, but we know them better than that. They ain't gonna give up that easy, particularly not after he let Ampudia march out with all his men and arms."

Adam was even more stunned. "Taylor let the Mexican Army go scottfree?"

"Yep, just like he did at Matamoros. They left this morning."

"He's insane!"

"Yep. We had them right where we could have beaten them, once and for all, and he let them go," Buck said in a bitter voice. "I rode over and told Ben where we were this morning, and he said Taylor's chief of staff wrote Washington a glowing report about the victory at Monterrey and how Taylor's army had broken the back of the Mexican Army in the north. Hell, Taylor's army didn't take Monterrey. We Rangers did! And now he's saying thank you kindly, boys, and sending us home."

And Adam knew why. Taylor didn't want the "troublemakers" in his occupation army. The Rangers were good enough to do his dirty work for him, but not good enough to share in the rewards. No, the Texans' methods of dealing with the enemy would not fit in with the Army's conciliatory policy concerning the Mexican population. Taylor was a fool if he thought he could live peaceably with the Mexicans just because he had won a few battles. He didn't know their devious natures. They would never accept occupation sitting down. And because of that damned fool, Taylor, he was trapped in this house with his enemy—unless he wanted to leave now and risk being crippled for the rest of his life. Well, Taylor could occupy northern Mexico by his absurd methods, but he and Buck would occupy this enemy household by theirs, at least until he was able to travel again. Then, Adam noticed something.

"Where are your guns?" he asked Buck.

"In my room, down the hall, with the rest of my things."

"You left your weapons where a Mexican could get to them?" Adam asked in total disbelief.

"Hell we don't need guns around here. Ain't nobody gonna bother us. Ain't nobody around except Anita and her grandfather, two women servants, and an old gardener, and the servants are all scared to death of us."

"Maybe you can discount the old man and the servants, but what about *her?* Have you forgotten that she pulled a gun on us?"

"Anita?" Buck asked in utter disbelief. "Hell, if she was gonna kill us, she could have done it that first night. Or she could have just let you die, for that matter."

Adam wondered why she hadn't just let him die. She certainly didn't have any love for him, not the way she openly scorned him. Or fear. Did she have some devious plan of her own?

"Where are *my* guns?" Adam asked.

"In my room."

"Bring them to me."

"Why?"

"If you want to take the risk of having your throat

cut some night, that's your business, but I don't trust that Mexican as far as I can throw her! She may be setting up a trap for us."

Buck could only shake his head in disgust. In his heart, he knew Anita was incapable of treachery.

When Anita came to change Adam's dressing later that day, the first thing she saw was the huge Paterson Colt lying on the table beside Adam's bed. She shot Adam a scornful look, then bent to change his bandage without a word. Adam suspiciously watched her every move, until the procedure became too painful for him to remain in his half-sitting position on his elbows. He fell back to the bed, his lips tightly compressed and his forehead beaded with sweat.

"I can give you something for the pain," Anita said, schooling herself to keep her tone of voice cool and seemingly indifferent.

"What?"

"Jimson weed."

Adam recognized the name of the plant whose leaves had a narcotic effect. It was used for that purpose in Texas, too. But if not given in just the exact amount, the drug could be lethal. "No. I don't want anything."

"Are you afraid I will poison you?" Anita asked in a mocking voice.

Adam glared at her, answering in a tight voice, "That possibility has occurred to me."

Adam expected Anita to get angry, or deny that she would do such a thing, but she did neither, instead calmly returning to the task at hand. When she had finished, she disposed of the soiled bandage, straightened the linens, put up her supplies, and tidied the room, acting as if Adam didn't even exist, while Adam watched her every move wearily.

Anita walked to the door, opened it, and turned. Looking Adam directly in the eye, she said, "You can rest in peace, *Tejano*. Which is more than my people can do when you are around. If I should decide to kill you, I would not sneak behind your back to do it. I would do it to your face."

After Anita had left the room, Adam stared at the door, knowing that he had wrongly accused her. Anita was a fighter, but she would never sink to cold-blooded murder. That was the coward's way out, and, above all, Anita was not a coward.

Two days later, when Anita was changing Adam's dressing, Buck stood behind her, peering over her shoulder. "Looks a hell of a lot better, Adam. Ain't near as red and angry-looking."

Adam muttered something unintelligible beneath his breath and continued to glare at Anita, as he always did, particularly when she got too close to him and his senses heated, as if he could ward off his unwanted attraction to her with his eyes alone.

But today her presence was even more threatening than usual. He could smell her scent surrounding him like a sensual blanket, not the heavy, flowery essence that the women of quality back in South Carolina wore, but a faintly musky sweetness that sent his pulses pounding with primitive desire. As she bent over his leg, her low-cut *cámisa* fell away from her slightly, and he could see her full breasts, the color of golden honey and jutting forward proudly, almost impudently. Then when she moved, he got a tantalizing glimpse of the rim of one dark nipple. The sudden urge to taste that sweet flesh, to take that enticing nipple in his mouth came over Adam, and his desire rose yet another notch.

Clenching his teeth, he tore his eyes away from the tempting sight and found his eyes on the long, lustrous pigtail that fell over her shoulder, its tip lying on his lower belly. With just the thin sheet covering him, Adam became acutely aware of it brushing back and forth across him as Anita bandaged his leg, seemingly scorching him right through the material, then became miserably conscious of her slender fingers touching his thigh as light as a butterfly's wings, and therefore all the more arousing.

Horrified, Adam felt a familiar heaviness flood his lower belly and knew what was coming. "For God's sake, hurry up!" he snapped.

But it was too late. Adam could feel his manhood growing and slowly rising, and he knew that Anita must be aware of what was happening, for his throbbing erection tented the sheet as if someone had thrust a pole beneath it. He struggled with all his will to stop what was happening, but trying to force his arousal down was as impossible as trying to stop the sun from rising. Damn her, he thought viciously.

Anita would have had to been blind not to have noticed his erection at her close proximity. She was worldwise enough to know that men's organs behaved this way when they were aroused, but what shocked her was her own reaction. A tingle of excitement ran through her clear to her fingertips, and a peculiar warmth formed deep in her belly. Suddenly she found it difficult to breathe. Anita's passion had never been aroused. The closest she had come to feeling even a flick of physical desire had been that thrill when Adam had suddenly appeared in her courtyard, and that had been more emotional than physical. The only man who had ever kissed her had been Adam, and then in anger. She remembered his tongue thrusting in and out of her mouth, and a sudden weakness invaded her.

With a will of their own, her eyes slowly traveled up Adam's broad chest with its dark, springy curls, across his muscular shoulders, then up the tanned column of his throat and across his strong chin. It was the first time she had allowed herself to really look at him and was forced to admit that he was a magnificent male specimen, as lean and sinewy-muscled as a powerful mountain lion. Even the dark bristles on his chin couldn't detract from the rugged beauty of his well-shaped male features. Then, as her eyes met Adam's blazing green ones, Anita felt that glittering anger like a slap in the face.

Yes, she thought, *he desires me, and he knows I know it and hates me for it.* Furious with herself for allowing her own passion to be awakened by this half-savage, her eyes narrowed and she glared back, stunning Adam as he watched the hot smoldering in her dark eyes turn as hard and icy as a glacier.

Anita turned her attention back to Adam's leg and quickly finished the dressing, taking satisfaction in hearing Adam's sharp intake of breath as she tied the two ends of the bandage with uncharacteristic roughness. Then, feeling a twinge of shame for deliberately causing him pain, her anger at herself rose even further. He was her enemy, one of the hated *Tejanos* who had just subjected her people to a shameful defeat. He deserved pain for what he had done, she thought, coming to her own defense. But she knew, deep down, that causing him pain was at odds with her healing art. Suddenly torn by conflicting emotions, Anita wanted to hit back, *had* to hit back at the arrogant *Tejano* who threatened the defensive wall she had so carefully built around herself. She flipped the sheet over his leg curtly and rose to her feet, then stared at the outline of his bold erection with deliberate contempt.

Anita's open scorn of the rigid proof of his masculinity had the same effect as a dash of ice water on Adam's burning senses. His proud organ shriveled and lay limply between his legs. It was a humiliating experience, being unmanned by this haughty girl. Then, when she glanced up at him with a smug smile on her face, Adam longed to jump from the bed and throttle her. He glared at her back with unmitigated fury as she proudly walked from the room.

Adam glanced over to where Buck was standing at the window gazing out, relieved that his friend had walked away before his body had betrayed him and Anita had scorned him. He couldn't have born Buck witnessing her unmanning him. Damn the little bitch! Teasing and taunting him. She knew how she affected him, and she had enjoyed humiliating him. Well, he wouldn't give her the opportunity to do so again.

"From now on, I want you to change my dressing,"

Adam announced.

Buck turned from the window, a surprised expression on his face. "Me? Hell, I don't know nothing about changing dressings."

"It's not all that difficult. The Rangers change each other's dressings when we're out in the field all the time."

"Yeah, but their wounds weren't as serious as yours. And they didn't have a splint on their leg. What if I knocked it out of place? Besides, I don't know nothing about those poultices Anita has been putting on it to draw out the infection."

"She can mix the poultice, but you apply it."

"Why in the hell are you so determined that I do it?" Buck asked in exasperation.

"Because I don't want that Mexican touching me again!"

Buck didn't like the way Adam said "Mexican." Although he had heard his friend use that contemptuous tone innumerable times, had used it himself when referring to his enemies, he highly resented Adam scorning Anita, the very woman who had saved his life. "Well, that's too damn bad, because I ain't gonna mess up your leg by doing something I don't know nothing about."

As Adam opened his mouth, Buck cut across his words in a firm voice. "Save your breath. It won't do you no good to argue with me. I ain't changing your dressings, and that's final."

"Then I'll do it myself!"

"Like hell you will! Your fingers ain't small enough to get between that splint and dressing any more than mine are. You'll mess up that splint, too. I

100

see any signs of you tampering with that bandage, I'll hogtie you to the bed."

Buck turned and stormed from the room, leaving Adam seething in frustration.

Buck was present the next day Anita changed Adam's dressings, and Adam strongly suspected his presence was in support of Anita, and not to offer him any comfort, something that irritated him to no end. Adam steeled himself against Anita's touch and her nearness, using every bit of his iron will to fight down his dark attraction to her, for despite her humiliating him the day before, his body still wanted her, something that shocked him and angered him even more. He forced himself to endure, and, to his vast relief, Anita didn't dally. It was almost as if she was as anxious as he to get the chore done and over.

Then, to Adam's frustration, Anita didn't leave the room. Instead she turned to Buck. "He needs a bath. Do you think you can manage it?"

"A bath?" Buck asked in astonishment. "Hell, we bathed him when I brought him here. What's he need another bath for?"

Adam's eyebrows rose at Buck's revelation. Anita had bathed him, seen him naked, washed him like a baby? Adam was already in a foul mood and thought this the ultimate insult. She had no right to invade his privacy, particularly when he was unable to defend himself.

"Because he stinks," Anita bluntly answered, well aware of the angry look on Adam's face. She could have clarified her accusation by pointing out that it was the foul odor coming from the wound and not necessarily Adam, but she didn't. She was still wanting to hit back at him.

"Well, that's just too goddamned bad!" Adam threw out. "If you don't like the way I smell, you can stay out of this room!"

Anita turned, her black eyes meeting Adam's blazing ones evenly. "Then that's just exactly what I will do," she said with a calmness that infuriated Adam all the more. "I will not change your dressing again until you have bathed."

Anita turned and walked to the door with Adam's eyes boring into her back. As she opened it, she threw over her shoulder, "And shaved. You look like a javelina with all those long, black bristles on your face."

As the door closed behind her, Buck stroked his beard self-consciously, then looked across the room at Adam. His eyes glittering with fury, his lower face covered with almost two weeks' growth of black bristles, and his thick hair uncombed and hanging across his forehead, Adam did look like a wild man. Unlike the majority of the Rangers, Adam was a man who generally kept up his appearance, and Buck was accustomed to seeing him that way. "I guess we'd better do what she says."

"Like hell we will! No woman orders me around. Hell will freeze over before I'll bathe for that bitch!"

Buck winced at the ugly word. Feeling his own anger rise in Anita's defense, Buck forced it down. As furious as Adam was, there was no telling what he might do if Buck challenged him. Besides, Anita had been a little insulting, Buck admitted, telling Adam out-and-out that he stunk. Seems like she could have been a little more delicate about it. But then, he never could understand women's preoccupation with bathing. As far as he was concerned, a bath a week was sufficient, and it hadn't even been a week since they'd bathed Adam. Buck shrugged his shoulders. "Suit yourself."

But as another day passed and Adam stubbornly clung to his resolve, Buck began to worry, afraid that not having his dressing changed, Adam might be endangering his recuperation. But no amount of pleading or reasoning would change Adam's mind. He staunchly refused a bath.

It wasn't until the third day that Adam finally relented, and then only because he couldn't stand the stench himself. He felt as if he were suffocating in it, and the unaccustomed beard on his face was itching like crazy. With Buck's help, he bathed, washed his hair, and shaved, but still the odor still clung, having permeated the bed linens.

"Go out in the hall and see if can find that maid to bring us some fresh linens so we can change this bed," Adam instructed Buck.

"Change the bed?" Buck looked at Adam as if he'd lost his mind. Then, recovering from the surprising request, he admitted, "I ain't never changed a bed, much less one with a man in it."

"Neither have I, but we'll figure it out."

Buck looked down at the splint on Adam's leg doubtfully. "I don't know if we should try it by ourselves. We might get that splint out of alignment.

We don't want that bone mending wrong and leaving you crippled. I think we'd better get Anita to help us."

Adam had hated having to back down to Anita's demands, hated even more to ask for her help, but the threat of being crippled for life was a powerful one. Grudgingly, he agreed, snapping, "All right! Go get her!"

When Buck walked back in with Anita, carrying her basket of supplies and fresh linens thrown over one arm, Adam glared at her, fearing that she would throw his capitulation in his face. But, to his surprise, she made no comment, and the look on her face was totally devoid of all expression, puzzling him.

Anita was wise enough not to bait Adam any further. She, too, had become worried over the bandage not being changed for so long and had regretted her threat. Not that she really cared if the *Tejano* lived or died, she told herself firmly. She just hated to see all her hard work go for naught, and she had never lost a patient.

Efficiently, she changed the dressing, vastly relieved to discover that the wound was still healing despite its neglect, and then, with Buck's help, changed the linens on Adam's bed. Despite her resolve to remain totally indifferent to the savage Texan, Anita again felt the stirring of desire, acutely aware of his powerful muscles rippling beneath the smooth skin on his back as she pushed the bottom sheet up to him. Then, as she and Buck carefully rolled Adam over the bunched sheets, she found she couldn't take her eyes off his bare chest, the dark hairs there tapering to a fine point where the sheet lay across his hips, seemingly pointing like an arrow to that part of him that had excited her before.

As she bent over him and smoothed the top sheet down, Anita became acutely aware of his scent. No longer did Adam stink. The smell was that of leather, which seemed to have permeated his skin from his long hours in the saddle, soap, and a faint masculine essence that sent her senses reeling and her heart racing. Even when she stepped back from him and could no longer smell the strangely disturbing scent, she was painfully conscious of him. Shaved and bathed, with his hair freshly washed and falling about his well-shaped head in dark, lustrous waves, she had never seen him looking so handsome. And those vibrant green eyes against his dark tan was startling, making a little catch come to her throat every time she glanced at them. Not even the jagged scar at the top of his forehead could detract from his rugged beauty. If anything, it just added to his appeal.

Suddenly realizing that she was staring, and terrified that Adam would catch her looking at him like a hungry cat, Anita tore her eyes away, furious with herself. Abruptly, she turned away and began straightening the room, hoping to distract herself from the disturbingly handsome man on the bed. But the activity didn't seem to help. She was still acutely conscious of him, his powerful masculinity attacking her senses in waves that sent shivers rushing over her.

Filled with disgust at herself, she bent to pick up the dirty linen on the floor, planning on making an immediate exit, when Buck swooped them up in his large arms. "I'll carry these out for you, Anita."

Anita looked up. *"Gracias,* Buck." Then suddenly curious, she asked, "Is that a nickname? Buck?"

Buck wanted to deny it, but looking into Anita's dark eyes, he found he couldn't. He sensed she'd know he was lying and think less of him for it. "Yes," he admitted reluctantly.

"Then what is your real name?"

A dark flush rose on the giant's face. He shuffled his feet and then answered in acute embarrassment, "Magnus Rufus."

"Magnus Rufus?" Adam asked in surprise from the bed. "I didn't know that."

Buck whirled and said angrily, "No, you didn't, and don't you dare go telling any of the boys!"

"Why not?"

"Why not?" Buck asked in an incredulous voice. "Why, if the boys knew, they'd laugh me right out of the Ranger service."

Adam shrugged his broad shoulders. "It's not such a bad name."

"Like hell it ain't!" Buck threw back. "How'd you like to have a handle like that? I don't know where my ma and pa ever got those names. They ain't even in the Bible. And I ain't been called that since I was a kid, not since I was old enough to clobber any kid who called me Magnus." Buck shook his shaggy head, a look of total disgust on his face, muttering, "Magnus. Christ!"

"I don't know why you're ashamed of it," Anita commented. "Magnus means 'great' in Latin. I think it suits you perfectly."

"Latin?" Buck asked in astonishment. "How'd you

know that?"

"Because Latin was one of the subjects I studied."

Adam's eyebrows shot up in surprise at Anita's words. He knew Mexican women weren't educated, not even the high-class ones. Had she been taught Latin so she could read her Catholic Bible? But she had distinctly said *one* of the subjects she had studied. He was filled with curiosity. "And what other subjects did you study?" he asked.

"Many others," Anita answered evasively.

"What others?" Adam persisted.

Anita didn't want to tell Adam that she had been as well educated as the men of her class for fear he would ask why, and that was information she would never divulge to him. She would never tell the hated *Tejano* that she was an outcast amongst her own aristocracy, that her grandfather had deliberately given her a man's education so that she could take care of herself and manage the ranch after he died. Undoubtedly, the arrogant savage would take fierce delight in throwing her shame in her face.

"*That* is none of your business, *Tejano*," she answered haughtily, then turned and walked regally from the room.

Adam stared at the open doorway, again seething in frustration.

Chapter 8

Over the next two weeks, a steady stream of Rangers came and went to the hacienda to tell Adam and Buck good-bye before departing for Texas. Since Anita had taken the two Texans into her home willingly, she didn't deny the hated enemy entry. If nothing else, her good breeding prevented her from doing so. Mexicans prided themselves as much on their hospitality as any southerner.

Anita had expected the Rangers to be as crude, surly, and arrogant as her patient. To her surprise, she discovered Texans could be well mannered, even gentlemanly when they chose to be. Therefore, a polite, but cool cordiality existed between Anita and the visiting Rangers.

Anita's relationship with Buck was an entirely different matter, however. The night that they had worked together to save Adam's life had given them a special bond, which slowly evolved into a friendship.

Adam, watching the interplay between Anita and the other Rangers, was both perplexed and frustrated. Anita seemed to have called a truce of her own with everyone but him. That it was he, as much as herself, that kept the war between them going hot and heavy was something that Adam refused to admit. He convinced himself that the others were blinded by her exotic beauty and lulled into a false security by her femininity and therefore, did not recognize Anita for what she was—their enemy. And so, as Adam became increasingly irritated, he blamed his anger on his friends' stupidity and not his resentment at being singled out.

The Ranger officers were among Adam's visitors, and since Sam Walker had been the first on the scene and his enlistment had expired the earliest, he was the first to come to say his good-byes.

As Walker and Buck seated themselves beside Adam's bed, Sam's blue eyes twinkled as he said, "You sure you're not just pretending to be sick, Adam? So you can hang around here a little longer? That was a mighty pretty señorita who greeted me at the door."

Adam scowled deeply. "For Christ's sake, Sam. She's a Mexican!" he snapped.

"Hell, you must be sicker than I thought," Walker said with a laugh. "Since when are any women our enemies? Particularly one as beautiful as she."

Walker's gaze drifted to the door where Anita had disappeared after she had shown him to Adam's room. Seeing his friend's look, Adam tensed. Walker, with his dark red curly hair and dancing blue eyes was a good-looking bastard, and the Ranger captain could charm a bear from a tree when he set his mind to it. A new emotion came to the fore, one as old as time itself, the jealousy of one male vying against another for a female's attentions.

The new emotion shocked Adam, and he tried to deny it, saying, "Well, I guess every man has his own tastes. Personally, I don't think Mexican women are at all attractive. Their coloring is too high. They all look like painted-up whores."

"Don't you be calling Anita a whore!" Buck threw out hotly, coming to the edge of his chair in Anita's defense. "You wouldn't be alive if it weren't for her."

"I'm not the one beholden to her!" Adam shot back. "You are. Remember?"

"That still don't give you the right to be calling her dirty names. You know damned well that she's a lady."

"I'll call her anything I want!" Adam replied in a hard voice. "Just because she's got you wrapped around her little finger doesn't mean she's fooled me."

Walker eyed the two men thoughtfully, knowing that there was more here than met the eye. There had been a sharpness in Adam's voice when he had said that Mexican women didn't suit his tastes, a tone of voice that had had a warning edge to it. Walker strongly suspected that the rugged Texan was attracted to the girl and fighting it tooth and toenail. Did Adam feel the attraction as a betrayal to the memory of his wife, who had been killed by the girl's countrymen? And Buck? Why was he so protective? If he didn't know the giant better, he'd think he was attracted to the beautiful girl himself, but Sam knew Buck was devoted to his wife. Whatever, he'd better do something to change the subject. The two men looked like they were about to tear each other apart with their bare hands.

"Did you hear my news?" Sam asked, clearing his throat. "I've enlisted in the regular army." Walker grinned. "Had to take a demotion, though. I'm back to being a captain. I'll command Company C, United States Mounted Rifles."

Buck was the one who broke the fierce eye contact between him and Adam. He turned to Sam. "Yeah, we heard. But why the regular army—for God's sake!"

"I was in the army before I moved to Texas. I served with both Taylor and Worth in the Seminole War." Seeing the two Rangers' surprised expressions, he added, "Didn't I ever tell you that?"

Both men shook their heads, and Adam wondered if that was how Walker managed to get a jump ahead of the other Rangers in getting into the war, remembering that Walker's company was mustered in before Taylor had even officially called for volunteers. Had it been because he had known the two generals in Florida?

"Well, I guess it slipped my mind," Sam continued. "But I'm an old army man, so I'm used to army life. Besides, it's the only way I can be guaranteed staying in the fight. Taylor says he doesn't want any more volunteers, Ranger or otherwise. So I'm off to Washington. I want to see if I can get the strength of my company increased." Sam moved to the edge of his chair, saying, "Which reminds me. I didn't just drop by to say farewell. I'd like to know if you two would like to join up with me. Some of the other Rangers are doing just that, and I'd sure like to have you in my company."

Adam wanted to stay in the fight badly. His thirst

111

for revenge hadn't been satisfied, not by a long shot. But he wasn't that desperate. "Sorry, Sam. I could never take army life. Too many stupid rules and regulations."

"Same goes for me Buck chimed in. "Besides, the Army wouldn't let me wear my coonskin cap, and you know how strongly I feel about that."

Walker wasn't surprised at the two men's refusal. All of the Texas Rangers were independent men, but Adam and Buck were even more so, guarding their right to be individuals and make their own decisions with a determination that bordered on ferocity. "I figured you'd turn me down, but I wanted to try anyway. It's a shame you boys are going to miss out on the action."

"Maybe Taylor will change his mind about volunteers," Adam said hopefully.

"Even if he did, it wouldn't do you any good— unless you're willing to accept a role in the army of occupation. Since Mexico refused to surrender after the fall of Monterrey, President Polk is convinced that the only way to beat them is to take Mexico City itself. The war is over in northern Mexico. It's moving to the interior, and General Winfield Scott will be running that show."

"General Scott?" Adam asked in a shocked voice. "What happened to Taylor?"

"Polk has appointed Scott to take over the Mexican campaign. Taylor will command the army of occupation in northern Mexico, and Polk has ordered him to stay put in Monterrey."

"Why the change of plans?" Adam asked. "I heard that Polk despises Scott. Some people say that's why he passed over Scott and appointed Taylor to the Mexican campaign, even though Scott was the general-in-chief and Taylor's senior officer." Adam's brow furrowed thoughtfully, then he cocked his head. "Or is Polk disenchanted with Taylor for letting the Mexican Army get away at both Matamoros and Monterrey?"

"Well, it's true he's not too happy with Taylor's methods of fighting this war, but I'm inclined to agree with a lot of others who think Polk has come to fear Taylor more than he despises Scott, and that's why Polk is taking the campaign away from him."

"Why should Polk fear Taylor?" Buck asked.

Because Taylor is the hero of the hour, even more so after the victory here at Monterrey. There's a lot of talk among the Whigs about running Taylor for President in the next election. Naturally, as the Democratic Party's head man, Polk wants to keep the Whigs out of the White House."

"But Taylor's a general, an army man," Buck objected. "What would he know about running the country?"

"The American people have always had trouble differentiating between a general and a statesman," Adam remarked in disgust. "They don't understand that running an army and running the country takes two distinctly different talents. Look at how many generals have been elected President in the past. And Taylor is made of the same stuff as Andrew Jackson, a tough old fighter who appeals to the common man, and we all know where Andy landed up. In the highest office in the land. But the question is, how does Taylor feel about it?"

"I don't think Taylor came into this war with any political ambitions," Walker answered. "But there is no doubt in my mind that he's hearing the siren's call. After all, to become the President of one's country is an overwhelming honor, one few men could resist if given the opportunity. At any rate, Taylor is out of the war. One more victory would be all it would take to put him in the White House, and Polk is going to make damned sure that doesn't happen by keeping him here in northern Mexico. The war is over here."

Anita entered the room, carrying the supplies for changing Adam's dressing in her arms. Walker rose from his chair and said his good-byes to Adam and Buck, then pointedly made a charming exit to Anita, taking mischievous pleasure in seeing how much it irritated Adam.

While Anita performed the task, Buck watched her with concern. She had seemed deeply disturbed over the past few days, and Buck wondered if Adam's surly attitude was beginning to wear her down. Even now, his friend was glaring at her as if he could murder her.

Directing his attention back to Adam, Buck commented, "Sam's looking good, ain't he? He didn't have that peculiar gleam in his eyes, like the last time I saw him. I'm telling you, when he gets that look in his eyes, it gives me the creeps."

Adam tore his gaze away from Anita and looked Buck in the eye, saying in a tight, angry voice, "He only gets that look when he's talking about Mexicans." Adam paused, gazing off thoughtfully. "Damn, it makes me mad when people call him 'Mad

Walker.' If they'd gone through what he has, they'd hate Mexicans with a passion, too. No one can take that kind of humiliation and brutality and not be affected by it. You know, when Sam got back from Mexico and came to tell me Dan was still a prisoner, he told me everything that happened during those years, about the battle at Mier and how he was captured, about finding Dan in the prison there when he was brought in, about how they were marched through every little village in northern Mexico so the peons could spit on them and throw stones on them and call them filthy names, about finally overpowering their guards and escaping. He admitted they made a mistake after they escaped. They should have stuck to the roads and fought their way back to Texas. Instead they went into the mountains and got lost in that desert above Saltillo. They wandered around helplessly out there, burning up in the daytime and freezing at night, eating insects and rattlesnakes and cactus, going without water for days on end. They were too weak to fight when the Mexicans finally caught up with them."

Adam paused for a minute, staring out into space, and Buck knew he was remembering that Adam's brother, Dan, had shared all those horrors with Walker and that Adam had completely forgotten that Anita was present. He wondered if he should remind Adam, then thought better of it. These were things Adam had never told him, had kept locked deep inside him. Maybe getting it out of his system would help. But still, he hated for Adam to speak of the Mexicans with such strong hatred in front of Anita after all she had done for him. He glanced at Anita and saw her shake her head, signaling him not to stop Adam on her behalf. He smiled back in silent gratitude and held his silence.

"Then there was that death lottery, where they drew beans from a jar to see if they would live or die," Adam said, still staring out into space. "Sam said those who drew white felt too guilty to be relieved that they hadn't drawn a black bean, like they had somehow betrayed the others. And then they were forced to watch the execution of their friends. Sam said when they marched them out the next night, the executed were still lying where they had been shot, their bodies black and stiff. He never knew if the Mexicans buried them, or just left them there for buzzard bait."

Adam was in a world of his own making. As if in a daze, he continued Walker's grim tale. "The prisoners were marched to Perote in central Mexico and imprisoned in an old castle down there. One day Walker was struck by a guard because he wasn't hauling rocks fast enough. He said he went wild and attacked the Mexican. The other guards beat him to a bloody pulp and he almost died. A few months later, he and five others escaped and finally made their way home. Dan would have gone with him, but he was too ill to travel."

Adam turned his head, his eyes once again boring into Buck. "Have you ever seen your friends murdered in cold blood, Buck?" he asked in an angry voice. "Have you ever been lost in a desert, starving and dying of thirst? Have you ever been marched hundreds of miles with chains around your wrists and ankles, until your feet were cut to ribbons? Have

116

you ever been in a dungeon? Sometimes those men didn't see daylight for weeks at a time. It was cold and damp, infested with lice. Sam said the rats were so big that they had to fight them off for the crumbs of moldy bread and wormy meat the Mexicans fed them. And have you ever been whipped, Buck? Whipped until the flesh was shredded from your back and legs, your head battered until it was black and blue and swollen to twice its normal size? Dammit, if you'd gone through all of that, like Walker did, you'd be a little mad, too!"

Wisely, Buck held his silence, remembering that Adam's brother, Dan, had gone through all that, too, except Dan hadn't survived it, like Walker had. Had he, Dan might have been just as obsessed with his hatred, and now Adam carried that burden on his soul, a grim inheritance that demanded vengeance.

Anita had listened with keen interest while Adam related Walker's story. Despite her strong dislike for the Texans, she couldn't help but feel compassion for the men who had suffered so much. And who was this Dan that Adam had mentioned several times, she wondered. Obviously he was someone very close to Adam. Now, she better understood why Adam hated Mexicans so badly. But her people had their reasons, too.

A long silence prevailed in the room. Anita was the first to break it when she arose from where she had been bandaging Adam's leg. "Your Ranger friend is a fool if he thinks the war is over in northern Mexico."

Adam's head snapped around, and he looked at Anita as if he didn't know how she had come to be there. He shook his head, feeling foggy and confused and remembering nothing of his outburst. Then as the meaning of her words penetrated his brain, his eyes narrowed suspiciously. His hand flew out like a striking snake and caught her wrist, pulling her forward. "Were you spying on us?" he asked in a hard voice.

Anita jerked her arm and found that Adam's grip was like steel. Standing proudly, she said, "No, I was not spying. I overheard his words when I was walking down the hall." She glared down at Adam, adding, "Besides, if I wanted to know what was being said, I would not have to spy. I would stay in the room. This is *my* home."

Another suspicion took root in Adam's mind. Anita was a Mexican. Had she heard rumors of Mexican troop movements through the Mexican grapevine? Had the Mexicans regrouped and planning an attempt to take Monterrey back?

He yanked her closer, asking in a demanding voice, "Why did you make that remark? What makes you think the war isn't over in northern Mexico?"

"Because Santa Anna will gather an army and march on you."

Adam laughed harshly. "You crazy little fool. Don't you even know Santa Anna isn't the President of Mexico anymore? Hell, he was exiled to Cuba years ago."

"I know *exactly* where Santa Anna has been the last few years. But he's in Mexico now. Your government let him back in. It was they who gave him his return to power in Mexico."

Adam was so shocked by Anita's words that he didn't notice the bitterness in her voice, or that her eyes were glittering with anger. His head snapped around as he looked to Buck to confirm or to deny what he had just heard.

"It's true, Adam. Santa Anna is back. I heard about it at the Ranger camp a few days ago. He's been in Mexico ever since August."

"For Christ's sake! Why didn't you tell me?" Adam asked in an accusing voice.

"I figured you knew, that one of the Rangers who came visiting must have told you. Hell, it's all they were talking about. And it's true what Anita said. It was the American government that gave him safe passage through our naval blockade."

"But why?" Adam asked in mixture of disbelief and anger. "Why in the hell did they do it? Didn't they realize that he was the only man who could pull it together for Mexico?"

"He tricked them. He convinced Polk that if he'd let him through the blockade, he'd persuade the Mexicans to sue for peace. Instead, he overthrew Paredas, declared himself president, and took command of the army. He's already working on building it up."

Buck ran his fingers through his shaggy hair and hunched over in his chair. "Damn, I'd give anything to stay in this war. I'd give my eyeteeth to get my hands on that treacherous bastard."

"So would I," Adam answered with a low growl. "Santa Anna is the one who sent my brother to that prison where he died. If it weren't for him, Dan would be alive today. I've got a particular score to settle with Santa Anna."

So that was who Dan was, Anita thought. Adam's

brother. And Santa Anna had been responsible for his death. Adam hated him in particular among all Mexicans. Her heart raced at this unexpected news.

Neither man noticed the spark of interest that flickered in Anita's dark eyes at their words. By the time Adam turned his attention back to her, she had retreated behind her cool, indifferent facade.

"And I suppose that's why you think Santa Anna will march north?" Adam asked her, his voice dripping with venom. "That, like all Mexicans, you consider him your hero, your savior."

The look that came over Anita's face stunned both men. They had seen her angry, but never this furious. "No! Santa Anna is *not* my hero! He is a traitor to Mexico, a scourge on my people. Time and time again, he has betrayed us with his treachery, bleeding us dry of our treasury with his greed for luxury, and wasting our men in needless wars to satisfy his egomaniacal thirst for fame. He cares about no one but Santa Anna and his own power. He is totally unscrupulous, a man who thrives on turmoil and the blood of others, and yet so weak that he resorts to eating opium."

For Anita it was a long discourse, astonishing both Adam and Buck with its length and rancor. Adam had heard that there were Mexicans who hated Santa Anna almost as passionately as the Texans did. It surprised him to learn that Anita was one of them, but what surprised him even more was her knowledge of the man.

"You seem to know an awful lot about Santa Anna," he remarked.

"*Sí.* I make it my business to know *everything*

about him," Anita answered with a metallic glitter in her dark eyes.

"Why?" Adam asked curiously.

"*That* is none of your business, *Tejano,*" Anita answered in a hard voice. "But he will march north. Mark my words."

Again Adam laughed harshly. "You're wrong, Anita. You may know a lot of facts about Santa Anna, but you don't know a damnéd thing about military tactics. The United States is preparing to invade Mexico's interior, and Santa Anna is going to have to meet that attack to win this war. He can't be bothered with the northern provinces when the very heart of Mexico, the capital, is at stake."

"He will come," Anita answered with absolute confidence. "You'll see."

With that, Anita turned and walked from the room, as majestic and self-assured as any queen, and, strangely, both Adam and Buck found themselves believing her.

Chapter 9

A week later, John Coffee Hays appeared at the hacienda to visit Adam, and Anita found it hard to believe when the colonel introduced himself at her door that this was the commanding officer of the entire Texas Ranger force and the man she had heard described as a "living terror." Slimly built and of medium height, his mild hazel eyes sitting in a clean-shaven face that was almost boyish in appearance, he was soft-spoken and polite to the point of shyness.

After showing Hays to Adam's room, Anita remained, sitting in a chair by the window, both curious about the man himself and any news of the war that he might have. Seeing she was planning on staying, Adam shot Anita a hot look that clearly told her that her presence was not wanted, but Anita glared back her defiance, daring him to tell her to leave.

Bold, insolent bitch, Adam thought with renewed anger, wishing he was recovered enough to get up from the bed and physically expel her, for he knew nothing short of that could force her to leave once she had set her mind on staying. She was undoubtedly the most obstinate, frustrating female he'd ever had the misfortune to run across.

Hays was unaware of the silent battle taking place between the two antagonists. He settled into a chair beside the bed and said, "You're looking fit, Adam."

Adam tore his eyes away from Anita and turned his head to face the colonel, answering in a distracted voice, "Thanks, Jack."

"You're on your way back to Texas?" Buck asked the colonel.

"Yes, me and my company will be pulling out tomorrow. Would you like me to deliver a letter to Martha for you?"

"Sure would," Buck answered, his face lighting up at the mention of his wife. "I reckon she's wondering if I'm still alive, and I'd like to explain why Adam and I are being delayed."

"You don't have to stick around here because of me, Buck," Adam said tersely.

Hell, Buck thought in frustration, Adam was getting testier every day, snapping at everybody and everything. He was enough to try the patience of a saint. "I know, Adam. But you and me have always been partners. Why, if I went back without you, Martha would skin me alive."

"I'll be happy to take your letter, Buck," Hays said, settling the issue of whether Buck would stay or leave in his calm but authoritative manner "And there is something else I wanted to discuss with the two of you. I'm not as convinced as Walker that the Rangers are out of this war. Whether the Army likes it or not, they're going to need volunteers particularly men who understand the Mexican mind, like we Rangers do."

Anita's dark eyebrows rose in open skepticism at Hays's last words. She had to bite her tongue to keep from scoffing at the colonel's claim. Adam was well aware of her reaction, just as he was acutely aware of everything about her when she was present. He slashed her a warning look to keep her mouth shut, a look that Anita pointedly ignored. Damn, she was distracting, he thought. He couldn't even concentrate on what Hays was saying with her in the room.

Again, Hays was unaware of the silent struggle going on between the two. He continued. "I'm going to use all of my influence to see if I can't get us back in this war with General Scott, and I'm sure the governor will support me to the hilt. If I can get another company together, I'd like to have both of you in it."

Adam's head snapped around, the colonel's last words having finally captured his undivided attention. He shot a quick glance at Buck, seeing the giant's eyes light up with anticipation. What Hays was proposing was the answer to their prayers. Yet, both men believed in Anita's prediction that Santa Anna would march north to do battle with Taylor's army. Adam felt torn and knew Buck was feeling the same. They didn't want to miss any of the action by having to choose to stay in northern Mexico, or march with Scott's army into the interior.

"Well, what do you say?" Hays prompted when both men had remained silent for so long.

Adam decided to hedge. "We'd like to join your company, Jack, but I don't know how long this leg is going to take to heal. It's broken pretty bad, you know. It might be quite a while before I can ride any distance."

Hays frowned. "I didn't realize it was that serious." He paused, a thoughtful expression on his face, then said, "I'll tell you what. When I find out where our embarkation point is, I'll let you know. That might be months off. Then if your leg is healed, you can meet me there. It would save you the time of having to backtrack."

"Embarkation?" Adam asked in surprise. "Isn't Scott going to march overland, along the eastern coast of Mexico?"

"No, he's going to try for an amphibious assault."

"He's crazy! Adam blurted.

Hays chuckled. "That's what the military experts in Europe are saying, too. But then, they didn't think we could lick the Mexicans in our first encounters with them, either. Our victories at Palo Alto, Resaca de la Palma, and now Monterrey have given them pause."

"Wait a minute," Buck interjected, a suspicious scowl on his face. Back up there. Does that mean we'd be traveling on steamers?"

"Yes. Veracruz has been chosen as the target."

Adam glanced sharply in Anita's direction and hissed in a low voice, "Watch what you say, Jack. She's listening to everything."

Without even glancing over his shoulder, Hays said, "Don't get alarmed, Adam. I didn't let any big secret slip. It's pretty much common knowledge here in Mexico where the attack will take place. In fact, the Mexicans are already preparing for the invasion and shoring up their defenses in Veracruz. After all, it's the most logical spot to invade. It's a straight shot from there to Mexico City."

"And straight through mountains," Adam pointed out.

"There are mountains everywhere in Mexico," Hays answered. "One way or another, the American Army is going to have to cross them."

Buck had been contemplating the horrors of steamers and said in a determined voice, "You ain't gonna get me on one of those steamers, Jack. As much as I want to get in on the fighting, I ain't setting foot on one of them. Hell, they're dangerous! A man could get killed on one of those fool things."

Hays could have pointed out that a man could get killed fighting in a war, too, but he didn't. He gave Buck a penetrating look. "You're serious, aren't you?"

"You're damned right I'm serious!"

"To tell you the truth, Jack," Adam said, "I'm not too keen about getting on a crowded troop steamer, either. I have this fear of being in tight, closed places. I'd probably be a raving maniac by the time we reached Veracruz." But Adam didn't want to be left out because of something as stupid as the mode of transportation. He decided to try a long shot. "What would you say if we agreed to meet you in Veracruz?"

"You mean you'd travel overland, through hundreds of miles of enemy territory, just the two of you all alone?" Hays asked in an incredulous voice.

"Yes," Adam answered calmly.

Hays stared at Adam in disbelief for a moment, then laughed. "By God, you're men after my own heart. Just the kind of men I'm looking for. Bold and fearless. Okay, Adam. It's a deal. If you two can manage to get to Veracruz in one piece, I'll make a spot for you in my company."

"Thanks, Jack," Adam answered, feeling a tremendous relief, and Buck quickly echoed his words.

After Hays had left, the two men grinned across the space of Adam's bed at each other, pleased with the coup they had pulled off. Buck was the first to break their smug silence. "This way we won't have to sweat out your leg healing in time for us to leave with the other Rangers, and we can get in on all the fighting, both here and in central Mexico."

Adam frowned. He had been feeling smug because he had talked Hays into letting him and Buck meet them in Veracruz, instead of going by steamer with the other Rangers. "No, Buck, I don't think there will be any more fighting in northern Mexico. I was willing to admit to that possibility before I learned that Scott isn't marching overland. No, if the invasion is to be by sea, at Veracruz, Santa Anna will have to set himself up someplace between there and Mexico City. It wouldn't be a matter of Santa Anna simply pulling back, but moving his army halfway across Mexico to intercept Scott's army after he finished with Taylor's. In order to do that, he'd have to attack Taylor's army in the middle of the winter.

"He will come north," Anita said in a quiet but emphatic tone of voice.

Buck startled, having forgotten she was present.

Adam scoffed. "You're crazy if you think that. Bring his army halfway across Mexico, over the mountains, in the middle of the winter?"

"You *Tejanos* never learn, do you?" Anita asked in a scathing voice. "Have you forgotten Santa Anna marched his army across the barren stretch of land between the Rio Grande and San Antonio de Bexar in the middle of winter? You didn't think he would do it, not without forage for his animals. You didn't prepare because you thought he wouldn't march until spring, but he appeared on your doorstep in February—in the middle of the winter!" Anita's dark eyes flashed. "Don't make the mistake of underestimating Santa Anna the second time, *Tejanos*. I told you, he is devious. He never does the expected thing. He will come."

As Anita left the room, Buck watched her with dumbfounded wonder, and Adam with a frown of puzzlement.

Adam was confused. He could understand her hating Santa Anna for what he had done to Mexico, but Anita had sounded almost as if she had a personal vendetta against the Mexican President and was warning him and Buck not to fail the second time in defeating him once and for all.

Ben McCulloch had visited off and on with Adam and Buck, and on the day of his final departure, Adam said in exasperation, "I don't understand Taylor's logic. Dammit, we gave him Monterrey, and now he sends every Ranger home. Even you."

"You and Buck were out here at this *rancho* when it happened, but some of the Rangers were pretty mad when Taylor let Ampudia go and raised a little hell in Monterrey. I guess it was the last straw for Taylor. He said he didn't have time to police a thousand Rangers or to find things to keep them occupied. I agreed to return if hostilities commenced, and I don't think that will be very long. These negotiations aren't going to last."

"What negotiations?" Adam asked.

"Hell you are isolated out here, aren't you? Santa Anna has started peace negotiations, but I know it's just another one of his sly tricks. He's stalling for time to build up his army."

"And the American government is falling for it?" Adam asked in disbelief.

"When it comes to Santa Anna, they're as naive as newborn babes. Besides, you know how cunning that bastard can be. He's led the Mexican people a merry chase for over twenty-five years, jumping from party to party and betraying them all, one day a federalist, the next a centralist, then back again. Christ, he's the biggest opportunist this world has ever produced."

"Then you don't think the fighting in northern Mexico is over?" Buck asked.

"Not with Santa Anna back in the picture, and after what happened the other day, I'm even more convinced. Taylor received word from Scott that he wanted nine thousand of Taylor's troops for his invasion into central Mexico, mostly his experienced regulars. Well, it really shook the old man up. One of his officers told me he was so upset that he spread mustard over his meat, his bread, his potatoes, even his dessert, and then ate it without a word. Considering how cool Taylor usually is, that says a lot." Ben shook his head. "Now, I admit we Rangers haven't always seen eye to eye with Taylor, but, dammit, the old man deserves better than that. They're stripping him, leaving him wide open to the enemy."

"Then he's going to send Scott the troops he requested?" Adam asked.

"I don't know. The last I heard he was ignoring the request, and he's ignoring Polk's order to stay put, too. He's making plans to move on to Saltillo."

Buck grinned. "Maybe, a little of us rubbed off on him. Now *he's* disobeying orders.

"Well, if Scott presses the issue, Taylor will have to send him the troops." Ben rose. "So I may be seeing you boys sooner than you think. Hell, I may be back before you even get out of that splint, Adam."

"I hope not," Adam answered fervently. "I want to be able to ride by then."

The splint didn't come off for another two months, but the dressing was removed for the final time two weeks later, leaving a puckered mass of scar tissue the size of a silver dollar on Adam's thigh.

As Adam looked down at it, Anita said, "Does

the scar upset you, *Tejano?*"

Adam winced. It irked him to no end that Anita refused to call him by his name, as she did Buck, but persisted in calling him *Tejano,* and always with such utter contempt. "No the scar doesn't bother me. I have others," Adam answered tersely, then admitted grudgingly, "To be honest, I'm surprised that it isn't larger, considering how infected it was."

Anita made no acknowledgment of Adam's oblique compliment of her skill, but proceeded to pack her supplies in her wicker basket. Adam was fascinated with the basket's contents. There were dried leaves of every possible shape and size, pieces of bark and roots, dried mushrooms, jars of powders, and bottles of elixirs, even something that looked suspiciously like mold. None were labeled, and Adam wondered how Anita knew one from the other, for all the roots looked alike, as did the powders and elixirs.

"Where did you learn how to use all that stuff you keep in that basket?" he asked, curious.

"I told you. I have the gift for healing."

"The gift, perhaps, but you still had to learn from someone."

"*Sí.*" Anita admitted. "I was taught by an old mestizo servant, who learned the art from her Yaquí mother."

"Yaquí? That's a Mexican Indian tribe, isn't it?"

"*Sí,* but not just a tribe. They are a nation unto themselves, so fierce that no one has been able to conquer them. Some of the cures that she taught me go back to ancient times."

As far back as the Aztecs? Adam wondered, his

gaze drifting over Anita's golden skin. Then he remembered that Anita was talking about a servant, and not an ancestor.

"Is she the one who taught you to dress that way?"

"What way?"

"Like a common peon. Even I know that upper-class Mexican women don't wear *camisas,* ankle-length skirts, and sandals, not even in the privacy of their homes."

Anita shrugged. "They are comfortable."

The motion, while casual, had a seductiveness to it that made Adam's heart quicken. His gaze slowly swept over the smooth skin of her shoulders, up the long, graceful column of her neck, then dropped to the rise of her proud full breasts revealed in the low-cut blouse. He stared at the lush mounds. God, he wanted to taste her.

Then realizing what he was doing, he jerked his eyes away. "And what do others of your class think of your attire when they come to visit?"

"I do not care what the others think. I do and say as I please." Anita paused, then seeing Adam's scowl, asked, "Do you think only you *Tejanos* can be independent? That only you can set your own code of rules?"

"You're a woman," Adam objected. "A woman should be more . . . more—"

"Subservient?" Anita asked in a biting voice. "No. I am not like the others, weak and dependent on the male, clinging, silent, stupid. I live by my own dictates, not society's, not any man's. I am different. I am me. Anita!"

Yes, Adam thought there couldn't be another like her in the whole world. She was more than different. She was unique. A mixture of puzzling contradictions, possessing both the haughtiness of a queen and the earthiness of a peasant. Not only did she attract him physically as no woman ever had, not even his wife, but Adam found her fascinating. He knew she was unusually intelligent and longed to talk to her, to delve into her complex mind and see what she was thinking, what she was feeling, what made her tick. But she held herself away from him, hiding her thoughts and emotions behind the cool, indifferent mask she set on her face, something that frustrated him to no end. Yes, she excited him, fascinated him, and frustrated him as no woman ever had, her spirit as elusive and haunting as a ghost.

Adam was so deep in these thoughts that he did not realize he was again staring. Under that piercing gaze, a look that seemed to be trying to peer into her soul, Anita felt very uncomfortable. She allowed no one to invade that inviolable part of her, and yet this *Tejano,* this man who disturbed her as no one ever had, was getting too close, bringing all her defenses rushing to the fore. She stiffened and glared at him, saying in a cold, hard voice, "You are rude, *Tejano.* Am I so different that you must stare at me, as if I were a freak?"

Adam's hand flew out with lightning-fast swiftness. Catching her small wrist, he jerked her down so roughly that Anita fell halfway over him. Holding her tightly against his chest, he glared into her face. "Don't call me *Tejano.*"

"Would you prefer gringo?" Anita asked with a sneer

"No. Call me by my name, like you do Buck."

"Buck is different."

"Why?"

"He is a *compadre*, an *amigo*,"

"And I'm still your enemy?"

"*Sí.*"

"Why? Why do you single me out? Why do you hate me so much?"

"Not just you. I hate all men who use guns to attain power."

"I'm not trying to attain power. I use my guns for protection. The men I seek have weapons."

"And what about the other Mexicans? Those who have no weapons? You use your guns, your physical prowess, to intimidate them. You use your strength against the weak."

Adam was finding it difficult to think with Anita's soft breasts pressed against his chest, her face so close that their lips were just inches apart. With supreme will, he battled the desire that was rising in him and forced himself to concentrate on their conversation. "Are you talking about the peons?"

"*Sí.*"

"Hell, you're an aristocrat. Since when does the Mexican aristocrat give a damn about the peons? You've kept them in virtual slavery ever since your ancestors came to this country."

"That will change. Someday Mexico will belong to all Mexicans."

"Yeah, Adam said with sarcasm in his voice. "When hell freezes over."

"And *that* is when I will call you by your name, *Tejano*."

Anita pulled away, turned, picked up her basket, and walked from the room. Adam watched with a mixture of frustration and anger. The Americans had won every battle in their war so far, but he had yet to win one skirmish with this Mexican. And she was a woman — for Christ's sake.

The next day, out of the blue, Anita started calling Adam by his name.

The following month crawled by for Adam and was sheer hell. As his irritability increased day by day, he told himself that his tension was due to his confinement, his old fear of being hemmed in coming to fore. Although he could move about — for Anita had provided him with a crude crutch — those movements were limited to the upper story, since he couldn't manage the steep stairs with the cumbersome splint. There he paced like a caged tiger, snapping and snarling at everyone so much so that Anita's housekeeper, Maria, refused to take *el Diablo Tejano* his meals anymore.

But it wasn't just Adam's confinement to the upper floor that was wearing on his nerves. More than his limited mobility and utter boredom, it was *who* he was confined with. Anita. He found that he couldn't keep his eyes off her when she was around, his gaze drifting over the seductive sway of her hips, the mesmerizing movement of the single, thick braid of lustrous raven hair that hung down her back, the graceful column of her neck, the black eyes that could flash with anger or glitter with scorn, the high cheekbones, the tiny, shell-like ears, the golden tint of her flawless skin, then lingering—always lingering—on the sensuous curve of her full bottom lip and the proud thrust of her breasts. Even when she wasn't in the room with him, Adam was tormented by an acute awareness of her presence, smelling her sweet scent which floated in the air, hearing the tantalizing sound of her deep, throaty voice drifting from the hallway. She was a temptress sent to torture him with her exotic beauty and bold sensuality, leaving a constant aching in his loins and his nerves a tight coil deep in his belly.

He tried to fight it, reminding himself that she was his hated enemy, scourging himself with the belief that his attraction itself was a betrayal to the memory of his Anglo wife—the woman he had loved. When that didn't work, he told himself that he was above animal lust, but that didn't ring true, either. Adam was a strong, young man with healthy sexual urges, and he couldn't deny his sexuality any more than he could deny any other part of him. He had already discovered that he couldn't take Anita by force, nor would he woo her with seduction. Both were beneath him. There seemed to be no escape from the torment but escape itself. He had to get away from her, put a vast distance between them, and the sooner the better.

And so, the day that Anita removed his splint and pronounced his leg healed Adam's first words to Buck were, "We'll leave as soon as we can get packed up."

"No, that would not be wise, Anita interjected.

"The knee is stiff. Your leg needs exercising. And it is still weak. You will need to walk with your crutch for another day or two."

"I'll carry the damned crutch with me."

Buck ignored Adam's retort and asked Anita, "You don't think he should travel yet?"

"No, the jarring of a horse on the newly mended bone might snap it again. To be safe, I would suggest waiting a few more days."

"We leave today," Adam repeated stubbornly.

"Like hell we will!" Buck snapped. "I didn't sit around here for two months waiting for your leg to mend to have you snap it the first time you try to mount. That's your left leg, you know, your mounting leg. You'll be putting your full weight on it. Besides, what's the hurry? We ain't got no place to go. Nothing is going on out there that we're gonna miss."

"Has it ever occurred to you that maybe we've outstayed our welcome?" Adam asked, taking another approach. "That Anita might be glad to see us leave."

Buck frowned, making his bushy eyebrows meet over the bridge of his nose as he pondered this possibility.

But before he could respond, Anita said, "I would prefer that you stay for a few more days. I do not want to see my efforts ruined by a precipitous departure."

"Then it's settled," Buck said in a firm voice. "We're staying."

From his peripheral vision, Adam caught the fleeting look of relief in Anita's dark eyes and

137

wondered at it. Had it been, as she had said, that she didn't want to see her careful work of the past two months destroyed, or because she would miss them, miss him. Adam felt a surge of immense satisfaction at the last thought, and then seeing the cold mask fall back into place over Anita's face, silently cursed himself for a fool.

"Work," Anita said to Adam in a dispassionate voice. "Exercise that leg. Get the circulation going." She turned and busied herself with tidying up the room.

Adam pulled himself up with his crutch and stood, grumbling, "This is a damned bunch of foolishness." But he was shocked at how weak the limb was. He *did* need the support of the crutch.

As Adam limped stiffly from one side of the room to the other, Buck asked, "Where will we go when we leave here?"

"Saltillo, I guess. Didn't you tell me that's where Taylor has moved the bulk of his army?"

"Yeah, he marched out to occupy the city two days ago." Buck grinned, adding, "In direct disobedience to Polk's order to stay put in Monterrey. And he ain't sent Scott the troops he requested, either. Maybe we underestimated him."

"I think he knows that Polk is trying to sabotage his chances at the presidency. He's stalling for time, hoping to get that one last battle in before he gives up his best troops."

"Well, it don't look like Santa Anna is gonna accommodate him. Hell, it's been two months since Ben left, and Santa Anna hasn't budged. He's still down there at San Luis Potosi, drilling his army."

"The truce didn't end until a few days ago," Adam reminded him.

"Hell since when did a truce stop Santa Anna from attacking?" Buck spat. The giant gazed off, a thoughtful expression on his face, then said, "Maybe we'll just be wasting our time sticking around here. Maybe Santa Anna won't march north. Maybe we just ought to go back to Texas and wait for Hays and his company to pull out."

Adam's eyes shifted to Anita, standing at the window and gazing out at the Sierras. He observed her thoughtfully for a moment, then turned his attention back to Buck. "We can wait around a little longer. Scott can't begin his campaign until Taylor gives him the troops he wants. And if Santa Anna comes, he'll have to march through the San Luis Potosi Pass. It's the only way he can get through the mountains that separate him from us. Saltillo guards that vital pass. If anything happens, it will have to take place somewhere around there."

"Then we just go to Saltillo and wait to see if Santa Anna shows up?"

"Yes."

Anita turned and walked from the room. From the corner of his eye, Adam saw the strange metallic glitter in her black eyes and the feline smile on her lips, giving her beautiful face an almost diabolical appearance. The hair rose on his nape, for he sensed that look boded ill for someone.

Chapter 10

That night, Adam stood at his window admiring the breathtaking view of the Sierra Madres in the distance. The dark, jagged peaks were topped with snow that glowed in the moonlight against a backdrop of an ebony sky in which millions of glittering stars twinkled.

A soft knock sounded at the door, bringing a deep frown to Adam's face. The only one who ever knocked on the door was Anita, but she never came to his room at night, one propriety—perhaps the only one—that she stringently obeyed.

He turned and crossed the room, limping slightly on his stiff leg. Opening the door, he saw Anita standing in the dark hallway. Had he only imagined it, or had there been a brief flickering of apprehension in her eyes when the door had swung open? If so, there was none there now. Her face was its usual mask—cold, impassive, making the beauty of her face look as if it were a bust carved in bronze instead of flesh and bone.

"We must talk," Anita said, her words more a demand than a request.

The low, throaty timbre of her voice throbbed in the air and sent an answering throb coursing through Adam's veins. The passion that he had been struggling to keep at bay surged to the surface, startling him with its intensity.

Holding his arms rigidly at his sides to keep from touching her, Adam answered thickly, "It's late. Come back tomorrow."

It had taken all of Anita's considerable courage to prepare herself for the bold proposition she had come to present to Adam. At his curt reaction, she wavered. What if he should refuse? No, she couldn't let herself weaken at this point. Not even the fear of his rejection could turn her away from her resolve. It was a matter of revenge and family honor. "No. We will talk now," Anita persisted, sidestepping him and walking into the room, passing so close to him that her skirt brushed his legs and Adam was engulfed in her heady, sweet scent.

Adam's senses reeled; he fought a brief but fierce battle with himself. He turned to find Anita facing him, an intense expression on her face.

"Shut the door, Adam. The servants have big ears, and what I have to say is none of their business. It's between you and me alone."

Adam's curiosity overrode his desire. He pushed the door closed, his eyes never leaving Anita's face.

As soon as the lock had snapped in place, Anita drew a deep breath to fortify herself. "There is something I want from you," she said.

Adam frowned. "Are you talking about payment for your services? I thought Buck told me you had refused to accept anything for treating me."

"I did. That is not what I'm talking about. I want . . . I want to go with you when you leave here."

This was the last thing Adam had expected. "Go with me?"

"*Sí.* I, in return for your taking me with you, will cook your meals, wash your clothes, and clean your house."

"I don't need a servant," Adam replied, still puzzled by her strange request.

"I am not proposing to become your servant. I am proposing to become your camp follower."

"You don't know what you're saying, Anita. Camp followers do much more than cook and wash clothes. They serve the men they follow in much more intimate ways. Those women are their lovers and mistresses."

Why did he have to make it so difficult for her? Anita thought. When she had offered to become his camp follower, she had hoped he would read between the lines. "I am aware of that." She took a deep breath and said in a deceptively calm voice that showed none of the inner turmoil she felt, "I will do that, too. Become your mistress."

Adam felt the calmly spoken words like a physical blow; his breath left him in a rush. His eyes dropped from her face to sweep over her body hungrily before he realized what he was doing. Jerking his eyes away, he said in a ragged voice, "I'm not interested."

Anita's dark eyes flashed. "You lie! I am young, but not naive. I have seen the way you look at me, not just a moment ago, but from the very beginning. I know what it means when a man looks at a woman that way. You desire me. And I have not forgotten the way your body reacted to my touch that day I was changing your dressing."

Anita's bold, candid reminder stripped Adam of all pretense, and it angered him. Wanting to punish her for disarming him, he said in a hard voice, "Not desire, Anita. I *lust* after you. There's a difference."

Adam's harsh words cut deeply. Since the day her mother had died, Anita had been very careful to let nothing penetrate the hard shell she had built around herself, not pain, not disappointment not anything, and yet Adam's words did hurt. She wondered why no other man could wound her, unaware that deep down she secretly wanted him to care. She forced herself to keep her face impassive and her voice calm as she replied, "*Sí*, I know. You hate me because I'm a Mexican. But that doesn't change anything. Your body refuses to acknowledge the hate in your soul. You still want me."

It occurred to Adam that perhaps Anita felt the same about him. He knew her well enough to know that her hot blood ran just below the surface. He had seen it erupt more than once in anger. That the desire might be mutual filled him with a great deal of satisfaction. "And you? What do you want from me?"

The smug smile that was spreading across Adam's

lips was wiped away by Anita's next words. "I told you. I want to go with you. I want to see Santa Anna defeated once and for all, and the gringos will do it—eventually. I want to be there when it happens, to witness his downfall."

"Go with me?" he asked in an incredulous voice. "Into battle?"

"No, not into battle. I know that's impossible. But I *would* fight in this war if I could. I would give anything to be a man and meet Santa Anna on the battlefield—or face-to-face anywhere. I would kill him!"

Adam was stunned by the fierce intensity on Anita's face and her passionate words "Why? Because of what he's done to Mexico?"

"Partly," Anita admitted. "He's a scourge on the Mexican people. He keeps the country in a turmoil, whether he's ruling or not. He thrives on unrest, on others' misery. That alone would be enough to make me hate him."

"But not enough to make you want to kill him. Your reasons are much more personal, aren't they?"

"*Sí*, they are," Anita admitted.

Adam waited for Anita to explain, but she was stubbornly silent. "I want to know why, Anita," Adam said in an adamant voice. "I want to know your reasons."

"You don't need to know my reasons. It's enough to know I hate him as much as you."

"No, it isn't enough!" Adam answered angrily. "Not for me, it isn't. You're proposing to prostitute yourself—"

"No! I merely propose a barter. I am *not* prostituting myself."

"The hell you aren't! You're selling your body like a common *puta*."

"No! A *puta* sells her body to any and every man. I offer myself to you, and only you, and not for money, but in return for taking me with you. And I can be much more than a mistress to you. I can help to bring Santa Anna to his downfall."

"How?"

"I'm a Mexican. I can be your ears. Mexicans will say things, divulge things that they would never say within a gringo's hearing. I can bring you information on Santa Anna's movements."

"You'd spy on your own country?" Adam asked in a shocked voice "Why, that's treason!"

"No! I spy on Santa Anna! It is *he* I want to see destroyed, not Mexico. This war would already be over if it were not for him. He keeps it alive, not the people, and to satisfy his lust for power, not national honor." Anita stepped forward, her dark eyes glittering with the intensity of her beliefs. "Don't you see? Even if Mexico should win this war, we would still lose. Santa Anna would continue to bleed the country, inflict even more misery upon its people. He must be destroyed—before he destroys Mexico!"

"You're rationalizing, Anita. Santa Anna might be keeping this war going, but he didn't start it."

"No, but others did, others as power hungry and selfish as he. They are no better than him. They don't represent the people, either. Your country offered us a fair price for the land they wanted, a land the Mexican government could no longer govern. That money could have been used to improve the lot of the Mexican people. And it could have been done without the loss of our national integrity, too. France sold your country the Louisiana Territory without loss of face. But President Paredes put his hatred for the gringos before the good of Mexico. No, *they* are the traitors to the Mexican people — not me!"

The fervency of Anita's impassioned speech convinced Adam that she sincerely believed in what she said, but what she was proposing was impossible. "No, Anita. I can't drag you along with me. War is no place for a woman.

"Mexican women follow their husbands and lovers to war," Anita argued. "They travel with the Army. When a battle is to be fought, they are left behind, but close enough to know that the battle is being fought and to learn of its outcome immediately. They are there on the scene, but not in the battle itself."

"The American Army doesn't allow camp followers."

"They have washerwomen. One, at Fort Texas, was a heroine. The gringos call her the Great Western."

Adam's head snapped up in surprise at Anita's knowledge. What she had said was true. According to army regulations, four laundresses were assigned to each company. The women were the wives of rank and file, hired by the army, with their own pay and rations. Taylor had these women with him. Most were shipped ahead of the Army from Corpus Christi to Port Isabel, but a few, like the woman Anita had just mentioned, had traveled cross-country with the army in the baggage train. "The Great Western," so called because of her unusual height and size, had been one of the latter and had distinguished herself with her great courage during the bombardment of Fort Texas, having one bullet pass through her bonnet and another through her bread tray when she served as matron of the hospital.

"How did you know about the Great Western?"

"The Mexicans are not the only ones who talk. The gringos do, too. And while most Mexicans cannot speak English, many of them understand it. There is little that escapes the notice of the Mexican peasants in this war, on both sides. Gossip is the only form of entertainment they have, the only form they can afford. So, you see, there *are* women with your army. And not all of them are Anglos. There are Mexican women in your camps, too. The mistresses of the officers. Maybe your army does not allow it, but they are there nonetheless."

"I won't be serving with the American Army. I'm a Texas Ranger. And we *don't* have women in our camps."

Anita shrugged, saying, "Then I'll stay in the nearest town or village. There's hardly anyplace in Mexico where there's not at least a small hamlet nearby. Besides, I've heard that your *Tejano* camps are crude, that you don't even have tents. A simple adobe hut would be better than that. I'll cook for you and wash your clothes, just as the Mexican camp followers do."

"Dammit, you're not a camp follower, a lowly peon. You're an aristocrat! You're not used to such hardships."

Anita drew herself up to her full height. "I am as strong as they are! And I can do anything they can. I'm not afraid of hard work. I told you, I'm not like the other women of my class."

"You're really determined, aren't you?" Adam asked in a scathing voice. "Nothing is too low for you. You'd slave for me, whore for me—"

"If you insist upon calling me that ugly name, yes!" Anita flared out, her beautiful black eyes flashing. "There is *nothing* I wouldn't do to see Santa Anna dead. Nothing!"

"Why?" Adam demanded, taking quick advantage of Anita's distressed, excited state. "Why do you hate Santa Anna so much?"

"Because he killed my mother!" Anita shrieked. "Her soul cannot rest until I have avenged her death!"

Adam's dark eyebrows shot up in surprise. He knew Santa Anna had no qualms about murdering his political enemies, but he had never heard of him harming a woman. "He murdered your mother? Why?"

Realizing that she had revealed more than she intended in the heat of the moment, Anita stepped back behind her protective wall. The icy mask fell over her face. "He did not kill her with his own hands," she admitted in a voice as hard as flint.

"She killed herself. But he—and he alone—is responsible for her death."

"She committed suicide?" Adam asked in a horrified voice, then, without even thinking, blurted, "How?"

The memory of the night her mother had killed herself came rushing back and, with it, the haunting vision of her mother's dead body, a mental picture that was so vivid she could see the flickering candlelight casting eerie shadows over the gruesome scene, could smell the candle wax, could hear the wailing of the wind outside the window.

Adam watched as Anita's eyes turned glassy and the color drained from her face, leaving it deathly pale. When she swayed on her feet, Adam stepped forward and caught her arms, asking in alarm, "Anita? What's wrong? Are you ill?"

Adam's voice brought Anita back to the present. "No. No, I am not ill," she muttered.

"You looked so . . . so strange."

"I was thinking of my mother."

"You were going to tell me how she killed herself," Adam reminded her, sensing that her strange behavior had something to do with her mother's death.

"No! I was *not* going to tell you anything. That's none of your business. We'll *never* speak of my mother again. Never!"

Anita whirled and walked to the window, staring out at the night. Adam stared at her stiff back in puzzlement. He could understand her being upset, but why was she being so adamant in refusing to speak of her mother? But there was one thing that he understood. Like him, Anita wanted revenge, and the need to revenge the death of a loved one was something that he understood only too well. The only difference between him and Anita was that she hated one particular Mexican, while he hated them all.

"That's why I chose to ally myself with you," Anita said, as if she were reading his mind, still staring out the window. "You're a *Tejano*. You hate Santa Anna as much as I do. A *gringo* would never understand. They fight for greed, not revenge. The *gringos* may bring about Santa Anna's downfall, but if anyone can kill him, it will be a *Tejano*."

"It would be an unholy alliance, Anita. A Mexican and a Texan? Have you forgotten that you hate me, or that I hate you?"

Anita turned. "No, I haven't forgotten. We are still enemies. There's too much bloodshed between our peoples for that to change. But enemies can become allies, providing they both hate their mutual enemy enough."

Yes, Adam thought, he supposed if the Mexicans could ally themselves with the Comanches, their ancient enemies, against the Texans, then he could unite himself with Anita. And undoubtedly, their alliance would be just as uneasy as the Indians' and the Mexicans', both guarding their backs while they went for their enemy's throat.

Aware of Anita watching him expectantly, Adam said, "There's just one problem with this insanity, Anita. You're expecting something from me that I may not be able to deliver. It's true Santa Anna is on the top of my list. I want to see him dead as much as you do. But that doesn't mean I'll ever get the opportunity to kill him. This is war, and war is fought between armies, not individuals. I may never get close enough to kill him. None of us Texans may. Nor am I going to chase him down exclusively. Your war may be against him personally, but mine is against Mexico. For me, he's just a part of it. Number one, but not all."

"I know all of this," Anita said with a sigh of resignation. "I want his death, but I don't fool myself into thinking that it is necessarily the way it will turn out. I may have to settle for only a taste of revenge, his downfall. But when it comes, whether it's his death or his downfall, I want to be there — not hundreds of miles away, but close enough that I can see the smoke and hear the guns and know that he is being beaten. Only then, can I feel that I was a part of it."

At that moment, Anita looked somehow vulnerable, and Adam got a fleeting glance of the sensitive woman behind the stone wall. But when she raised her eyes and met his, there was no sign of weakness there, only one of firm resolve, She'd made her proposal, and no matter how shocking it might be, she wouldn't back down. Now it was up to Adam to accept, or to reject it.

Adam knew that it was insanity, that he should out and out refuse, but his mind was no longer in control. Seeing the exotic beauty before him, and knowing she could be his for the taking, the passion that had been seething just below the surface rose in a need too strong to deny any longer. In a voice ragged with desire, he asked, "When would our alliance begin? Now? This minute?"

A victorious flicker appeared in Anita's dark eyes and then disappeared as quickly as it had come. "If you wish."

Adam's eyes slowly raked her body, then returned to rest on the thick, long braid that was draped over one shoulder. He had stared at that braid innumerable times, wondering how it would look undone, with her hair hanging free. "Unbraid your hair," he said thickly. "I want to see it hanging around your shoulders."

Without hesitation, Anita picked up the thick, lustrous braid and began undoing it, her eyes never leaving Adam's face.

Adam watched each movement of her slender fingers as if mesmerized. When she had finished, she shook her head, and the waist-length hair fell about her shoulders in a shimmering waterfall of soft, black waves.

As if in a trance, Adam stepped forward and raised his hands, smoothing the long tresses, amazed at its silkiness. Catching a handful of hair on each side of her head, he felt its heavy weight before one hand slid through it to cup the back of Anita's head. His mouth came down on hers in a bruising, demanding kiss, while his other hand dropped to her tiny waist, molding her soft body to his hard length in a crushing embrace.

As his tongue plunged into her mouth, plundering the sweetness there, his lips grinding against hers, Adam felt Anita stiffen in his arms. He pulled back and gazed down at her, seeing the hard, cold glint in her black eyes.

No, dammit! Adam thought. He wouldn't allow her to hide behind her icy wall, to play the part of a sacrificial victim. There was passion in her. He'd seen it in her burst of fiery anger and he'd bring it forth if it killed him. He'd work at her until she wanted their union as much as he, until her body was clamoring for release as much as his, until she begged him for it.

With supreme will, Adam forced his raging passion down and lowered his head, seeing the lightning-fast flicker of anger in Anita's eyes before it disappeared behind an expression of stony resignation. His lips brushed her forehead, her temples, her eyelids with feather-like kisses that startled Anita with their gentleness, while his hands caressed and stroked her back.

When Adam's lips nibbled at the sensitive corner of her mouth, his tongue flicking with erotic promise, a shiver ran through Anita. She had completely discounted the passion Adam had awakened in her, thinking he would pounce on her as swift and unconcerned for her feelings as an animal. She had prepared herself for a brutal assault on her body, for pain, for humiliation, thinking it would only make it easier for her to hate him, that it would nip in the bud any desire she might have for him. But Anita had never expected this tender seduction. His sensuous caresses on her back, her hips, fingertips brushing ever so lightly the sides of her breasts, his warm, mobile mouth playing and coaxing over her lips was attacking something much more vulnerable than her body—her senses. One she could survive; the other threatened the woman she so carefully protected. No, this would never do. She had never credited the savage Texan as being capable of gentleness or tenderness. She had made a terrible mistake.

Anita opened her mouth to tell Adam that she had changed her mind, but the feel of the tip of his tongue slowly brushing back and forth across her lips, back and forth across her teeth, robbed her mind of the thought. Then, when he slipped into her mouth, exploring her small teeth, his tongue sliding the length of hers, then swirling around it, Anita could no longer think at all. Every fiber of her being was focused on the new sensations that he was invoking. Anita had never known a man's kiss could be so pleasurable, so intoxicating, so exciting. Her legs turned to water beneath her as she sagged, then strained against him, his tongue gliding in and out in an endless kiss that brought her to her tiptoes in a silent plea for more and more.

A smile of satisfaction crossed Adam's lips when he broke the long kiss and heard Anita's soft moan of protest. But he wanted more than the victory of one small skirmish in their clash of wills. He had laid his battle plan very carefully. He would have no less than total capitulation. When he had finished, there would be no more walls between them.

Adam's mouth left a fiery trail of kisses down the

slim column of Anita's throat, his tongue sliding across her collarbone before he nuzzled the valley between her breasts, his hands stroking the soft flesh through her *camisa*. Suddenly anxious to see as well as touch her, Adam deftly untied the ribbon that held up her *camisa,* sliding it down her arms, then unhooked her skirt. As her clothing fell to the floor in a soft whisper, Adam bent, swooped Anita up in his powerful arms and carried her to the bed, laying her on it.

Stepping back, Adam looked down, sucking in his breath as the impact of Anita's nakedness hit him. Hungrily, his eyes feasted on the high, full breasts with their dark nipples, the unbelievably tiny waist, the gentle flare of her hips, lingering on the dark curls between her thighs before sweeping back up to gaze at her face. With the color of her cheeks heightened by her aroused passion, her long black hair fanning out around her, her skin the color of warm honey, her dark eyes smoldering with desire, Adam thought that she looked like some dark pagan goddess of love. His goddess, by damn!

Adam tore off his clothes impatiently, popping buttons, boots hitting the floor with dull thuds, tossing one article of clothing one way, then another. From the bed, Anita watched as Adam revealed his magnificent body to her. When he stood briefly poised over her, her eyes quickly ran over him, seeing the muscles in his broad shoulders and arms rippling beneath his smooth skin, then following the dark hair on his chest as it tapered to a fine line over his taut abdomen, then flared again at his groin. Her breath caught as she stared at his erection, bold and proud and seemingly enormous. Without the sheet to hide it, it seemed very threatening, as did his entire body, vitally alive, every powerful muscle primed for action. A tingle of fear ran through her. She jerked her eyes away and looked up. Then seeing the green eyes blazing in his tanned face, that fear was instantly replaced with an incredible excitement, her own passion rising like a monumental wave and engulfing her. A choked sob escaped her throat as she lifted her arms in silent invitation.

Adam didn't hesitate for a split second. When he lay down beside her and took Anita in his arms, the searing touch of bare, feverish flesh against bare, feverish flesh made both gasp in shock. And then Anita's hands were tangling in Adam's thick hair as she lifted her head for his kiss, wanting more, sensing that she had just begun to taste the delights of the mysteries between a man and woman.

Steeling himself to go slow, Adam didn't disappoint her, his kiss demanding, then coaxing, his tongue plundering wildly, then soothingly, alternating between savage possession and sweet seduction, rousing her unbelievingly, then backing off until Anita was sobbing in sexual frustration.

His dark head descended, his tongue dancing erotically across her passion-heated skin, then laving the soft mounds of her breasts before his lips closed over one dark, pointed peak. Anita felt a bolt of fire rush to her loins, a sudden wetness between her legs as Adam worked his sorcery, his tongue an instrument of exquisite torture. She clutched the back of his head, holding him a prisoner there, arching her back, feeling as if he was sucking the marrow from her bones, the life from her body.

Adam slipped lower, determined to explore every inch of this exotic goddess, his tongue tracing each rib before it swirled around her dainty navel, hearing Anita's gasp of pleasure. As he moved even lower, dropping fiery kisses over the golden skin on her abdomen, the soft, dark curls between her legs, the insides of her thighs, a tingle of alarm ran through Anita. She yanked on his head, muttering, "No!"

Adam raised his head, gazing at her with eyes glazed with desire. Her incredible softness, the smooth silkiness of her skin, the heady scent of her womanliness so close to his nostrils was intoxicating him. He longed to taste her sweetness, but in some little corner of Adam's dulled mind, he knew that would shock Anita's sensibilities and ruin everything. And Adam wanted her now with every fiber of his being, not just her body, but all of her. He wanted to possess her fully, completely, irrevocably, lay claim to that inviolable part of her that she guarded so fiercely, brand her for life.

Adam slid up her body, stopping to dally at her breasts again, then mouthing the pulse beat at the base of her throat. Anita was floating on a warm, rosy cloud, her hands smoothing over the powerful muscles on Adam's back and shoulders, marveling at the differences in their bodies, his so hard, hers so soft, but still, in many ways so much alike. She could feel his heart pounding against hers and his rock-hard manhood throbbing against her thigh, seemingly in unison with that throbbing place deep within her.

As Adam shifted his weight and slipped his hand between her legs, his fingers sliding through her slickness, parting the engorged, aching lips, seeking and finding the core of her womanhood, Anita tensed at that intimate act, suddenly coming to her senses. No one had ever touched her there. Her eyes flew open, and she started to object, but the protest never came. As Adam's skillful fingers teased and tantalized, a warmth invaded her, searing her from head to toe, while waves of sweet rapture washed over her body, and she muttered instead, *"Madre de Dios!"* before the waves turned to powerful undulations that rocked her body and left her gasping for breath.

Anita's passionate response fired Adam's burning desire. Unable to deny himself any longer, he rose over her, slid his hands beneath her hips, and lifted her, entering her slowly, carefully. He came to a dead halt, shocked by her tightness, torn between his intense need to satisfy his raging desire and his fear of ripping her in two. His hesitancy did not suit Anita. She had tasted of ecstasy, and now her sensitized body was screaming for release, every nerve ending on fire, a fire that she knew only Adam could quench. It was she who lunged, impaling herself on him.

With the sound of Anita's strangled cry in his

ears, Adam found himself plunging in, tearing through the fragile barrier and buried deep inside of her velvety heat, the untutored muscles there gripping him like greedy hands From then on, Adam had no control over what was happening. Anita was a wild thing beneath him, moving frantically in the rhythm as old as time, sobbing incoherently, her legs like a vise around his hips, her nails raking his back, her sharp teeth nipping at his shoulders and neck, her lips raining torrid kisses over his face. Her heated frenzy invaded him, and Adam pounded back, his powerful thrusts deep and true, feeling like he was drowning in molten fire before he was caught in a flaming inferno that sent him spiraling up like a sky rocket, hearing a roaring in his ears and seeing stars bursting behind his eyes, before he exploded in a shattering release that seared his brain.

When Adam emerged from the dark abyss that he had been plunged into, his first awareness was of their sweat-slick bodies, then their rasping breaths, then their hearts pounding one against the other. The room still spun dizzily around him as he raised himself weakly on his elbows and looked down at Anita. Seeing her dazed eyes and the look of total awe frozen on her face, he knew that she had experienced the climactic explosion, too.

Fearing he would crush her with his weight, Adam rolled to his side, too spent to even notice that his leg was aching from the strenuous exercise. It took all of his remaining strength to roll to his side, blow out the lamp beside the bed, and pull the covers up over them. But even as his eyes were closing in exhaustion, he reached for Anita, pulling her to him, wanting her close even while he slept.

Adam never knew if it was minutes or hours later when he was awakened by Anita slipping from his embrace and leaving the bed. Groggily, he raised himself on one elbow, seeing her quickly dressing in the shaft of moonlight coming from the window.

"Come back to bed," Adam muttered thickly.

"No. It's over for tonight."

Anita padded softly to the door, then turned, saying in her deep husky voice "Our bargain is sealed."

Adam stared at the door as it softly closed behind her, as stunned by her cold, unemotional words as he had been by her earlier uninhibited passion.

Chapter 11

The small bedroom was awash with brilliant sunlight when Adam awoke the next morning. But Adam took no cheer from its warmth. His thoughts were dark and brooding.

He had been a damn fool to let his passion rule his reason. Damn! He couldn't drag a woman along with him, all over Mexico, for the duration of the war. That they, two enemies, had agreed to their unholy alliance because of his lust for her and Anita's lust for personal revenge made it even more insane. If only he could take back the night, or at least figure out some way he could back out gracefully. But Adam knew that he couldn't. Anita had put the seal on their bargain—as she so coldly called it—with her virginal blood, and Adam was a man of his word. To renege at this point would be no better than treachery.

He had to hand it to her, Adam thought bitterly. Anita was clever. She had neatly manipulated him into an impossible position, trapped him with a woman's oldest weapon—her body. Dammit, she was nothing but a calculating, cold-blooded bitch!

Adam scowled, knowing that he would have to amend that last thought if he was to be totally honest with himself. Yes, she was cold-blooded—and hot-blooded, too. He had suspected a deep passion in her, had deliberately set out to bring it forth, but he had never dreamed of the depths of that passion. Never had he experienced such a tremulous, white-hot, explosive climax, so much so that it was almost frightening in its intensity, its total mindlessness. He had awakened a sleeping tiger by prodding it, then had all but been devoured by it. And then, when it was over, when he thought he had broken down her icy barrier once and for all, she had coldly announced that the bargain was sealed, leaving Adam feeling as if he—and not her—had been the sacrificial victim.

Yes, she had used him, Adam thought with a sardonic twist on his lips, and would continue to do so. That he had given Anita her weapon against him—his own lust—made it even worse. For one so young, she was incredibly ruthless. Where had she learned it?

Adam's thoughts zeroed in on Anita's grandfather. He had not seen the old aristocrat since that day before the Battle of Monterrey. Had he any idea of what was going on? Did he know that Anita had brought the enemy into the sanctuary of his own home, that a steady stream of hated

Tejanos had come and gone, that Anita had come to Adam's room at night and made an unholy bargain? Surely the old man couldn't know the latter. Mexican men, particularly upper-class Mexicans, were fiercely protective of their women's virtue, so much so that they practically imprisoned them and set guards over them, their *duennas*. But Adam had seen no *duenna,* either. Why hadn't the old man lived up to his responsibilities to his granddaughter? If nothing else, he should have been watching over Anita, and if he had been doing his job, Adam wouldn't be in his present predicament. Was the old man really so ill that he was still confined to his room, or was he afraid to come out and face his enemies, leaving Anita to deal with them?

The thought that Anita's grandfather might be hiding behind her skirts infuriated Adam. He flung the covers aside, swung from the bed, jerked on his clothes, and went down the hall with murder in his eyes. The door to Anita's grandfather's room was slammed open without even the courtesy of a knock. Stepping into the room, Adam came to a dead halt.

Anita's grandfather lay in the middle of his massive bed, propped up by pillows, looking as dignified as a king sitting on his throne. Rather than showing surprise or shock at Adam's forceful entry, the elderly aristocrat looked as if he had been expecting Adam, as if he had summoned the Texan, instead of Adam bursting into his room

163

unannounced.

"I was hoping you would come," the Mexican said calmly, his dark eyes meeting Adam's evenly. "The fact that you have tells me much of your character. A lesser man would have taken what my granddaughter had offered and then left, with no word to me, like a thief in the night."

Adam was totally taken aback by the elderly man's words. "You know of your granddaughter's outrageous bargain?" he asked in shocked disbelief.

"*Sí*. Anita has never kept anything from me. She has always been totally honest, sometimes to the point of being disconcerting."

"Then you approve of what she's done?" Adam thundered, his anger on the rise again. "What kind of a man are you? She's sold her body to me . . ." Adam thumped his broad chest. "Her enemy!"

"Ah, you are angry with me. That, too, tells me something of your character. To answer your first question, no, I do not approve. But I am sure you know by now that Anita does as she pleases. There is nothing I can do that will change her mind." The old man sighed deeply. "It has always been so with my granddaughter. She has a mind and a will of her own. And so, since I cannot change anything, I am resigned."

"Then there's absolutely nothing you can do?"

"Like what, señor? Lock her in her room? No nothing short of chaining her would stop Anita now. And I am afraid that is my fault. I take blame for it. I have instilled my hatred into her to the point that the burden of revenging the disgrace Santa Anna placed on our heads is as much her responsibility as mine. It is a matter of family honor, señor. But I never dreamed that Santa Anna would return to Mexico. He had been exiled for life. I was content with that, and so was Anita. When your country let him back in, it opened old wounds."

Adam's attention had locked on one word. He cocked his head. "You said Santa Anna disgraced your family. In what way?"

"Then Anita didn't tell you?" the elder man asked in surprise.

"She told me her mother committed suicide because of Santa Anna. She refused to tell me why, or give me any further details."

The Mexican nodded his head. "Sí, I should have known that she would not divulge that information to anyone, under any circumstances. She is much too proud to admit how deeply her mother's death hurt her, to tell of her shame and disgrace. Just as I am reluctant to speak of it." Anita's grandfather paused and stared at Adam, as if he was peering into the younger man's soul. Finally, he said, "But I think, in view of the unusual circumstances, you should know." He pointed to an easy chair beside the bed. "Sit down, señor. This may take some time."

Adam was about to burst with curiosity. He

walked to the chair and sat, leaning forward with his elbows resting on his knees, his full attention on the old Mexican lying on the bed.

"How much do you know of Santa Anna's rise to power?" Anita's grandfather asked.

"Not much," Adam admitted. "I never even heard of him until the Texas Revolution."

"Santa Anna is not a *hidalgo* as I am, one of the upper class of Mexico. His parents were of the middle class, and his father tried to apprentice him as a merchant. But Santa Anna aspired for much more. He wanted power, and in Mexico, a military career was the best, if not only way, to achieve that end. So, at fifteen, he became a cadet in the Royal Army of Spain. His climb from the ranks to general was not made by any military genius on his part, or any noteworthy service, but rather by hanging on the coattails of others rising to power. And he was very adroit at switching sides according to how the political wind was blowing, repeatedly betraying the very men to whom he owed his success.

"In '28, when Santa Anna was commander-in-chief, Spain refused to recognize Mexico's independence and tried to take the country back. Santa Anna was sent to meet the invading Spanish Army. He left his headquarters at Veracruz, leaving the city totally unprotected, and marched to Tampico to fight off the Spanish. It was here that he started calling himself The 'Napoleon of the West.' a ridiculous claim, for most of the victories he took credit for were fought by General Mier y Teran, a true military genius. Thanks to that man, Santa Anna's campaign was successful, and he was hailed by the people of Tampico as the 'Conqueror of Tampico.' "

The old *hidalgo* paused and stared out into space for several minutes, collecting his thoughts before he continued. Adam squirmed impatiently in his seat. Finally, the Mexican said "It was there that my daughter Teresa met Santa Anna. She was in Tampico at the time, visiting relatives of my deceased wife, and naturally, she attended many of the victory balls and dinners given in Santa Anna's honor. She was young and beautiful and caught Santa Anna's eye. He wooed her. But not as a gentleman. He convinced her to sneak away from her *duenna* and meet him secretly in his headquarters at night. They had several meetings, and I don't have to tell you what transpired. He seduced her, and when Teresa returned to Monterrey, she was with child."

Adam sprang to his feet. "Anita is Santa Anna's daughter?" he asked in a mixture of disbelief and horror.

"*Sí*. And now you know why Anita would not tell you. She is both ashamed and horrified that she was fathered by that monster."

Adam sat back down, stunned by the news. But then, he should have guessed Santa Anna's part in disgracing Anita's mother and, thereby, her family. The man was a notorious womanizer, his lust for

167

women ranking only after his lust for luxury and power. Adam had heard on his campaign during the Texas revolution that Santa Anna had sent special couriers ahead of him to arrange for a pretty woman for the night. His pursuit of women brought his downfall at San Jacinto, if rumor could be believed. According to some of the Texans who fought at the battle, Santa Anna was caught by surprise that afternoon because he was occupied with a mulatto girl in his tent, a yellow-skinned slave from one of the nearby plantations. Adam had heard Buck and the others laughing about it and saying that the president-general had been caught with his pants down in more than one way, and the Texans were so grateful to the slave girl that they later dedicated a song to her, "The Yellow Rose of Texas."

A sudden thought occurred to Adam. "Then your daughter didn't kill herself when she discovered she was pregnant?"

"No, Teresa was not nearly as concerned as I was. She insisted that Santa Anna loved her and that he had promised to marry her as soon as he could. According to her, he had explained that his duties as General-in-chief were much too pressing for him to take time out for a big wedding and a lengthy honeymoon, as she deserved."

"And she believed that rot?" Adam asked in an incredulous voice.

"Ah, señor, Teresa was very young and very naive. Remember her upbringing. She had been sheltered all of her life. She trusted with the innocence of a child. She was flattered at having a general, the hero of Mexico, take notice of her. And do not forget Santa Anna's effect on the gentle sex. Women of all ages found him fascinating. At that time, he was in his early thirties, at his prime. He was tall, broad-shouldered, and handsome, in a dramatic manner. Teresa was enthralled with his good looks, his elaborate uniforms, his lavish way of living, his charisma. After all, if Santa Anna could charm all of Mexico into believing him, do you not think he could charm one small girl?"

"All right," Adam conceded, "so she was gullible. But what about you? Surely you knew he was lying through his teeth."

"At that time, I knew almost nothing of Santa Anna. We here in the northern provinces were isolated from the rest of Mexico. The government paid little attention to us, much as they did your Texas. And in turn, we paid little attention to the constant upheavals in central Mexico. The government switched hands so often that by the time we learned of a man's rise to power, he had fallen and another had taken his place. My chief concern was my *rancho,* not politics. All I knew was Santa Anna was a powerful general and the hero of the hour, a man with whom I could align my family, if necessary. And since I had no choice in the matter, it was necessary. I wrote to him, expecting him to be a man of honor since he had risen to

169

the rank of general, and told him of my daughter's condition. Ah, señor, I was as naive in that sense as my daughter. Three times, I wrote. None of my letters were acknowledged. By then, I knew that my daughter had been duped. In my fourth letter, I challenged Santa Anna to a duel. The honor of my family demanded that much of me. The coward never answered that letter, either."

"What about your daughter? Didn't she get suspicious when Santa Anna never answered any of your letters?"

"Teresa never knew of my letters and I didn't have the heart to tell her the truth, that Santa Anna had played her for a fool. You see, she was my only child. I doted on her, particularly after her mother died. I was trying to protect her from the ugly truth. I broke the marriage contract I had made for her when she was a child, explaining that she had married an officer in Tampico against my knowledge and that her husband had been killed in battle shortly thereafter. I don't think her betrothed or his family believed my story, nor did anyone else in Monterrey. Too many people in this area had relatives in Tampico. Mexico can be a very small country when one is trying to hide something," the *hidalgo* ended bitterly.

Adam sat back in his chair "But didn't Teresa get suspicious when so much time had passed and she heard nothing from Santa Anna? Didn't she question why he wasn't fulfilling his promise to her?"

The old aristocrat pushed himself higher on his pillows before answering. "She was totally blinded by infatuation. She kept making excuses for him. First, he was too busy fighting the country's enemies, then, when he became President, too busy with establishing the government. She lived in a dream world of her own, fantasizing on how Santa Anna would come and marry her, and make her the highest woman in the land. She spent months planning the wedding and the state dinners and the elaborate balls that she would have. She was pleased that Anita was his daughter, firmly convinced that lie would acknowledge her as his. She even named Anita after him."

"But somewhere along the line, she came to realize that Santa Anna had lied to her," Adam pointed out.

"*Sí*. For sometime I had known that Santa Anna was already married when he seduced Teresa. I made it my business to investigate him thoroughly. Surprisingly, for a man who thrived on public attention, he managed to keep his private life very quiet. He had married a commoner, an Inez Garcia. She and their five children lived in almost virtual seclusion on his estate between Veracruz and Japala. One of his sons died as a child. It was rumored that another son was mentally deficient and that Santa Anna was ashamed of him. Perhaps, that is why he hid his family away. At any rate, it was not common knowledge that he was married until his wife died and he made such

171

a show of grieving for her. The hypocrite! He didn't even wait until the official mourning time was over to marry a fifteen-year-old, a girl young enough to be his own daughter."

"Dammit, I know all that!" Adam said impatiently leaning forward in his chair. "Get to the point!"

A flush rose on the old man's face. "Forgive me, señor. When I speak of Santa Anna, I tend to get carried away. That was long after my daughter's death, and has nothing to do with my story."

"You were going to tell me how your daughter learned the truth," Adam prompted.

"When Santa Anna marched to Texas to subdue the rebellion, he passed through Monterrey. Teresa, although I had kept her much in seclusion since her return from Tampico, managed to slip away from the hacienda. I was waiting for her when she returned that evening. She was devastated. It seemed she had planned to go to Santa Anna, expecting him to be thrilled to see her. She never reached his camp. On her way through the city, she overheard one of his officers ridiculing Santa Anna for claiming to be such a connoisseur of women, while he had married a lowly, plain-faced commoner. Teresa questioned the man and found out the truth. Her dream world was suddenly shattered."

Anita's grandfather gazed off into space for a long moment. When he resumed talking there was a haunted look in his eyes and his voice was

172

choked with emotion. "I suppose I should have watched Teresa closer that night. I knew that she was terribly upset, but I never dreamed she would kill herself. Frankly, I didn't think her capable of self-destruction. She was always so childlike, so dependent upon others for everything. Taking one's life is not an easy thing to do, you know. It takes a certain amount of determination and a grim courage of sorts. I never credited Teresa for having either. She hung herself from the rafters in her room with a sheet she had torn into strips. It was Anita who found her later that night. She was awakened by a storm and had gone to her mother for comforting. It was not a pleasant sight, señor. Certainly not one for the eyes of a five-year-old."

Adam grimaced, remembering Anita's strange behavior when he had asked her how her mother had killed herself. Now he knew why she had turned so deathly pale. She had remembered seeing her mother hanging from the rafters. Adam had seen men who had been hung. It had been a gruesome sight, their faces black and bloated, their swollen tongues hanging from their mouths, their eyes protruding, their clothing stained where they had soiled themselves. The sight had sickened him, a grown man. How much more traumatic would it be for a child to see her own mother that way? Shame crept over him for his thoughtlessness. He wished to God that he had never asked her.

"And then I made yet another mistake," Anita's

grandfather continued, unaware of the expression of self-disgust on Adam's face. "I should have gone after Santa Anna that night, murdered him in his sleep if need be, while he was nearby, while I had the opportunity. But I was so grief-stricken that I never even thought of him until a week later. By then he was gone."

"You probably wouldn't have gotten anywhere near him," Adam commented. "He had his *Zapadores,* his crack troops, with him. They also acted as his personal bodyguards."

"*Sí,* I know. But even if I died, I would have liked to have tried."

"And where would that have left Anita?" Adam countered.

"*Sí,* I finally came to realize that. That is why I had to settle for trying to destroy Santa Anna politically and not by assassination. For years, I spent every *peso* I could scrape up to lend support to his enemies. It didn't matter that some were no better than he, power hungry and greedy. When Santa Anna was finally exiled after Herrera came into power, I thought both the country and I were rid of him for good, that I could settle down and lead a reasonably contented life, that I could go back to being a simple *ranchero*. Then your country let him back into Mexico. Now thousands more will die, on both sides. That was a stupid thing for them to do."

Adam agreed heartily, but the American government letting Santa Anna return to Mexico was not

174

the issue here. Anita and her welfare were. "Now Santa Anna is back and he's our problem," Adam pointed out. "But he's yours and mine. Not Anita's! She shouldn't be burdened with seeking revenge. It's"—Adam's brow furrowed as he searched for the right word—"it's unnatural."

"Why is it unnatural?"

"For Christ's sake! She's a woman!"

"Ah, but don't you see? I would have made the same mistake with her that I made with Teresa, protecting her, shielding her from the realities of life. And you know what the disastrous results were when Teresa was faced with the ugly facts of her predicament. She could not cope. I swore that I would never make the same mistake with Anita. We cripple our women when we overprotect them, make them so dependent on us. They remain children all their lives. No, señor, I was determined that I would raise Anita differently. I took Anita from her *duenna* and placed her under the care of a servant, an old *mestizo* who was wise in the ways of the world. It was from her that Anita learned her healing skills, and much more. She saw the other side of life, the side that is not so pretty. Misery, death, poverty. By the time she was eight years old, she was wiser than the old women of our class. That is when she came to me and demanded to know why her mother had committed suicide and the truth of her birth."

"And you told her? An eight-year-old?" Adam asked in a mixture of disgust and anger.

The old man threw up his hands in exasperation. He glared at Adam. "You have not been listening to me, señor! We are not talking about a child. We are talking about Anita! I have already told you that she has always been strong-willed. By then, she was wise, too. Even if I had wanted to, I could not have lied to her. She would have seen right through me. I told you, she insisted on an explanation. Then she demanded to know what I intended to do about punishing Santa Anna for what he had done to her mother. From then on, she knew everything I was doing. Together, we planned our strategy, like two generals laying out their battle plans."

Adam shot to his feet. "She doesn't just want his downfall. She wants his death!" he exploded.

The old aristocrat was totally unruffled by Adam's outburst. He gazed up at the tall Texan towering over his bed and answered calmly, "Sí, we both do. But as you pointed out, getting near enough to Santa Anna to kill him is impossible. He has too many enemies. He guards himself too well. So we settled for taking away his power, his life-blood. Without that, he is but a shell of a man."

Adam turned and walked to the window, staring out at the mountains in the distance for a long while. Finally, he said, "Well, if you wanted to toughen Anita, you certainly succeeded. She's as hard as those mountains out there."

The Mexican sighed deeply. "There are other

reasons why I have raised Anita as I have. Even if I wanted it for her, Anita could never live the life of one of the women in our class, under the protection of a husband. She has a double taint. Her illegitimacy and her mother's suicide. No *hidalgo* would marry her, despite her beauty. That is why I have seen that she had an education as good as any man, why I have taught her everything I know about running a *rancho*. When I am gone, this *rancho* is all she will have."

Adam turned from the window. "Why would no *hidalgo* marry her? For Christ's sake, it's not her fault that she's a bastard, or that her mother committed suicide."

"No, it is not her fault, but we both know that too often the child pays for the parents' sins. In Mexico, among our class the family of the son sues for the girl's hand when they are still children. Marriage is an alliance between families. No one has sued for Anita's hand. They fear she has common blood in her veins, blood that they do not want mixed with theirs. But even more, they fear that she may pass her mother's weakness down to her children. In Mexico, suicide is considered a grievous sin, one so serious that the Church will not bury the person in consecrated ground. It is believed that those who take their own lives are possessed by the devil, and no one would consort with the devil or his issue. To do so would condemn them to the fires of hell."

"That's absurd!" Adam snapped. "If anything,

177

Teresa was . . ." Adam searched for a kinder word than insane. ". . . mentally disturbed at the time."

"*Sí*, and that, too, carries a stigma, does it not, in both your country and mine?"

Adam couldn't deny it. The mentally unstable were hidden away by their families, and many people, even in the so called civilized countries of the world, considered them possessed by the devil. That, too, was an ugly fact of life.

"I see you understand, señor. But do you realize what would happen to Anita if Santa Anna wins this war and remains in power? He knows that I was instrumental in his downfall. He will seek his own revenge. He will strip Anita of her only heritage, this *rancho*. That she is his daughter would not matter to him. He has bastards all over Mexico and Texas whom he cares nothing about. No, he would use his revenge as an excuse to satisfy his greed, leave Anita penniless and at the mercy of my in-laws, the very people who did not watch out for and keep her from him."

"And you? What would he do to you?"

"Ah, señor, we both know Santa Anna's methods of dealing with his enemies. He has them murdered. But I am afraid time will cheat him of that pleasure. I am old and very ill. I do not believe that I will live past a few more weeks. That I am even alive today is testimony to Anita's great skill in healing. By rights, I should be dead. No, señor, I do not fool myself. Anita thinks that I am getting better, but I grow weaker every day.

178

The second attack will come. Soon. And when it does, I will not survive. At least I have that much to be thankful for. Anita will not be here. If she were, she would fight to save me, and she would lose. She would never forgive herself. Failure is something she cannot accept. That is, perhaps, her only weakness."

Adam took a long, hard look at the old man. Before he had been too angry, and then too occupied with everything Anita's grandfather had been telling him, to notice how gaunt the proud old aristocrat had become, the ashy coloring of his skin, the dusky, almost purplish lips. Adam wondered how Anita could possibly think the old man's condition was improving, when even he could tell it had worsened. Had it been because she had seen him day by day and not noticed how he had slipped downhill, or was she lying to herself? Or did she know and was only putting up a good front for the old man's sake?

"I'm sorry," Adam said. "I shouldn't have barged in on you that way."

"No, I am glad you came to me, and it is obvious that I could not go to you. Perhaps now you will understand Anita better, perhaps even treat her more . . . more gently. She is tough, but she still has a woman's tender heart in her."

"Look, if you think I'm trifling with Anita's heart — forget it! She approached me about becoming my mistress, remember? My interest in her is just . . . just pure animal lust. Nothing more! We made an agreement, but we're still enemies. There's no tender emotional involvement on either side."

If the proud old *hidalgo* was shocked by Adam's frank, almost brutal words, he gave no sign. Instead, he replied calmly, *"Sí,* but even an enemy can be treated with a certain amount of respect. A worthy adversary can be as essential to a man as a trusted friend. It adds a little spice to one's life."

Adam looked at the old man as if he had lost his mind. What in the hell was he talking about, a worthy adversary? Hell, Anita was a Mexican, his enemy, not an opponent in some silly game.

I see you do not understand, señor. But someday you will. In the meanwhile, I only ask that you do not mistreat her."

"I'm not in the habit of mistreating women!" Adam snapped. His eyes narrowed. "Besides, I thought you said you weren't going to try to protect her."

A flush rose on the Mexican's face. *"Sí,* I am afraid I was falling back into an old habit. Perhaps we should change the subject."

"To what?"

Anita's grandfather shrugged, then answered, "Ranching, perhaps. Anita tells me you are a *ranchero,* too."

Adam frowned. He couldn't remember telling Anita that. Perhaps Buck had. The two were so damned chummy. "Yes, I have a ranch back in Texas," Adam answered without enthusiasm. He glanced out the window, then said, "But I'd never guess you were a rancher from looking out there. I haven't seen many cattle around."

"No, there are not many around the old man admitted. "I sold most of my herd to support Santa Anna's political enemies. It has only been since he was exiled that I have turned my attention back to the ranch. But I have been concentrating on quality, not quantity, by improving my stock with interbreeding."

"Yes, Anita told me you had traveled to Reynosa to pick up some bulls you had ordered from Europe. Seems like a waste of money to me, particularly if you were short on cash."

"No, señor, it is not a waste of money. That is the difference between Mexican and Texan *rancheros*. We have been in the cattle-raising business much longer than you and know the importance of introducing new strains into our herds periodically. Too much interbreeding drags a herd down. That is what happened to your longhorns. At one time, they were good Spanish cattle, but they have interbred too much. Now they are scrawny, their meat tough and stringy."

"Yeah, but they're free," Adam countered. "Besides, the United States' demand for beef is growing so fast that they'll buy anything, even if it is tough and stringy."

"But it will not always be that way, señor. Someday, someone will cross good cattle with your longhorns and come up with a breed of cattle that will be superior. That man will demand the highest

181

prices, and the market for your longhorns will drop out."

"Then I'll just sell the damned things for their hides and tallow," Adam answered irritably.

The Mexican frowned. No respectable rancher would sell his cattle for their hides and tallow, except in dire circumstances.

Seeing the look on the elderly man's face, Adam said, "Look, I have a ranch, but I'm just not that interested in ranching anymore. Maybe you're right about all that breeding stuff, but frankly, I don't give a damn. Besides, I don't think you're up to just passing the time of day. I came here to get some answers to some questions. Nothing more."

"And you got your answers?"

"I did."

Adam turned and walked to the door, all too aware of the proud old Mexican's eyes on him. A feeling of shame crept over him. He turned and said, "I didn't mean to be rude with my abruptness. It's just that I can't continue with my life as a rancher until I've settled a few scores down here. Right now, that's my only concern."

"*Sí*, I understand," Anita's grandfather answered sadly. He lay his head wearily back on the pillows and closed his eyes adding, "Only too well."

When Adam returned to his room, Anita was waiting for him. "You went to see my grandfather didn't you?" she asked in an accusing tone of voice.

"Yes. He told me everything

The color drained from Anita's face. "Everything?"

"Everything."

Anita felt betrayed. Of all people for her grandfather to speak to of her shame, why had he picked this man, the only man capable of hurting her. Undoubtedly, Adam would throw it in her face, scorn her, humiliate her, use her shame like a weapon. "He had no right to tell you! Anita spat angrily.

"He thought, under the circumstances, that I should know. And I'm glad he did. It answered a lot of questions." Adam decided to take a different approach with Anita. Perhaps she would listen to reason if he approached her more gently, as her grandfather had suggested "Anita, I can understand you hating Santa Anna. He was your father, and he turned his back on both you and your mother. I know that must have hurt you —"

"He is *not* my father. I have no father."

"Anita, be reasonable. I admit I wouldn't be proud to call him my father, either, but you can't deny your parentage."

"I have no father!"

"Anita, you're not the only one who's been hurt by Santa Anna's thoughtless lust. He's left a trail of illegitimate children all through Mexico and Texas. And your mother wasn't the only upper-class Mexican he betrayed, either. I heard, when the Alamo was under siege, he became enraptured with a beautiful young señorita in Bexar, but her *duenna* was much better at guarding her charge than your mother's was. He couldn't seduce her, so he married her in a mock ceremony with one of his soldiers disguised as a priest. She bore him a child, too. He banished them both. So you see there are others who have been hurt by Santa Anna besides you and your family, but you don't see them going out and risking their necks to get revenge on him, do you? Hell, if that were true, half of Mexico would be after him."

"I do not care what the others do! They are sniveling cowards—like him! I am Anita! He is a scourge on all women just as he is a plague on my country. Only one woman has ever been strong enough to get her revenge on him. I will be the second. But I will not be satisfied with just humiliating him. I will see him destroyed!"

Adam's curiosity was aroused. "What woman humiliated him?"

"A *puta* named Louisa. After spending several nights in his bed in the palace, Santa Anna refused to pay her. She stole his medals and distributed them to the peons in the slums of Mexico City. Santa Anna had to spend several thousand pesos to get his beloved medals back, as if they were anything to concern himself with." Anita scoffed. "He bestowed most of the stupid things upon himself."

"And so you align yourself with a *puta?*"

"I would align myself with the devil himself to get revenge on Santa Anna!"

Yes, Adam thought grimly. And he knew just who that devil was. Him.

"Besides," Anita continued, "you are a fine one to talk. You tell me I should not seek revenge because I am one of many. What about you? Do you think your brother is the only *Tejano* who died in one of Santa Anna's prisons?"

Adam was livid. He stepped forward and caught Anita's shoulders. Shaking her, he thundered, "Who told you about Dan? Buck?"

Suddenly Anita regretted her harsh reminder of Adam's loss. Beneath his anger, she could sense his anguish. For a moment, she wavered, considering apologizing for bringing up the painful memory. Deep down, she didn't want to hurt Adam, despite the fact that he represented everything she hated. Then realizing what she was doing, putting Adam's feelings before her need for revenge, she quickly regained control, pulled away from him, and looked Adam directly in the eyes. "No. I overheard you mention him to Buck that day when you learned that Santa Anna had returned to Mexico. If you can seek revenge for the death of your brother, then I can seek revenge for the death of my mother. Some might take such outrages lying down, but not you, nor I. Neither of us are cowards."

Adam frowned at Anita's oblique compliment. But then, maybe she didn't consider it a compliment. Apparently she considered a coward even lower than the devil. "Then you won't change your mind? You're still going along with me?"

Anita's dark eyes glittered with anger. "The bargain was sealed last night. Are you trying to back out?"

Well, so much for trying gentleness on Anita, Adam thought in exasperation. "All right!" Adam snapped. "If you want to risk your neck to get your revenge, then that's fine with me. We leave tomorrow, at sunrise." Adam glared down at her, saying in a hard voice, "But don't expect me to be worrying about your safety, or to be coddling you."

"I have not asked either from you!" Anita threw back. "All I have asked is that you take me with you. From there, I can take care of myself."

With that, Anita turned and walked from the room, leaving Adam again feeling totally defeated.

Chapter 12

Anita was mounted and waiting for them when Adam and Buck emerged from the hacienda early the next morning, her belongings packed in a small wicker basket strapped to the back of her saddle. Not only was Anita prepared to leave, but Adam's and Buck's horses were saddled and waiting, too.

As Adam walked to his horse, he eyed Anita's peasant clothing with disgust and then came to a halt, staring at her bare calves in shock as he realized that she was mounted astride, and not sidesaddle.

Seeing his look, Anita asked, "How did you expect me to travel? Dressed in my riding suit and mounted sidesaddle? How could I blend in with the ordinary Mexicans and learn of anything if I were that conspicuous? No, I am nothing but just another Mexican camp follower who has attached herself to a gringo protector for the duration of the war."

Adam glanced across at Buck to see his reaction to Anita's blunt words. He had taken the bull by the horns and told Buck of his pact with Anita the night before, going into great detail why Anita wanted revenge, but glossing over just what she had offered him in return, and letting the giant come to his own conclusions. Buck was no fool. He had been outraged that Adam had taken Anita as his mistress on Anita's behalf, thinking the position as his mistress demeaning to her. Then Adam had told Buck in no uncertain terms if he didn't like the way things were going they could split up. Buck had backed down, but Adam knew that his friend wasn't happy with the new arrangement, and now, hearing Anita put it so bluntly, Buck had a stricken look on his face, torn between two loyalties.

Seeing the giant's expression, Anita said gently, "No, Buck, don't blame Adam. He isn't taking advantage of me. This was my idea. And please, don't judge me too harshly. I only do what I have to do."

"I ain't judging you, Anita," Buck answered, shuffling his big feet awkwardly. "It's just that . . . that the new arrangement is gonna take some getting used to."

"It will take some getting used to on all our parts," Anita said, shooting Adam a meaningful look. "Just consider me a new partner in your venture. And I promise that I won't be a burden."

"I wasn't worrying about that," Buck answered, misery written all over his face.

"I know. But the other is none of your concern. That's between Adam and me."

Adam was infuriated by Anita's concern for Buck's sensibilities. It made him feel like a first-class heel, and yet he knew that Anita would be using him as much as he would be using her. "You're damned right it's none of his business! If he doesn't like it, he can pull out. I've already told him that."

Anita looked Buck directly in the eye. "It would distress me greatly to see your friendship with Adam come to an end because of me, but I will not back out. Can't you accept our agreement, that I'm Adam's mistress, by my own choice?"

Buck wasn't accustomed to such frankness. He blushed in embarrassment.

"Please, Buck, it's very important to me," Anita said in a soft voice, an intense expression on her face.

"All right, Anita," Buck agreed reluctantly. "I'll keep my nose out of it. I don't want to lose either of your friendships."

"Nor do I want to lose yours," Anita replied.

"For Christ's sake," Adam exploded, his perplexing jealousy over their friendship coming to the fore, "if we're going, let's go! The war could be over before you two stop your silly yapping. So the three of us are partners now. That's settled and I don't want to hear any more about it!"

Adam swung his saddle bags from his shoulder to the back of his horse, then slipped his short rifle and two Colts into their holsters. Mounting, he galloped away angrily, leaving Anita and Buck no choice but to follow.

By the time they reached the crest of the hill that overlooked the hacienda, Adam was far ahead with Buck riding hard to catch up with him. Anita turned her horse and reined in, looking down at the place that had been her home since birth, a sad expression on her face.

"*Adiós,* Grandfather," she said softly. "I know you won't be here when I return. I love you, even though I may not have shown it as much as you would have liked. But I think you know that's something I can't help. It's become my way." Anita paused, then said, "I won't let you down. I'll see our family's honor revenged. I promise."

Anita blinked back the tears swimming in her eyes, squared her small shoulders, and turned her mount, galloping her horse after the two Rangers riding away in the distance.

When she caught up with them, Buck shot her a compassionate look, having guessed that she had been saying good-bye to her home and her grandfather. Anita gave him a grateful smile in return. Adam, however, lost in his dark, brooding thoughts, hadn't even noticed her absence.

When they approached a small village about ten miles from Monterrey, Adam reined in and said to Buck as the giant brought his horse up beside Adam's, "We can buy our supplies for the trip up there."

Anita moved her horse forward from where she had been following the two men, and said, "Let me go. Once they have seen who your are, they will charge you three times as much for everything, out of spite, if nothing else."

"She's got a point there, Adam," Buck said. "Hell, sometimes those greasers won't even sell to us." Then realizing what he had let slip out, Buck grimaced and said, "Sorry, Anita. I mean Meskins."

"No, don't try to change your language because of me, Buck. I know you mean no personal offense. Besides, I think your use of the term is more habit than anything. No, it's not what you call someone, but how it's said. Even 'Mexican' can be an insult from some people's lips," Anita ended, slashing Adam a meaningful look.

Her effort was not lost on Adam. "All right, Anita," Adam said in a brittle voice, "suppose you go and see if you can get any better deal out of those *Mexicans*."

Anita ignored Adam's sarcasm. She kneed her mount, but as it started to move away, Adam caught her arm. "You'll need money."

Anita knew better than to tell Adam that she had money or to offer to share the expense of their supplies. Neither man's ego would survive that insult. Although it went against her grain, she held out her hand.

As she moved away the second time, Buck said, "Wait a minute, Anita. Do you know what to buy?"

Anita wheeled her horse. "*Sí.* I have camped out with my grandfather before. We need staples. I assume you'll provide fresh meat. Those guns do kill something besides men, don't they?" she pointedly asked Adam, then whirled her horse and rode away without awaiting an answer.

Buck glanced across at Adam's furious countenance. Bewildered, he shook his shaggy head, wondering, if Anita had wanted to come along, ,then why did she continue to bait Adam? She acted almost as if she wanted to start a fight with him. And if Adam had wanted to take her along, why was he acting so sour about everything? They sure didn't act like any lovers he'd ever seen.

The two men dismounted and waited, and waited. Glaring at the small village, Adam asked, "What in the hell is taking her so long?"

"Oh, you know women," Buck answered from where he had settled down propped against a tree trunk. "She's probably looking over all those fancy doodads that women like to moon over."

Not Anita, Adam thought. Any woman who ran

around in peasant clothing by choice wasn't going to dally looking over female adornments. She didn't give a damn what she looked like. And yet Adam had to admit that she looked more beautiful in her simple clothing than any woman he had ever seen. She didn't need rich clothing to enhance her beauty. She was even more beautiful than Beth had been.

The thought shocked Adam. How in the world could he possibly compare Anita to his wife? Damn, first he had betrayed Beth's memory with his body, and now he was betraying it with his mind. The two women were nothing alike. Anita's dark beauty was too flagrant, almost vulgar, while Beth had been the epitome of southern beauty, pale, golden-haired, blue-eyed, soft-spoken. It was like comparing a pristine dove to a gaudy peacock. Or a gamecock, Adam thought, remembering Anita's fiery spirit that emerged in spurts from behind her icy barrier. No, there was nothing womanly about Anita, besides her body, that is, nothing soft, gentle, serene, soothing. Her grandfather was wrong. Anita didn't have a woman's heart in her. It was just like the rest of her—made of stone.

"Here she comes now," Buck said, rising to his feet and startling Adam from his brooding thoughts.

Anita rode up and reined in, a pleased smile on her face, a smile that looked more like a smirk to Adam. She handed him back the pesos, deliber-

193

ately letting them fall one by one in his hand so he could count them.

Adam glanced at the gunnysacks tied to her saddle and asked in surprise, "You got all that for just two pesos?"

"*Sí*. I told you I could be helpful."

"By God, those greasers *have* been stealing us blind!" Buck said hotly, eyeing the bulging sacks in disbelief.

While Buck distributed the supplies between their horses, Adam swung into his saddle and asked Anita, "What took you so long?"

"Bargaining takes time," Anita replied.

"You didn't have to bargain. Just buy! I'm not exactly poor, you know."

"It wasn't in consideration of your purse," Anita reported sharply "In Mexico, peasant women are expected to dicker over the prices. You just don't go to the marketplace or a store and buy. That would arouse suspicion."

"Then what about that horse you're riding?" Adam asked, his gaze sweeping over the golden bay. "That's first-class horseflesh. And that saddle is studded with pure silver. Don't you think that's going to arouse suspicion? Mexican peons ride burros bareback."

"If I rode a burro I wouldn't be able to keep up with you. Besides," Anita said with an elegant shrug, "when they see I am with *Tejanos*, they will just assume that you stole the horse and saddle for me."

Buck burst out laughing, the sound rumbling from his huge chest and exploding in the air, startling the horses. But Adam failed to see the humor in Anita's words. He gave her a scorching look, then kneed his horse and galloped away, calling over his shoulder, "Come on! We've lost enough time!"

Adam led the way that day, heading southwest toward Saltillo, driving them fast and hard, perhaps in hopes of discouraging Anita, and perhaps in hopes of goading Buck into an argument on her behalf. Neither happened. Anita was an expert equestrian with amazing stamina for a woman, and had no trouble keeping up with the grueling pace that Adam had set.

That evening, as soon as her horse was tended to, she began gathering firewood. When Buck started to help her, she stopped him. "No, Buck. This is part of Adam's and my agreement, too. A camp follower prepares the fire and does all the cooking."

"But you've have a hard—"

"Please," Anita cut across his words. "Don't interfere."

Buck sat down beside Adam, grumbling under his breath, "Don't seem right, her doing all the work."

Even Adam was feeling a little guilty, but dammit, this was her idea, he thought in self-defense.

Grudgingly, he said, "If we're partners, then we'll take care of the horses."

"If you like," Anita replied indifferently.

Both men knew it was a poor exchange. They watched, silent and uncomfortable, as Anita expertly and, with her usual cool efficiency, built the fire and prepared the evening meal. But when they took their first bite of the food Anita had dished out for them, both were secretly glad that Anita had insisted upon doing the cooking. The stew was delicious, a huge improvement on the usual camp food to which the men were accustomed.

"Say, Anita, what did you use in this stew, anyway?" Buck asked, as he shoveled the food into his mouth. "Even Martha can't make rabbit meat this tender and juicy."

"I'm sure it's just your imagination, Buck. Food always tastes better when one has been in the open air. Personally, it tastes a little bland to me."

Adam thought the food perfectly spiced, but instead of saying so, said sourly, "Well, for Christ's sake, don't go feeding us that hot food you Mexicans eat. It'll burn a hole clear through our stomachs."

Buck shot Adam an angry look, but Anita only shrugged and replied calmly, "I'm aware you aren't accustomed to spicy food. I took that into consideration when I cooked this. That's why it tastes so bland to me."

When Anita started gathering up the dirty

dishes, Buck came to his feet. "I'll help you with the dishes," he said, hoping to make up for Adam's rudeness in some small way.

"Do you help your wife wash dishes at home?" Anita asked.

"Well . . . no, but—"

"Then you will not help here."

To Adam's relief, there were no awkward questions concerning sleeping arrangements. The late fall air was cold, and as soon as the dishes were done, everyone rolled up in the blankets and huddled as close to the fire as they could safely get. Later that night, they were aroused when a bull wandered into the camp and settled down beside the fire.

"Where in the hell did he come from?" Buck asked, propped on one elbow and staring at the bovine in disbelief.

"He is a *ladino,* a tame bull that has gone wild," Anita explained. "Leave him alone. He is old and harmless. All he wants is to share the heat of the fire with us."

"Are you crazy?" Adam asked, staring at the animal's broad rump, which was facing him. "You expect us to sleep with a wild bull?"

"He is cold, too!" Anita retorted.

"Yeah, and I reckon we don't really have any choice," Buck said. "He's dead to the world, and, personally, I don't feel up to tangling with a bull over who's gonna get to sleep by the fire, even if he is an old bag of bones."

Anita and Buck lay back down. Reluctantly, Adam did the same, after switching ends in his bedroll. If he was going to be forced to sleep with a bull, he'd be damned if he'd do it with his face in its rump.

But Adam found sleep elusive, despite the lulling crackling of the fire and its soothing warmth. The bull snored, even louder than Buck, sleeping on the other side of the fire. To make matters worse, they weren't even snoring in unison, the loud, annoying noise a steady rumble in the still night air.

Then, as a log popped and a few cinders flew through the air and fell on the bull's rump, Adam smelled singed hair just before all hell broke loose. The bull shot up on all four feet, bellowing in outrage. Hind legs came flying out at Adam as he sat up, one razor-sharp hoof barely missing his head. The three hapless humans scrambled for safety as the enraged bull went berserk, bucking, twisting, and turning, scattering blankets, camp utensils, saddles, even the burning logs everywhere.

Adam and Buck dove for their Colts, and soon the roars of their guns were added to the furious bellows of the bull and the frightened squeals of the horses. But not one bullet found its mark, both men repeatedly missing the wildly twisting, bucking target as they dodged wicked horns and sharp hooves. Finally, as the last bullet flew through the air, so close that it nicked one of the animal's horns, the bull turned and tore off into the woods, leaving the ground shaking in its wild flight.

Adam looked about the camp in disbelief, then seeing his blanket had fallen next to a burning log and had caught fire, yanked it up and beat the fire out on the ground. As he stared down in disgust at the singed blanket, Anita broke into gales of laughter.

Adam whirled and glared at her. "What's so damned funny? We all could have been killed!"

Anita sank to the ground, holding her sides, rocking as she laughed. "You two," she answered between gasps for air. "You're *los Diablos Tejanos* . . . supposed to be so fierce and deadly with your guns . . . and yet . . . and yet you couldn't kill one old, half-crippled bull."

Neither man answered. Shame-faced, Buck bent down and picked up his coonskin cap, shaking the dust from it, while Adam stormed off into the woods in search of more firewood.

The next day was unseasonably hot and humid. As they wove their way over narrow, rocky paths between almost-barren hills, the sun beat down on them unmercifully from a cloudless, searing-blue sky. Sweat trickled down their foreheads and dampened their clothing.

Adam glanced across at Anita riding beside him, seeing her *camisa* was plastered to her body and clinging to her full, high breasts like a second skin. From his height, he could see the beads of perspiration lying in the valley between those proud mounds, glistening like diamonds in the sunlight. The sudden urge to taste those salty drops of moisture overcame him, and his heat rose. Muttering a curse beneath his breath he tore his eyes away from the tempting sight. Then Adam frowned, realizing for the first time that Anita wore no head covering.

"You should have bought a sombrero for yourself yesterday when you were buying those supplies. You've nothing to protect your face from the sun."

"Mexican women don't wear sombreros," Anita pointed out. "Besides my skin doesn't burn. I'm too dark."

Adam's gaze swept over the golden skin on Anita's face. Now he knew where she got her high coloring, from her father. He wondered how much of his hated enemy lay within her. Certainly not her regal carriage and her immense pride. That part of her was pure *hidalgo,* as were her aristocratic features and her fierce thirst for revenge. Yes, that was part of her Spanish heritage, for no one could be more vengeful than a Spaniard. Perhaps, considering her bloodlines, her seeking revenge wasn't unnatural after all.

But Adam still couldn't forgive her for using him to attain her purpose. If she had proposed to become his mistress out of mutual desire or out of a need to be taken care of and protected, he could have accepted it. Honest lust or survival he could understand. But she didn't give a damn about him, or herself, as far as he could tell. All she cared about was her revenge, so much so that she was willing to risk her life for it by deliberately placing herself in a war zone.

Buck could have pointed out that Adam was no different, that the two were as alike as two peas in a pod from that standpoint. For years, Adam had had no concern for his life. His desire for revenge was what kept him going, his life force. But even if Buck had pointed that out, Adam wouldn't have accepted it, for what was really eating at his vitals was Anita's indifference to him. Deep down, he wanted her to care and show it.

That afternoon, they spent two hours looking for water under the searing sun, following a maze of twisted, baked canyons whose floors were so dry that the ground was cracked. Not even a puddle of muddy water could be found. Even Anita, who was accustomed to the hot Mexican climate, was feeling the effects of the sun, the tip of her nose and the back of her neck tinged with pink. Her throat was so dry it ached, and the heat drained all energy from her. The rocky walls of the canyons reflected the heat like a huge oven, so that every breath of air seemed to sear her lungs and she was drenched with perspiration.

When they finally emerged from the maze and saw a line of trees in the distance, Buck squinted his eyes to see against the glaring sunlight and said, "Those are cottonwoods. There must be water there. Those damn things won't grow no place else. They're about the thirstiest trees I've ever seen."

"Well, let's hope they're not so thirsty that they didn't leave any water for us," Adam commented, then kneed his mount, galloping off toward the trees.

When they rode beneath the shade of the rustling leaves, they slowed their horses, relishing the feel of the cool shade after the scorching sun. But the shade did nothing to relieve their intense thirst. Their mounts pranced impatiently beneath them, tossing their heads and pulling on the reins. Knowing the animals smelled water, they gave them their heads, and the horses trotted off through the thick woods, finding the small stream that ran through it as true as an arrow.

Before their mounts had even come to a full halt, the three were out of the saddle. They fell to the ground, lying on their stomachs and drinking thirstily from the stream while their horses slurped noisily beside them.

Finally Adam raised his head, tossed his hat aside, and ducked his face in the water, splashing water on his neck and head, then sat back on his heels, shaking his head and sending glittering water drops flying in a shower around him. He glanced around, seeing animal prints in the wet sand beside him. Recognizing one as those of a big cat, he quickly scanned the woods behind them, his hand going to one of his guns, then realizing the horses would have smelled a cougar if there was one lurking about, removed it and relaxed.

He glanced down at Anita and saw she was still drinking. Placing his hand on her shoulder, he said, "Don't drink too much too fast. It will make you sick."

Anita raised her head. "Buck is still drinking."

It was true. The giant was making as much noise as the horses. "Yeah," Adam replied, "and if he gets a bellyache it will be his own fault. He knows better. I just thought I ought to warn you."

Anita knew that drinking too much after a long thirst and when one was overheated could cause stomach cramps, but she had never been so thirsty in her life. She fought back the urge to ignore Adam's warning and cupped her hand, splashing water over her face and neck. But she still felt miserably hot and sticky. If the two men had not been present, she would have stripped and waded into the stream.

Buck sat back, his beard dripping water down his shirtfront. Looking about him, he said, "This

203

looks like a good place to make camp for the night."

Adam would have preferred to get another hour or two of traveling time in. He glanced at Anita, wondering if she could hold out that much longer, then cursed himself for taking her comfort into consideration. Besides, she looked in better shape than Buck and this might well be the last water they'd find before they reached Saltillo.

"Okay," Adam agreed. "But let's make camp back at that clearing we rode through."

While Buck tended the horses, Adam sought out small game in the woods and Anita gathered firewood. By the time she had the fire going, Adam returned with two skinned rabbits. As soon as the evening meal was simmering over the fire and Anita had baked flour tortillas over a hot stone and placed them aside, she rose and walked to her small wicker basket, removing a bar of soap, a towel, and a fresh change of clothing.

Turning to the two men, she said, "I'm going farther down stream for a bath. If you get hungry before I return, help yourselves."

Forty-five minutes later, the tempting aroma of the stew simmering over the fire became too much for the men. Deciding not to wait for Anita, they dished up two plates and ate. But, while Buck was wolfing down the food as if he hadn't eaten in days, Adam couldn't enjoy his meal, despite his hunger and the taste of the delicious food. Ever since that morning when he had become aroused by the sight of Anita's damp *camisa* hugging her breasts like a second skin, he had been battling his desire for her. Now he was tormented by fantasies of her bathing in the stream. Time and time again, his eyes drifted in the direction she had gone. That she could arouse him with no visible effort on her part irritated him, but what really filled him with disgust was he was actually worried about her being off in the woods alone, something he had pointedly told Anita he would not do. He remembered the footprints he had seen earlier. Like all animals, cougars watered at dawn and dusk, and it was growing late. And these hills were crawling with bandits, unprincipled men who had no scruples about attacking a lone woman, be she Mexican or not.

Adam put his plate aside and rose. "I think I'll go see what's keeping Anita."

"Yeah, I've been worried about her, too," Buck replied. "Seems she should have been back by now."

"I didn't say I was worried about her!" Adam snapped defensively. "I just thought . . . I'd remind her the stew is cooking down. If she wants to eat tonight, she'd better do it while there's some left," Adam said in a terse voice, using the first excuse he could think of for seeking Anita out.

As Adam walked away, Buck shook his head in exasperation. He'd hoped once Adam was in the saddle and out in the open again, his mood would improve, but he was just as testy as when he'd been cooped up. And Buck knew damn well Adam had been worried about Anita. He'd seen it on his face as plain as day.

Adam met Anita coming up an animal trail that wove through the woods to the stream. Seeing her braid was wet, he assumed that washing her hair must be what had taken her so long.

Seeing Adam approaching her, Anita stopped, a surprised expression on her face. Then her dark eyes narrowed suspiciously. "Did you come to spy on me in my bath?"

The accusation infuriated Adam, for in truth he had been spying in his mind with his fantasies. "No! If I wanted to watch you bathe, I wouldn't have to spy. You sold your body, remember? Made yourself my woman. If I wanted to look at your nakedness I wouldn't have to sneak around to do it. That's my right now."

Adam's hard words stung, but Anita knew she had no one to blame but herself for his contempt, if that's what had aroused his anger. Then she realized that perhaps he had other reasons for seeking her out. Had he thought to make love to her? A tingle of excitement rushed over Anita at the memory of Adam's sensual lovemaking; a delicious warmth filled her. She had discovered, much to her surprise, that she could give herself up to passion, lose herself in it, enjoy it to the fullest and still keep the woman she guarded inviolable. One was of the body, the other of the spirit. No, that part of her was not endangered by Adam's passion nor her own. It was those gentle, tender feelings that had nothing to do with physical desire, feelings she had deliberately suppressed, that threatened her.

Then Anita remembered something. When she and Adam had suddenly met on the path, the expression on his face had been one of profound relief, and not the intense look of a man bent on satisfying his desire. Had he feared for her safety? The thought excited and warmed her even more than the promise of sensual delights.

"Why did you come then?" Anita asked, steeling herself to keep her expression impassive and reveal none of the trembling excitement she felt. "Were you worried about me?"

Adam would never admit to Anita what he couldn't even admit to himself, that he cared. The first and foremost rule he lived by was never show your weakness to the enemy. He replied in a harsh voice, "Don't start getting any silly ideas about our relationship. I told you in the beginning that I wasn't going to worry about you, and even if I did, it would just be concern of one ally for another, and nothing else. That's all we are, Anita. Temporary allies. Nothing more!"

Adam's eyes bored into Anita's. "Now if you'll excuse me, I'll do what I came down here to do.

Wash up a bit myself."

Adam sidestepped Anita and walked past her down the trail. Anita stared at his broad back, feeling more than just disappointment. His harsh avowal that he had no tender feelings for her had hurt deeply, much more deeply than she was willing to admit.

The three were just preparing for bed when they heard an ominous sound in the distance. "That sounds like thunder," Buck remarked. "Think there's a storm coming?"

Adam gazed off, seeing sheet lightning in the distance through the trees, then answered, "Maybe, maybe not. You know how it is in Texas a lot of times after a particularly hot day. You'll see lightning and hear thunder in the distance, but nothing ever comes of it."

But it soon became apparent that a storm was approaching. The wind that preceded it rattled the branches of the cottonwoods all around them and lightning flashed and cracked, then flashed again. Thunder rolled, and balls of phosphorescent light—St. Elmo's fire—hovered over the horses' heads and danced down their manes and tails.

Buck threw back his blanket, pulled something from his saddlebags beside him, and rose. Walking to Anita, who was rolled up in her blanket a few feet from him, he placed the oilskin over her.

"Here, Anita. You can have my parka. Might keep some of the rain off."

"What about you?" Anita asked. "Won't you need it yourself?"

"Aw, hell, I'm used to sleeping in the rain. I don't even bother with it."

"In that case, *gracias*," Anita replied.

Lying in his bedroll, Adam frowned. Leave it to Buck to think of something so chivalrous, he thought sourly. And he supposed Buck's thoughtful consideration would make him look even more like a heel in Anita's eyes. *He* was supposed to be her protector, not Buck. Well, he hadn't wanted her to come along, Adam reminded himself. And he'd told her he wasn't going to coddle her. Maybe sleeping in the rain would be good for her. When she found out what rugged lives they led, maybe she'd go back to where she belonged. Damn Buck! Why didn't he mind his own business?

Buck had hardly crawled back into his bedroll next to Adam's when the rain came, buckets and buckets of it. Lying on the ground with only his blanket for protection from the pouring downfall, Buck grumbled, "Now ain't that just like nature to be so contrary? I would have given my right arm for a drink of water this afternoon and now I'm drowning in it."

Adam didn't bother to answer. The only sounds were the crash of thunder, the loud cracks of lightning, and the heavy pattering of rain. Then he said, "Water is seeping beneath my bottom blanket. I think we're lying in a little ravine. Do you want to move?"

"Naw, we got this puddle of water nice and warm now. If we move to another we'll probably catch cold."

"Yeah, I guess you're right," Adam replied lazily.

Both men shifted their positions and closed their eyes, oblivious to the deafening noises all around them and the rain pounding down on them.

Anita, warm and dry on the higher ground she lay on and beneath Buck's huge poncho, had heard the brief exchange between the two men. She could only shake her head at the rugged Rangers' absurd reasoning.

Chapter 13

The first thing Adam became aware of when he awoke the next morning was the raindrops glittering on the cottonwood leaves above him. The second thing he noticed was the tempting aroma of fresh-brewed coffee in the air. He rose on one elbow and looked about the camp, his eyes going immediately to the fire burning at the center. He knew Anita had to have built it, for he could hear Buck snoring loudly behind him. How had she managed to find enough dry wood? he wondered. After that downpour last night, it must have taken some time-consuming searching. And what was she doing up so early? He would have thought after the past two days of grueling riding, she would have welcomed the opportunity to sleep late. Unless she hadn't been able to sleep because of the miserable sleeping conditions.

The last thought brought a smug smile to

Adam's face. Maybe now Anita would change her mind and demand to be taken back to Monterrey, back to her soft feather mattress and warm, cozy home, back to the comforts of the life she was accustomed to. But when Adam saw Anita coming from the side of the camp where they kept their supplies, his hopes were dashed to the ground. There were no signs of exhaustion on her face from having spent a sleepless night, and her walk was just as brisk and regal as ever.

Dammit, Adam thought irritably, didn't anything get her down? His muscles were stiff from sleeping in the rain on the hard ground, for the parched earth had absorbed the water like a thirsty sponge. His clothing was damp and rumpled and the day's growth of beard was itching like crazy. He felt like hell, and knew he looked it. Yet Anita looked as fresh as if she had just emerged from her morning toilet.

"Would you like a cup of coffee?" Anita asked from across the fire.

Adam startled. He had thought Anita unaware of his wakefulness, since she hadn't so much as even glanced in his direction. Had she been aware he had been scrutinizing her?

Anita had felt those glowering green eyes on her. It seemed Adam had awakened in his usual foul mood. If he had any other, Anita had yet to see it. He seemed to be perpetually irritable. But then, that suited her purpose. It made it all the easier to dislike him, and that was absolutely critical to her self-preservation. No, it would never do to let this strangely disturbing man get the upper hand over her emotions. To like him as well as be attracted to him physically could destroy her.

Buck came up out of his soggy blanket, looking like a rearing shaggy bear. "Did I hear someone mention coffee?"

Anita smiled at Buck across the fire, something that further irritated Adam. "*Sí*. Would you like a cup?"

"Boy, would I!" Buck replied, lumbering stiffly to the fire and accepting the tin cup from Anita, *his* cup of coffee, Adam noted sourly as he rose from his bedroll.

Buck took a big swallow of the steaming brew. "Ah, that's good! Ain't nothing like a cup of hot, fresh coffee to get a man going in the morning. And you make it strong, Anita. Just like I like it. Can't stand weak coffee."

Anita made no comment. Personally, she preferred her coffee a little weaker, but she had guessed that the Rangers liked theirs so strong you could practically stand on it. Seeing Adam walking over to the fire, she picked up the pot and poured another cup for him.

As she handed it to him, their fingers brushed. Adam felt a bolt of electricity run up his arm at the brief physical contact. He glanced sharply at Anita to see if she had felt it, too, but her face

213

was its usual mask. Damn her, he thought. She was a temptress sent straight from hell to torment him. Deliberately, he turned his back to her and walked away without so much as a thank you.

Anita ignored Adam's rudeness and began preparing breakfast, pulling the shawl she had wrapped around her closer, as there was a cool nip in the morning air.

Seeing her motion, Buck remarked, "Guess it won't be so warm traveling today. That storm must have been a norther passing through. Feels real good to me."

"I'm afraid I have thin blood," Anita answered. "The heat doesn't bother me nearly as much as the cold."

Adam frowned. Was that what had awakened her so early? Had she been cold? Then realizing that he was worrying about her, this time about her comfort, he shook his head in disgust.

Soon the tantalizing aroma of frying bacon and baking tortillas was added to that of the coffee, making both men's stomachs rumble and their mouths water in anticipation.

Then, as Anita started breaking eggs into the frying pan, Adam asked in surprise, "Where did you get those?"

"They're quail eggs. I found them in a nest under some bushes down by the stream this morning."

Adam remembered the cougar prints and felt a

214

rush of fear. "What in the hell did you go down there for?"

"I needed water to make coffee," Anita answered calmly.

"Dammit, don't you know there are wild animals around here and they water at that stream? You could have been attacked!"

Anita wondered at Adam's strong reaction. Did an ally feel that protective of another? Or did he care, after all? Or was he just thinking of her as a weak, defenseless woman, not a special woman, just a woman who needed a man's protection? Well, she wasn't that kind of a woman. She didn't need any man to protect her.

"I know there are wild animals, but they didn't bother me."

"They?" Buck asked in alarm, his hand with the cup in it stopping in midway to his mouth. "What animals were down there?"

Anita shrugged. "A few javelinas, a deer, and," she sliced Adam a pointed look, "a *puma*," using the Mexican term for cougar.

"A *puma!*" Buck exclaimed. "Damn it, Anita! Don't you know they're dangerous? As far as that goes, those javelinas can be pretty mean sometimes, too. You should have taken one of our guns with you."

"I do not need a gun to protect me!" Anita threw back hotly. "I told you, they didn't bother me. They knew I was no threat to them."

Both men could only stare at Anita. Did she feel even a flicker of fear, Adam wondered when he had recovered from her shocking revelation. No, she was incapable of feeling even something as elemental as that emotion. He had been right in his estimation of her. She *was* made of stone.

Two days later, the three rode into Saltillo. It was obvious that the American Army was there. Blue uniforms were seen everywhere as they weaved their way through the narrow, twisted streets to the southernmost outskirts of the city, their eyes locked on the pass through the towering Sierras that Santa Anna would have to travel—if he came.

As she had done before, Anita went ahead into a sleepy village, this time to secure them lodging. When she had found what she wanted, she had no trouble convincing the Mexican peons who lived there to vacate and move in with their relatives across the city for a few months. The handful of pesos that she paid them would feed the entire lot for almost a year.

When Anita led Adam and Buck to their new lodgings, Adam looked around him, relieved to see that the farmhouse sat away from the rest of the village and would offer them some privacy and that there was a lean-to beside it for the horses. The interior of the adobe building pleased him

MORE PASSION AND ADVENTURE AWAIT... YOUR TRIP TO A BIG ADVENTUROUS WORLD BEGINS WHEN YOU ACCEPT YOUR FIRST 4 NOVELS ABSOLUTELY *FREE*
(AN $18.00 VALUE)

Accept your Free gift and start to experience more of the passion and adventure you like in a historical romance novel. Each Zebra novel is filled with proud men, spirited women and tempestuous love that you'll remember long after you turn the last page.

Zebra Historical Romances are the finest novels of their kind. They are written by authors who really know how to weave tales of romance and adventure in the historical settings you love. You'll feel like you've actually gone back in time with the thrilling stories that each Zebra novel offers.

GET YOUR FREE GIFT WITH THE START OF YOUR HOME SUBSCRIPTION

Our readers tell us that these books sell out very fast in book stores and often they miss the newest titles. So Zebra has made arrangements for you to receive the four newest novels published each month.

You'll be guaranteed that you'll never miss a title, and home delivery is so convenient. And to show you just how easy it is to get Zebra Historical Romances, we'll send you your first 4 books absolutely FREE! Our gift to you just for trying our home subscription service.

BIG SAVINGS AND FREE HOME DELIVERY

Each month, you'll receive the four newest titles as soon as they are published. You'll probably receive them even before the bookstores do. What's more, you may preview these exciting novels free for 10 days. If you like them as much as we think you will, just pay the low preferred subscriber's price of just $3.75 each. *You'll save $3.00 each month off the publisher's price.* AND, your savings are even greater because there are never any shipping, handling or other hidden charges—FREE Home Delivery. Of course you can return any shipment within 10 days for full credit, no questions asked. There is no minimum number of books you must buy.

4 FREE BOOKS

TO GET YOUR 4 FREE BOOKS WORTH $18.00 — MAIL IN THE FREE BOOK CERTIFICATE T O D A Y

Fill in the Free Book Certificate below, and we'll send your FREE BOOKS to you as soon as we receive it.

If the certificate is missing below, write to: Zebra Home Subscription Service, Inc., P.O. Box 5214, 120 Brighton Road, Clifton, New Jersey 07015-5214.

GET
FOUR
FREE
BOOKS
(AN $18.00 VALUE)

ZEBRA HOME SUBSCRIPTION
SERVICE, INC.
P.O. Box 5214
120 BRIGHTON ROAD
CLIFTON, NEW JERSEY 07015-5214

even more, for instead of it being the usual one large room, there were three, the two small bedrooms flanking the central room.

Anita motioned to one bedroom. "Buck, you can take that room. Adam and I will sleep in the other."

Adam winced at her candid reminder that she was his mistress, but Buck, who had become more adjusted to the new arrangement than he, lumbered to the doorway and peeked in. "This sure beats anything we've had when we're on Ranger business."

"We won't be staying here all the time!" Adam snapped. "This will just . . . just be our headquarters."

Anita ignored Adam's pointed reminder that she would not be accompanying them on their forays against the enemy. Directing her attention to Buck, she said, "It's not much, but it will shelter us from the elements. And when it's cleaned up, it will look much better. The first thing I need to do is replace those mattresses. They're probably infested with bedbugs. Buck, would you mind dragging them out into the yard for me so that I can burn them?"

Adam resented the fact that Anita had asked Buck for a favor and not him. His puzzling jealousy came to the rise. "Now, wait a minute!" he snapped. "This house is your idea. Don't go getting any nesting ideas and think you're going to

217

run our legs off helping you get it fixed up. We've got business to attend to in Saltillo."

Anita turned, saying, "I only want to make this place more habitable. And as soon as Buck has removed the mattress, you two can leave. Frankly, I don't want you here while I'm cleaning. You'll only get in the way."

Buck felt a twinge of homesickness, remembering how many times Martha had chased him out of the house when she had serious cleaning to do. He gave Adam a challenging, heated look. "I'll drag them out for you, Anita. Adam may not mind sharing his bed with a bunch of biting bedbugs, but I don't cotton to the idea. And I sure don't want you straining your back trying to lift those heavy mattresses," he added, his voice heavy with disapproval of his friend's attitude.

Ten minutes later, Adam and Buck rode away. They spent the rest of the day seeking news of the war. To their disgust, they discovered that nothing, absolutely nothing, was going on. The war had come to a complete standstill. It was dark by the time they rode back to the farmhouse, and even Adam had to admit that the little building looked inviting with the cold night air blowing down from the mountains and chilling them to the bone.

When they stepped into the building, the warmth from the fire in the fireplace across the room surrounded them like a welcoming blanket. And then, the two men looked about them, wondering if they had entered the wrong house. The place didn't look the same. Gone were the cobwebs, the dust, even a new table and chairs sat where the old rickety ones had been. The floor, where it could be seen between the colorful straw mats, was swept so clean that it shone as if it were made of stone, and not packed dirt. There were new curtains in the small windows, and the newly scrubbed pots and pans hanging on the side of the fireplace gleamed in the firelight.

"Sit down," Anita said from the bedroom doorway. "Dinner is ready. It will be ruined if it simmers any longer."

Almost as if in a daze, both men walked to the table and sat, still looking about them in disbelief, while Anita served them their food. Finally, Buck said, "Damn, Anita. It's amazing what you did with this place. How'd you get all this done in so short a time?"

Anita shrugged.

"Where did you get the new table and chairs?" Adam asked.

"At the same place I got everything else, the marketplace."

"How'd you get them here?" Buck asked.

"I hired a wagon and two boys to help me. They carried in the heavier things, including the two new corn-husk mattresses."

Adam winced, remembering his irascible behavior that morning, then asked, "How did you buy all this stuff?"

"I have money with me."

"We'll pay you back," Adam replied.

"That won't be necessary. As you said, this house is my idea."

"I said, we'll pay you back," Adam said in a hard, carefully measured voice.

Anita fought down her fierce pride and answered, "If you insist. It cost eight pesos. That includes the food."

"You got all this for eight pesos?" Buck asked in amazement.

"Sí."

"And a little bargaining?" Adam threw in sarcastically.

Anita looked him directly in the eye. "And a little bargaining," she said, then turned, adding, "Now eat. Before your food gets cold."

When they had finished eating and Anita was gathering up the dirty dishes, she said, "There is a wooden tub behind that screen in the corner. And there's hot water over the fire."

"You telling us we gotta take a bath?" Buck asked, a wary look on his face.

"I would prefer that you do. The bed linens are clean."

"But it ain't even Saturday," Buck objected.

Adam sat back with a smug smile on his face, thinking to enjoy the struggle of wills between the two. He knew of Buck's aversion to bathing. His friend insisted that anything over one bath a week was downright unhealthy. But to his amazement, Anita not only maneuvered the giant behind the screen, but after he was dressed in fresh clothing, managed to talk Buck into letting her trim his long, shaggy beard, something that, to Adam's knowledge, not even Martha had been able to do.

When she was through, Buck stroked his beard with one hand, saying in a horrified voice, "Christ Anita! You scalped me."

"You look very handsome, Buck," Anita responded.

A flush rose on the giant's face. No one had ever called him handsome. He wasn't gullible enough to believe Anita. He knew she was exaggerating. But still, the compliment pleased him. He averted his eyes, grumbling, "Yeah, well, I may look better, but I feel downright naked."

Anita laughed softly and turned to face Adam. He knew what she was expecting. Dammit, he should refuse to bathe, just on principle. But the thought of a hot, relaxing bath was too appealing. He rose, saying irritably, "Come on, Buck. Help me empty that tub. If I'm going to have to bathe, I'll be damned if I'll do it in your dirty water."

"Hell, at home, the boys and I all use the same water," Buck objected.

"This isn't home, and I'm not one of your boys!"

"All right. You don't have to get so testy about

221

it," Buck said, lumbering across the room. "Just seems like a waste of water to me."

Long after Anita and Buck had retired to their separate bedrooms, Adam sat and stared at the fire, fighting a battle with himself. A part of him wanted to go into the bedroom and claim what was his by right of his and Anita's agreement, while another part argued that to do so would only cement their crazy alliance further. Maybe if he didn't collect on his end, Anita would pull out, Adam thought. But Adam knew in his heart that Anita didn't care if he bedded her once, or a hundred times. She had settled in, and she wasn't going to budge. So what was he gaining by denying himself? Not a damned thing but aching loins and guts that felt like they were tied into a million knots, for he wanted her as much, if not more than before. The memory of their one night of passion played on his mind and tortured his body. Anita had told Buck that she was his mistress. Then that's what she'd be. His woman. Nothing more!

Adam rose and walked to the bedroom, his heart already racing in anticipation.

As he pushed the door open, the light from the inner room suddenly bathed the bed. Anita sat up and pushed her long black hair back from her face, saying in a groggy voice, "I thought you weren't coming."

Adam's throat turned dry as he realized, with

just a little shock, that Anita was naked. He stared at the proud breasts with their pert, dark nipples, then jerked his eyes away, answering in a thick voice, "I thought about it."

"It would change nothing, you know."

"I know. That's why I changed my mind."

Adam shifted his weight, all too aware of his manhood straining uncomfortably against the tight confines of his pants. His movement drew Anita's attention to that part of him.

Seeing the telltale bulge, Anita pushed back the covers. "Stop fighting it, Adam. We're together in this. Besides, I've discovered that I enjoy making love."

For the second time, Adam was shocked, this time at Anita's candid admission. Women didn't go around openly admitting to something like that. Not respectable women. To the contrary. They seemed to find the act repulsive, or at least Beth had. She had submitted to her wifely duties with a grim resignation, showing absolutely no interest, much less enthusiasm, and leaving Adam always feeling a little dirty when it was over. But Anita had said she enjoyed it. Considering her passionate response, Adam didn't doubt her sincerity. But still, her blatant admission was unsettling. He had never met a woman like Anita before, totally honest and without guile.

"Close the door and come to bed."

The throaty tone of Anita's voice floated in the

air and surrounded Adam. Combined with the tempting vision of her beautiful, naked body and her smoldering dark eyes that promised heaven and more, Adam's blood pounded in his temples and was answered in his loins. His simmering heat burst into a flaming inferno of need, blocking out all rational thought and destroying the last vestiges of resistance. He closed the door.

Before Adam could even begin to remove his clothing, Anita climbed from the bed and began unbuttoning his shirt. Her boldness stunned Adam, for no woman had undressed him as a prelude to making love. Beth would have never thought of doing something so unladylike, and the prostitutes that Adam had on occasion visited after her death to relieve his lustful needs hadn't considered it part of their services. He started to push Anita's hands away and to object but found he couldn't. The feel of her fingers brushing the heated skin on his chest was highly erotic, the darkness only increasing his awareness of her touch.

Anita pushed Adam's shirt from his shoulders and down his arms, smiling with pleasure when she felt his powerful muscles trembling beneath her fingertips, his response to her touching him exciting her. "Sit on the bed, so I can take off your boots," she instructed, giving him a gentle shove.

As if in a daze, Adam sat, the corn husks in the mattress rustling beneath his weight, lifting one foot, then the other as Anita stripped him of his boots and socks.

"Now stand," Anita said softly.

Adam's heart pounded in his chest, and his mouth turned dry, knowing she meant to strip him of his pants, too, to remove the last barrier between his and her nakedness. He stood, his legs feeling incredibly weak as Anita deftly undid his belt buckle. As she unbuttoned his pants, he sucked in his breath at the feel of her fingers touching his bare belly, traveling lower and lower toward that part of him that was aching and pushing against the material. When the last button gave way, his rigid manhood sprang free from its confinement, and to Adam's utter surprise, Anita took the throbbing flesh in her hand.

"You are built like a stallion, *Tejano*," Anita said in a deep, throbbing voice.

While Adam was again shocked by Anita's bold words, he felt a tingle of pride run through him. He was a man, with a man's ego, and proud of his manliness. But he made no comment on Anita's compliment, and he knew without a doubt that she meant it as that, nor did the use of the hated *Tejano* rile him. He was lost in sheer sensation as she stroked his rigid length, her fingertips leaving a trail of fire over that ultra-sensitive part of him.

Anita enjoyed touching him, marveling at how his manhood hardened and grew even larger under

225

her ministrations, the skin a velvety soft covering over a shaft as hard as steel. Stroking him excited her unbearably, sending a rush of heat over her, then centering in that throbbing place between her legs.

Adam felt his skin stretched so tight that he feared he would burst. He reached to still Anita's hands, only to find she had disappeared like a wraith as she bent and pushed the tight pants down his legs, leaving the muscles in his thighs trembling as her hands trailed down them. He gritted his teeth against the exquisite sensation, then, when she reached his ankles, stepped from the pants and reached for her. Pulling her to her feet and then into his arms in a tight embrace, his breath caught at the feel of her soft, womanly curves pressed against him, and the room spun dizzily around him.

His kiss was hot and ravenous, with none of the tender seduction he had previously used with Anita. His passion was ungovernable, his hunger for the sweetness of her mouth overriding all thought of gentleness. Anita answered him with her own raging passion, needing no gentle inducement. She was as hungry for him as he was for her, her small tongue dancing around his, then straining her body against his when his tongue slid in and out in a sensual pattern that mimicked that which was to come, making small whimpers of delight at the back of her throat, a sound that excited Adam to a feverish pitch.

They fell to the bed on their sides, still locked in that torrid kiss, bodies straining one against the other, their hearts pounding in unison. Then Adam broke the kiss, rolling Anita to her back, his lips dropping fiery kisses over her face, down her throat and across her shoulders. His hands swept down her body like wildfire, leaving a burning trail in their wake, then back up, cupping her full breast in one hand and squeezing its softness. He bent his head, his tongue laving the warm, silky skin, breathing deeply of her intoxicating scent before his mouth closed over her dark nipple, teeth gently nipping it, then rolling it around his tongue. Anita moaned in pleasure, the sound exciting Adam even more.

As he feasted at her breast, then took its twin in his hot mouth, Anita clasped his dark head to her, almost smothering Adam in her softness as she held him fiercely, glorying in the waves of exquisite pleasure washing over her. As that throbbing deep within her became almost unbearable, she writhed her lower body against his, wanting him, needing him inside her.

The feel of Anita's soft belly brushing back and forth against his hot, rigid length where it was trapped between them was an agony for Adam. He pulled back, leaving Anita's breasts and slipping downward between her open legs, his tongue dancing wildly over the feverish skin of her abdomen, then swirling in the dark curls between her thighs, drawn as irrevocably to the honeyed recess of her womanhood as a bee to the nectar in a flower.

Through her spinning senses, Anita guessed his intent. She stiffened, muttering thickly, "No!"

But it was too late, Adam had already slipped his hands beneath her, cupping her buttocks and lifting her to his mouth, his tongue flicking like a fiery dart and sending an electrical jolt dancing up her spine.

She pulled on the dark hair on his head, gasping, "I said no!"

Adam raised his head and gazed up her body, her proud breasts standing like twin hills on her chest, his blazing eyes meeting hers. "Why not?" he asked in a voice rough with desire.

It was an act that seemed too intimate to Anita, even more so than their joining. "It's . . . it's unnatural."

Adam wondered why he was so determined to taste her there, to explore her most intimate secrets with his tongue. It was something he had never done to a woman, would have never dreamed of doing to Beth. But no woman excited him the way Anita did, aroused his passions to the heights she did. Her womanly scent, was driving him wild. "It's no more unnatural than our alliance," he threw back, then dropped his head.

Anita struggled, her heart racing in her chest, but Adam held her hips firmly, ignoring the frantic tugs she was giving his hair, feasting on her there as hungrily as he had on her breasts.

"You are an animal!" Anita sobbed, desperately fighting the sensations that were threatening to engulf her, knowing what he was doing must be terribly wicked. It felt too wonderful to be anything else.

Adam laughed, a laugh that sounded like the devil himself to Anita's ears. She tried to steel herself to him, to remain indifferent and impassive, to feel nothing, but the defenses she used so well to protect the inner woman were useless on her body. Under Adam's erotic attack, she was as helpless as a grain of sand in a windstorm. The feel of his hot tongue darting here, there, swirling around the swollen bud of her desire, then dipping lower to explore her innermost secrets, in and out like a flame of fire, excited Anita as nothing ever had. She rolled her head as the waves of glorious sensation washed over her and became powerful undulations that shook her body, her breath coming in ragged gasps, feeling consumed in fire.

Through his own dazed senses, Adam was aware of Anita's soft thighs tightening on his head as if she would hold him prisoner there. Her capitulation excited him even more than her salty-sweet taste and her heady scent, his turgid manhood lengthening another inch and threatening to burst. When he felt her spasms of joy and heard her cry out, he couldn't wait any longer. He had to bury

229

himself in her.

Adam entered her when those spasms were still rocking her body, and she felt his powerful, deep thrust like a lightning bolt, sending sparks racing up her spine and bringing forth another breathtaking climactic response. He steeled himself against the feel of her hot muscles grasping him, fearing he would be pushed over that fine brink before he was ready. With supreme will, he fought for control, his body breaking out in a sheen of perspiration as he clenched his teeth, determined that this time he would be the one to set the pace, to dominate, that he would master her once and for all.

Then as Anita stilled beneath him, staring up at him with glazed eyes, he smiled and began the exquisite, slow movements calculated to tease and tantalize, then going at her hard and fast, then slow again. He withdrew his entire length, taunting her with the tip of his manhood until she begged for release, then entered her damp, tight heat with excruciating slowness, taking delight in her eyes widening as she felt his immense pulsating length filling her. Then lying deep within her, he paused. It was a mistake. Anita engulfed him, surrounded him, melted around him, her scalding heat burning him like a branding iron. His passion surged to the surface in a powerful, hard, intense pitch of excitement. He drove into her over and over with the unbridled force of his need, pouring himself into her and reaching for her very soul in his possession, groaning and muttering her name repeatedly.

They rode that hot crest of passion, Adam lifting Anita to a wild, swirling turbulence. She felt her senses expanding, an unbearable tension filling her, and knew the time for release was near. She shifted her hips to meet the spiraling, urgent heat of his deep, powerful plunge, then cried out his name as she was flung into a dark, mindless void among swirling colors and exploding stars, totally unaware of Adam shuddering above her as he reached his own climactic burst.

There was a long silence in the room as both slowly drifted back to reality. Feeling incredibly weak, Adam struggled up on his forearms and looked down at Anita. Seeing the blissful smile on her face, a strange warmth suffused him at the knowledge that he had given her immense pleasure.

The feeling stunned him. What in the hell was wrong with him? he wondered with no small horror. He had meant to master her, conquer her, not please her.

Then as Anita opened her eyes, the thick, dark lashes sweeping up like twin fans, and she said in a soft voice, "That was very nice," the peculiar warmth inside Adam intensified.

Filled with self-disgust, Adam grunted something unintelligible and rolled to his back. To his dismay, Anita cuddled up to him, pressing her soft, warm curves to his side. Then something happened that startled Adam. Incredible as it seemed, he felt his body responding to her touch. He had never had such recuperative power in the past. Twice in one night perhaps, but never had his body recovered so rapidly. But then, Adam had never had a lover like Anita, passionate and wildly exciting.

As if his body had a mind and a will of its own, and with something akin to helplessness, he turned to her, and she welcomed him with open arms.

Chapter 14

The next month passed like an eternity for Adam and Buck, and the two men grew increasingly impatient and restless. Only Anita was content to wait for Santa Anna to make his move.

"Maybe he ain't coming," Buck grumbled to Adam as the two men sat at the table one night. "At least, not to Saltillo. Taylor moved a portion of his army to Victoria, between Monterrey and Tampico. Maybe we should go there too. Maybe that's where the action is gonna take place."

"No, I don't think so," Adam answered. "If Santa Anna comes, it will have to be through that pass out there."

"Then how come Taylor moved to Victoria?"

"He's avoiding Scott, still putting off sending him his best troops. Taylor was supposed to meet Scott at Camargo, down on the Rio Grande, but Taylor sent word that he had urgent business in

233

Victoria and couldn't make it."

Buck chuckled. "So Taylor is still disobeying orders."

"Yes, but he can't do so indefinitely, not without risking court-martial."

"Well, I wish something would happen soon. Looks like we're gonna have to spend both Christmas and New Year's in this stinking place."

"You should have gone back to Texas with Ben. That way you could have at least have spent the holidays with Martha and the boys."

"Hell, it's beginning to look like Ben ain't gonna come back, either." Buck rose heavily to his feet. "Well, I guess I'll go on to bed. It's pretty bad when you ain't got anything more exciting to do than sleep." He turned to Anita where she was sitting in a rocking chair and mending one of Adam's shirts. "Good night," he said.

"*Buenas noches*, Buck," Anita answered, raising her head and smiling at the giant.

As Anita lowered her head to return to her sewing, Adam sat back and watched, something he found he enjoyed doing when she wasn't aware of it. Her movements were always so graceful, no matter what task she was performing, whether it was sweeping the floor, grinding corn, scrubbing clothes, ironing, washing dishes, or cooking. Yes, she was certainly keeping up her end of their bargain, seeing to his every physical need, slaving for him. Except in bed. There Adam found himself slaving to satisfy *her*.

Adam had never figured out his compulsion to pleasure her or the immense satisfaction it gave him, but he was forced to admit that, while Anita planned on using him to meet her purpose and was still cool and aloof out of the bedroom, she was totally unselfish and uninhibited in bed. She gave Adam as much pleasure as she received, perhaps even more. Adam had never known such ecstasy, such total fulfillment. But Adam still wanted more, much more.

A month later, Taylor was back in Saltillo, and fast on his heels, on February 4th, Ben McCulloch and his small company of Rangers arrived from Texas, passing through Monterrey on their way. As soon as Adam and Buck heard the news, they sought out their old friend and invited him to dinner.

If McCulloch was surprised to find Anita with the two men, he hid it behind his usual stony mask, and as soon as the dishes were cleared away, the three men got down to business.

"So Taylor was glad to see you back," Adam commented.

"Yes. According to his chief-of-staff, Taylor has been asking where in the hell I was for over a month now. Without the Rangers to act as scouts and guides and to carry messages, the army has

235

been paying through the nose. Couriers have been killed, dispatches interrupted, reconnoitering parties cut off and captured. Taylor finally admitted that he doesn't know how to deal with these Mexican guerrillas."

"And did you say Scott is finally going to get the men he demanded?" Adam asked, feeling a twinge of disappointment. As long as Taylor refused to send the troops, he had felt safe hanging around northern Mexico. But if the plans for the invasion of central Mexico were being put into action, he and Buck were going to have to make a decision. They couldn't be in both places at once.

"Yes, Taylor stalled for as long as he could," Ben answered. "Of course, Taylor has been reinforced with that army General Woll marched down from San Antonio, but they're green troops. Scott stripped the old man of all but six thousand troops, almost all volunteers, and you know how Taylor feels about volunteers. But I've got to hand it to the old man. He's still fighting the powers that be. He was ordered to fall back to Monterrey, you know."

"I feel kinda sorry for him," Buck said. "It seems to me like he's getting a rotten deal."

"He is," Ben agreed, "and he's bitter about it. But he's got more guts than we ever gave him credit for. Despite everything, he's not falling back—and Polk be damned! He's still hoping for one more battle, one more victory, particularly

236

after what happened to that message Scott sent to him."

"What message?" Adam asked.

"You haven't heard about that?" Ben asked in surprise. Then he shrugged his shoulders, saying, "Well, I guess the Army is keeping it quiet. When General Scott arrived at Camargo and discovered Taylor was still in the interior, he threw military etiquette out the window and sent Taylor a second message, this time ordering him to send his seasoned troops to the coast and outlining his entire proposed campaign into central Mexico. Scott sent the dispatch by a military messenger who was captured by a group of Mexican *vaqueros* and brutally murdered. Hell, you don't have to be a genius to know what happened to that dispatch. By now, I'm sure Santa Anna knows that Taylor has been stripped of his best troops."

Adam and Buck exchanged excited glances before Adam looked over to where Anita stood and read her lips as she whispered, "He is coming." Then his gaze shifted upward, and he shivered at the diabolical gleam in her dark eyes.

Unaware of the drama going on around him, McCulloch continued. "So my guess is the war in northern Mexico isn't over after all. Hell, you know Santa Anna won't be able to resist the temptation to crush Taylor's army before he goes to meet Scott. Now the only question is, when? Will he march in the dead of the winter, or wait

237

until spring?"

Adam remembered Anita telling him that Santa Anna had marched in the dead of the winter, surprising the Texans at the Alamo. "He won't wait until spring."

"He'll have to come through that mountain pass out there. It's full of snow," McCulloch argued.

"A little snow won't stop Santa Anna," Anita remarked.

Ben gave Anita a sharp, suspicious look, and Adam said, "Relax, Ben. Anita hates Santa Anna as much as we do. He's made a few enemies south of the Rio Grande, too, you know. Anita is on our side in this."

"I see," Ben muttered, not knowing how to take this surprising news. He turned his attention back to the two men. "So how about it, boys? Are you joining my company?"

"That depends, Ben." Adam frowned. "Have you heard anything from Hays?"

"Yes. He's still working on trying to get a company together."

"You see, Ben," Adam explained, "we promised Hays we'd meet him in Veracruz if the governor authorized him to call up a new company."

"Veracruz?" Ben asked in surprise.

"Yes, Jack wants to get in on the fighting in central Mexico, and, according to him, the target is Veracruz. We made all these plans back in Monterrey, before he left for Texas."

Ben grinned. "You're sneaky, aren't you, boys? Or rather, I should say greedy. You want to get in on the fighting up here in the north *and* in central Mexico."

"That's right," Adam admitted frankly. "Have you heard anything about when Scott plans to invade?"

"Well, I guess that's no secret. After that message to Taylor was interrupted, even Santa Anna knows that. Scott plans on invading this spring. He wants time to get his army out of the lowlands before the yellow fever season starts."

"Spring?" Buck asked in a shocked voice. "Are you talking about the middle of March? Hell, that's just six weeks away!"

"I'm afraid it is," Ben answered. "Looks like you boys are going to be in for a tight squeeze if you expect to see all the action. Santa Anna can split his forces, leave part behind to stall Scott while he concentrates on Taylor, but you can't. Unless you two intend to split up."

"We wouldn't never do that!" Buck said hotly. "We're partners!"

When Adam and Ben both chuckled, a sheepish look came over the giant's face as he realized Ben had only been teasing.

"Ben," Adam said, leaning across the table and giving his friend an intense look, "you can see why we can't sign up with you for a regular enlistment, not if we're going to get down to central Mexico to meet Hays, like we promised. But we'd sure like to serve with you. Dammit, Santa Anna is coming! I can feel it in my bones. Is there anyway we can join up with you for a short enlistment, say a month?"

"You're not the only ones balking at a long-term enlistment," McCulloch informed the two men. "Taylor wanted the boys to sign up for a year, but they flat refused. He was so desperate for our services that he finally violated regulations and agreed he'd take them on their own terms. Most of the boys signed up for six months, a few for three, but none for as short a time as a month." Ben gazed off thoughtfully for a moment, then smiled. "But what the hell! The company is short-handed, and I'm pretty desperate myself. You're in, boys."

Buck threw back his head and laughed with glee, then slapped McCulloch so hard on the shoulder that it almost knocked the newly promoted major from his chair. "Thanks, Ben. I knew you wouldn't let us down."

"Yeah, sure, Buck," McCulloch muttered, rubbing his aching shoulder.

"Thanks, Ben," Adam said quietly.

"You're welcome, Adam. You'd do the same for me. Besides, if Santa Anna comes and we beat him, the whole campaign into central Mexico might be called off. Maybe we can end this war right here." Ben chuckled. "Sure would make

Walker and Hays mad if they landed in Veracruz and found out that the war was over, wouldn't it?"

"Yeah," Buck agreed. "And then we could all go home to Texas."

A painful expression came over Anita's beautiful face at Buck's last words. The thought that Adam might go back to Texas, walk out of her life forever, distressed her deeply. Somehow, someway, the *Tejano* had managed to slip through her defenses.

Ten days after McCulloch's visit, Anita raced her horse up to the small farmhouse, flew from the saddle, and ran to the house, her long black braid trailing her like a streamer. Throwing open the door, she cried out excitedly, "Santa Anna is here!"

Adam and Buck, cleaning their guns at the table, looked up in surprise at her sudden entry, and then as her words registered, Adam's gun clattered to the table as he dropped it and shot to his feet. "What in the hell are you talking about?"

"Santa Anna is at Encarnación. I heard it at the market place in the village."

"Rumors? Christ, Anita, we've been hearing rumors for over a week now," Adam responded irritably.

"No, this is no rumor. It's fact! Some deserters from his army wandered into the village last night. Santa Anna's army has reached Encarnación."

241

"Deserters? Where are these men?" Adam asked, picking up his gun.

"I wouldn't tell you even if I knew," Anita answered defiantly, her small chin thrust out and her eyes suddenly blazing. "The villagers have taken them in and are hiding them from Santa Anna. Do you think I would turn those poor men over to the Rangers for questioning? No, they've suffered enough. They're crippled with frostbite and ill. It's enough that you know Santa Anna has arrived."

As Anita turned her back to him and walked into their bedroom, Adam stared at her in frustration. Damned if he could figure her logic, he thought. She wanted to see Santa Anna completely and totally defeated, yet she protected his soldiers with a fierceness that stunned him. True, as deserters, they were no longer fighting men, but the information that could be gained from them might save thousands of lives on both sides, her precious Mexicans as well as Americans. Hell, women didn't know a damned thing about fighting a war, unless it was on a one-to-one basis, like it was between them, Adam added wryly. And at that Anita was an expert.

Several days later, the Rangers were ordered to join Taylor at Agua Nueva, a large Mexican ranch that lay between Encarnación and Saltillo. Here, Taylor had pulled up his advance column of fifteen hundred men.

As Adam quickly packed for his and Buck's departure, Anita walked into the bedroom and announced, "I am going, too."

Adam felt an icy fear clutch his chest; his breath left him in a rush. He looked up from his saddlebags and spat across the bed, "Like hell you are!"

"I told you that I wanted to be close enough to see the smoke and hear the cannons when the gringos met Santa Anna. That won't be possible here in Saltillo. There are several small villages on Agua Nueva. I'll stay at one of them."

"You're crazy! We don't know where this battle will take place. It could be anywhere between here and Encarnación. You could get caught right in the middle."

"I won't get caught. The Mexican grapevine will keep me informed."

"No! You're staying here in Saltillo!" Adam thundered. Seeing Anita open her mouth, he cut across her words. "And I don't want to hear another word about it!"

Adam swung his saddlebag over his shoulder and walked to the door, aware of Anita's angry gaze on him. At the door, he turned, saying in a hard voice, "You stay put, Anita. You hear? So help me God, if you move one inch off this farm — I'll throttle you!"

Anita's icy mask fell in place over her beautiful face. "As you wish," she replied tightly.

243

Adam's eyes narrowed as he studied the rigid form of the girl standing before him. Anita looked furious, and very beautiful. The sudden urge to kiss her good-bye rose in him. Adam forced it down, knowing if he gave in, Anita would use his weakness against him. The next thing he knew, he'd be taking her to Agua Nueva. He whirled and walked from the house, an uneasy feeling creeping up his spine.

Adam didn't have long to ponder over his uneasiness over Anita. The Rangers had barely set up camp at Agua Nueva when McCulloch chose Adam, Buck and four other Rangers for a special mission. Within minutes, the group was riding out for Encarnación, their orders to cross the thirty-five-mile desert and pinpoint the location of Santa Anna's army and determine its strength.

About six miles out, they captured a Mexican deserter who claimed that Santa Anna had twenty thousand men with him. The deserter was sent back to Taylor with one Ranger, and the others rode on to substantiate the information, for the Mexicans tended to exaggerate everything, and the Rangers doubted that Santa Anna could amass that large an army in so short a period of time.

Avoiding the road for fear of running into an enemy patrol, they pressed on through the rugged country, fighting the thorny chaparral which

244

seemed determined to block their progress every inch of the way. Around midnight, they rode through the enemy's picket lines undetected, dismounted, and cautiously approached the Mexican camp, the darkness concealing their approach. Lying on their stomachs, they looked down from the top of a small hill to where the Mexicans were encamped on a vast plain and saw the hundreds of campfires that stretched for miles and miles, a chilling sight.

Adam gave a low whistle and whispered to Ben, "So that deserter wasn't exaggerating."

"Not this time," Ben answered. "With all those fires going, there's got to be between ten and fifteen thousand men down there." McCulloch turned to his side and said in a low voice, "Spread out, boys, and scout the perimeters. See how good a head count you can get in the dark. Report back in an hour."

Silently, the Rangers shimmied back from the top of the hill and then crept from campfire to campfire, counting bedrolls and cannons and slitting the throats of a few careless sentries. When the Rangers reported, McCulloch had a good idea of how many men Santa Anna had, but he wanted to be positive of Santa Anna's strength. He was a man who performed his duties with meticulous detail.

"The rest of you men go back and report to Taylor what we found," McCulloch said. "Adam and I will stick around until daylight and see if we can get a more accurate count."

"I'll stay, too," Buck offered.

"No, you go back with the others, Buck," Ben said in a firm but kindly tone of voice. "The less of us there are, the less likely we'll be discovered. Ordinarily, because of the risk, I'd send all of you back. But I'm covering myself. With two of us, there's a better chance of at least one of us getting out of here alive."

Buck knew that getting killed was the easy part. If captured, Ben and Adam would be cruelly tortured before they died. Buck could have asked Ben, Then why risk Adam, your best friend? But Buck knew the answer. Like a good commander, Ben had not even taken their friendship into consideration. He had chosen Adam because he knew Adam was the best man. Both men were quick thinking and cool under fire, crack shots and expert horsemen. But even more important, the two were so perfectly attuned to each other that they didn't even need to converse to communicate their thoughts. When they worked together, it was almost as if they were two parts of a whole. But that still didn't stop Buck from fearing for Adam. Hell, the place was alive with Mexicans. To compound Buck's worries, there was that recklessness in Adam that had concerned Buck for some time. He was too daring. He took too many risks. It was almost as if he didn't care if he lived or died.

It had been that way ever since his wife died.

As the others started creeping back to where they had left their horses, Buck whispered to Adam, "You be careful!"

"Stop worrying, Buck. I'm not going to get myself shot up again, if for no other reason than to deny Anita the pleasure of poking around on me again."

"I'm talking about getting yourself killed!" Buck snapped.

"Hell, that wouldn't do me any good either. Anita is so stubborn, she'd probably resurrect me."

Buck frowned, not liking Adam's criticism of Anita. Then it occurred to Buck that Adam was joking, albeit sarcastically, but, still, it had been a long time since Buck had heard his friend joke about anything. The strange dread Buck had been feeling vanished, and the giant crept away to join the other departing Rangers.

Chapter 15

The next day, Adam and Ben were back in Taylor's camp with the information that the general had requested. Shortly thereafter, because he felt the area would be easier to defend, Taylor pulled his army back to a tight little valley where a *rancho* named Hacienda Buena Vista sat.

Three days later, when Santa Anna and his army arrived on the scene, Adam was greatly relieved for the distraction. Now he could concentrate on fighting, and not on worrying about Anita, something that he couldn't seem to help and that irritated him. But to Adam's disappointment, the Rangers didn't take much of a part in the battle. During the next two days, other than one foray the Rangers made to chase a company of Mexican dragoons back to their lines, the Battle of Buena Vista was an artillery combat that waxed and waned and wore on Adam's and the other Rangers' nerves.

On the second night of the battle, when they were rolling their bedrolls out on the hard ground in the bone-chilling cold, Adam said to Ben, "You know, I saw something this morning when we chased those lancers back to their lines that's puzzled me all day. I only got a glimpse of it, but it looked like a flag with a shamrock on it. That's an Irish symbol. What's an Irish flag doing flying in the middle of a Mexican Army?"

"I saw it, too," Ben answered, "and I was just as curious. Curious enough to ask one of those prisoners about it. He said it was the flag of a new artillery battalion manned by American deserters, mostly Irish, who fight for the Mexicans. They call themselves the San Patricio Battalion."

"Irish?" Buck asked. "Why in the hell would they want to fight for the Meskins? Why, they can't even talk it."

"The Mexican government has been passing circulars around luring all immigrants in the American Army since the beginning of the war," Ben explained. "The Mexicans know the immigrants feel downtrodden and unwanted in the States. That's why the Army has so many of them, because they can't find jobs anywhere else. With the Irish, the Mexicans have an added enticement. They appeal to their Catholic conscience by portraying the American expedition against Mexico as a crusade against the Church."

"Hell, those Irishmen are crazy if they think the

Meskin government is gonna give them anything," Buck spat. "They don't even take care of their own. There ain't no one more downtrodden than the Meskin peon." Buck lay down and pulled his blanket up over his massive shoulders, then muttered, "Dammit, not only do we have the Meskins to fight, but our own deserters, too. What's this world coming to?"

"If I know Santa Anna, he did that on purpose," Adam commented from where he was rolled up in his blanket. "Any man who has a fanatical interest in such a bloodthirsty sport as cockfighting would take perverse pleasure in seeing old comrades-in-arms kill one another."

"The bastard!" Buck muttered, rolling to his side.

The morning came in a gray pall, the weak sun unable to penetrate the thick smoke that still hung over the battlefield. The bone-weary Americans took their positions and waited for the Mexican attack to come. It never did.

Finally, puzzled by Santa Anna's delay, Taylor sent a party of Rangers forward to investigate. When they reached the ground where the fighting had been the heaviest the day before, what they found both surprised and horrified them. Santa Anna and his army had sneaked away, giving Taylor the victory that he so coveted. Behind him,

Santa Anna had left the pockmarked battlefield littered with the mangled and dead bodies of hundreds of men from both sides.

But it was the sight of the American dead that sickened the Rangers. The Mexicans had stripped them of all valuables, leaving no covering except for scanty remnants of clothing, then stabbed and mutilated the bodies horribly, while not one Mexican body had been defiled. Even more disturbing was the expression frozen on many of the Americans' faces, one of horrified disbelief, telling the Rangers that those men had survived the battle, but died at the hands of the Mexicans while begging for mercy.

Enraged by what he saw, Buck spat, "Those goddamned greasers! They're no better than the Comanches, butchering the bodies like that and robbing the dead."

Adam looked around him, grim-faced and tight-lipped with his own anger. He didn't bother to point out that the majority of Santa Anna's army were Indian conscripts, as savage and barbaric as their northern cousins, if not more so.

McCulloch turned to one Ranger, "Go back and tell Taylor what we found. Tell him I'm scouting on ahead to make sure Santa Anna is in retreat and not trying to trick us out of our defensive position." As the Ranger ran for his horse, Ben called, "And tell him to get a burial detail up here!"

Turning to the other four men, Ben said, "Come on, boys. Let's see what that sneaky bastard is up to."

The Rangers followed the trail Santa Anna had left almost to Encarnación. What they saw convinced them that the Mexican Army was not only retreating, but retreating as fast as they could, finding discarded guns, abandoned baggage wagons and cannons, deserted wounded who had died and those who had been too weak to keep up, the latter watching the Rangers fearfully as they passed.

Finally, Ben reined in, saying, "You boys go on back. I'm going to ride a little farther, but there's no need for all of us to go. I'm pretty sure I'm only going to find more of what we've seen."

As the Rangers wheeled their horses, Ben said to his lieutenant, "Alston, you tell Taylor I said if he wants these wounded prisoners, he can damn well come and get them himself. This Ranger company isn't taking any more prisoners," the major ended, his eyes glittering with anger at the outrage he had witnessed earlier.

When the Rangers rode away, Adam and Buck lagged behind, both deeply disturbed by the massacred prisoners of war they had seen on the battlefield. As they passed an abandoned Mexican farmhouse that sat on the eastern corner of Agua Nueva, a mud hut that was no more than a hovel, a movement caught Adam's attention from the corner of his eye. His hand flew to his gun and he whirled his horse, then stared at the golden bay that had stepped out from behind the hut and was munching on the dried winter grass at the corner of the hovel. He recognized that horse. A series of emotions followed one another so rapidly that it was impossible to tell where one ended and the other began: utter disbelief, icy fear, and then cold fury.

Finally realizing that his friend was no longer riding beside him, Buck turned his mount and called to Adam,

"What's wrong?"

Adam didn't answer. He slammed his gun back into his holster, kneed his horse, and rode up to the hovel. Reining in a few feet from the door, he glared at it before he thundered, "Dammit, Anita! Get out here!"

A long moment passed with no response from within the hut. Buck rode up and, not having noticed the bay, looked at Adam as if he had lost his mind.

"Anita! I'm warning you. If I have to come in there after you — you're going to regret it!"

The flimsy reed door slowly opened, and Anita stepped out. She quickly looked Adam over and felt a surge of relief to find he was unharmed. A sudden urge to run and embrace him in sheer joy seized her, stunning her with its intensity. Then, remembering Adam's dictate that she stay in

253

Saltillo and the way he was ordering her around now, she recalled her anger, and her black eyes flashed.

"What in the hell are you doing here?" Adam shouted, so loud that Buck cringed.

The angry look on Adam's face would have terrified even the bravest of men, but not Anita. She faced him squarely, then said, "I told you I wanted to be close enough to hear the cannons and see the smoke. I was. I also saw the Mexican Army when they passed this morning. Santa Anna rode in his coach, surrounded by so many lancers that I couldn't hardly see the wood, while his poor soldiers staggered behind him in exhaustion." Anita's dark eyes flashed as she said angrily, "He's gone! You let Santa Anna escape!"

Both men felt Anita's accusation like a blow. Adam recovered first, spitting out, "We didn't let him escape. He sneaked away in the middle of the night, like the coward he is." He gave her a hard look. "But that's not the issue here. I told you to stay put in Saltillo!"

Adam watched as the mask fell over Anita's face and her lips tightly compressed. When she stepped behind that hard wall of hers, cold and stubbornly silent, it infuriated him. It was a barrier that he couldn't penetrate, not with reason, not with threats. Nothing he did or said seemed to have any effect on her, He might as well be pounding at a mountain. He could contend with the heated

254

Anita, but never this Anita.

"You know, you've got a lot of your father in you, Anita," Adam ground out. "You use people to get what you want. And you deliberately led me to believe you were staying in Saltillo. You're just as ruthless and deceitful as Santa Anna."

Adam had meant to goad Anita into anger, but his ploy misfired. She turned deathly pale at his accusation, and the fleeting look of pain in her eyes tore at his heart. Shame overcame him. Why had he said such a cruel thing? he wondered in self-disgust, knowing how mortified Anita was at being Santa Anna's flesh and blood. Had Buck not come flying to her defense, Adam might have swung from his horse, taken her in his arms, and asked forgiveness.

"You take that back!" Buck said angrily, leaning from his saddle as if he were about to pounce on Adam.

Anita had recovered from Adam's hurtful words. "No, Buck. I did deliberately deceive Adam. But I wouldn't have done so if he had kept his end of our agreement. And, yes, I would do anything to get revenge on Santa Anna, including use people, if need be. He knew that from the beginning, too." Anita's eyes shifted and met Adam's levelly. "But I'm not the only one who uses people."

Adam knew Anita was referring to him. While she used him to satisfy her lust for revenge, he used her to satisfy his lust for the flesh. But was that all it was on his part? Adam wondered. His need for her seemed to be changing into something more, something elusive that he couldn't quite put his finger on. Adam refused to delve any deeper on such thoughts. They were too disturbing.

"All right," Adam admitted in a hard voice, "so we're two of a kind, and I refused to bring you to Agua Nueva. But you're going back to Saltillo right now. Get your things together."

"No! I won't leave. There are two wounded Mexicans inside, stragglers who were too weak to keep up. I won't desert them, as Santa Anna did. Despite what you think of me, I'm *not* like him."

At Anita's surprising revelation, Adam looked sharply at the open door, then started to dismount.

Anita quickly stepped before the open doorway, barring it with her small body. "No! Stay away from them!"

There she goes again, Adam thought in exasperation, protecting Santa Anna's soldiers. But this time they weren't innocent deserters. These were men who had tried their damndest to kill them yesterday, maybe even had taken part in that horrible butchery he had just seen. "These aren't deserters, Anita. They're prisoners of war. Now step aside," Adam commanded, again starting to dismount.

"No, I won't step aside! I won't let you touch

them!"

It was more Anita's demeanor than her words that shocked Adam. She looked like a fierce lioness protecting her cubs, her black eyes glittering dangerously. Adam sat back in his saddle, demanding, "Why not? Hell, you act like you think I'm going to murder them in cold blood."

Anita's small chin rose another inch in defiance. "And that is precisely why I won't step aside. I won't take that risk. *Los Diablos Tejanos* are notorious for not taking prisoners. I won't let you harm them. I won't!"

The accusation had the ring of truth about it and stung, bringing Adam's anger to the rise again. As Anita stepped back into the hut and shut the reed door in his face, he glared at it, then turned in his saddle, saying to Buck, "Stay here with her. I'll tell Alston to have Taylor's men pick up these two wounded when they round up the other prisoners. Then take her back to Saltillo."

"Me?" the giant asked in astonishment. "Why me?"

"Because if I got within two feet of her right now, I'd strangle her!"

"But what about Ben? What's he gonna say when he gets back to camp and I ain't there?"

"Don't worry about Ben. I'll explain everything."

Adam whirled his horse and rode off, wondering just how he *was* going to explain Buck's absence. What could he tell Ben? That he'd gotten himself mixed up with a Mexican girl who was so obsessed with getting revenge on Santa Anna that she jeopardized her own safety, that he had absolutely no control over her, that she defeated him at every turn. Hell, Ben would laugh in his face.

Damn her! She kept his guts tied in knots. He couldn't understand her. She was incredibly passionate at night, then by day, cool and distant—until she flared in anger—as fiery as a volcano one moment, the next as cold and hard as a glacier. Yet he knew she had compassion in her. Her concern for the ill, the poor, and oppressed of her country proved that. And she was capable of a warm relationship. Her deep friendship with Buck was testimony to that. But she showed none of these qualities to Adam. With him, she was either fire or ice, with no in between. Once, just once, he wished that she would look at him with warmth in her eyes, not passion, or scorn, but genuine warmth.

As it turned out, Adam didn't have to explain Buck's absence to Ben, thereby saving him the humiliation of having to admit to his friend he had a woman on his hands he couldn't handle. The major didn't return to camp until the next morning and then, after reporting to Taylor, fell into his bedroll and slept twenty-four hours straight through. By that time, Buck was back in camp.

When he finally arose, Ben took Adam and

258

Buck aside. "The war in northern Mexico is over, There's no need for you boys to hang around here, and I know you're anxious to get down to Veracruz and meet Jack. If you want, you can leave."

"We still have time to serve on our enlistment," Adam reminded him.

"We're the only ones who know how long you signed up for, and Taylor's too excited about his victory to notice a couple of Rangers missing."

Adam fought down his rising excitement. "Thanks, Ben," he said with a broad smile, clapping his friend on the back.

"Sure thing, Adam," Ben replied. "And you two take care, you hear?" He turned and walked away.

Fifteen minutes later, as Adam and Buck turned their horses onto the main road to Saltillo, Adam turned to Buck and said, "We'll go back to Saltillo, pick up Anita, take her to Monterrey, and then make a beeline over the Sierras for Veracruz. Hopefully, we won't miss out on too much going on down there."

But when Adam outlined his plan to Anita that night, she had different ideas. She drew herself up to her full height and said, "No. I will not go back to Monterrey. I'm going with you."

"Didn't you hear me?" Adam asked in a hard voice. "We're going to Veracruz, hundreds of miles away, through mountains—in dead winter! It will be a grueling trip. A dangerous one. Hell, Buck and I might not even make it."

"If you can make it, I can make it," Anita countered. "And I won't slow you down."

"You're damned right you won't, because you're not going!"

"We have an agreement," Anita reminded him in a tight voice. "I told you in the beginning that I wanted to be there when Santa Anna was defeated, when his power was destroyed. Neither has happened. He is still *presidente*. Are you going back on your word?"

Adam had been pushed to his limits, "You're damned right I am!"

Anita's eyes flashed. "If you won't take me, I'll go by myself. I will see Santa Anna's downfall, not hear about it. You can't stop me. No one can!"

"Then go by yourself and see if I give a damn!" Adam thundered, the angry words bouncing off the walls of the small room and making Buck cringe. Then Adam spun on his heels and stormed from the house.

Adam was still pacing in the dark before the small adobe house ten minutes later, so frustrated that he was oblivious to the biting cold, when Buck emerged. He watched Adam's agitated walk for a few minutes, then said quietly, "We're gonna have to take Anita with us."

Adam whirled around. "Are you crazy?" he roared. "Drag a woman all that distance, through those mountains? Besides the deep snow in those

260

passes, we'll have to contend with Indians and bandits. The Sierras are crawling with both of them. Even if we manage to make it through all that, we'll still have hundreds of miles to travel through enemy territory. We could run into a Mexican patrol any minute. No!" Adam said, firmly shaking his head. "She's not going. It's too dangerous, too risky."

"I know, but we're still gonna have to take her. If we don't, she'll take out on her own, just like she did the other day. Her chances of making it would be a hell of a lot better with us than by herself. Hell, Adam, can't you just imagine what would happen to her out there all by herself?"

Adam could think of a score of things that could happen to Anita if she attempted the trip into the interior by herself—all disastrous. Dammit, she'd maneuvered him again. Why couldn't he say to hell with her and make it stick? Why couldn't he turn his back on her and simply walk away? To be brutally honest with himself, he wasn't sure he *could* leave her behind at Monterrey. Not for good. She seemed to have some mysterious hold on him, one that had nothing to do with their agreement.

"Come on," Buck said, "let's go back in and tell her. Besides, it's freezing out here."

Adam followed Buck into the house, knowing that he really had no choice. Like it or not, Anita was going with them. Why in the hell couldn't she be like other women, content to wait at home? War and revenge were men's business.

Anita was standing by the fireplace when the two men walked in. She shot Adam a hot, accusing look.

Adam hated to back down. The words stuck in his craw. He glanced at Buck, hoping he would make the announcement, but the giant was stubbornly silent. He threw up his hands, spitting out, "All right! You can go."

If Adam had expected any sign of gratitude, or even relief, on Anita's face, he was doomed for disappointment. With her usual, perplexing manner, she did a complete turnaround, behaving as if the whole argument had never occurred, saying calmly, "Tomorrow I will go to the market and buy both of you serapes and sombreros."

Buck was as puzzled at her sudden turnabout as Adam and confused by her words. "What do we want with serapes and sombreros?"

"You can't go into the heart of Mexico dressed like gringos. You'd be too conspicuous. The serape will cover your sidearms, since you insist upon wearing them," she said, slicing Adam a scornful, oblique look. "And we can stain your faces and hands so that your skin will be darker." She turned her full attention on Buck, studying him thoughtfully for a moment, then said, "And we will have to dye your hair and beard black. It will make you look more Mexican."

262

"Dye my hair?" Buck exploded, the loud noise shaking the walls. "Like some whore?" Then, realizing he'd stepped out of bounds by mentioning a whore in Anita's presence, Buck's face turned beet red, for he still afforded Anita the respect of a lady despite all his cursing.

"Anita's right," Adam said, scrutinizing the giant and saving Buck from having to make an awkward apology. "If we're going into the interior, we'll need disguises, and your hair is much too light. It *would* attract attention."

"But what about Adam's green eyes?" Buck objected, directing his question to Anita. "They'll show up, too."

"There are green-eyed Mexicans," Anita replied, "particularly around Mexico City, where the Spanish influence is so strong."

Buck scowled deeply, then reluctantly agreed. "Okay, I'll do it." Then as a sudden thought occurred to him, he asked, "But what about our horses? Peons don't go around riding good horseflesh like ours." He glared at Anita, saying, "And I ain't riding no jackass! So don't even suggest it."

"No," Adam agreed firmly. "We're absolutely not getting rid of our horses. We'll need good animals to make it through those mountains."

"Our mounts will be no problem," Anita replied calmly. "The upper classes aren't the only ones who ride good horses in Mexico. There are those who ride animals that have been stolen." She shrugged her shoulders. "You won't be simple peons. You'll be *bandidos*."

"*Bandidos?* Adam gasped.

"*Sí.* The mountains all over Mexico are full of them. And if anyone should happen to notice your guns, that would explain them, too. Bandidos carry guns everywhere with them, just as you do."

"That's just great!" Adam spat sarcastically. "Now that we've figured out how to keep from being recognized, we'll have to worry about being shot at by the authorities."

"What authorities?" Anita asked. "The Army? Since when does the Mexican Army worry about *bandidos?*"

Anita had a valid point. The Mexican government had never been up to handling its outlaw problem. The highwaymen ran rampant all over the country, feared by the upper and middle classes and terrorizing the peons.

After Anita had left the room, Buck turned to Adam and said in disgust, "I never thought I'd live to see the day when I'd pretend to a Mexican bandit. Me! A Texas Ranger!"

With a deep scowl on his face, Buck turned and lumbered off to his bedroom. Adam put another log on the fire and walked to his and Anita's room. There, the two undressed in the dark, an uncomfortable silence surrounding them, both acutely aware of their clashes of will over the past days.

264

Adam was the last to climb into bed. Deliberately, he reclined a distance from Anita, lying stiffly on his back and staring at the ceiling. He wouldn't make love to her, he vowed firmly. Not after she had deliberately disobeyed him and then forced him into agreeing to take her into the interior with him. Dammit, a man should have some control over his woman.

Anita was very aware of Adam putting distance between them. She knew he was angry with her. He didn't understand, she thought, feeling a painful ache deep inside her. Seeing to her revenge wasn't something she wanted to do, It was something she *had* to do. It was a promise she had made to her mother's memory, to her grandfather, but, more important, to herself. Her soul couldn't rest until it was done. And Adam, of all men, should understand that. It was their mutual thirst for revenge that had bonded them in the first place.

But that was no longer what held Anita to Adam. There had been another reason why she had been so fiercely determined to go with him. She couldn't let him go. The thought of him walking out of her life was too unbearable. She knew it was inevitable in the end, that he would go back to Texas and leave her to face a life of emptiness, but that was in the future. This was now, and she wouldn't ruin what time she had left with him worrying about it or letting him keep her at a distance. Not here in bed. This was the only place they weren't at odds, the only place they blended, the only place she could let down her defenses, if only for the moment. His passion for her was all she had.

Anita rolled to her side and gently kissed Adam's shoulder, whispering, "I'm sorry if you are angry with me, but I only do what I must."

Anita's kiss felt like a hot brand on Adam's bare skin. Despite his vow, he was hungry for her. He fought his rising passion. Her intoxicating scent, her warmth, the promise of paradise that throbbed in her throaty voice were too much for him. She was a fever in his blood for which there was no cure but her. Wordlessly, he turned to her.

Chapter 16

The next day was spent in preparation for their long trip to Veracruz. For the men, still living by their Ranger code of survival on the dangerous frontier, this meant caring for their mounts and weapons. While they were busy currying the horses until their coats shone, re-shoeing them and treating any small wound that might fester, then sharpening their knives and cleaning their guns, Anita was left to make the more practical preparations, at least in her opinion.

Anita could accept the preparation of their mounts for their trip. After all, the horses were going to be their means of transportation. But the Texans' preoccupation with their weapons was something she couldn't understand any more than the American soldiers. While her feelings for Adam were undergoing a drastic change, she hated his weapons, particularly his guns, those vile instruments that served no purpose but death and destruction. Oh, she knew they were an ugly necessity of war, but she couldn't fathom Adam's insistence on carrying such an awesome arsenal, nor his almost loving care of the lethal instruments. To her, they were a testimony to his savagery, his love of violence, something she despised and was at odds with the new, tender feelings for him that were emerging. So while Adam and Buck occupied the better part of their time with their weapons, Anita—seething just below the surface of her cool facade—was left to travel to the marketplace to purchase their supplies, cook in preparation for the trip, and then pack everything.

That evening, the small house was filled with mingled odors of gun oil and fresh-baked tortillas, and the men were still busy cleaning their guns at Anita's usually spotless kitchen table. She looked at the smelly, messy oil smeared all over the top of the table and the wads of oil-soaked flannel that littered the floor and shook her head in disgust, then said, "It's time to put your guns away. Our meal is ready."

"Just dish me up a plate and set it aside," Adam answered in a distracted voice. "I'll eat later."

"No. You will eat now."

Adam shot Anita a sharp look. The words had been said with a commanding tone of voice that brought his male ego to the rise. Dammit, did she think she was going to lead him around by the nose like some tame bull? It was bad enough that she manipulated him at every turn and that he was at her complete mercy in bed, but he'd been damned if he'd let her boss him. "I said I'd eat later," he answered in a carefully measured voice that was vibrating with threatening undertones. "This is important."

"Your body is just as important as your weapons. What good will they do you if you starve to death?" Anita answered with a calm logic.

"I'm hardly starving!" Adam threw back.

"You have eaten nothing all day," Anita pointed out.

Buck glanced uneasily from Adam to Anita. For the life of him, he couldn't understand their relationship. He knew the two were lovers at night, but during the day, they either ignored each other or fought like cats and dogs. Even stranger, they both seemed to enjoy their clashes, deliberately goading each other into a fight. Buck had uncomfortably witnessed more than a few of these violent verbal confrontations, and he could never figure out if they were paying him a compliment by being so open in front of him, or if they were so involved with each other that they completely forgot he was there.

"She's right," Buck said, quickly entering the conversation and hoping to avert what looked to be developing into another of the couple's endless arguments. "We ain't eaten all day, and I'm as hungry as a bear. We can finish cleaning these guns after supper."

"No." Anita said in a firm voice. "After we have eaten, I must dye your skin and you should try on the clothing I bought you to see if it fits. If there are any alterations to be made, I must do them tonight, or else our departure will be delayed tomorrow." Seeing Adam was about to object, she quickly added, "Your disguises are just as important to your survival as those guns."

It was a point that Adam couldn't argue with, although he would have dearly loved to. With a deep scowl on his face, he helped Buck clear the table.

After they had eaten and the dishes were put away, Anita carried a big pot to the table and set it down. "You had better strip off your shirts. This dye might stain them permanently."

Grudgingly, Adam complied, baring his magnificent, steel-muscled chest. Buck, however, hesitated, his deep southern-hill manners, which dictated that he keep himself properly clothed before a lady at all times, coming to the fore. A deep flush crept up his face. Then, with obvious reluctance, he bared his massive upper torso.

Anita was well aware of his embarrassment. Hoping to ease his discomfiture, she turned her attention first to Adam, staining his face, neck, upper shoulders, and chest with a wad of flannel that she had soaked in the dark brown solution in the pot.

"Where did you get the dye?" Buck asked Anita, watching in amazement as Adam's skin tone darkened another shade with each brush of the wet flannel.

"I made it from plants I collected. We Mexicans are very adept at making dyes."

Back in Texas, Adam thought, the calicos that the women wore on the frontier quickly faded after a few washings, but even the poorest Mexican peon's clothing retained its vibrant colors. Even the threads they used to embroider the colorful flowers and designs on their clothing never looked washed out. The Mexicans did excel in their dyes, the colors always brilliant and lasting. Then a sudden thought occurred to him. "How long will this dye last?" he asked, pushing Anita's hand away. "I don't want to go through life looking like a Mexican."

The words stung, reminding Anita only too well of Adam's scornful attitude toward Mexicans, and therefore herself. With supreme will, she covered her hurt and answered calmly. "It should wash off in a few months. Now close your eyes, so I can do the lids."

Carefully, Anita wiped Adam's eyelids, noting his thick, long eyelashes, eyelashes that seemed out of place with the rest of his rugged, masculine features. Then when she had finished and Adam

271

opened his eyes, Anita's breath caught. The deeper skin tone made his eyes stand out even more, the pure crystalline green almost jumping out at her. *Dios*, they were beautiful, she thought. She could gaze into them forever. Reluctantly, she turned her attention to Buck.

Since there was so much hair on Buck's face, it didn't take long to dye the giant's skin. While the two men were soaking their hands and lower forearms in the solution in the pot, Anita prepared the dye for Buck's hair.

When she set the second pot on the table, Buck looked down at the coal-black liquid and frowned. "You sure this stuff is gonna wash out in a few months? Martha may not like me with black hair."

Anita could have pointed out that as much as Buck disliked bathing it was very possible it might last longer, but didn't. Instead she said, "*Sí*, it will wash out. And we will probably have to redo the roots from time to time as it grows out."

It was a much more time-consuming task to dye Buck's thick hair and beard than it was to tint both men's skin. Even his bushy eyebrows were dyed, and when Anita had finished, he looked even more ferocious and bearish.

Adam glanced at Anita's small hands. They were black from the dye. "How are you going to get that off?" he asked.

"I have something that will bleach them."

"Good," Buck said, the worried expression on

his face replaced with a broad smile. "If my hair ain't back to its normal color by the time I go back to Texas, we can use that."

Anita wasn't too sure the bleach would be safe to use on hair. It might make it fall out. She tried to imagine Buck bald-headed and bare-faced. The mental picture wouldn't come. Buck wouldn't be Buck without all his hair. She smiled fondly at the giant. "I don't think that will be necessary."

The smile irritated Adam, as it always did when Anita smiled at Buck with genuine warmth. He rose from the table and said in a hard, clipped voice, "Where are those damn clothes you wanted us to try on? I want to get this foolishness over so I can get back to cleaning my guns."

"I left them on your beds," Anita answered, totally ignoring Adam's dark scowl and carrying the pot of dye to the door to throw it away.

Both Adam and Buck walked to their separate rooms. Within seconds, Adam was back, carrying the clothing in his hands, and his face looking like a stormcloud. "What in the hell did you buy this charro suit for?"

"That is what the *bandidos* in Mexico wear," Anita replied.

"I know. But I'll be damned if I'll wear one."

"Why not?"

"Because they're downright gaudy, that's why! I've never worn velvet in my life, much less an embroidered jacket. And the pants aren't even sewed at the sides. They're held closed by gold buttons. It's indecent! And I'll be damned if I'll wear those silver bells or those monstrous hung spurs on my boots. I'd look like a goddammed Gypsy!"

Anita secretly thought the *bandidos'* dress a little overdone, too. Their charro suits lacked the elegance of the well-tailored suits the *hidalgos* wore that were decorated with just the right amount of embroidery. But, nevertheless, the suits were what the Mexican outlaws wore. They deliberately dressed to gain attention, strutting around like peacocks before their hens in their flamboyant finery. "If you are to impersonate a *bandido*, you must dress like one," Anita replied in a maddeningly calm voice. "Or else take the risk of arousing suspicion. Of course, you could leave your weapons behind and dress like a peon. I could easily exchange that suit, if that's what you decide."

Anita knew full well Adam wouldn't leave his precious guns behind. She wasn't surprised when he snorted, turned, and stormed back into the bedroom to don the suit.

By the time Buck and Adam returned, Anita had cleared the table and washed the dishes. They walked from their respective bedrooms almost simultaneously.

"God Almighty, Anita!" Buck exclaimed, his face beaming behind his new black beard. "I've never had such a fancy suit. Sure wish Martha could see me now."

Personally, Anita thought the giant looked ridiculous. The flagrantly flamboyant suit was so tight on his big frame that he looked as if he had been poured into it, leaving the material gaping open between the buttons on his pants. Anita had searched long and hard for a suit large enough to fit Buck. Finding something big enough to fit his girth had not been as much a problem as his height. There were heavy men among the *bandidos*, men who looked just as ridiculous as Buck in their tight suits. But no Mexican was as long limbed as the giant. The pants and sleeves were inches too short.

"I'm sure Martha would think you look very nice," Anita responded graciously.

Buck flushed. Then a wide grin spread across his face. "Yeah, I reckon she would," he admitted, unabashed. "She ain't never seen me so gussied up. Never did have me a classy Sunday-go-to-meeting suit like this one. And this sombrero," Buck said, holding up the giant hat. "I ain't never seen such a fancy one. Why, it's got gold coins sewed all around the brim." He fingered one of the dangling coins, asking in an awed voice, "You reckon they're real gold?"

From across the room, Adam shot Buck a look of total disgust. He had expected him to show better sense than to be impressed with something so obviously gaudy. "Hell, no, they're not real.

They're just painted gold."

Buck shrugged his massive shoulders. "Well, they're still pretty and shiny, even if they ain't real gold."

Anita turned her attention to Adam. She had never seen him in a suit of any kind. All he ever wore was a dark cotton shirt, twill pants, and a leather vest. The skintight charro suit fit his lean physique to perfection, outlining every sinewy, powerful muscle, and his darker skin tone made the shirt look dazzling white in contrast. Combined with his thick, dark hair and striking green eyes, he looked very masculine, very handsome, and very exciting.

Unaware of Anita's complimentary thoughts, Adam twisted his shoulders and complained irritably, "The jacket is too tight. I can't even move my arms."

Anita could see the material straining across his impressive shoulders, and had the waist-length jacket been designed to button, Adam wouldn't have been able to close it over his broad chest. "I can split the seams under the armpits," she replied. "That's what the bullfighters do with the jackets of their suits of lights to give them more freedom of movement."

"What about the sleeves and pants?" Adam asked, still disgruntled. "They're much too short."

"I was afraid they might be. That's why I bought a length of black velvet that matches the suits. I will have to sew a band of material at the bottom of them."

"Won't that be rather obvious?"

"Not if I cover the seam with embroidery."

"More embroidery?" Adam snapped in disgust. "Christ! All we'd need is a red sash around our waists and we *would* look like a couple of wild Gypsies."

Anita knew Adam was balking more at the suit being Mexican than its tightness or excessive decoration. Her patience with him was at its end. "If you can think of a better idea, you're free to do it!" she snapped back. "Or you can go to the marketplace tomorrow and see if you can find a suit to fit you. Or you can dress as a peon and leave your guns behind. I don't care what you do!"

Adam loved it when Anita flared out at him. With her dark eyes flashing and her golden skin flushed with anger, she was vitally alive, and very beautiful. And when she stood stiff with anger, she had a way of thrusting out her chest, making him acutely conscious of her lush, proud breasts. He stared at those heaving mounds. His desire rose, sudden, hot, and urgent.

"Well, what will it be?" Anita demanded, when Adam continued to stare at her.

Buck stepped between the two, saying to Adam, "We ain't got time to go looking for suits tomorrow. We need to get out of here. Let Anita do the alterations."

It was a moment before Adam responded. "All right!" he snapped, his ire now aimed at Buck. He had completely forgotten what the argument was about. If the giant hadn't been present, he would have swept Anita up in his arms and carried her to the bedroom. At that moment, Adam fervently wished his friend a hundred miles away.

By the time the two men returned to the room from changing back into their western clothing, Anita was already cutting strips of velvet to add to the sleeves and pants of their suits.

Seeing she was occupying the table, Adam frowned and said, "I hope you're not planning on using the table all night. It's the only place we can clean our guns."

Anita bit back an angry retort. She knew damned well he didn't need a table to clean his guns. *Dios*, he was in a testy mood tonight. "I will only use it long enough to cut out the material. Then I will sit by the fire. The light is much better there. Until then, why don't you two check out the saddles I bought for you. I put them in the lean-to. Perhaps they will not suit your taste, either, since they are studded with silver," she ended in a biting tone of voice.

"What saddles?" Adam asked in surprise. "What in the hell are you talking about?"

"Your new Mexican saddles. *Bandidos* do not ride western saddles. They are as much a part of your disguises as those clothes."

It was a point that the Rangers couldn't argue with, yet neither man had even thought of it. "Gosh, Anita," Buck admitted readily, "I didn't even think of that. Sure is a good thing you did." He paused, then asked, "But how did you carry two saddles back from the marketplace on your horse?"

"I didn't. I hired a wagon to bring them here."

"I didn't see no wagon," Buck answered in surprise.

"No, you were busy in here when I returned — cleaning your guns," Anita answered sarcastically, shooting Adam a look of pure disgust.

The effort wasn't wasted on the tall, dark Ranger. Adam frowned, realizing for the first time that he and Buck had been amiss in their preparations, spending their time on their weapons while Anita had seen to every detail of their disguises. And then, he had done nothing but criticize her selections. A niggardly feeling of guilt rose in him. Hoping to make up for his earlier irascible behavior, he said, "I see no reason to check the saddles out. I'm sure they're fine."

"Yeah," Buck agreed, feeling a little guilty himself. "You sure know more about Mexican saddles than we do." Then as a sudden thought occurred to him, he turned to Adam and asked, "But what about our saddles? How are we gonna carry them with us? Why, it'd take a pack horse just for them."

"You cannot take them with you," Anita announced. "I exchanged them for the new ones. Of course, it wasn't an even exchange. They were much too plain and worn to bring a good price."

Both men were shocked by her words. Those saddles were well broken in, and the two were as much attached to them as they were their battered hats. Considering the time the two Rangers spent in their saddles, it was almost as if Anita had sold their comfortable home right out from under them.

Buck was the first to recover. "You sold my saddle?" he asked in a horrified voice.

"*Sí.* You could not take them with you. Why would *bandidos* be carrying western saddles with them?"

"We could have carried them on a packhorse. With a tarp over it, no one would know what's under there," Adam said angrily.

"You would buy another horse and drag it halfway across Mexico just to carry your saddles?"

Both men knew it would be totally impractical. They planned on traveling light, carrying their supplies with them. Having to fool with dragging a packhorse behind them would slow them down. But Adam couldn't help feeling resentment at Anita's boldness, selling something so personal as his saddle. "You could have at least asked for our permission!" he snapped.

"You were busy!" Anita threw back. "Besides, what difference would it have made. If you could not take them with you, it was better to sell them than leave them to rot."

Adam's scowl deepened. True, it wouldn't have made any difference. If it had to be done, it had to be done. Apparently, Anita had thought things through much more thoroughly than had he and Buck. They had been too excited at the prospect of getting into the fighting in central Mexico even to consider that it might mean making sacrifices. The knowledge didn't sit easily with Adam. He was a man who prided himself on his logic, and yet Anita, a woman no less, had been acting much more logically than he.

Ignoring the dark expressions on both men's faces, Anita took the suits from their hands and carried them and her sewing materials to the rocker by the fire. Seating herself, she said in a frosty voice, "You can have the table now."

While Anita made the alterations on their suits, the two men meticulously cleaned their guns. As soon as they laid aside their last pistol, Buck rose and ambled off to bed, muttering "Good night" as he walked heavily to his room, leaving the two alone.

The firelight danced over the walls of the room, and the only sounds were the crackle and pop of the fire. For several moments, Adam watched Anita as she concentrated on her embroidering, the needle flying in and out of the velvet as she quickly and skillfully sewed the design. Finally, he broke the silence. "It's time for bed."

"Go ahead," Anita answered without even raising her eyes from her work. "I need to finish this tonight, if we are to leave in the morning."

Adam didn't want to go to bed without Anita. In part, his reluctance stemmed from the desire she had aroused in him earlier. But there was another, more perplexing reason. He had become accustomed to her lying by his side. If he awoke during the night, knowing she was there comforted him. Adam couldn't understand his feelings. He certainly wasn't afraid of the dark. But her presence seemed to put his mind at rest and soothed his soul. He rose and walked to their bedroom, then turned at the door and gazed back at her for a long moment.

Feeling his eyes on her, Anita glanced up. Was it her imagination, or was there a yearning in his expression? Did he desire her company? *Dios*, how she wished it were true. Then she could let her true feelings for him come forth, give in to her hidden yearnings to smother him with love. Anita laughed bitterly to herself for entertaining such fanciful ideas. The only thing Adam wanted her for was to satisfy his physical needs. She was his mistress and would never be anything more. Well, if he wanted her body, this was one time she would deny him, and their bargain be damned.

Her fierce pride demanded it of her, particularly after his cutting criticism of everything she had done that day. She forced herself to meet his gaze levelly and said in a deliberately cool tone of voice, *"Buenas noches."*

Adam felt a keen disappointment. He had been hoping she would change her mind. "Good night," he muttered.

Closing the bedroom door behind him, Adam wondered if Anita was angry with him for the way he had behaved that evening. If so, he really couldn't blame her. He had been even more ornery than usual. He pondered over why he went to such lengths to provoke Anita. He knew, in part, he did so because it was the only way he could draw her out from behind her cold, indifferent wall. Only then was her full attention focused on him. But there was more to it than that. He actually enjoyed their clashes. They excited him, sending a surge of energy running through him that made him feel as if he had suddenly come alive. Was his picking fights with her some sort of strange perversity?

Adam lay on the bed and stared out at the darkness, feeling very alone and very confused.

In the next room, Anita gave in to her deep emotions, and a silent tear trickled down her cheek.

* * *

283

The three rode out of Saltillo the next morning just as the sun was rising over the majestic Sierra Madres, the towering, snowcapped peaks a dazzling white in the sunlight. The men's Colts and Bowie knives were packed away in their saddlebags, since those special weapons would be a dead giveaway that they were Texans, but they carried the rest of their weapons openly. Mexican *bandidos* armed themselves as heavily as the Rangers. Adam had even packed away his battered hat, along with his old clothing. But not Buck. Beneath his oversize sombrero with its dangling coins, the giant had stuffed his ratty coonskin cap, insisting upon wearing his good-luck charm and adamantly refusing to throw it away, as Anita had suggested, much to his horror and Adam's amusement.

When they reached the road leading to the valley where the Battle of Buena Vista had been fought, Adam glanced over at Buck and saw the deep scowl on his face. "Are you having second thoughts about this?" he asked the giant.

"What?" Buck asked, torn from his thoughts.

"I asked if you're having second thoughts about this trip into the interior. You look worried."

"It ain't that. I was thinking what might happen if we ran into any of the boys out on patrol. If they saw us in these *bandido* disguises, they might shoot first and ask questions later."

Adam shook his head in disgust, thinking

284

Buck's concern much exaggerated and totally groundless. Anita, however, could see the truth in Buck's words. Perhaps now the giant Ranger could see the other side of the coin, that of the pursued instead of the pursuer.

She examined the two men riding beside her with a critical eye, then said, "A Ranger might mistake you for a *bandido*, but up close, any Mexican would be able to tell you are not one of us."

"How?" Buck asked in surprise. "In these get-ups we look just like 'em."

"You may look like Mexicans from a distance, but your mannerisms are not Mexican. We have very distinctive movements, the way we shrug our shoulders, the way we use our hands when we speak, the way we hold our heads. And there are differences in the mannerisms of the different classes. A peon's body portrays subjection. He hangs his head and slumps his shoulders. He is hesitant to speak to strangers. In fact, all Mexican men are aloof and suspicious of outsiders to some degree. For those reasons, it would better for you to stay in the background as much as possible, at least until you have mastered our mannerisms. Let me do the mingling and the talking. A woman asking questions would not arouse as much suspicion. We are much more curious creatures."

More nosy creatures, you mean, Adam thought. But he could see the wisdom of Anita's words.

There was much more to an effective disguise than clothing and saddles. Again, she had been more perceptive than he. He gazed across at her thoughtfully, thinking there was much more to her than met the eye. She had a keen intelligence and a logical mind that he wouldn't expect to find in a woman. Along with her boldness, these were traits that both frustrated and fascinated him. She was like no woman he had ever known. Was it because of the way she had been raised by her grandfather, or were these traits an inherent part of her? And how could a woman with such masculine traits be so damned desirable? She was a puzzle to him.

The next day, as the three approached one of the passes that would take them through the Sierras to the eastern coast of Mexico, Anita suddenly reined in and dismounted.

Adam pivoted his horse and asked, "What's wrong?"

"Nothing. It's just that I have never seen snow up close before. I am curious to see what it feels like," Anita answered, walking to one of the scattered patches of snow.

She bent and scooped up a handful. "It's heavier than I thought it would be."

"That's because it's half melted and packed," Adam explained.

"You have snow in Texas?" Anita asked in surprise.

"Not the part of Texas we're from. In the ten

years I've lived there, it's only snowed once, and then not enough to cover the ground."

Anita was curious to know more about the place where Adam lived. "And where in Texas is your ranch?" she asked, dropping the snow and wiping her wet hands on her shawl.

"About ten miles north of the Nueces River."

Anita frowned. Adam's answer had really told her nothing. She mounted, asking, "Are there mountains there?"

"No, the land is flat and covered with mesquite brush, much like the territory around Reynosa."

Anita frowned. Having been born and raised in Monterrey, she was accustomed to seeing mountains all around her. She didn't know if she would like living in such a flat land. And then she remembered she would never see Adam's homeland, that when the war was over, he would go back to Texas and she would never see him again. A deep depression came over her.

Adam didn't notice Anita's silence and withdrawal as they climbed higher and higher over the tortuous, twisting trail they were following. When they reached the pass itself, the ground was covered with a mantle of white and it was snowing.

This time it was Buck who reined in suddenly, saying in an awed voice, "Would you look at that? I ain't seen so much snow since I left the Georgia hills. Real pretty, ain't it?"

His words brought Anita out of her dark brooding. She looked about at the softly falling snow and the pristine winter scene in wonder. "Why, it's beautiful!"

Adam stared at Anita in disbelief. The expression on her face was almost childlike, and her eyes were sparkling with excitement. This was an Anita he had never seen, never dreamed she held hidden behind her forbidding wall. Then he became aware of her clothing. He and Buck both wore serapes that were almost as thick and heavy as blankets, while she had only two cotton shawls wrapped around her.

"It may be pretty, but it's going to be damned cold for you," he said in a voice made gruff by his concern. "You should have bought a serape for yourself."

"Mexican women do not wear serapes," Anita pointed out.

"That might be true, but you're not accustomed to this harsh cold like the Mexican mountainwomen are. You admitted yourself that cold bothers you more than heat. What if you should get sick?"

Did he think her a liability? Anita wondered. Would he change his mind about taking her along and turn back? No. She would not allow that. "I will not get cold, and I will not get sick," she answered in a firm voice. "I am just as hardy as any Mexican mountainwoman."

With that, Anita kneed her mount and rode

away, leaving Adam to stare at her back in exasperation.

But despite Anita's words, she did get cold. Even with the two shawls wrapped tightly around her body and head, leaving only her eyes exposed, she was freezing. To her utter dismay, it was even worse that night. The wind coming down from the mountains all around them was a icy blast, and despite the heat of the fire they had built and the blanket she had wrapped up in, she was miserable, her hands and feet numb with cold.

Suddenly she felt herself being pulled under Adam's blanket, and his arms wrapped tightly around her.

"What . . . what are you doing?" she asked in surprise.

"Sharing my body heat with you," Adam answered gruffly.

"I'm not cold," Anita denied adamantly, clenching her teeth to keep them from chattering.

"You have got to be the most stubborn woman I have ever met. And the most stupid. Even animals have enough sense to share their body heat in bitter cold like this."

"I said I am not cold!" Anita insisted, trying to push away from him.

Adam muttered a curse under his breath and tightened his grip on her. "And I say you're a damned liar. My God," he said, slipping his hands under her blanket, "you feel like ice."

"I do not need you to warm me," Anita answered hotly, afraid he would throw her weakness in her face later.

"The hell you don't!"

"Will you two cut it out?" Buck groaned from where he was rolled up in his blanket. "How am I supposed to sleep with you arguing all night?"

"We won't keep you awake," Adam answered, glaring down at Anita, "because there isn't going to be any further argument. This is one time she's going to do what I say."

Adam's words had the same effect on Anita as waving a flag before a bull. She glared at him, silently struggling to free herself, pushing, twisting, turning, gouging. But her efforts were a waste of energy. Adam's powerful arms about her were like two bands of steel. Even worse was the fact that his heat was surrounding her, warming her and insidiously weakening her will. Despite her objections, she didn't want to go back to her cold bed. When he pinned her thrashing legs down with one hard-muscled thigh, she gave up her fight, knowing it was useless to struggle against his superior strength. As her frigid body greedily absorbed the heat radiating from him, a delicious languor invaded her. *Dios*, she wished she could stay like this forever, locked in Adam's strong arms. But even more, she wished that he could love her. But she knew such could never be the case. With this sad thought in mind, she closed her eyes and drifted off to sleep.

Adam held her close, briefly savoring the only victory he had yet to win in their running battle of wills. But the realization that he had done so only by his superior strength soon took the joy out of his victory. He wanted more than a physical surrender from Anita. He wanted her total capitulation, in spirit as well as body. What's more, he wanted it to be given freely.

Deep down, Adam knew Anita would never give him what he wanted. But what he didn't know, or refused to acknowledge, was what he really wanted from Anita was her love.

Chapter 17

The trip through the Sierras was long and tortuous. In some places, the horses had to labor through snow three feet deep, and everywhere, the icy wind howled down from the mountains, chilling them to the bone. For three days, they were followed by a huge pack of wolves, until they finally got close enough for Adam and Buck to shoot them, the two men giving Anita a startling demonstration of their sharpshooting as the vicious, snarling animals were methodically dropped to the ground. When they descended from the mountains into a lower altitude, the snow was melting, turning the ground into mush and the rivers into raging torrents. But despite all this, they rode onto the lush, verdant coastal plain outside of Veracruz nine days later, gaunt and exhausted from their grueling trip.

They would have never made it in that time if Adam hadn't pushed them hard and unrelentingly, from dawn to dusk, and then some. During the trip, Anita had earned the respect of both men. Not once did she lag behind or complain about their punishing pace, the bitter cold, the discomforts, and Adam marveled at her strength of will and endurance, wondering if it was her legacy from her stalwart Indian ancestors.

Adam was also forced to admit, grudgingly, and only to himself, that he and Buck might have never made it without her. It was Anita who went ahead into the villages to see if there were Mexican soldiers stationed there, who ferreted out information on troop movements and the presence of bandits in the area, on which pass was blocked with snow or which trail was the safest and easiest. Every time she returned, Adam was amazed at the wealth of information that she could find out in so little time.

As they emerged from a heavily wooded area about five miles from their destination, they brought their mounts to a dead halt. Before them, the dusty road that led to Veracruz was crowded with Mexicans going to the city.

Toothless, gray-haired old men and women, children of all ages, women, many with babes in arms, all carrying their meager possessions on their backs, trudged wearily down the road. Intermingled among them were the men driving small flocks of sheep and pigs, an occasional lumbering ox, and small Mexican carts piled high with household furnishings.

Looking the crowd over, Adam said, "The battle for Veracruz must be over. They're going back to the city. I wonder who won?"

"No, they are not going back," Anita corrected him. "These are country peons, not city." Moving her horse forward, she said over her shoulder, "Wait here. I will find out what is going on."

Ten minutes later, Anita was back. "The Americans have been amassing all winter on Lobos Island, a little coral island about a hundred eighty miles south of Tampico. Then, several days ago, an American warship was seen off the coast here at Veracruz, close enough to the fortress in the harbor to fire its cannons at it. They are expecting the Americans to attack at any minute. The authorities have ordered everyone in the outlying area into the city behind the protection of the walls."

"Well, I'll be damned," Buck said in astonishment. "We beat the Army here."

"Yes," Adam answered, just as pleased with this surprising news, "and thank God, the war is still on. I never mentioned it, but I was a little worried that Mexico might have surrendered after we defeated them at Buena Vista. News travels slow in those mountains we just came from. For all we knew, the war could have been over, and we would have made that horrible trip for nothing."

"Santa Anna cannot surrender even if he wanted to," Anita informed the two men. "The Mexican legislature was suspicious of the ease with which he slipped through the American blockade. They suspected a conspiracy. Then, when he evacuated Tampico last October, allowing the American Navy to capture it without a single shot being fired, they were angered because Santa Anna had given the enemy a foothold in central Mexico from which to invade the interior. The Mexican congress passed a resolution saying for any Mexican even to speak with an American official was treason and punishable by death. Everyone in Mexico knows who that resolution was aimed at, and Santa Anna's hold on the government is too shaky for him to defy them."

"When did you learn all that?" Adam asked.

"One of the wounded that I took in at Agua Nueva was a Mexican officer. He told me."

"You've known all this time, while I've been worrying about the war ending while we were in those mountains?" Adam asked in an accusing voice. "Why in hell didn't you tell me?"

"I didn't know you were worried, and you never asked," Anita replied, with an elegant shrug of her shoulders.

Buck laughed at the look of total exasperation on Adam's face, then hearing the sound of hoofbeats rapidly approaching, turned in his saddle. "Jesus! Look what's coming. A Meskin patrol. Let's get out of here!"

"No!" Adam said sharply. "Stay where you are.

If we run, they'll get suspicious."

The crowd in the road scattered in every direction, clearing the way for the lancers. It was either that or be run down. The cavalrymen in their brilliant uniforms and tall shakos rode past without giving Adam, Buck, and Anita a glance, their saddles creaking and reins jangling, leaving a flurry of dust in their wake.

Before the crush of Mexicans could close back in behind them, Adam spurred his horse. "Come on. Let's follow them. They can clear the way for us."

As Adam and Anita galloped away, Buck shook his shaggy head, thinking that his friend was getting more like McCulloch every day, boldly rushing in where angels feared to tread. What if one of the lancers turned and saw through their disguises? Reluctantly spurring his own horse, Buck followed.

As it turned out, more than one of the lancers did turn in their saddles and look to see who had the audacity to follow them so closely. Adam gazed back at them steadily, as if he had every right to be there. Invariably, it was the lancer who broke eye contact and turned his attention back to the road before him. Not until the dragoons had almost reached the gates of the city did Adam veer his horse and ride off the road, Anita and Buck close on his heels.

As the three came to a stop at the crest of a hill overlooking the city, Buck said in exasperation,

"Jesus, Adam, that was a crazy thing to do. Anita told us to stay in the background. What if those lancers had seen through our disguises?"

Adam shrugged and answered, "But they didn't."

Anita was a little angry at Adam for taking such a risk, too. "You only got away with it because you are dressed like *bandidos*. Only those swaggering, egotistic fools would do something so bold and daring."

Adam didn't particularly like being told he had the same characteristics as a *bandido*. It had been Mexican bandits who had murdered his wife. The only defense he could find to Anita's accusation was to pretend it had all been a deliberate act. "Didn't you say we should learn the Mexicans' mannerisms? Well, that's what I did. I behaved just like a *bandido* would be expected to behave."

"Gosh, I never even thought of it," Buck said in astonishment, swallowing Adam's excuse and looking at his friend with a new respect.

But Anita wasn't fooled. She knew Adam had reacted as Adam. *Dios,* he was too daring for his own good, taking foolish, unnecessary risks.

Dismissing the subject, Adam turned his horse and looked down at the scene below him. The city of Veracruz sat beside the grayish-green waters of the Gulf of Mexico, completely surrounded by a fifteen-foot wall, the only buildings visible the huge churches with their high bell towers and domes. In the harbor, perched on a coral reef about a thousand yards offshore, sat the massive San Juan de Ulua, an ancient fortress that had once been a Spanish castle, its white walls shrouded in mist.

"Well?" Buck asked impatiently. "Are we going into Veracruz or not?"

"Definitely not," Adam replied. "That place will be a death trap when the Americans start shelling it."

"How are they gonna get close enough to shell it, with that big fortress sitting out there in the harbor?" Buck countered.

Adam studied the harbor thoughtfully, then said, "You're right. Veracruz is impregnable by sea. Our ships could never get past that fort. They'll have to invade the coastline, either north or south of the city. Come on. Let's do a little scouting. Maybe we can figure out the most likely landing point and form a welcoming party for General Scott."

They rode north for about ten miles and, finding the coastline too rugged for an amphibious landing, retraced their steps and headed south. When they reached a long stretch of broad beach where the ground gently rose to rolling sand dunes about three miles from the city, Adam reined in and looked about him.

"If I were Scott, this is the spot I'd pick," Adam said. "It's about as good a beachhead as he's going to find, and it's close enough to the city to see it, yet far enough away to be out of gun range."

"Yeah, it's the best spot for landing boats we've seen," Buck agreed. "But I bet those sand dunes back there are crawling with Meskin soldiers."

Adam scanned the dunes in the distance. All he could see was the blowing sand and the sea oats that were sprinkled on the dunes waving in the brisk breeze. Above them, several sea gulls circled and cawed, angry at having the solitude of their beach invaded by humans. Adam glanced up at them, wishing he had their view. Then, spying the steep hills about half a mile inland, he said, "Let's backtrack and ride up to those hills. If the Mexican Army is concealed in those dunes, we'll be able to see them from there."

The hills were heavily wooded, the limbs of the scrubby trees twisted grotesquely by the steady wind from the gulf. Here they were concealed from view from both the city and the beach below them. When they looked down at the dunes and discovered that they were completely deserted, Adam frowned and said, "I don't understand it. Why don't the Mexicans have someone down there? They've left the best beachhead totally unprotected."

"Beats me," Buck answered, with a shrug of his massive shoulders.

Because the hill gave them an excellent viewpoint of both the beach and the city with its harbor, they decided to camp there and wait. That night, they slept with the smell of salt in their nostrils and the sound of the surf in their ears.

About noon the next day, Adam sighted a sail on the horizon. It soon became apparent that this was no lone merchantman making its way to Veracruz. Within an hour, the entire sky was filled with canvas as the Gulf Naval Squadron came into view. By midafternoon, the troop transports were in position, and the soldiers climbed over the sides and into the bobbing surf boats, while the people of Veracruz stood on the walls surrounding the city, the sailors on the visiting ships in the harbor hung from their rigging, and the men on the American men-of-war offshore all watched anxiously. At 5:30 P.M., a cannon on the flagship roared, a signal for the amphibious assault to begin.

Adam, Anita, and Buck watched the landing from their hilltop. Once the boats hit the beach, the men scrambled over the sides and splashed into the water, wading in, their muskets and cartridge boxes held high over their heads. When they reached the beach, they dove to the sand, expecting to be greeted by a hail of musket balls from the dunes. None came. The only sounds were the roaring of the surf behind them and the shrieking of the sea gulls above them. The beach was as deserted as it had been the day before.

As the men on the beach lay in the sand fearfully awaiting an attack, Buck said, "I ought to ride down there and tell them to stop worrying. There's not a greaser within miles of them."

"And get your head blown off for your trouble?" Adam snapped. "If they see anyone coming from those dunes at them, they'd riddle them. Sit tight. They'll figure it out."

The three on the hilltop watched as a patrol was sent out. After carefully searching the beach and finding it empty of the enemy, word was sent to General Scott on the *Massachusetts* to proceed with the landing. The sun went down, a flaming ball of fire that turned the beach a warm, rosy color, then darkness fell, suddenly, without any dusk, as happens in the tropics. Throughout the evening, the surf boats went back and forth, back and forth from the troop transports until, by 10:00 P.M., all of Scott's men were on the beach.

Throughout the entire landing, the sea had become increasingly rough, and shortly after the last man stepped ashore, the storm that had been threatening all evening broke. Thunder rolled and lightning split the heavens, but there was little rain in the storm. It was mostly wind. But what a wind! It didn't howl. It shrieked like an enraged woman, an ear-splitting sound that grated on the nerves.

The gnarled trees around Adam, Anita, and Buck's camp twisted in every direction, sending broken limbs flying through the air, and the three had to rush to weigh down their supplies to keep them from being blown away. Throughout the night, the storm raged and was still going strong the next morning. The three looked down from their hilltop and saw the entire gulf was filled with angry whitecaps and leaden, reflecting the gray, overcast sky above, while the surf was a foaming mass of rolling water where the waves were crashing against the beach.

Seeing that some of the troops on the beach were beginning to pull out, Adam said, "It looks like they're marching on Veracruz. I'm going down there to find Hays."

"What about me?" Buck asked.

"You stay here with Anita."

Anita saw the disappointment on Buck's face. "That's not necessary. I'm not a child, requiring a nursemaid. I can take care of myself."

Adam knew only too well how capable Anita was. Strangely, her independence irritated him. It didn't seem natural. Women were supposed to be dependent upon men. More and more, he found himself wanting to protect her and finding, to his chagrin, that she didn't need protecting. Yet, his rational self told him that if Anita had been like other women, she would have never survived the trip over the mountains, nor would he and Buck, with her dragging them down. But still . . . Adam shook his head in frustration, not really knowing what he wanted from her.

"No, Buck stays here," Adam said in an adamant voice. "If a patrol comes up here looking around, I don't want you by yourself."

When Anita started to object, Adam gave her a hard, warning look. Quickly, Buck intervened. "No, Anita. He's right. Besides, he ain't gonna be gone that long. Ain't no reason for both of us going."

Considering the issue closed, Adam turned, walked to his horse, and quickly saddled it. As he started to mount, Anita asked, "You are going like that? Dressed like a Mexican?"

In his haste to get away, Adam had completely forgotten that he still had on his charro suit. Quickly, he stripped off the jacket, handing it to Anita to keep it from blowing away.

"Here," Buck said, whipping off his coonskin cap and offering it to Adam, "wear this. They'll never mistake you for a greaser with it on."

The last thing Adam wanted to put on his head was Buck's smelly skin cap. It would be much too close to his nose. "No, Buck. It might blow away. I'd hate to lose your lucky charm."

"Hell, it ain't like those broad-brimmed sombreros we've been wearing. It won't blow away."

"It's too big for me," Adam argued.

"It ain't too big. It may sit a little lower on your head, but that will keep the sand out of your eyes."

From the corner of his eye, Adam saw Anita's

expression. To his surprise, she was smiling, but not her usual cynical smile. Her lips were curved with genuine amusement, and there was a humorous sparkle in her eyes that he had never seen before. The sight was startling, and before he could object, Buck had slammed the coonskin cap on Adam's dark head.

Despite the wind, the smell of the old musty, sweaty animal skin surrounded Adam like a shroud, and it was all he could do to keep from gagging. Vowing to remove it as soon as he was out of sight, he quickly mounted and rode from camp.

But Adam never removed the cap. When he rode onto the beach and full force into the brunt of the wind, the coonskin did offer some protection to his face. Here in the open, without the trees to serve as a barrier, there was a sandstorm such as Adam had never seen, the gritty material stinging his skin, coating his lips, clogging his nostrils, and so thick that he could hardly see ten feet in front of him.

He was almost on top of the picket who had been posted before either man realized that the other was there. "Halt!" the surprised sentry called out, the sound flying past Adam's ears in the high wind.

"Don't shoot!" Adam cried out. "I'm an American."

The sentry stepped closer, straining his eyes to

see through the swirling sand, his musket pointed with deadly intent at Adam. Then, seeing the coonskin cap on the stranger's head, the young soldier relaxed, muttering, "Well, I be damned. You are one of us."

"How about pointing that thing someplace else, son. That gun aimed at my chest is making me a might nervous," Adam said, seeing the frightened picket's finger still twitching on the trigger.

"Oh, sure, mister," the youth mumbled, lowering the musket.

"I'm looking for Colonel Hays. Can you tell me where his outfit is bivouacked?"

The youth's brow furrowed. "I ain't heard of no Colonel Hays."

"He's with the Texas Mounted Volunteers," Adam explained.

"Ain't heard of them, either."

"Maybe your commanding officer can help me. Can you direct me to him?"

"General Worth? Yeah, he's back there," the picket said, pointing vaguely to the rear of him, "behind that sand dune."

"Worth?" Adam asked in surprise. "Are you speaking of T.J. Worth? The same General Worth that fought at the Battle of Monterrey?"

"Yeah, he was at Monterrey." The soldier squared his shoulders, saying proudly, "And our division was the first to hit this beach."

Adam's dark eyebrows rose at this information.

But then, he reminded himself, he shouldn't have been surprised. Taylor had sent Worth into Monterrey first, too, and the general had proved himself — with a little help from the Rangers. Pleased that his old acquaintance and commanding officer was present, Adam nodded and turned his horse in the direction of the sand dune the picket had pointed out.

The dune was a mere dark blur in the blowing sand, and Adam's horse almost stumbled over more than one soldier wrapped in canvas on the ground in an effort to escape the stinging sand. Other troopers stood around slapping viciously at themselves and scratching everywhere, muttering curses.

Mosquitoes? Adam wondered. In this wind? Then, as he felt a bite on his hand, Adam realized what was happening. The sand was alive with voracious fleas, and the wind was stirring them up as much as the sand.

He heard the general's tent before he actually saw it. The flapping noises the canvas was making sounded like sharp cracks from a rifle over the howling wind. When Adam pulled up in front of it, the tent looked as if it would be ripped from its stakes any moment, despite the fact that it sat behind the protection of a tall dune.

Adam dismounted and asked the sentry standing before the tent, "Is this General Worth's headquarters?"

The soldier looked at Adam suspiciously, then nodded curtly.

"Would you tell him that Adam Prescott would like a moment with him? You might add that I fought with him in Monterrey, in case he doesn't remember my name right off."

Shooting Adam another distrustful look, the sentry stepped into the tent, then returned shortly. "The General said to come in, sir."

Adam smiled, noting that the soldier's demeanor had taken on an air of respect. Apparently, he hadn't expected the general to agree to seeing a rough-looking character like himself.

Adam dismounted, ground-tied his horse, and, ducking his head, pushed back the tent flap. Seeing him enter, General Worth rose from where he was seated behind a small table and smiled broadly, offering his hand. "So it really is you."

Adam accepted the general's hand and gave it the customary shake. "I was afraid you might not have remembered me."

Worth's bushy gray eyebrows rose. "Not remember the man who saved my life?" he asked in a disbelieving voice. "No, Adam. I'm not an ingrate. Nor could I ever forget any of the Rangers. Without you men giving me your best at Monterrey, I'd still be bucking for that grade."

"Your promotion was long overdue, General. An officer of your caliber should have gotten it a long time ago."

Worth thought so, too, but graciously deferred from saying so. Instead, he motioned to a camp stool. "Have a seat and tell me what you're doing here in Veracruz."

Adam sat on the stool, took off Buck's cap, and placed it on the sand. "My partner and I agreed to meet Colonel Hays here. I was wondering if you could tell me where he's bivouacked? That picket out there didn't seem to know."

The ruddy-faced Kentuckian frowned. "I wasn't aware that Colonel Hays was in General Scott's command. I know for certain that he and his men didn't take part in the landing last night. But then, it's possible he's on his way. The campaign hasn't gone exactly as planned, you know. General Scott only got half of the men he had requested; the transports he ordered were canceled by mistake; only a third of the munitions and half of the surf boats arrived. Then our sailing time was delayed by bad weather. Because of our transportation problems, many of the troops were left behind on Lobos Island, and some haven't even been shipped from Brazos Santigo. Hays could be down there, still awaiting transportation."

Adam didn't like what he was hearing. "If the Rangers are still down on the Rio Grande delta, how long might it take before they arrive?"

"I have no idea. A few weeks, possibly a few months. As I said, things haven't been going smoothly." The general shook his gray head, saying in a worried tone of voice, "And it doesn't look like our luck is getting any better. If this storm could have held off for another day or two, we could have landed our wagons, supplies, and horses. Now we're stuck out here in a virtual sandstorm, being eaten alive by fleas, with only a four-day supply of boiled beef and sea biscuits in our knapsacks. We don't even have our artillery. The weather seemed so balmy when we sailed. We thought we had left the bad weather behind us."

"These *nortadas* have a way of showing up when least expected," Adam commented.

As if to prove its perversity, an usually strong gust of wind caught the tent, seemingly sucking the canvas from its moorings and raising the roof. Both men looked up, expecting to see the tent go flying away, before the roof fell back down with a loud snap.

Dropping his eyes, Worth asked Adam, "Is that what they call these storms, *nortadas?*"

"Yes, the Mexicans call them that. In Texas, we call them northers, but they're the same thing. A strong north wind. But in Texas, the air is cold, feeling like it came right off the north pole. I guess the air warms up by the time it reaches this latitude."

The general gave Adam a thoughtful look, then said, "I'm curious. Why didn't you and your partner wait to ship out with the rest of your regiment?"

"We made these plans with Colonel Hays back in October, when I was still laid up with my broken leg. Since we didn't know how long it would take the bone to heal and were afraid we'd miss the sailing, we agreed to meet him down here as soon as I was able to travel. But now I can see where our coming on down here was rather hasty. I guess we should have gotten back in touch with Jack." Adam looked the general in the eye and candidly admitted, "I guess we were so anxious to get in on the fighting, we didn't even stop to think things through. We never dreamed we'd get here first. We rode into Veracruz two days ago, ahead of everyone."

A startled expression came over the general's face. "Are you saying you traveled overland? You didn't come by a neutral merchantman?"

"No. We left Buena Vista three days after the battle."

"Buena Vista?" the general asked, even more shocked. "You were at the Battle of Buena Vista?"

"Yes, sir. My partner and I served with Major McCulloch. He cut our service short so we could get down here and meet Hays."

"But we just heard about the battle the day we sailed from Lobos Island by special courier. And that man rode day and night. You must have done some hard traveling yourself."

"Yes, we did. We made it in eleven days."

"Eleven days? Over the Sierras? In dead winter?

That's . . . that's extraordinary," Worth commented, for lack of a better word.

"Not really, sir. Not when you stop to consider that Santa Anna moved his entire army over the mountains in a little over three weeks. And they were on foot."

But not that distance, Worth thought, still amazed at the Texans' arduous trek.

Adam picked up Buck's cap and rose. "Well, sir, I'd better be going. I know you have important things to do."

"I'm sorry that I couldn't give you any more information. What will you do now?"

"Wait around for Hays to show up, I guess," Adam answered, then added, "and hope it's soon."

Adam stepped from the tent, the wind slapping him in the face and the sand stinging his exposed skin. Putting Buck's coonskin cap on, he mounted. As he rode back through the army camp, he was glad that he wasn't stuck down here on the beach with the troops. The blowing sand and howling wind were bad enough, but the fleas seemed to have gotten even worse. The wind must be blowing them, too, Adam thought. Christ! The little devils were all over him!

When Adam returned to the hill above the beach, he discovered that Buck and Anita had moved their camp to the opposite side of the hill where the wind wasn't so strong. They had even managed to start a fire, the thick smoke trailing the ground in the stiff breeze.

Adam dismounted and unsaddled his horse, passing on Worth's information to a disappointed Buck, stopping every now and then to scratch an irritating flea bite. Handing Buck back his cap, he said, "Thanks. It was a big help after all."

Buck looked down at his cap, then said in a horrified voice, "It's covered with fleas!"

Adam glanced down and saw the black specks all over the fur. Suddenly, he realized what had happened. When he had set the cap on the sand in Worth's tent, the fleas had swarmed to it. "I'm sorry," Adam said lamely. "The beach is crawling with them."

"And is that why you are scratching yourself?" Anita asked. "They are all over you, too?"

"Yes," Adam admitted, scratching a bite on his chest through his shirt.

"You will find a stream about a hundred yards down the hill," Anita said. "Go down there and bathe. I will bring you fresh clothing, then boil those clothes you have on."

Buck shook his cap violently. A bucket of sand fell out, but not one flea. They clung to the fur with a fierce tenacity. "Damn! How am I gonna get them out of my cap? You can't boil coonskin."

"Give it to me," Anita said calmly. "I will fumigate it in the smoke."

As Adam made a beeline for the stream, he

heard Buck muttering, "Hell, my cap is ruined. Now it's gonna smell of smoke."

Personally, Adam thought it would be a vast improvement.

Chapter 18

During the time that the Americans were encircling Veracruz and began bombarding it and the harbor, Adam, Anita and Buck moved their camp to a high hill which overlooked the city. Here they could see over the walls and into Veracruz itself as the four American batteries pounded away, day and night.

It was a living hell for the people of the city. Houses collapsed under the exploding shells and buried the occupants alive, or drove them into the streets where they were cut down by flying metal. Survivors huddled beside half-crumbled walls, while children cried pathetically for dead parents or from empty stomachs, since the city's food supply had been cut off.

Viewing the shelling from the hill, Anita was heartsick at what she saw. The night bombardment was the worst, the light from the multiple fires

314

dancing eerily over the crumbled walls of the houses and the rubble in the streets, the shells shrieking in the still night, their fuses leaving spiraling trails of bright red stars before they exploded and lighted up the rooftops, bringing more death and destruction.

"The fools," Anita hissed one night. "Why did the authorities order the people in the outlying areas into the city? And why didn't they let the people leave when Scott offered them safe conduct? They would have been better off in the open. Now the innocent die. And for what?"

Adam heard the anguish in her voice. He remained grimly silent, a niggardly feeling of guilt gnawing at his conscience. What in the hell is wrong with you, he asked himself angrily. Those are Mexicans down there, your enemies. They showed no compassion for your wife or your brother, or those wounded Americans they butchered at Buena Vista. But these thoughts gave him very little comfort.

Then a few nights later, when Anita heard the news that General Scott had refused the Mexicans' request to let the women and children leave the city, she was furious. "Why did Scott refuse?" she demanded of Adam, her black eyes flashing dangerously. "What kind of an animal is he, to murder helpless women and children? He is nothing but a butcher!"

"Scott had his reasons," Adam replied, tight-lipped. "The Americans have already had several clashes with Mexican reinforcements trying to reach the city. If those reinforcements get inside those walls, it might take months before Veracruz surrenders. And Scott doesn't have that kind of time. His commitment is to his men and winning this war. He's got to get his troops out of the low country before the yellow fever season starts. Otherwise, he'll lose his entire army and his whole campaign will be a failure. This is war, Anita," Adam reminded her bluntly. "You wanted to see Santa Anna defeated, and this is how it's done. If you can't take it . . . then go back to Monterrey!"

Adam swung on his heels and walked away, swallowed up by the darkness. Anita turned to Buck, the tears on her cheeks glistening in the firelight. Seeing the giant's discomfiture, she said, "I will not attack you, amigo. What Adam said is true. In my heart, I know if Santa Anna wins this war, not only will the people of Veracruz suffer, but all of Mexico. But it is so hard to watch. Those are my people down there. I feel their pain, their sorrow."

"If it's gonna tear you up like this," Buck said gently, "then maybe you ought to go back to Monterrey, like Adam suggested. It ain't gonna get any prettier, you know."

"I can't go back. I *must* see this through. The soul of my mother cannot rest until she has been avenged. My family honor demands it of me. And even if this were not true, my conscience would not allow me to run. That monster, Santa Anna, must be crushed, once and for all. I cannot afford the luxury of hiding from the truth, like an ostrich with its head in the sand. What must be done, must be done."

Anita turned and walked away. Buck frowned. If Anita felt so strongly for the Mexican people, then why had she sided with the Americans? Surely, her desire to get revenge on Santa Anna wasn't worth the anguish she was going through in seeing her people suffer. She was a puzzle that Buck couldn't understand. He had never known anyone as complex or as intense as Anita.

The next day, Veracruz surrendered, much to everyone's relief, and over the next few weeks, while Scott prepared for his march into the interior, Adam and Buck waited for Colonel Hays and his men to appear. Then, watching the American Army pulling out for their march on Mexico City, they became more and more anxious.

One morning, Buck entered the small adobe house, saying in a dispirited voice, "Well, General Paterson and his division left this morning to join General Twiggs."

"Yes, I know," Adam replied. "We saw them pass."

Buck sat down in a chair, hunched over. "Well, I guess General Worth will pull out next. Then we'll be left sitting here with the occupational forces.

What in the hell is taking Hays so long?"

"I don't know, but I can tell you one thing," Adam said in a firm voice, coming to his feet. "We're not going to wait around here any longer. There have already been several cases of yellow fever reported."

"*Sí*," Anita agreed. "If we stay here any longer we may all die of the *vomito*. There is no cure for it, you know."

Buck knew that there was no cure, nor did anyone seem to know what caused the dreaded disease that plagued the wet, tropical areas the world over. The victim died horribly of internal hemorrhaging, hence the black vomit that was associated with the disease as well as the telltale yellow pigmentation of the skin. Buck shuddered and asked, "Where are we gonna go?"

"To the most logical place," Adam answered. "To Japala, with the Army." Turning, he said over his shoulder as he walked to the door, "I'm going to have a talk with General Worth. Maybe he can use us as scouts until Hays shows up."

Thirty minutes later, Adam was seated in the general's headquarters in Veracruz. "What can I do for you, Adam?" Worth asked, after he had seated himself behind his desk.

Adam didn't beat around the bush. "Colonel Hays hasn't shown up, and we don't want to sit around waiting for him any longer. Hell, we came down here to fight! At this rate, Hays might not show up until the war is over. I was wondering if you could use a couple of good scouts?"

General Worth frowned, then said, "I'd like to oblige you, Adam. Believe me, no one knows better than I what extraordinary scouts you Rangers are. But I'm afraid it's impossible. General Scott won't be using any civilians as scouts, not even Rangers. His engineering corps will do that job for him."

"That's what Taylor said before he left Corpus Christi, but he changed his mind," Adam pointed out.

"Scott won't change his mind. You see, there is a vast difference in the two commanders. General Scott is a stern disciplinarian. He believes in doing things according to army regulations, and army regulations call for the engineers to act as scouts. He doesn't bend. He's all spit and polish. That's why he's called, Old Fuss and Feathers. But don't get me wrong. While he isn't the leader of men that Taylor is, he's a brilliant strategist and a capable administrator. You'll see no slackness in his command, no indecision. He'll take Mexico City come hell or high water. You watch and see."

"But that's just it! I don't want to watch and see. I want to be a part of it."

"You could enlist. I'd be more than pleased to have you in my command. In fact, I can almost guarantee you a position as a field officer."

Adam laughed harshly. "No offense, General,

319

but army life isn't for me. The fighting is okay, but all that spit and polish and regulations goes against my grain."

General Worth wasn't at all surprised by Adam's honest answer. Like all frontiersmen, the Ranger was a rugged individualist. But Worth was disappointed. The Ranger was good officer material. Unknown to Adam, Worth had watched him carefully after Adam had saved his life. What the general had seen had impressed him, and he had wondered why Adam didn't have a Ranger company of his own. He possessed the same charismatic qualities as the Ranger captains, qualities that set him apart from the other Rangers, exuding a quiet confidence, brave, quick-witted, cool under fire, so persevering and persistent that retreat was unthinkable and defeat unbearable. Yes, Adam had the makings of a top-notch officer.

While Worth had been thinking these things, Adam had a sudden idea. He sat at the edge of his chair, asking, "If we can't scout for you, then how about letting Buck and me spy for you?"

"Spy?" General Worth asked in surprise. "You mean obtain information for us?"

"Yes."

"But how do you intend to do that?"

"Disguise ourselves as Mexicans. That's how we got down here. And remember, we speak fluent Spanish. We'll just blend into the population and watch and listen. You'd be surprised at the information you can pick up from the Mexican peons."

"But won't they get suspicious? Two strange men hanging around?"

"We're not just two men. We have a Mexican girl with us. She lends us a certain credibility. We'll just observe, and she can ask the questions. With so many Mexicans displaced by the war, no one will be suspicious of three strangers wandering about. And Anita can ask questions without arousing suspicion. Everyone knows how gossipy women are."

General Worth had heard that Adam had been taken in by a Mexican girl when he was wounded in Monterrey. He wondered if this Anita was the same girl and why she was traveling with the two Rangers, but his good manners prevented him from asking. "Well, this puts a different light on everything. Surely, not even Scott, could object to having you ferret out information for us if you're willing to take the risks."

"We're willing," Adam assured him. "We'll travel ahead of you, like we're running before the American Army. If we find out anything that may be of importance to you, either Buck or I will report it to you. There's only one thing we want in return."

"What's that?"

"We want to be present at the battles, to observe if nothing else."

"Reap the fruit of your toils, so to speak?"

"Sort of. At least that way, we could feel that

321

we had some part of it."

"I'm afraid I can't promise you that, Adam. I can only speak for my part in this war. My division may not participate in all the major battles."

"Then I guess we will just have to settle for tagging along with you," Adam said with a grin, feeling pleased with himself for coming up with this ingenious plan, "and hope that you see a lot of action."

General Worth laughed at Adam's audacious words. "There may be times when I won't be available to take your reports. Perhaps I should introduce you to one of the junior officers. Then, if I'm not around, you can report to him." The general pursed his lips thoughtfully, then said, "Yes, I think I know just the man. Captain Robert E. Lee. He's the commanding officer of the engineers. As Scott's head scout, he'll be able to incorporate the information you bring in with his own findings."

Adam waited impatiently while General Worth sent for Lee, anxious to get back to Buck and Anita and tell them of the arrangement he had made. When the young captain stepped into the office and Worth introduced them, Adam was impressed with the soft-spoken Virginian. There was something about the captain's bearing that spoke of greatness, something more than his obvious good breeding and his keen intelligence. Perhaps that quality of greatness was bred into him, Adam thought, upon learning that Captain Lee was the son of the famous cavalry hero known as Light Horse Harry.

Fifteen minutes later, Adam was on his way back to the small adobe house where Buck and Anita waited. He burst into the house and excitedly related his news to the two.

"Are you crazy?" Buck thundered when Adam had finished. "You can't ask Anita to spy. If the Meskins caught her at it, they'd kill her. Even faster than you and me."

"No, Buck," Anita said firmly. "I told Adam I would help gather information. If spying will help end this bloodbath sooner, then I will do it."

Buck whirled and walked to his room, grumbling under his breath. Anita picked up a candle holder and walked to her and Adam's bedroom. Adam followed, torn by sudden doubts.

Closing the door behind him, he watched while Anita set the candle down on the chipped table beside their bed and began to unbraid her long hair. "Buck is right," Adam said in a decisive voice. "I guess I never stopped to think about it before, but it is too dangerous for you. If the Mexicans ever caught us, they'd kill us, but if they caught you . . . " Adam shuddered, thinking of all the horrible methods of torture the Mexicans might devise for Anita. To them, she would be a traitor as well as a spy.

Anita whirled, her long hair flying out around

323

her like huge black wings. "No! I won't let you leave me behind. Not now! Not after making that terrible trip over the mountains. I've earned my right to be there when Santa Anna is defeated. You cannot cheat me of it!"

I'm not trying to cheat you of anything! I just don't want to see you hurt."

The black eyes narrowed. "Why? I'm just another Mexican. What difference does one more dead Mexican make to you?"

Adam flinched at Anita's hard words. He knew she wasn't just another Mexican, one of the enemy. Not any more. She was . . . Adam scowled. He couldn't identify what Anita was in his life. A fellow conspirator? An uneasy companion? A passionate lover? They all fit, and yet none really described their relationship, and Adam couldn't put a finger on the emotions that were emerging — or refused to.

"All right!" he spat in frustration. "There will never be any reasoning with you. But if you get caught, remember that I warned you."

Anita felt an immense relief. She couldn't bear to be left behind, and it wasn't just her desire for revenge that was driving her. No, she couldn't bear to be parted from Adam, not yet. She was fighting for every precious minute she could spend with him, stolen time whose memories of which would have to sustain her the rest of her life after he had gone back to Texas. Yes, for that, and for her revenge, she added a little belatedly, she would be willing to take the risk of spying. Careful not to reveal her feelings, she answered, "I will not get caught. And I won't argue with you. Not tonight."

The next morning, Anita announced that she would go to the marketplace to buy new disguises for the two men, pointing out that if they were to mingle with the peons, they must dress like them.

When neither man objected, Anita said, "And you must practice acting like peons. Remember what I said? Their bodies speak of subjugation. You must remember to slump your shoulders and bow your heads. Never look anyone in the eye. And if someone of authority speaks to you, look afraid."

Adam and Buck frowned. Both were fearless, proud men. Playing the role of a peon wouldn't come easy to them.

"I will trade our horses for a cart and burro," Anita continued.

Adam's head snapped up. "Like hell you will!"

"I know you don't want to give up your horses, but peons travel by cart, or on foot."

"Dammit, we'll need swift horses if we're going to deliver the information we ferret out to the American Army," Adam countered. "We'll just have to run the risk of arousing suspicion."

Anita found she couldn't argue with Adam's

logic. If they couldn't get the information to the Americans swiftly, there would be no point in spying. She put her keen mind to work, then said, "Then we will have to disguise the horses, too."

"Disguise them?" Buck asked in surprise. "How are you gonna do that?"

"You'll see."

That afternoon, Anita set to work on the horses to make them look less impressive. First she denuded their sleek coats of large patches of hair with a preparation she had concocted, then skillfully painted what appeared to be ugly sores and scratches over their hides, and finally splattered them with mud. Adam and Buck stood by and watched with something akin to horror the transformation of their well-tended mounts into what appeared to be run-down nags.

"I hope to hell you know what you're doing," Adam said, a look of pure disgust on his face. "What if their hair doesn't grow back in? I wouldn't be caught dead with such a miserable-looking horse back in Texas."

"The preparation I used to denude them is harmless. It won't damage the hair roots."

As Anita picked up a pot, dipped her hand in it, and began to smear something on the sores she had painted on the horses, Buck asked, "What's that?"

"Honey. It will draw flies and make the sores look even more realistic."

326

Both men groaned in disgust. Not only were they going to have to ride such disreputable mounts but contend with a swarm of voracious flies, too.

"What about your saddle?" Adam asked. "With that silver studding, it's likely to arouse suspicion."

Anita shrugged. "We won't be riding saddles. We'll ride bareback, like the peons do."

"Bareback?" Adam thundered. "You're crazy if you think I'm going to ride all the way to Mexico City bareback!"

"Yeah," Buck agreed heartily. "By the time I reached Mexico City, I'd have honest-to-God sores on my rump as big as those false ones you painted on my horse."

"Then I'll have to remove the silver inlays, nick the leather here and there, and scuff up all of our saddles to make them look more worn looking," Anita relented. "Even then, they might arouse suspicion." She stepped back and gazed at the horses thoughtfully. "In fact, the horses might still arouse suspicion, too. Despite their disguises, anyone with an eye for good horseflesh could tell they are not nags. You can't hide a horse's spirit."

"You're forgetting that a peon hasn't got an eye for good horseflesh," Adam pointed out.

"That's true," Anita admitted. "At any rate, this is the best we can do."

* * *

The three left Veracruz the next day, taking the National Road to Japala, the two men dressed in the white, pajamalike attire, sandals, and straw sombreros that the Mexican peons wore and riding their miserable-looking mounts. But the two had stubbornly refused to leave their sidearms behind, or even pack them away in their saddlebags with their trusted Colts. To Anita's chagrin, the single-shot pistols were still strapped to their hips beneath their long serapes.

Mounted on their good steeds, they passed the lumbering wagons and trudging troops of General Patterson's division, then General Twiggs, finally melting into the crowd of Mexican refugees fleeing before both advancing armies, taking care to slow their mounts to a lumbering gait that would resemble that of a worn-out nag. In the cool mountain air, a blessed relief after the humid, sweltering heat they had felt in Veracruz, they camped amongst the Mexicans that night, Adam and Buck staying inconspicuously beside their fire while Anita circulated through the crowd for information.

On the third night, Anita returned with a smug smile on her face. As soon as she was seated beside them, Adam asked, "What did you learn?"

"Santa Anna and his army are ahead of us. He has established his headquarters near a sleepy village named Cerro Gordo."

"Big Hill? Hell, that could be anywhere between

here and Mexico City."

"No, the village was named for the mountain that dominates it, El Telégrafo, because the rise was once a link of visual communications set up by the Aztecs between Veracruz and Mexico City. Twelve thousand of Santa Anna's army are entrenching themselves there and laying cannons on the summits of Telégrafo and the neighboring hills."

"Santa Anna doesn't even have twelve thousand troops!" Adam spat. "Not after the beating he took at Buena Vista. The Mexicans are exaggerating again."

"You forget that we are talking about Santa Anna!" Anita snapped back. "The man who can charm the Mexican people into anything. He has convinced them that he won the battle at Buena Vista, not the Americans. The Mexican government even gave him a medal for it. And he has raised more men for his army and marched them a thousand miles to meet your gringos. He is there, at Cerro Gordo, waiting."

Anita's words proved true. The American troops found Santa Anna and his army waiting for them at Cerro Gordo, and a fierce battle took place. But again, Santa Anna fled in the face of defeat, and Adam and Buck, who had brazenly joined Worth's men were a part of the patrol that pursued the fleeing Mexicans for ten miles to keep them from reforming.

That night, Adam and Buck returned to their camp to give Anita the good news. As they related the details of the battle, the scowl on her face got deeper and deeper. Then, when they had finished, she exploded. "I don't care if it was a great victory for your gringos! I don't care if three thousand Mexicans were captured! You didn't capture Santa Anna. He escaped your clutches— again!"

As she turned and walked angrily away, Adam and Buck exchanged miserable looks. Knowing that they had failed took the joy out of the victory for them. But strangely, it was not knowing that they had failed to capture Texas's old enemy that made them feel so low. It was Anita's disappointment in them that made them feel so dispirited.

Chapter 19

The day after the victory at Cerro Gordo, the American Army moved on to Japala, about thirteen miles farther inland. Adam, Anita, and Buck rode ahead of the column and long before they reached the town, they could see it, sitting like a jewel on the side of a hill, the domes of its churches gleaming in the sunlight. All around them, the mountains were covered with a lush tropical growth, the summits towering into the sky and surrounded by fluffy white clouds. One mountain dominated the scene, Orizaba, whose jagged peak was perpetually covered with snow that was dazzling white in the sunlight.

They passed fields of newly sprouted maize and pastures in which fat sheep and cattle grazed; then riding into the outskirts of the town, they saw listless Indians sitting outside their mud hovels and watching them, dull-eyed, from beneath the shade of banana trees. Their horses' hooves clattered on the cobblestone street as they rode into the city proper. Here the homes were substantially built of brick covered with plaster, many two-storied and painted in pastel colors, with flat tile roofs and courtyards in the center. And everywhere, over the houses, up the trees, along the walls, grew the vine with its large purple morning-glory-like blossoms from which the medicine *jalap* was made and from which the town had taken its name.

Buck looked around him appreciatively, thinking that this picturesque town with its cool mountain air, its lush tropical foliage, and its breathtaking view of the Sierras a vast improvement over some of the places he had seen in Mexico.

Japala offered no resistance to the Americans, much to the battle-weary soldiers' relief, and the army settled down on the outskirts of the city for the night.

Later that evening, Adam returned from headquarters and announced to Anita and Buck, "General Worth's regulars have been ordered to move thirty miles west to the next stop. We'll go ahead of the troops, as we usually do. If we find the Mexican Army at Perote, we're to report back to the general."

Buck's head snapped up. "Did you say Perote?"

"That's right," Adam answered tightly.

Buck searched his friend's face, wondering how Adam felt about going to the town that housed the prison where his brother had died, but Adam's expression was closed, his face totally unreadable.

332

The only hint of how Adam might be reacting had been his terse answer.

Early the next morning, the three packed up their meager belongings and their supplies and rode out, passing through the main plaza on their way out of the city. Even at this early hour, the square was already crowded with peons laying out their simple wares in the open market and was flanked on one side by the abandoned National Guard barracks and on the other by a church whose bells were pealing in the crisp morning air.

At one side of the plaza, a blue-cassocked priest rushed to the church, scowling at the peasants busy in the plaza from beneath his flat, broad-brimmed hat. On the other side of the square, a group of aristocrats on their way to mass picked their way haughtily through the crowd, their faces full of distaste for the lowly all around them. Seeing both the padre's and the wealthy Mexicans' expressions, Anita thought bitterly that there was only one thing missing from the scene to keep it from being symbolical of all Mexico: the arrogant soldier pushing his way through the plaza, shoving aside any unfortunate peon who got in his way. The poor of Mexico were caught between the three groups and were forced to endure the insolence of the rich, the tyranny of the military, and the extortion of the church. None cared about the plight of the lower classes.

No, Anita thought, this war wasn't against Mexico. The Americans fought the Army and the aristocracy, and not the people of her country. She felt no qualms in aiding the gringos. Yes, she wanted more than seeing Santa Anna destroyed. Mexico had many enemies beside the hated *presidente*. She fervently hoped, if the Americans won, that the power of the aristocracy, the military, and the church would be crushed, freeing her people.

Turning down the road to Perote, the three passed a drove of pack mules loaded with huge bundles of firewood being taken to the market, the halters of each tied to the braided tail of its predecessor and driven by two small Mexican boys. The steep mountain road climbed almost straight up the rugged Sierras, higher and higher, passing through thick, foglike clouds that dampened their exposed skin and clothing. Looking back down behind them from this dizzying height, not a touch of brown or green could be seen. It looked as if the entire world was carpeted with fluffy white cotton.

Higher they climbed, feeling giddy from the lack of oxygen in the thin mountain air, their ears ringing. Buck glanced over at the thick pine woods besides them, blinked his eyes in disbelief, then said to Adam, "Maybe it's just the altitude and I'm seeing things, as well as hearing them, but I could have sworn that I saw some Mexican troops over there."

"No, it's not your eyes playing tricks on you. I

saw some farther back. They're some of Santa Anna's troops, fleeing from the battle."

"Do you think they're retreating to Perote? That Santa Anna will make another stand there?"

"No, they seemed too disorganized to be retreating. As for there being a garrison at Perote, that remains to be seen."

"Goddammit, I don't like being up here with all these soldiers around us," Buck said, looking about him uneasily.

"Relax," Adam said in a soothing voice. "They won't bother us. They're just Mexicans running from the American Army, just like we're supposed to be doing."

When the sun went down that evening, the three stared at the glorious sight below them in silent awe. The clouds hovering around the mountains turned to gold, then rose colored as the jagged peaks took on the blood-red color of the fiery orb. Then darkness fell, like a curtain, sudden and inky black. They slept that night under a blanket of a million glittering stars, looking close enough to touch, the pungent smell of pine in their nostrils. In the woods all around them, the Mexican soldiers fleeing from their defeat at Cerro Gordo huddled around their small fires, feeling cold, hungry and dispirited.

The next day, the road to Perote became rougher and narrower, passing through woods in which stunted pine trees sparsely grew and then, barren ground. Riding into the city, the trio looked around at the gloomy sight. A dusty, smoky haze covered everything, coating the houses with their peculiar slanted log roofs with soot, and a fine white sand blew like snow in the cold mountain air. Adam stared grimly at the gray, grizzly walls of the fortress which sat a mile from the city. The ancient Spanish castle not only guarded the road to Mexico City, but had served as one of the most notorious prisons in Mexico. Thousands upon thousands of political prisoners had died within those walls in its slimy, rat-infested dungeon, and his brother had been one of them.

The three quickly learned that the fortress had been abandoned shortly before by its garrison and that the people of Perote were anxious to help the Americans. They did not like Santa Anna, and when asked of his whereabouts, replied that he was hiding in the mountains somewhere around them.

The next day, General Worth and his men marched into the town, and the general and a platoon of soldiers searched the crumbling fortress and found several American prisoners captured at Veracruz and two Mexican generals who had been imprisoned by Santa Anna for their failure to hold the port city. The Americans also found a military gold mine, fifty-four cannons and a cache of much needed supplies and ammunition that had been left behind by the Mexicans.

Once again, Adam, Buck, and Anita settled down beside Worth's army and waited, and waited, growing increasingly impatient and restless each day.

One day, as the three sat in the gloomy little hovel that they had taken refuge in, Buck grumbled, "Where in the hell is Scott and the rest of the Army? Has he forgotten we're perched up on this cold, barren mountaintop?"

"I don't know," Adam said, laying down his coffee cup and rising from the table. "But I'm going to pay General Worth a visit and see if I can find out what the delay is."

Adam returned later that afternoon and slumped into a chair, saying glumly, "Scott had problems. Big problems. He hasn't been able to move his supplies from Veracruz because of the lack of wagons and horses, and the few miserable wagon trains he managed to get together were so badly harassed by guerrillas and bandits that barely half of them made it through to Japala. Scott's troops can't contend with their hit-and-run tactics."

"Well, where in the hell is Hays?" Buck responded. "If he and the boys were here, we could put an end to that. If there's one thing we Rangers know, it's how to deal with a bunch of sneaky bandits and guerrillas."

"I asked Worth if he had heard anything about Hays, but he doesn't know any more about his whereabouts than we do. Hell, I doubt if Scott even knows where the rest of his army is being held up. But I can tell you one thing. Those reinforcements better show up fast. Otherwise, this whole campaign is going to fall flat on its face."

"Well, it don't seem to me like we're doing so bad for ourselves. We beat the Mexicans at Cerro Gordo, didn't we?"

"Yes, but a good third of Scott's army here in Mexico are pulling out on him."

"Pulling out?" Buck asked a shocked voice. "What in the hell are you talking about?"

"According to Worth, there were almost four thousand volunteers whose enlistment of one year ran out. They wasted most of that time waiting on Lobos Island to be shipped out. More than ninety percent of them refused to sign up again. They said they had no quarrel with Scott, but they'd had it. They'd had enough of going hungry, of bloodshed and disease, of going without pay. Their grudge is against the government who won't send enough men, supplies, and ammunition to do the job. Scott ordered them to go back and get out of Veracruz in a hurry, before the yellow fever season really sets in. A few days ago, seven regiments marched out, grinning and cheering, being envied by the troops left behind at Camp Misery."

"Camp Misery?" Buck asked. "Where's that?"

"That's what the troops named their camp at Japala. The volunteers aren't used to such crude living conditions, like the regulars and us Rangers.

They're growing restless and bored. They've taken to roaming about the countryside, unchecked by their officers, who are getting just as mean-tempered, terrorizing and pillaging the villages. Scott tried to discipline them by making an example of several of the offenders and giving them thirty lashes, but it didn't have any effect on them. They're sneaking Mexican alcohol and going on wild binges. Hell, they're crazy to drink that potent stuff the Mexicans brew. It can pickle your brain with one swallow."

Buck remembered the charming city of Japala and the beautiful countryside surrounding it. "Hell, if they think they got it bad, they should have been in that hellhole down in Camargo. At least they ain't burning up in a pit surrounded by hot rocks and getting eaten alive by ants, like Taylor's men were."

Adam made no comment to Buck's I observation. Instead, he rose and walked to the door, saying over his shoulder, "I'm going for a walk."

As the door closed behind him, Anita and Buck exchanged worried glances. "He's going to the castle again," Anita said quietly.

"Yeah, I know," Buck answered grimly. "Dammit, I wish to hell we could get out of here! This place is gloomy enough, but it's downright gruesome the way Adam keeps visiting that prison. The longer we stay, the more he broods about his brother's death. That place is haunting him."

"Tell me about his brother."

"He ain't never told you about Dan?" Buck asked in surprise.

"No. All I know is what I have overheard. How did he get captured?"

"It happened about six years ago, when Mexico sent a military force to attack San Antonio. The Meskins captured the city and held it for ten days. When they left, they took fifty-three prisoners with them as hostages. Dan was one of them."

"He was picked at random?"

"No, the Meskins captured the district court. Everyone present there that day was taken hostage, including the judge. Dan was a lawyer, just like Adam, you know."

"No, I didn't know Adam was a lawyer," Anita answered in surprise. She frowned. "I thought he was a rancher."

"He is now. He gave up his law practice in San Antonio with his twin brother to take up ranching."

"Dan was his twin?"

"Yeah, his identical twin. I guess that's one reason Adam took his death so hard. They were awfully close."

"But didn't Adam do anything to try and free his brother?"

"Hell, yes, he did! The Rangers mounted a force to go after the Meskins, and he and I rode with them. But we never did catch up with the Meskin

Army. The ground was so boggy from recent heavy rains that they escaped over the border before we could do any more than skirmish with their rear guards," Buck ended bitterly.

"But what about ransoming him? Didn't Adam try that?"

"They weren't being held for ransom. Those goddamned Meskins were holding them and threatening to kill them if we retaliated. And, by God, that's just what we did! We formed an army and went after them."

"Why did you do something so foolish?" Anita asked angrily. "They said they would kill the hostages if you tried that."

"Because that's what the Meskins have always done to their Texan prisoners!" Buck retorted hotly. "They did it at Goliad, and they did it to Dawson's men."

Anita had heard of the infamous massacre at Goliad, something she considered a blemish on her country's honor and had been perpetrated by her archenemy, Santa Anna, but she had never heard of this Dawson. "Who is Dawson?"

"He was a Texas Ranger captain. He and his company were the closest to San Antonio when the Meskins retreated with their hostages. They went after 'em, but the Meskin Army caught 'em in the open and surrounded 'em. Those Rangers didn't have a chance of a snowball in hell. There were only fifty of 'em and fifteen hundred

Meskins. The Rangers surrendered. As soon as they'd laid down their arms, the Meskins cut them down. Slaughtered them right on the spot. Hacked 'em in so many pieces, you couldn't tell what parts belonged to what man."

Anita cringed. Her stomach lurched. She was forced to admit that the Texans had their reasons for hating her people, too. There was so much injustice and unnecessary cruelty on both sides.

Buck was unaware of her reaction and her pale face. He was too caught up with his remembered anger. "That's why we didn't trust the Meskins to kill the hostages anyway. But by the time we reached the border, so many men in the Army had deserted that we didn't have enough men left to invade Mexico. Most of the men who had joined the army were just riffraff, looking for excitement and plunder. All that was left was a couple of hundred Rangers. What good were we against a force that large? The general in charge of the expedition decided to turn back, except most of the Rangers refused to. They decided to invade Mexico themselves. Sam Walker was one of 'em. Hays tried to talk him out of it, but he wouldn't listen. And I was scared to death Adam would go with 'em. I had a devil of a time talking him out of it. Thank God, I was successful, or else he would have been captured like Walker and all the others in the Mier expedition. Then he would have shared their fate."

Buck paused, then asked, "Do you remember that day when Adam got so angry at me for saying Walker had a weird look in his eyes when he talked about Meskins? How Adam went on and on about everything Walker told him had happened to him?"

"*Sí*, I remember."

"Well, the reason Adam got so upset was he knew his brother went through all that, too. The Meskins threw all the Mier prisoners in with the hostages they had taken. Dan experienced all those horrible things Sam did, too,—the death lottery, the march across the desert, the escape and recapture, the long march into Mexico and imprisonment here at Perote. Only Dan didn't escape the second time with Walker. He was too weak with dysentery to go along. But he tried it later on his own. His Meskin guards caught him trying to dig a tunnel under the walls. They beat him to death right then and there. Adam heard about it from one of the other prisoners who was later released. When he heard the news of Dan's death, something inside him seemed to die."

"*Sí*," Anita commented sadly, "I have heard that identical twins are so close that they can tell what the other is thinking, feel what the other is feeling, that if one dies, a part of the other dies, too."

Buck stared at Anita in horror, a shudder running through him.

Anita dropped her eyes and fidgeted nervously

343

with her skirt, a behavior so uncharacteristic of her that Buck frowned in puzzlement. Then in a hesitant voice, she asked, "Who is Beth?"

"Didn't Adam tell you about her, either?" Buck asked in surprise.

"No."

Buck's brow furrowed. "Then how do you know about her?"

"Adam talks in his sleep. He has called out for her in the night."

Buck grimaced, thinking how insensitive it was of a man to call for his wife while sleeping beside his mistress. But then, he remembered that Adam hadn't known what he was doing. Aware of Anita waiting patiently for his answer, he said, "She was his wife."

Anita was stunned. Adam had a wife? But then she had suspected that the woman Adam called out for was very close to him. Still, she felt very hurt and very betrayed, and a pain unlike none she had never known filled her—until something occurred to her. Buck had used the past tense when he had spoken of her. "Then, she died?" Anita asked.

"Yes."

Anita felt a rush of relief, then asked, "How did it happen?"

"It ain't a pretty story," Buck warned in an ominous tone of voice.

"Still, I want to know."

Buck hesitated for a moment, then said, "Shortly after Adam received word of Dan's death, a gang of Meskin bandits under General Canales raided across the Nueces, and Adam's ranch was one of those hit. When his *vaqueros* deserted him, Adam was left to defend himself and his wife against more than thirty men. Adam picked off a good dozen of the bandits before a bullet grazed his head and knocked him senseless. The last thing he heard before he lost consciousness completely was his wife's terrified screams. When he regained consciousness, his head was covered with so much blood that the Meskins must have assumed he was dead."

So that's where he got the scar on his forehead, Anita thought.

Buck continued his grim tale. "When Adam regained consciousness, he found Beth's body lying outside in a puddle of blood. She had been dragged outside, stripped naked, and raped by God only knows how many of those bastards before she hemorrhaged to death. Adam's unborn child died with her."

Anita was horrified "She was pregnant?"

"Yeah. She was about six months along. The rest of Adam seemed to die along with her and the baby."

Anita's rising hopes were dashed to the ground. She had been a fool to think that Adam might eventually come to love her, a Mexican, one of those who had cruelly murdered the woman he loved. Now she knew why he called out her name. He still loved her.

The knowledge tore at Anita's heart, and yet, perversely, almost as if she were punishing herself for being so stupid and letting her defenses fall to the rugged Texan, she asked, "She was very beautiful, wasn't she? Blonde and blue-eyed?"

Buck had thought Beth one of the most beautiful women he had ever seen, but now, looking at Anita's exotic coloring, Beth's beauty seemed pale in comparison. Then Buck realized that Beth had failed to measure up to Anita in many other ways, too. He remembered Martha saying that Beth had not been a good choice for a wife for Adam, that she lacked the strength and fortitude a frontiersman's wife needed. The remark had come as a surprise to Buck, for his wife rarely said anything critical about others, and then he had promptly forgotten it. Now he could see the truth of Martha's words. Beth had been beautiful and sweet, but weak and clinging. Adam needed a strong woman by his side, a fighter, a builder, a hawk like himself and not a pretty, meek dove. He needed a woman like Anita.

"Wasn't she?" Anita persisted.

"Yeah, she was pretty, but—"

"And Adam loved her very much, didn't he?"

Buck assumed that Adam loved his wife. That was why a man married a woman, wasn't it? But if he felt any love for Anita, Adam certainly never showed it. He never looked at her with tenderness, or spoke to her with soft words, or showed her any kindness or gentleness. And Buck had heard the anguish in Anita's voice and knew that she was all too aware of Adam's lack of feelings for her. The realization that Anita loved Adam and was hurting because that love wasn't returned tore at the giant's heart. Why was Adam so blind? he asked himself angrily. Couldn't the young fool see that Anita was more woman that Beth could have ever hoped to be? Was Adam doing what so many did to their dead loved ones, setting Beth on an altar to be worshiped, forgetting her faults and weaknesses and making a saint out of her? Why did people suddenly reach perfection in the minds of others only after they had died?

Seeing the torn expression on Buck's face, Anita said, "You don't have to answer that question. I know the answer."

"Maybe I shouldn't have told you about Beth," Buck said, feeling miserable.

"No, I'm glad you did. Now I understand Adam much better. He's been deeply hurt by the loss of his brother and the death of his wife and child. His soul is scarred."

And scars never heal, Buck thought glumly.

Anita turned, picked up her shawl, and wrapped it tightly around her head and shoulders. As she walked to the door, Buck asked, "Where are you going?"

Anita turned, answering, "To find Adam."

"Why?"

"Because he needs me," Anita answered simply. *But the young fool don't deserve you,* Buck thought bitterly as Anita walked out the door.

Anita saddled and mounted her horse, turning into the blowing wind and biting sand as she rode to the castle. She dismounted before the cracked, towering walls and walked through the gate and the courtyard, shooting a hard look at the crowd of sightseeing soldiers there who were crowding around a Mexican guide showing them the bone fragments that had been embedded in the cross where the prisoners had been executed. Such gruesome curiosity disgusted her.

Inside the castle, she passed the beautiful chapel with its stained glass windows and went down the damp stairs, the steps becoming slippery with slime the deeper she went. Once she had reached the dungeon, she walked down the narrow, musty-smelling passageway, the candles in the wall sconces casting eerie shadows over the sweating stone walls. She found Adam just exactly where she had expected to find him, squatting inside a cell and staring at a hole in the sand beside one wall. She sensed, as Adam had, that this was his brother's cell, that Dan had removed the stone flooring and placed it in the corner where it still sat, that the hole had been dug by him, that Dan had met his violent death here in this narrow, dank cell.

Seeing her from the corner of his eye, Adam snapped, "What are you doing here?"

Anita ignored the harsh tone of Adam's voice. "I've come to be with you."

"I don't want your company. Go away!"

"No, I won't leave," Anita answered firmly. "It's not good to mourn alone. Nor is it good to brood on your brother's death. Brooding won't bring him back."

"No, but it can serve to remind me why I'm here," Adam said with an ugly snarl. "To kill *Mexicans!*"

Anita flinched at Adam's hard words, but she refused to run from his hate and anger. She could feel it in him, the two black emotions, roiling inside where there was no escape, no release. An intense urge to go to him and take him in her arms to comfort him rose in her, a need that was so powerful it was a physical ache deep within her. But Anita knew better. Adam would never allow her to show him compassion, much less her love. So she stood and patiently waited, ignoring the bone-chilling, damp air, the rank stench, the rustling of what she knew must be rats in the dark shadows.

Finally, after an hour, she bent and touched Adam's shoulder, saying gently, "Come. It's growing late. Buck will be worried about us."

To her surprise, Adam didn't argue. He rose and

349

walked from the cell without a word, or a glance in her direction.

Anita followed him up the slimy stairs and out of the castle, mounted and rode behind him through the cold night to their lodgings, feeling the burden of his sorrow as her own.

Adam didn't dine with Buck and Anita that night. Instead, he retired to his and Anita's bedroom as soon as he returned from the castle. When the dishes were dried and put away, Anita went to him, a look of purpose on her face.

Lying on his back in the bed and covered with a blanket to his chest, Adam glared at Anita as she walked in and softly closed the door behind her. When she started to undress, he turned on his side, deliberately and coldly turning his back on her.

Anita hesitated, then strengthened her resolve to comfort him and finished undressing, slipping beneath the covers and pressing her soft curves against Adam's back, while her arm folded around his waist. Adam felt contact of their naked flesh like a branding iron.

He shoved Anita's arm away and spat, "Not tonight! I'm not in the mood."

"Then I'll put you in the mood," Anita replied, undaunted, her husky voice throbbing with sensual promise as her arm snaked around Adam's hip and she fondled him intimately.

Adam sucked in his breath sharply, then hissed,

"Dammit, Anita, there's a time and a place for everything! And lust has no place in what I'm feeling tonight. Now, cut it out!" Viciously, he shoved her hand away.

Suddenly Adam found himself rolled to his back and Anita lying half over him. She looked down at his surprised face and said, "You are wrong, Adam. This is what you need. Trust me."

"A *Mexican?*" Adam scoffed. "I'd sooner trust—"

Adam's words were cut off as Anita bent and kissed him, her small tongue plunging into his mouth and swirling around his. The hunger for Anita that always lay just beneath the surface came to the fore. Adam struggled to push it down, trying to jerk his mouth away. But Anita would have none of that. She held his head firmly in her small hands, her tongue darting in and out, ravishing and arousing in an endless passionate kiss that destroyed Adam's resistance and drugged his senses.

While he was still spinning in a mindless daze, Anita broke the kiss, raining torrid kisses over his face, tongue dancing down the pounding pulse in his throat, then mouthing and nipping his broad shoulders. At the feel of her artful tongue licking the flat nipple on his chest, then gently grazing it with her teeth, Adam gasped as he felt a bolt of fire shoot to his loins. He reached for her, but Anita eluded his grasp, slipping lower.

Following the line of dark hair down his taut abdomen, Anita stopped to pay homage at his navel, her tongue dipping in and out like a fiery dart, then circling lazily before continuing her arousing exploration. Anita's hands brushed across Adam's groin, tantalizingly close to that throbbing part of him that ached for her touch, to stroke the insides of his thighs. Then the powerful muscles there quivered as Anita placed love bites over them, her tongue soothing the tiny stings.

Reaching for his rigid manhood, Anita stroked the hot, velvety skin, feeling him growing even larger and hotter under her ministrations. "See," she whispered huskily, "you are alive. I won't let you bury yourself with your brother. Graves are for the dead."

The mention of his brother was like a dash of ice water on Adam's heated senses. He tensed, reason flooding back, and then gasped as Anita lowered her head and placed featherlike kisses over his turgid flesh.

Adam was both shocked at Anita's bold, surprising action and furious with himself for his weakness. He reached for her head, his hands tangling in her long dark hair that fell over her face and his groin like a black satin curtain. But Adam discovered he didn't have the strength to stop her. The feel of her tongue tracing his hot length, dancing around him, swirling over the tip while her small hands stroked the twin sacs heavy with need left him helpless beneath her erotic assault.

"No!" he managed to choke out, but Anita ignored his protest, knowing it was false, for Adam's hands were now exerting a gentle downward pressure on her head, a silent, eloquent plea for her to continue now, a willing captive to her exciting lovemaking.

A red haze fell over Adam's eyes; a roaring filled his ears, he was feeling as he could no longer contain himself, that he would burst out of his skin. It was heaven; it was hell, this exquisite torture Anita was subjecting him to. And then, when she rose, straddling him and locking both knees firmly at his hips, slowly descending, taking him into her inch by inch in a sweet vise that seemed to squeeze the life from him, Adam did think he would explode. He clenched his fists and ground his teeth, his groan mingling with Anita's gasp of pleasure as she felt his immense maleness filling her.

As Anita began her movements, slow, languid, incredibly sensual, Adam gave up his passive role, his hands rushing over her silken thighs and hips, then rising to caress her breasts. When Anita's movements quickened, Adam countered them, his powerful thrusts deep and true, and Anita felt as if she had been impaled on a bolt of lightning. The tempo increased, Adam placing hot, greedy kisses and nipping her shoulders and breasts, then, with a snarl, pulling Anita's head down and kiss-

353

ing her, fiercely, demandingly. Riding that white-hot crest of passion, breaths gasping, hearts pounding, Adam held them at the summit, both trembling with intense anticipation, before they soared over in a shattering explosion that seemed to rip the heavens in two and shook the earth.

When reality finally returned for Adam, Anita was still lying over him limply, her dark head beside his on the pillow. The fury in Adam that Anita had buried beneath an onslaught of unbelievable erotic delights again rose to the surface, an anger that was aimed more at himself than her. Again, she had used his passion against him, wielded it like a weapon with her uninhibited lovemaking. Christ! Had she no shame? Was there nothing she wouldn't do to bring him to his knees?

Catching her shoulders, Adam raised her to glare in her face, asking in a hard, biting voice, "Where did you learn that?"

Anita was still dazed, her eyes still dulled in the aftermath of her explosive release. Adam shook her. "I asked you where did you learn that *puta's* trick?"

It was the hard, ugly accusation, and not the shaking, that brought Anita to her senses. The words hurt, deeper than Anita would ever admit. She had meant to give Adam a respite from his morbid brooding, to give him a release from the emotional turmoil within him, to soothe his tortured soul in a loving that would be as much an act of healing as a profound gift of love. She had been a fool to think that he would accept anything from her, and she would never admit to her true feelings. Her fierce pride demanded that much of her.

Fighting back the tears that stung at the back of her eyes, Anita rolled from Adam, staring at the crude timbers in the ceiling above her. Her seemingly cold withdrawal after her passionate love-making infuriated Adam even more.

He hovered over her. "I asked you a question."

Her dark eyes flashed before Anita answered, "I have treated delirious men. They rave about many things. They tell of their deepest desires, their hidden fantasies."

"*Mexican* men!" Adam said, his voice heavy with scorn.

"Men are the same the world over!" Anita snapped back. "Do you deny that you enjoyed what I did to you, that I pleased you?"

Adam wanted to deny it, but the words wouldn't come. Despite all his faults, he wasn't a hypocrite. He too, had sexual fantasies, but he would have never dreamed of asking a respectable woman to love him the way Anita had, for fear it would shock her sensibilities and leave her repulsed. Yet Anita had done it freely, with no reservations.

Without answering, Adam lay back down, his thoughts once again occupied with the enigma that was Anita. How could she give so freely, so openly, then retreat into her icy shell, offering him nothing, not even a glimpse of what lay within her?

Adam didn't realize it, but Anita had been successful in distracting him from his morbid preoccupation with his brother's death. He spent the better part of that night puzzling over Anita. And one question was foremost in his mind. Why had she done it? The next day, Adam made another visit to the castle. Again, Anita followed him, appearing at his side in the cold, damp bowels of the dungeon as suddenly and silently as she had done the day before.

Adam didn't ask her to leave, nor did he resent her presence, finding it somehow comforting, almost as if she were taking his grief upon herself, sharing the burden with him.

Finally becoming aware of her trembling in the cold, Adam turned and placed his arm around her small shoulders, leading her from the gloomy, dank cell. Anita didn't object. She sensed that they had finally put Dan's soul to rest that day. Now if she could only find a way to bring peace to Adam's tortured soul. *Dios!* It was not easy to love this savage *Tejano*. But, despite everything, she did.

Chapter 20

Three weeks after the battle of Cerro Gordo, Scott ordered General Worth to take Puebla, the next stop on the way to Mexico City. Since they had heard no news of Hays, Adam, Anita, and Buck again went ahead of the Army to gather what information they could.

Puebla was the second largest city in Mexico and sat in a valley surrounded by the Sierras, a city filled with church spires and domes, beautiful castles, theaters, universities, and even a convent. The fountain in the main plaza was particularly impressive, made from beautifully carved basaltic stone and surrounded by six full-size, carved statues of dogs and tigers with open mouths, from which the water spilled.

Anita found them quarters off the plaza, close enough to hear the tinkling of the water in the fountain in the still of the night, and the next day, they prowled the city, keeping their eyes and ears

357

open. It soon became obvious that Puebla would offer no more resistance to the Americans than Japala had. Santa Anna had already been there to demand more troops and supplies and to exhort the people of Puebla to protect their city from the invaders. He had been firmly repulsed. The populace had no desire to fight for Santa Anna and hated him even more than they feared the Americans. A few days later, Worth's army marched into Puebla amongst blaring bands and flying pennants and settled down and waited for the rest of Scott's army to appear.

Again the delay played on Adam's and Buck's nerves, and one day Buck asked his friend in a disgruntled voice, "Well? What are we gonna do? Sit around here until the spiders weave cobwebs on us? Hell, Santa Anna is probably in Mexico City by now."

"I've been doing some thinking about that," Adam admitted. "Worth isn't going anywhere, not without Scott. The next stop is Mexico City itself, and Scott isn't going to attempt to take the capital until the rest of his army shows up. How about us going back to Japala and seeing if Hays has arrived yet?"

Buck perked up like a dog who had just heard the word "bone." "Sounds good to me."

"It may be a waste of time," Adam warned.

"Hell, anything is better than sitting around here and twiddling our thumbs."

The three left Puebla the next day, but they

never reached Japala. Passing through the gloomy mountaintop town of Perote, Adam spied a head of fiery red hair that could only belong to one man. Sam Walker.

After the three Rangers had greeted each other with handshakes and a lot of back-slapping, Walker stepped back and asked, "What are you two doing down here?"

"It's a long story," Adam answered, then proceeded to tell his old friend everything that had happened to him and Buck since Monterrey. The captain listened, both amazed and a little envious that the two had managed to take part in Taylor's last victory, Buena Vista, and Scott's first, Cerro Gordo. "So we decided to leave Pueblo and go to Japala to see if Hays has arrived yet," Adam finished.

"Well, you can save yourselves a trip," Walker replied. "We docked in Veracruz less than a month ago. Hays wasn't with us, nor was he at Japala."

Adam shook his head in bewilderment. For all practical purposes, Hays and his Rangers seemed to have disappeared off the face of the earth.

Walker's blue eyes twinkled. "Why don't you boys ride along with me until Hays shows up?"

Adam eyed Walker's navy blue, army uniform, a wary expression on his face. Seeing his look, Walker laughed. "Don't let the uniform fool you. We may be technically classified as regular army, and I may have a few new recruits in my command, but my tactics haven't changed. Me and my boys still operate like Texas Rangers."

"What about your commanding officer? Won't he have something to say about two civilians riding with you?" Adam asked.

"The Army leaves me pretty much alone. I've been assigned the job of keeping the road open between Japala and Perote, a task the Army can't handle. They're used to fighting an enemy that stands still. All this hit and run, hit and run has got them chasing around in circles like a hound dog chasing a flea on his tail. They don't care how I do it, just as long as I keep the guerrillas out of their hair."

"Then you won't be going with Scott on his campaign to Mexico City?" Buck asked.

"I'm afraid not," Walker answered, a hint of disappointment in his voice. Then he brightened, saying, "But fighting these guerrillas is just the kind of action we Rangers are used to. The only difference is they're hiding in the mountains and jungles, instead of the chaparral. So what do you say, boys? You want to ride along with me for a while? I've only seventy men in my company, so I could sure use you. Scott is moving his headquarters to Puebla in a couple of days, but he's not going anywhere, not until the rest of his men show up, and that might take months. Right now, the only action going on down here is against these guerrillas, and I'm running that show."

Neither Adam or Buck needed any further urging. "All right, Sam," Adam answered, "we'll ride with you until Hays either shows up or Scott marches on Mexico City."

"Then you won't stay with me, even if Hays doesn't arrive on the scene?" Walker asked in surprise.

"No. Buck can if he wants to, but I'm going with Scott."

"Why? You can kill just as many Mexicans here as in Mexico City."

Adam had come to Mexico to do just that, kill Mexicans. But somewhere along the line, seeing Santa Anna destroyed had become his top priority. It was almost as if Anita had infected him with her obsession. Adam glanced at Anita, waiting patiently on her horse a distance away, then said, "I want to be there when Scott defeats Santa Anna. It's a promise I made myself and . . . someone else."

Walker assumed that someone was Adam's brother. Then, spying Anita in the distance, his eyes widened. A big grin spread across his handsome face and a teasing twinkle came to his eyes as he said, "I see you brought that beautiful little señorita with you."

Adam always stiffened when one of his Ranger friends noticed Anita. At first it had been because he was embarrassed at having a Mexican mistress and he was afraid they would taunt him about making one of the enemy his woman, but this time his stiff demeanor was one of protectiveness. "Yes, I did," he answered tightly, a warning look

361

in his eye. So help me God, Adam vowed silently, if Walker insults Anita in any way, I'll slug him.

Walker saw the warning gleam in Adam's eyes and assumed he was warning him away from the woman he had claimed for his own. He laughed heartily. "You didn't fool me one bit with that act you put on back in Monterrey. Despite all that talk about not being attracted to her, I could see you were smitten." Walker gazed back at Anita thoughtfully, then said, "But if you brought her over the Sierras with you, she must be as tough as she is beautiful."

"She is," Adam admitted freely, feeling a strange twinge of pride. The new emotion surprised him. He had always thought of Anita's toughness as a blemish on her femininity, a characteristic that frustrated him at every turn. For the first time, he was forced to admit that he had come to respect her strength, and yes, even to appreciate her exasperating stubbornness. How dull life would be if she agreed with everything he said, if she were meek and mild-mannered, if she cowered to him. Adam almost laughed out loud at the thought of Anita cowering. Not his fierce little game cock. She was afraid of no one, and Adam was glad for it.

Adam and Buck refused Walker's offer of lodgings within the castle, where the captain made his headquarters. Instead, Anita found another little rundown house in the town for them and performed her special magic in making it homey.

362

For the next month, Adam and Buck rode with Walker and his company, feeding the guerrillas, who fought under a flag bearing skull and bones and the words "no quarter," a dose of their own medicine. They brought back booty, captured Mexican horses, ammunition, and supplies, but no prisoners, a fact that shocked the Americans, who still didn't understand the grim rules of war that the Texans and Mexicans fought under.

But Anita understood. Since Buck's revelation of how Adam's brother and wife had died, she knew only too well the devil that rode Adam's back. She fervently wished it could be different between their people, just as she wished it could be different between her and Adam. It was something she held close to her heart, revealing nothing of her secret longing.

When Adam and Buck heard that the rest of Scott's army had arrived and that the American forces were pulling out of Puebla, they left Walker, and the three rejoined Worth's army, taking their place at the head of the troops and spying before them. Three days later, after crossing the continental divide, they topped the rise overlooking the Valley of Mexico. Here, ten thousand feet above sea level, they paused.

Adam had seen some sights in Mexico. With its thick jungles, towering mountain peaks, deep gorges, and narrow passes, Mexico was a land both mysterious and beautiful. Even its deserts in the northern part of the country had a certain rugged beauty about them. But nothing surpassed the sight he now gazed down on.

The Valley of Mexico was fifty miles long and thirty wide and sat like a bowl among the majestic Sierras. The land below them was covered with a fine, early-morning mist, but not thick enough that it prevented them from seeing the orange groves, the small lakes, the lush green marshland, the isolated villages scattered all across it. In the center of the valley lay the capital city, called La Ciudad de Mexico by the Mexicans. It was surrounded by huge walls, its lofty spires and domes towering above the walls and the mist and glittering in the brilliant sunlight.

Anita was the first to break the awed silence, her voice even huskier than usual. "Cortez may have stood on this very spot three centuries ago."

"Yes, he very well could have," Adam answered, wondering if the Spanish conquistador had been as awed as they at his first sight of Mexico City. Certainly he was as excited at reaching his goal, if not more so. "You know," Adam said thoughtfully, "it's said that history repeats itself. I believe it's true. Cortez burned his bridges behind him when he sank his fleet at Veracruz, and now Scott, following the same trail to Mexico City, is doing the same thing. He's completely abandoning his supply and communication lines, cutting himself off from the coast and escape, leaving his rear almost virtually unprotected. His army will have to live off the land and get their munitions from those they capture from the Mexicans."

"Yep, it took a lot of guts to do that," Buck commented.

"Yes, and undoubtedly, there will be those who will call his bold, decisive action foolhardy," Adam added.

"The world called Cortez a fool too," Anita pointed out, "and he persevered."

Yes, Adam thought, in the long annals of history, time and time again, the brave, bold men who had forged forward against impossible odds and had been called fools for their intrepid actions, had turned out to be the victors, the conquerors, the men of vision. Cortez had proved himself on this same spot. And he'd do everything in his power to see that Scott did the same.

The trio found lodgings in an isolated village near Mexico City. Adam and Buck scouted the area around the capital city while Anita questioned the villagers for information. That night, they sat in their little hut and exchanged what they had learned.

"The people here in the heart of Mexico are not like those in Perote or Puebla," Anita warned. "They have pledged their full support to Santa Anna. The fools think that he is their hero, their savior. Scott will meet with fierce opposition from both the people and the Army. Santa Anna has raised a force of thirty thousand men to defend

365

the city."

"Thirty thousand men?" Adam exclaimed. "Christ! The man's unbelievable. He never gives up, and he never tires."

"*Sí*, he is indefatigable, but *not* unbeatable."

"I don't know," Buck said in a doubtful voice. "Things aren't stacking up too good for Scott's army. The Mexicans have got us outnumbered three to one, and Santa Anna has the city fortified to the hilt. Every damned road leading into the capital is a series of strongholds."

"Well, I know one thing for sure," Adam said. "Scott can't attack from the east. That big hill that blocks the main road from Puebla is a fortress. If the Mexicans I overheard can be believed, there are more than thirty cannons and seven thousand of Santa Anna's best troops up there." Adam turned to Buck. "You scouted the south side of the city. Could Scott approach from that direction?"

"Hell, no. That whole area is nothing but marshland. His troops would be up to their knees in mud."

But the next day, Adam and Buck were stunned to learn that Scott had done just that, attacked through a sea of mud and that one of Scott's generals had gotten himself into a serious predicament and was trapped between two Mexican armies.

That night, in a small village about five miles east of San Geronimo where the Americans were

366

trapped, Adam, Anita, and Buck, who had taken refuge from a thunderstorm in an abandoned adobe hut, sat and talked before their fire made from dried corn husks.

Adam, who had just returned from a visit with General Worth, exploded. "Damn it all! I hope Santa Anna doesn't attack those troops at San Geronimo tonight. They're trapped out there, with no way to get back out."

Buck's head snapped up. "Did you say San Geronimo?"

"Yes, I did," Adam snapped irritably. "For Christ's sake, pay attention!"

"I *have* been paying attention, but you never mentioned San Geronimo. All I knew was those troops were stuck out there some place west of that lava field. And they ain't trapped. They can get out. That was one of the places I scouted when we first arrived. There's a ravine that leads from San Geronimo and curves around that hill Valencia and his army are on."

"Why in the hell didn't you tell *me* that?" Adam asked hotly, giving Buck an accusing glare.

"Because you never asked!" Buck snapped back. "Hell, did you expect me to tell you every little thing I saw when I was out scouting?"

Adam jumped to his feet. "Come on."

Buck struggled to get his big mass from the earthen floor where he had been sitting. "Where are we going? Back to Worth?"

"No, we haven't got time to get to him. You're

going to show me that ravine."

Anita watched as the two men rushed from the hut. Then the reed door slammed back open, and Adam stood in the doorway, glaring at her, the lightning flashing in the dark sky behind him making him look very fierce and dangerous.

He pointed his finger menacingly at her. "You stay put!"

Anita glared back.

"Dammit, Anita, I mean it! Don't you go taking off on your own like you did at Buena Vista."

The mask fell over Anita's face. "As you wish," she replied coldly. Then seeing the look of total exasperation on Adam's face, she relented. "I won't leave here. I promise. This is close enough for me."

When Adam and Buck reached the ravine thirty minutes later, Adam turned his horse westward, following it until it ended at the outskirts of the small village of San Geronimo. Because of the driving rain, the picket didn't see them until they were almost on top of him.

"Don't shoot!" Adam called. "We're Americans."

The picket peered through the sheet of water, then said, "You look like Mexicans to me."

"These are just our disguises. We spy on the Mexicans for General Worth."

An officer rushed from the darkness, asking in a brisk voice, "What's going on here?" Then seeing Adam and Buck, he asked the picket, "What are these two peons doing here?"

"They claim they're spies for General Worth, sir."

Both men stared suspiciously at Adam and Buck. "They don't believe us," Buck muttered.

"Show them your coonskin cap," Adam said loud enough for the two soldiers to hear.

Buck swept off his sombrero and proudly displayed his ratty cap. The soldiers' expressions turned from suspicious to amazed. "Now take us to your commanding officer," Adam said with authority. "We have important information for him."

The Texans were led to the Americans' headquarters that had been set up in the village church. Inside, the building was dimly lit, the candlelight flickering over the cracked adobe walls and the statue of the Madonna on the side altar, and smelled strongly of mold and incense. Before the picket could even open his mouth, Adam quickly identified himself and Buck to the commanding officer and told him about the ravine.

General Persifor Smith accepted their news with a calmness that marked him as the same breed of soldier as Taylor. "I thank you for your trouble, gentlemen, but I already know about the ravine. One of my soldiers discovered it a few hours ago. I intend to attack Valencia's rear at daylight."

Adam decided he liked the man's confident, decisive manner. "We'd like to go with you, sir."

Smith glanced at Adam's Mexican clothing. "My

men might mistake you for the enemy and shoot you."

"Do you have a couple of spare ponchos?" Adam asked.

Smith smiled at Adam's quick thinking. "I believe that can be arranged. I have several men who were wounded and will be staying behind. You can use their muskets, too, if you like."

Adam gave Buck an oblique glance, feeling as if he had just pulled off a great coup, and the giant grinned back at him.

That morning, before daybreak, Adam and Buck, along with General Smith's troops, caught the Mexican Army completely by surprise. Within seventeen minutes, the battle was over, and the Mexicans were fleeing. Then hundreds of the Mexicans turned from their ranks and came back to the Americans, falling on their knees and throwing their hands up in surrender. One fell before the young infantryman next to Adam, calling out frantically, *"No hay soldado! No hay soldado!"*

"What's he saying?" the young soldier asked Adam, his musket pointed at the Mexican's chest.

"He's telling you he's not even a soldier. He's one of those Indian conscripts that Santa Anna scraped up this past month. Before that, he probably never even held a gun in his hand."

"What should I do?" the infantryman asked, his face pale with indecision.

Adam wanted to say, "Kill him! He's a Mexican, isn't he?" but the words wouldn't come. The Indian was obviously terrified, his normally dark complexion ashen with fright, his limbs shaking. For the first time, Adam had an inkling of understanding of what Anita had been telling him all along. This poor wretch wasn't his enemy. He was nothing but cannon fodder, yet another of Santa Anna's victims.

Adam fought his own struggle with indecision. An officer rushed forward and saved him from having to make the choice. "Get that prisoner back to our lines, soldier."

As the soldier led the prisoner away, Buck strolled up to Adam. "I've just heard Santa Anna is pulling back to Churubusco and all of Scott's army is in pursuit."

"Including General Worth's?"

"Yep. What are we gonna do?"

"That's a stupid question. We'll stick to these guys like glue. They'll soon be in hot pursuit, too."

But before Smith's troops marched out, the general walked up to the two Rangers. "Thanks for the help, men, but I'm afraid you can't come with us from now on."

"Why not?" Adam asked in dismay.

"You're not army. If Scott knew I'd let you fight with my men here, he'd skin me alive. The only reason I did so was I was desperate for manpower."

"And you're not desperate now?" Adam asked bitterly.

"Not with all Scott's armies converging." The general paused, his eyes full of genuine regret. "I'm truly sorry to disappoint you. If it were up to me, I'd take you along without a moment's hesitation. I could use more sharpshooters like you. But General Scott is a stickler for regulations."

"Yeah, so I've heard," Adam answered glumly. "Well, thanks for letting us get in on what fighting we did."

The general turned and called an order for his men to move out. Adam and Buck stood by watching as the troops marched away, wishing with all their hearts and souls that they were going with them.

"Well, I guess we might as well go back to San Geronimo and pick up our horses," Buck said, when the troops disappeared from sight. "Anita is probably wondering what happened to us."

Anita, Adam thought. My God, he had completely forgotten about her! When she learned that Scott's army was marching on Churubusco, would she try to get closer to the city? Dammit, she'd better not move from that hut. She'd promised him. But that didn't make Adam feel any easier.

"Come on!" he said urgently. "Let's get back to that hut."

Buck stared at Adam in surprise as he took off at a dead run.

It turned out that Anita was still at the hut, much to Adam's relief. The three sat outside the mud hovel and listened to the continuous roll of the cannons in the distance and stared at the billowing black smoke rising in the sky. It was an agony for the two men who were accustomed to being in the thick of the fight, and Adam wondered how Anita could stand being so close and yet not close enough to know who was winning. His nerves were tied in knots.

It wasn't until that evening that word about the outcome of the battle arrived at the small village. Anita wandered over to the crowd of Mexicans chatting excitedly a distance away. When she walked back, Adam saw the deep scowl on her face as she passed by a fire. He knew that look could mean only one thing. His hopes for a victory were dashed to the ground.

When Anita stepped up to him and Buck, Adam forced the question from his lips. "We lost, didn't we?"

"No. The Americans won."

"We won?" Adam asked in surprise. "Then what in the hell are you looking so glum about?"

"Shh, keep your voice down," Anita warned, glancing quickly over her shoulder. "I could hardly look happy over a Mexican defeat in front of all those Mexicans. Step inside and I will tell you the details."

As soon as the reed door shut behind them, Anita said, "It was not an easy battle for your gringos to win. Churubusco was heavily fortified. For four hours, the battle ebbed and flowed, and your army was pinned down under a murderous fire coming from the San Patricio Battalion—"

"The San Patricio Battalion?" Buck interrupted in an angry voice. "I was hoping we'd wiped out those damned deserters at Buena Vista."

"I'm afraid not," Anita answered. "The gringos were dropping like flies beneath their fire. Then they managed to break free and take the bridge that crossed the river. Then they stormed the fortress. They won. It was a great victory. Santa Anna lost a fourth of his army, most taken prisoner."

"And Santa Anna?" Adam asked anxiously. "Did they capture him?"

"No, he got away," Anita answered bitterly. "The gringos captured eight of his generals, but *he* escaped."

The three stood in silence in the small mud hut, each brooding darkly.

Chapter 21

"Your General Scott is a fool!" Anita threw out angrily. "And your gringo peace negotiator, Nicholas Trist, is a blithering idiot! Now is the time to attack Santa Anna, to crush his might, once and for all. But what do you gringos do? Accept an armistice. Armistice, bah! It is only another of Santa Anna's tricks to gain time and strength. And Scott sits around doing nothing. Nothing! Stupid fool!"

Anita had been raving for over fifteen minutes, and Adam and Buck, and the better part of the American Army, heartily agreed with everything she said, and were angered with the delay. The truce had been a colossal mistake on the part of Scott, the majority of the troops considering it a betrayal to the men who had given their lives at Churubusco. Many of his officers had urged the general to at least move his forces into a commanding position and especially to occupy the heavily fortified Chapultepec Castle, but according to the terms of the armistice, both sides had promised not to improve their position, and Scott would not violate his pledge. While Adam agreed with Anita that Scott was a fool, he felt obligated to defend his fellow American.

Anita had read his mind, and before Adam could even open his mouth, she spat, "No! Do not tell me that was part of the agreement. You see how Santa Anna honors that agreement. While Scott sits around doing nothing, he is busy shoring up his defenses and bringing in more men. To make matters even worse, when Scott accepted the truce, Santa Anna made it appear as if the Americans had requested it, and not him. He has again convinced the Mexican people that he is their savior, and they are flowing to his side, so much so that some of the outlying provinces are threatening to secede if the Mexican congress accepts the peace terms. "Tears of rage shimmered in Anita's dark eyes. "Now, thousands more will die, both Mexicans and gringos. That slaughter could have been avoided if Scott had pressed on while he had the advantage. This war would have been over, once and for all. Now it will be a bloodbath for both our countrymen."

Anita rushed from the room, leaving Adam and Buck to brood over her dire prediction. Finally, Adam said, "Come on! Let's get out of here before she gets started again."

As they walked out the door, Buck grumbled, "I

don't know why she's blaming us. Hell, we ain't gringos. We're Texans. If Houston had been in command, we'd have taken Mexico City by now. He'd have seen right through Santa Anna."

"She isn't blaming us. Not personally. She's just frustrated and blowing off steam."

"Yeah, well she ain't any more frustrated than the American troops are. They're getting angrier and more sullen every day. If Scott don't do something quick, he's gonna have a rebellion on his hands."

The three had taken quarters in a little Mexican village close to where the American Army had bivouacked, and as Adam and Buck strolled through the camp, none of the soldiers paid any attention to them, despite their Mexican clothing. The Mexicans had agreed to sell supplies to the Americans as part of the armistice, and the camp was crowded with peons anxious to sell their fresh produce to the hungry troops.

The two men walked past a small stream where the soldiers were doing their laundry, many wandering around in their long johns while they waited for their uniforms to dry. Farther downstream, a group of soldiers napped under some trees in the distance, having decided to pass the time in oblivion while their laundry dried. Adam stopped and stared at the deserted, dripping-wet uniforms lying about on the bushes all about them, his look thoughtful.

377

"What are you staring at so hard?" Buck asked.

"Those uniforms." Adam looked at Buck. "It was the lack of uniforms that kept us from taking part in the battle of Churubusco, and I don't intend for it to happen again."

Buck's brow furrowed. "Are you suggesting we steal some uniforms?"

Adam grinned. "Why not? If we appeared on the scene, dressed in uniforms like ordinary soldiers, in the confusion of the battle the officer in charge there would only think that we'd gotten separated from our unit. And with all these Mexicans wandering around in this camp, the soldiers could never prove who stole them. I'm sure it's not the first thing that the Mexicans have helped themselves to."

Buck shot the napping soldiers in the distance a quick look. "Well, let's get a move on, before those boys wake up and catch us red-handed."

Finding a uniform for Adam proved to be no problem, but finding one that would fit Buck's gigantic size took some doing. They finally settled for a tunic that was a little tight in the shoulders and chest and a pair of pants that was a good six inches too short for Buck.

As the two slipped away in the bushes, grinning like two boys who had just swiped their mother's pie cooling on the windowsill, Adam said, "With those muskets and cartridge belts we picked up at San Geronimo, no one will even guess we're not

378

supposed to be there. And we can pick up a couple of forage caps anywhere. The soldiers are always laying them down and leaving them unattended."

"Not me," Buck responded firmly. "I ain't wearing one of those silly caps. I ain't going into battle without my lucky coonskin hat on."

In September, the peace talks had collapsed, and eleven days later, Worth's army attacked a *molino* where Scott had heard that Santa Anna had a secret foundry. To the dismay of both Adam and Buck, the Battle of Molino del Rey was over with before they even caught wind of an impending fight and turned out to be a total disaster for the Americans. True, they had taken the mill, but there was no foundry there. The entire story had been a rumor that Santa Anna had circulated to lure the Americans into a trap.

Despite the fact that the battle had been a disaster for the Americans, Adam and Buck smarted at having missed out on the action and were determined that they wouldn't miss the next battle. Hearing news that something big was brewing and that Scott was finally on the verge of attacking Mexico City, Adam paid a visit to General Worth on the pretext that he had important information for him.

When he returned to their quarters, Buck asked,

"What did you find out?"

"Scott is going to attack from the west. Tomorrow he'll start bombarding Chapultepec, but the attack won't come until the day after."

"Is Worth gonna lead the attack again?"

"No, General Pillow will, from Molino del Rey. Worth will be supporting him. After the castle has been taken, Worth is to lead the main assault against the Garita de San Cosme."

"There're two western gates," Buck pointed out. "What about the other one?"

"Quitman and his Marines are to make a feint on it, but the real thrust will be by the San Cosme Causeway."

"Who will we be tagging along with? Worth and his men again?"

"To start with. Then we'll play it by ear."

Adam turned to Anita and asked, "What do you know about Chapultepec?"

"What most Mexicans do, I suppose," Anita answered with a shrug of her shoulders. "The rise itself, Chapultepec, means Grasshopper Hill in Aztec. The castle atop it was once a resort for Aztec princes. Then the Spanish used it as a summer castle. In recent years, it has served as Mexico's military academy."

"Then it's never been a fortress?" Adam asked in surprise.

"Not until now," Anita answered.

380

At midnight the following night, after the castle on Chapultepec had been bombarded by Scott's big cannons all day, Adam and Buck dressed in their stolen uniforms and left to join Worth's troops who were beginning their march to the *molino*. Shortly after the two men had left, Anita slipped from the adobe hut, saddled her horse, and rode off in search of a place from which she could watch the impending battle, driven by a conviction of her own. If the Americans were ever to crush Santa Anna's might, destroy his hold on the Mexican people, it would be today, and she wanted to witness it.

In the predawn light, she found a hill overlooking Molino del Rey that was the perfect spot. From that viewpoint, she could see not only the *molino* and the cypress park behind it, but Chapultepec and the castle that sat on its lofty height.

There were others on the hill besides Anita and the curious Mexicans who had come to see if the Americans would again bombard Chapultepec. At the top of the hill, beneath a scaffold, thirty men stood on mule carts with nooses around their necks and surrounded by American guards. Anita learned that the prisoners were part of the San Patricio Battalion that had been captured at the Battle of Churubusco and been sentenced to hang. Now they stood where they could watch the action of their former comrades-in-arms, their eyes locked on the flagpole at the top of the castle turret, each knowing that the raising of the Stars and Stripes in place of the Mexican flag there would signal their death. Then the officer in charge of the execution would order the carts driven forward, leaving the prisoners dangling from the scaffold.

Anita turned her back on the prisoners and their American guards. It was not her concern how the gringos dealt with their deserters. She had come here to watch the battle, not a hanging.

At dawn, the bombardment on the castle resumed, the heavy cannons thundering over and over and over. Anita could see where the balls were hitting the castle, gouging out huge holes in the old stone and cracking the walls. Many of the shells were falling in the park between the castle and the *molino,* tearing up the ancient cypress trees that grew there and setting them on fire.

A sadness invaded Anita as she watched the rampant destruction. The Americans were scarring a castle that had taken the Aztecs scores of years to laboriously build, a building that had retained its beauty through centuries of weathering, and were destroying the proud sentinels that had taken nature hundreds of years to grow. The park and the castle would never be the same.

Her eyes dropped to the line of stone buildings at El Molino del Rey. Remembering what Adam had said, she realized that he and Buck must be somewhere down there. A sudden, overpowering fear seized her, startling her. Only briefly after the battle at Buena Vista had she felt any concern for Adam, and that had quickly passed. She had always been supremely confident in his and Buck's ability to protect themselves in the most dangerous of situations. But now, standing on this hill where she would be able to see everything, the danger seemed so much more real. A lesser woman might have fled, but not Anita. She had goaded the two men into the position that they were now in, playing on their mutual hatred of Santa Anna. If they could endure the bloody struggle, then she could watch. It was the least she could do. She stood, rooted to the spot, her eyes anxiously glued to the scene below her.

The battle for possession of Chapultepec and the castle that sat on top of it turned out to be a fierce and bloody victory for the Americans, and Adam and Buck were very much a part of it, their disguises standing them in good steed. With the other Americans they rushed through the beautiful park to the castle under a blistering artillery barrage, climbed the storming ladders that were thrown against the castle's walls beneath a steady, murderous fire, leaped over the top of the walls to the terrace, and ran into the ancient building, their boots pounding ominously on the polished marble floors of the Halls of Montezuma.

Plunging into a large antechamber with bayonets poised for the kill, the two Rangers came to an abrupt halt, shocked by what they saw. They found no Mexican soldiers here, only the boy cadets, and the cadets were fighting like demons. They watched as one thirteen-year-old struggled to cock his musket and was run through with a bayonet by an American. The Marine who had stabbed the boy looked down at the bleeding form at his feet in horror, for the first time realizing that he had killed a boy, and not a soldier.

When it was over, only seconds later, five boys were dead, and the majority of the others wounded. In this antechamber there were no shouts of victory. The Americans present were appalled by what they had been forced to do, or had unknowingly done in the heat of the battle. They walked from the room silently, ashen-faced, some with tears in their eyes.

"Damnation!" Buck muttered in a voice choked with emotion. "They weren't nothing but kids, some of 'em no older than my boys. What in the hell were they doing here?"

Just more innocents to be used as cannon fodder for Santa Anna, Adam thought angrily. Infuriated, he turned. "Come on! This thing isn't over yet."

* * *

On the hill overlooking the battlefield, Anita wondered why the American flag had not gone up over the castle. The Mexican tricolor had come down long ago, and she had seen the Mexican soldiers rushing from the castle gates. Then, as the Stars and Stripes rose and fluttered in the thick cannon smoke hovering over the castle, she fell to her knees, silent tears streaming down her face. She cried in sorrow for the Mexican's defeat, for they were her people, in joy for the American's success, for Adam, the man she loved with her whole heart, and Buck, her dear friend, were among them, but mostly she cried in relief, for watching the bloody struggle had been an agony for her.

Anita heard an anguished sob and wondered if it had come from her or from one of the other Mexicans on the hill. Then, hearing the order, "Carts, forward," she knew that the sob had come from one of those doomed to die. With the sound of the carts' wheels creaking and rocks crunching in her ears, Anita rose and walked from the hill without a backward glance at the gruesome scene behind her. She had already witnessed one hanging, and *that* was enough horror to last her a lifetime.

Chapter 22

Adam and Buck didn't return to the small adobe house on the outskirts of the city where Anita waited until the next day when Mexico City had finally surrendered after Scott's armies had made a determined drive up the city's causeways and into the heart of the capital itself. To Anita, the two men looked like hell with their tattered, blood-stained uniforms caked with mud and the dark circles beneath their bloodshot eyes. But she had never been so glad to see anyone in her life. It was all she could do to keep from running over and hugging them, particularly the tall, lean *Tejano* who had battered at her defenses just as persistently as the Americans had those of Mexico City. For once, Anita's cool indifference slipped, and a fleeting look of immense relief passed over her beautiful face before she regained her usual stand-offish composure, a composure that still angered and frustrated Adam. But however brief it was, Adam had seen the expression. She cares about me, Adam thought in utter surprise. Really cares, despite the cold front she puts up. A warmth spread over him, his lagging spirits suddenly soaring.

Unaware of the emotional undercurrents flowing around him, Buck hung his head and said, "I'm sorry, Anita."

"For what, amigo?"

"For several things. First of all, I promised you we'd catch Santa Anna this time, but that sneak got away again. We let you down."

Anita was even more disappointed than Adam and Buck at Santa Anna's escape. The general seemed to lead a charmed life. His troops could fall all around him by the thousands, and yet he always walked away totally unscathed. Anita wondered what powerful god protected him. Certainly not the one she prayed to.

Aware of Buck anxiously awaiting her answer, she said, "It couldn't be helped."

But the look of utter misery on Buck's face did not disappear, as she had expected. The giant shuffled his big feet, then muttered, "There's more. And this time you ain't gonna forgive us. There were cadets at Chapultepec. They were just boys. Some of them were killed in the fighting," Buck's eyes rose to meet Anita's. "We didn't know they were there," he said in an anguished voice.

"Honest to God, we didn't!"

"*Sí,* I have heard," Anita replied sadly. "Already my people have immortalized them. They are calling them *los Niños Heroicos,* the heroic children. The boys had been ordered to leave Chapultepec by their commandant, but they refused to go."

Adam was surprised by this bit of information. "Then Santa Anna wasn't using them for cannon fodder?"

"No, this time we can't blame him. Nor can the Mexican people truly blame the gringos for their death. If anything, the burden of guilt rests on Mexico herself. My country has always been strongly militaristic, making heroes of its soldiers and giving them undue power. The children, particularly the poor and middle class, see this. For them, a military career is their only escape from drudgery, their only means to attain wealth and power, even recognition. There is something wrong in a country where these things can only be achieved by being born into them, or gained by the deaths of others."

Adam and Buck retired to their rooms with these profound, sobering words still ringing in their ears. When they emerged fifteen minutes later, they were dressed in their Mexican disguises.

"We're riding into Mexico City to watch the proceedings," Adam said "Do you want to come along?"

Anita had forced herself to watch the battle, but

388

to view the capital city's official surrender was more than she could bear. "No. I will stay here."

Adam wasn't surprised. He knew that Anita was torn between her love for her country and her belief that its only hope lay in the defeat of its leader and its army. The strong urge to take her in his arms and comfort her rose in Adam, but there was nothing in Anita's demeanor that showed him she would welcome, or even tolerate, his compassion. She had again stepped behind her icy wall. Frustrated, Adam turned and walked from the room.

A few minutes later, as he and Buck rode toward the city, Buck asked, "Are we going back to Texas now?"

"The war isn't over yet, Buck. Just the capital surrendered, not the country."

"Yeah, but there will be peace talks. Ain't that why Polk sent that peace commissioner down here, to talk peace?"

"And who is Trist going to talk to?" Adam countered. "Santa Anna abdicated when he pulled out of the capital. There isn't a Mexican president right now. The only position that Santa Anna retained was chief of the army, and he'll never surrender as long as he has an army at his disposal."

"What about the Mexican congress?"

"They don't have any power. Besides, they're divided on the issue themselves. You heard what

Anita said about the outlying provinces threatening to secede if the government made peace. No, without a leader, the Mexican government has collapsed into chaos. No one has the authority to talk peace."

"Then what are we gonna do?" Buck asked irritably. "Sit around here in Mexico City and twiddle our thumbs again?"

"No, the fighting is over here. I was thinking that we'd rest up for a while and then go back down to Perote and see if Walker has heard anything from Hays. If not, we'll just tag along with him until the end of the war."

"Well, if we're going back to Perote, we'd better bypass Puebla. Last I heard those bandits and guerrillas that moved in when Scott pulled out have the city practically under siege."

"I imagine Scott will send someone to remedy that, now that the fighting is over with here."

Chapter 23

A week later, Adam, Buck, and Anita rode out of Mexico City and through the pass that overlooked the lush Valley of Mexico, the two men still wearing their Mexican disguises, since the mountains were filled with guerrillas. They gave Puebla a wide berth, following a narrow, twisted mountain trail around it. In the distance boomed the thundering of cannons.

Hearing the noise, Adam said, "Now I think I know where Santa Anna disappeared to. Listen to those cannons. That's heavy artillery, not the kind of light stuff the guerrillas drag around with them."

"You mean you think Santa Anna and his army have joined the guerrillas at Puebla?" Buck asked.

Adam cocked his head, listening as yet another cannon roared, the sound reverberating through the mountains. "I'd stake my life on it. Puebla is under full siege."

When they rode into Perote six days later, Buck looked at the gray walls of the grim fortress in the distance and the perpetually blowing sand, saying in disgust, "Of all the scenic towns in Mexico, you'd think Walker could pick a better place than this gloomy spot for his headquarters."

"Walker didn't pick it," Adam answered. "The Army did. He's a regular now, remember?"

"Yeah, now that you mention it, I reckon this would be the last place Sam would pick. That castle has gotta have bad memories for him."

Suddenly realizing what he had said, Buck sliced Adam a sharp look to see his reaction, remembering that the castle had bad memories for him, too. But to Buck's relief, Adam never even glanced at the prison where his brother had died.

The trio discovered that the house they had occupied before was still vacant and promptly moved in, Anita seeing to things almost as soon as she walked through the door. Adam and Buck quickly changed into their regular clothes, and when he emerged from their bedroom, Adam handed Anita the Mexican garments. "Burn these. I'm through with sneaking around disguised as a Mexican."

"Me, too," Buck said, coming from his bedroom. "They make me feel like I was running around in my nightshirt. Felt downright indecent sometimes." He yanked his coonskin hat further down on his head, adding, "And that damned sombrero practically ruined my cap. Got it all bent out of shape."

As far as Adam could tell, the floppy cap had never had any shape, although there did seem to be a few more kinks in its ratty tail.

"You might hang on to these serapes though," Buck said as he handed his clothes to Anita. "With winter coming on, they might come in handy."

"*Sí*, I will keep the serapes for you to wear, on one condition."

"What's that?" Buck asked.

Anita shot Buck's filthy cap a quick look, then answered. "That you turn it over to me to be washed — regularly."

As the two men walked from the house, Buck frowned. "What do you suppose she meant by that?"

"I haven't the foggiest idea," Adam lied adroitly.

They found Walker in his room at the barracks in the fortress. As soon as the three men had greeted each other and sat down, Walker said, "Well, tell me about it."

Adam related his and Buck's adventures since they had last seen the captain, with Buck adding a tidbit here and there. Again, Walker listened a little enviously. When Adam had finished, he asked, "What's been going on here?"

"Not much. All we've had with the guerrillas are

a few skirmishes."

"Have you heard any news about Hays?" Buck asked.

"Not a word."

"Hell, he must not be coming after all," Buck muttered in disgust.

"Is that offer to tag along with you still open?" Adam asked the captain.

Walker beamed. "Sure is. Me and the boys would be glad to have you."

A little over a week later, Adam heard a knock on the door. Opening it, he saw Walker standing there in the dark, grinning from ear to ear in the light cast by the open door.

"Didn't think this could wait until tomorrow," Walker said, his blue eyes twinkling. "I have a surprise for you." He stepped aside, revealing the slight figure of Colonel Hays.

"Jack!" Adam exclaimed, taking the colonel's offered hand. "You finally made it!"

"Damn, I'm glad to see you," Buck said, rushing up and clapping the colonel on the back so hard he almost knocked the smaller man down.

"I'm glad to see you boys made it, too," Hays answered, wincing as Buck gave him another hearty clap on the back.

"It's just like old times, huh, boys?" Walker asked. "And I brought along a little something for the celebration." Walker held up a bottle. "Some honest-to-God Kentucky bourbon. Of course, Jack here will have to settle for water, since he's a teetotaler."

Adam, Buck, and Walker settled down with their drinks at the kitchen table, while Hays sat and sipped a cup of hot tea that Anita had thoughtfully provided for him.

"Where in the hell have you been?" Buck asked Hays before the colonel could even raise the cup to his lips.

Hays chuckled at Buck's direct approach. "Believe it or not, I landed back up with Taylor. The Army sent me back to northern Mexico to put down the guerrillas that were harassing him."

"Was McCulloch still there?" Adam asked.

"No, shortly after the battle at Buena Vista, he resigned and went home. Texas gave him a real hero's welcome."

"How did you manage to get down here, if you were assigned to Taylor?" Adam asked.

"When Polk heard of the problem Scott was having with the guerrillas, he ordered me and the boys down here."

"How about that, boys?" Walker said, obviously proud of his friend. "By express command of the President himself."

Hays blushed modestly, making him look even more boyish, and continued with his story, "So we marched out and boarded our transports at Brazos

Santiago." Hays paused, then said, "That was a voyage I wouldn't care to repeat."

"You couldn't take being cooped up, either," Adam surmised.

"That was part of it," Hays admitted. "We Rangers are landsmen, and the boys got restless. A few got into fistfights with the sailors. Then some of them were just plain curious. They'd never been on a ship before and got to poking their noses around in places they shouldn't have, and the captains complained. And then there was that problem with our horses. The sailors resented having to take care of them and started mistreating them. But Rip Ford's horse put an end to that. He bit off an Irish sailor's ear, chewed it up, and swallowed it. From then on, the sailors treated our mounts with respect."

When the chuckles subsided, Buck asked, "Rip Ford? Who's he?"

"You and Adam don't know him. He's a frontier doctor who signed up with the Rangers for the first time at the beginning of the year. He was transferred to my staff as my regimental adjutant."

"Rip, did you say?" Adam asked. "Is that short for Ripley?"

"No, actually his first name is John. He's been keeping all the records and writing to the next of kin when a Ranger is killed. He signed the letters 'rest in peace,' but there got to be so many of them, he started putting down R.I.P. instead. Now the boys just call him Rip. He's a good man. You'll like him."

Hays frowned. "There's a lot of new boys in this group. Oh, some of the old, hard-core Rangers came along, but I had to meet my quota of five hundred men, so some of them are adventurers and a little hotheaded. They're fighters, but . . . well, they're unpredictable and a little hard to handle. When we docked at Veracruz, General Robertson, the commander there, sent us to Vergara, south of Japala. God, you've never seen such a hellhole. The wind blew constantly, stirring up the sand and blowing our tents away, making it impossible to eat. The boys got pretty restless and disgusted at not seeing action, and started taking potshots at things. There was another regiment there from Robertson's 9th Massachusetts Infantry. I guess they'd heard about the fights with the sailors on board ship and got a little nervous when the boys started shooting up things. They sent over a half of a keg of whiskey as a peace offering. That was a long, miserable month for all of us. I was glad when General Lane arrived and we finally got out of there."

Adam's brow creased. "Lane? I don't believe I've heard of him."

"General Jo Lane. He's my commander, and the first army officer I've served under who understands us Rangers and appreciates our talents. Our division is on the way to Puebla to raise the siege." Jack's black eyes gleamed with anticipation. "And catch Santa Anna if we can."

From the corner of his eye, Adam saw Anita come to sudden attention, her dark eyes lighting up as if a candle had been lit behind them.

"And guess what?" Walker said. "Me and my boys are going along. General Lane is taking us into his command. Now, all of the Rangers will be riding together again."

"You *are* still joining up with me, aren't you, boys?" Hays asked Adam and Buck.

Adam was glad Walker would be in the same division. That way, he wouldn't have to choose which of his friends to ride with. "That's what we came down here for."

The next day, Adam and Buck were mustered into Hays's regiment of Texas Rangers. That night, Anita informed Adam that she would wait wherever the Rangers were making their headquarters at the time, that she no longer wanted to be close enough to the battles to hear the cannons. Not knowing that Anita had witnessed the battle at Chapultepec and had agonized over it, Adam wondered at her change of heart, but he was so relieved that he wouldn't have to worry about her sneaking off on her own that he never questioned her decision.

* * *

Several days later, Adam and Buck, along with their brother Rangers and General Lane's division pulled out of Perote for Huamantla where Lane had learned Santa Anna had stored a large amount of guns and ammunition.

Because of his familiarity with the surrounding territory, Walker and his company led the column, and when Walker saw a column of Mexican lancers riding out of the town a few miles from Huamantla, the sight was too much of a temptation for him, and he and his men charged, leaving the Rangers and the rest of Lane's troops behind.

Buck had seen Walker's company dashing away from where Hays's Rangers rode in the middle of the column. "Dammit, there goes Sam!" Turning in his saddle, he said to Adam, "Ain't that just like him? He's just gotta be the first into every fight."

"Well, I hope he leaves some Mexicans for us," Adam replied a little testily.

Because they were slowed up by Lane's foot soldiers, it was almost forty-five minutes before Hays's Rangers rode into the town. The battle was going hot and heavy; dead littered the ground everywhere. Adam and Buck joined in the furious fight, firing their pistols, then slashing with their sabers. Seeing a column of lancers fleeing, led by a man who looked suspiciously like Santa Anna, Adam, Buck, and several of the other Rangers dashed after them. After chasing the Mexicans for several miles over a tortuous mountain trail, the Rangers were forced to give up the chase and turn around. By the time they rode back into Huamantla, the battle was over.

Adam noticed the silence first. A quiet after the battle with its loud noises was to be expected, but this silence was eerie and hung over the city square like a heavy cloak. He reined in and looked about him. Peering through the thick gunsmoke still floating in the air, he saw a crowd of soldiers and Rangers in front of a church across the plaza from him.

"What's going on over there?" he asked an infantryman who was getting a drink of water from the fountain beside him.

"Someone named Sam Walker got hit in that churchyard over there."

"Dammit," Buck said, "unlucky Walker has gone and got himself wounded again."

The two men swung from their horses and hurried across the plaza, sidestepping the lifeless bodies that lay there, and the medics bent over the wounded. A frightened, riderless horse galloped wildly through the square, the clattering of its hooves sounding inordinately loud in the strange hush. Adam and Buck jumped aside to keep from being trampled, muttering curses.

When they reached the crush of men outside the walled courtyard, Adam and Buck shouldered their way through and walked through the arched gate. Seeing that the church courtyard was filled with men, all grim-lipped and ominously silent, a feeling of dread crept over Adam. Recognizing the two Rangers as personal friends of Walker, the men stepped aside, clearing a path for Adam and Buck.

Adam came to a dead halt when he saw Walker. The young captain was lying facedown near one of the walls in a pool of blood. Unlucky Walker's luck had finally run out. The brave, bold Ranger was dead, shot in the chest and the back of the head.

With legs that felt as heavy as lead, Adam walked to his friend and dropped to his knees beside Walker's body. Gently, he rolled the captain over. The same blue eyes that Adam had seen flashing with anger, smoldering with hate, and twinkling with mischief in the past, now stared lifelessly up at him. Adam passed one hand over those eyes, closing the lids for the last time, then sat on the ground and slipped his arms around Walker's shoulders, holding his limp body against his chest.

Numb and dazed, Adam sat in the dust and held his dead friend, oblivious to the Rangers weeping openly all around him, to Hays, standing tight-lipped and misty-eyed a short distance away, to Buck, towering over them like a giant sentinel, his face ashen and drawn with grief.

Again the crowd parted, clearing a path, and General Lane walked through it. For a moment, he stood and viewed the scene in silent shock. Then, enraged, he shouted to the troops, "Avenge Captain Walker's death! Make the Mexicans pay! Pillage the town! Take or destroy everything you can lay your hands on!"

The Rangers in the crowd needed no further urging. Revenge was foremost in their minds. "Let's kill the dirty bastards!" one of them yelled. "All of 'em!"

"Avenge Walker!" another shouted, and his cry was taken up by the others, soldiers and Rangers alike, ringing through the courtyard, then the plaza beyond.

Within minutes, the courtyard was emptied, Texans and Americans alike rushing through the gate and into the plaza like a shot out of a cannon, then spilling into the streets, yelling with rage. The Mexicans heard them coming. There was a bestial tone in those cries that brought terror to their hearts and spoke of doom. They ran for the safety of their homes, barring their doors and beseeching God to protect them.

Adam never knew how long he sat there in the dust of the courtyard holding Walker's lifeless body in his arms, deserted by all but Buck. Walker's blood drained from his body, drenching Adam's shirtfront and soaking his pants while Adam stared out with dazed eyes, his grief engulfing him and numbing him to everything. To Buck, the hour seemed like a lifetime as he listened to the fearful noises beyond the walls: wood splintering, terrified screams, glass shattering, pistol shots, cries of pain, howls of anger. But what was even more frightening to Buck was Adam. He was almost as still and lifeless as Walker.

Slowly, ever so slowly, Adam's grief was replaced with rage. Like a living thing, it grew within him, spreading, feeding off his previous hate until he was no longer able to contain it. Then it burst loose in a spine-tingling, bloodcurdling cry that came from the depths of his anguished soul.

When the unholy cry of rage rent the silence in the courtyard, Buck jumped in fright. Then, as Adam laid Walker down and rose to his feet, Buck's blood ran cold at the murderous look on Adam's face. Adam walked from the courtyard, his stride coldly deliberate, his eyes glittering with hate, his pistols drawn. Buck followed, terrified that Walker's death had pushed Adam over the fine line that separated the sane from the insane.

Like a wild animal stalking its prey, Adam walked from the courtyard and into the first building he saw. Inside, he stopped to look around, seeing the soldiers smashing the furniture, ripping down the draperies, slashing the upholstery with their bayonets, while others frantically searched the house for loot. But Adam wasn't interested in the wanton destruction of property or plunder. He was looking for Mexicans to kill, to kill to avenge the death of his brother, to kill to avenge the death of his wife, his unborn child, his comrades-in-arms who had fallen at Monterrey, at Buena Vista, at Churubusco, at Molino del Rey and Chapultepec, and his friend. He no longer thirsted for revenge. Every fiber of his being lusted for it, a lust that could only be satisfied by a violent blood-letting.

Hearing terrified screams from the floor above him, he bounded up the stairs, Buck close on his heels. Soldiers ran down the hallways, darting from room to room, many with their arms loaded with loot. Following the sounds of the screams, Adam entered a large bedroom, its battered, splintered door hanging by one hinge. In a corner, three soldiers were stripping the clothes from an old, gray-haired woman who fought back weakly, pleading for mercy. In the center of the room another group of soldiers were tearing the clothes from a young girl who was scratching and kicking, all the while screaming in terror.

Down went the naked girl, thrown to the floor so hard that it stunned her. The soldier closest to her pounced on her, straddling her legs, his hand fumbling with the buttons on his pants as he held her down with the other. As the soldier plunged in, ripping the tender, virginal flesh, the girl screamed in pain, the shrill, piercing sound bouncing off the walls.

Adam stood, paralyzed, his eyes locked on the girl's anguished face as the soldier raped her, the sounds of her hysterical sobbing, his animalistic grunting, the cheers of encouragement from the other soldiers ringing in his ears. His mind reeled dizzily as he was transported back into another time, another place. That was Beth being raped. Beth sobbing. Beth's tears streaming down her face. No, the skin was too dark to be his wife's. This was a Mexican woman. Nothing but a dirty Mexican. And then, as the girl opened her eyes, pain-filled eyes as black as ebony, he thought, It's Anita! The soldier was raping the woman he loved!

Another cry of rage was born in the depths of Adam's soul, rose, and burst from him, one even more horrible than the earlier one, drowning out the cheers of the soldiers around him and echoing off the walls. The hideous sound brought terror to the hearts of the spectators, and they stared wordlessly at the man who towered over the pair on the floor, his face twisted into an ugly snarl, his green eyes glittering with rage, his clothes soaked with blood, the living picture of a fierce, avenging god. Only the man raping the girl and the victim herself were unaware of the sudden silence, the frozen fear that filled the room. Oblivious in his lust, the soldier continued his frantic movements, grunting, his face reddened and contorted.

"Get off her!" Adam ground out between

405

clenched teeth. When there was no response to his command, Adam thundered, "I said get off her!", then clubbed the soldier with his pistol so viciously that it knocked the man from the girl. Lying in a heap at the girl's side, the soldier looked up with dazed eyes, blood trickling from the cut on his temple. Adam glared at the man. "You goddamned animal! I ought to blow you away!"

With his pistol pointed menacingly at him, the soldier feared Adam would do just that. Terrified, he struggled to his feet, stumbling in his haste, then tore from the room.

Adam whirled, aiming both of his pistols at the frozen spectators. "Get out! Get out before I kill every goddamned one of you!"

The soldiers were too terrified to move. One had lowered his pants in anticipation of his turn to rape the girl. The sight infuriated Adam even more. "Get out!" he roared, firing his pistol and splintering the floor at the man's feet.

The soldiers never stopped to consider that Adam's remaining pistol only held one shot, that if they rushed him, they could overpower him with their numbers, and even if they had, not one would have tried. They knew, to the man, that the tall Texan needed no weapons. As furious as he was, he could tear them apart with his bare hands. The shot only served to galvanize them. They turned and ran, shoving and pushing to get through the door, the half-naked soldier not even bothering to pull up his pants as he shuffled awkwardly behind them.

As Adam lifted his hand to fire his second pistol, Buck jumped forward, knocking his arm down. "Take it easy, Adam. You can't go around shooting soldiers. They're Americans!"

"They're animals!" Adam snarled back.

Adam turned, seeing that the old woman had crept to the girl's side and was cradling her limp body in her arms, rocking her and crooning, oblivious to her own nakedness and shame in her need to comfort the younger woman. Slipping his guns back into their holsters, Adam quickly crossed the room, yanked a spread from the bed, and placed it over the old woman's shoulders, covering both women. When the old woman looked up in surprise, Adam gazed down into her dark eyes, eyes that seemed to mirror the soul of the war-ravaged Mexican nation. Fear, anguish, bewilderment, sorrow, pain, he saw them all. Shame rose to the surface of his battered emotions.

I'm sorry, he wanted to say, but the words came out a strangled croak. Adam spun on his heels and hurried from the room, down the stairs, and out of the house, with Buck fast on his heels.

When Adam stepped back into the plaza, he saw what he hadn't noticed when he crossed the square fifteen minutes earlier, and it was a scene straight from hell. Soldiers and Rangers alike were breaking into stores and smashing the barred

407

doors of private homes, ransacking them and carrying the loot into the streets. What was judged valuable was set to the side, while the rest was thrown in a huge bonfire in the middle of the plaza: furniture, clothing, books, linens, mattresses, paintings, everything and anything that would burn. More than half of the men were drunk, having broken into the *cantinas* first and consumed every drop of liquor they could find, and these staggered around laughing, cheering, swearing, taking potshots at the buildings and trees, shouting threats at the terrified Mexicans whom they were chasing through the streets.

Adam looked across the plaza, seeing some soldiers carrying statues from the church and smashing them in the streets, while others brought out the pews and threw them on the fire. Even a crucifix was tossed in the flames. The old padre, trying to protest this outrage, was clubbed senseless, his blood added to those who had fallen earlier and littered the plaza, along with the dead, already bloated carcasses of the horses that had fallen in the battle.

Other Mexicans tried to protest this wanton destruction of their property. Like the priest, they were clubbed or run through with bayonets, while their women ran screaming through the streets fleeing from the men chasing them and bent on rape.

In the center of the plaza, four wagons of

captured ammunition sat. The Americans were swarming over the wagons, tossing the ammunition down to the soldiers below them, who smashed the guns against the cobblestones and the fountain and demolished the barrels of black gunpowder, strewing it over the streets.

"Come on!" Buck said in an urgent voice. "Let's get out of here before those idiots get the bright idea of setting those ammunition wagons on fire. Christ! They'll blow the whole town to bits, and them with it."

Adam didn't need any urging, He, too, wanted to get away. The wanton destruction, the brutality, the senseless beating and killing were making him sick to his stomach. Stripped of all restraint, these were no longer civilized men, or even human beings. Men without compassion, men without mercy, men without conscience, they had reverted back to their animalistic state, and there was nothing that he and Buck could do to stop the rampage. Once set into motion, it would have been as impossible as trying to stop the water flowing from a fractured dam with one's bare hands, or the tides of the ocean.

Adam and Buck shoved their way through the crowd in the plaza, stepping around the forgotten dead who had fallen in battle. It took some doing to find their mounts. Frightened by the smell of blood and the crazed troops, they had run off to one of the side streets. There they stood, wall-eyed and trembling.

Once mounted, the two men galloped into the countryside, taking a winding road into the mountains and leaving the horrible noises of the pillage of Huamantla behind them. Buck breathed in the pine-scented air, thinking the sweet smell a blessed relief after the nauseating odors of fresh blood, gunsmoke, fear and death. When they slowed to a canter, he turned in his saddle and looked back. The smoke from the bonfire rose ominously over the rooftops of the city, making a thin, twisting dark trail against the setting sun, a sun that was bloodred. Turning back, he glanced over at Adam. The tall Ranger stared straight ahead, sitting as still and stiff as death itself in his saddle.

When darkness fell, they camped off the side of the road, Adam performing his camp duties mechanically, ominously silent. He still had not spoken a word when the two men rolled up in their blankets to sleep, and Buck was worried sick, remembering Adam's strange stillness and silence after Walker's death, and the murderous rage that had followed. When Buck heard the troops from Huamantla marching down the road beside their camp, yelling and singing in their drunkenness, he tensed, fearing that it would trigger yet another eruptive rage in Adam, and Buck wasn't sure just who that anger would be aimed at. Nervously, he glanced to the side, seeing that Adam appeared unaware of the loud noises as he lay on his back and stared at the sky. Buck felt like he was sitting on a time bomb that might explode at any second.

Adam's emotions had taken a battering that day, assaulted from every side, but he wasn't on the verge of insanity, as Buck feared. He was silent and withdrawn because he was struggling to come to terms with three profound realities, truths that he had suddenly come face to face with.

The first was Walker's death. It seemed impossible that such a dynamic, vitally alive man could cease to exist in just a few short seconds, that he would never again talk across the campfire with his friend, ride beside him, share in his bold exploits, see his twinkling blue eyes, or hear his laughter, and yet he had closed Sam's eyes himself and held his lifeless body in his arms. Walker was dead, and nothing could bring him back to life. That was cold reality.

His love for Anita was real, too, a deep love that he could no longer deny. He had tried to fight his feelings for her, telling himself that he was betraying the memory of his beloved wife, but now he was forced to admit that his vow to avenge Beth's death had been motivated more by guilt than love. From the very beginning, their marriage had been strained. Beth had hated Texas, hated the frontier life with its hardships, its wild savages, its endless struggle with the Mexicans, its loneliness. She had begged him constantly to take her back to the safe, comfortable, gay social life

411

that she had left behind in South Carolina, but Adam had not wanted to give up his dream for a cattle empire, or the challenge it presented him. He had told himself that she was still a child, that as she matured, she would change. When she had been killed, he had been assailed with guilt, knowing if he had done as she had asked, she would still be alive. Now he realized that his vow to avenge her death had been to assuage that guilt, falsely rationalizing that if he killed her murderers and their kind, he could make it up to her. For the first time, he was forced to admit that their marriage had been a mistake, that Beth could have never been the wife he needed because she simply didn't have it in her. A frontier wife had to be strong, independent, capable of standing beside her husband when he was there, or carrying the burden when he wasn't. The dangerous Texas frontier was no place for the weak and fearful, and certainly no place for a petted, pampered princess. He needed a helpmate, and not a pretty ornament, a real woman, a woman like Anita. That, too, was truth.

But it was the third reality that Adam found the hardest to come to terms with, the violence and brutality that he had seen that day at Huamantla. He knew that looting, pillaging, rape, rampant destruction, and murder had always been an ugly part of war. Huamantla wasn't the first time that innocent civilians had suffered or been killed in cold blood, nor would it be the last. He could understand the Rangers' thirst for revenge. Like him, they had come into the war hating the Mexicans, with old scores to settle, and had known Walker personally, had grieved for his death. But Lane's soldiers had not known Walker and were newly arrived in Mexico. Before Huamantla, they had not fought in any major encounter with the enemy, had not seen their comrades-in-arms die at the hands of the enemy. They hadn't had time to develop the deep, abiding hatred for the Mexicans that the Rangers had, and yet they had been just as violent, just as brutal as the Rangers. What was their excuse?

Excuse? The thought hit Adam with the force of a physical blow. Was that all hate was? An excuse to revert to barbarism? Did the Rangers use it as a pretext to commit outrages against the Mexicans, as a cloak to hide their love of violence, their inherent brutality, their uninhibited fury, their bigotry? If that were true, then he was just as guilty. It was a shattering thought, one that Adam couldn't accept. No man, and certainly not one who claimed to be civilized, wanted to admit that there was a bit of a sadist, a bit of a barbarian, a bit of a devil in him.

Surely the Texan's vengeance was justified, he told himself. They had had outrages committed against them, too. Righteous wrath had its place in the world. Every civilization on earth punished those who had perpetrated crimes against their society. But Adam knew, deep in his heart, that his wrath wasn't justified, nor was the majority of his Ranger friends'. Like him, they hated all Mexicans, not just those who had committed crimes against them, and many times, innocent bystanders had suffered, just as they had suffered at Huamantla. Were they nothing but violent brutes, savages, as the Americans sometimes accused them of being?

Adam's soul-searching was causing him pain. Facing the ugly truth of oneself always hurt. He sank into a deep abyss of self-disgust and despair. Then he remembered the niggardly feeling of guilt he had felt while watching the bombardment of Veracruz, his hesitation in telling the soldier to kill the Mexican Indian trying to surrender at Contreras, his anger when he saw the dead and wounded cadets at Chapultepec. Those feelings had been his suppressed conscience crying out to be heard. Perhaps there was hope for his soul after all; perhaps some vestiges of the man he had once been lay deep within him. He had allowed his outrage over the murder of his loved ones and the killing of his friends to narcotize his conscience, to blind him to justice, to smother his compassion. Could he turn back? Or was he already too addicted to hate, violence, bigotry?

Long into the night, Adam struggled with these thoughts. By morning, he still had not found the answers. The shocking, shameful episode at Huamantla had lanced the deep, festering wound in his soul. The healing process had begun, but it would take time.

Chapter 24

The day after Huamantla, General Lane's troops, with the Texas Rangers in the lead, fought their way through the guerrilla-infested El Penal Pass to the American garrison at Puebla and, two days later, drove off the besiegers.

As soon as the siege had been lifted at Puebla and the Rangers had settled in, Adam went to Colonel Hays, announcing that he had come on personal business.

Hays sat behind his battered desk and motioned for Adam to have a chair across from him. "Personal business?" Hays asked with a frown. "I was hoping that you had come to accept that captaincy position I'd offered you."

Adam didn't want a captaincy, particularly now. To do so would make him responsible for his men's actions as well as his own, and Adam was still struggling to come to terms with his own injustices against the Mexican people, much less taking on the guilt of others. "I came to ask you if I could be excused from my duties for a few days. I'd like to go to Perote and bring Anita back here to our new headquarters."

Hays' frown deepened, and Adam guessed what the colonel was thinking. Since when did Rangers drag their mistresses around with them? "I intend to make her my wife," Adam announced.

Hays' head snapped up. "Your wife? You're going to marry her?"

Seeing the shocked expression on Hays' face, Adam stiffened. "Yes, I am," he replied in a terse voice.

"Perhaps . . . perhaps you should give the matter more thought," Hays said in a carefully guarded tone of voice.

"Why?" Adam snapped. "Is it inconceivable that I've fallen in love with a Mexican?"

Hays saw the angry glint in Adam's eyes and knew that the tall Texan was coming to the defense of the woman he loved. *Walk easy,* he warned himself. *You're treading on eggshells.* "Adam, I'm speaking to you as an old friend, not your commanding officer," Hays said quietly. "I can well understand why you're attracted to her. Anita is a beautiful woman and obviously well bred. Besides that, there must be something very special about her if she can demand such devotion from two hardened Mexican-haters like you and Buck. But marriage is a risky business, even under the best of circumstances. Stop and consider what life in Texas would be for her as your wife. I don't have to tell you how Texans feel about Mexicans and mixed marriages. She'd never be accepted. You'd both be ostracized."

Hays' words gave Adam pause. Would he be doing Anita as much a disservice as he had done Beth by taking her back to Texas with him? Then Adam remembered that Anita had always lived on the fringes of social acceptance due to the taint of her questionable paternity and her mother's suicide. There were many forms of prejudice. But Anita had risen above the snobbishness of her own class and continued with her life. No, he and Anita didn't need the approval of others, not as long as they had the support of a few loyal friends. And they would have that. They had Buck, and Adam felt certain that Buck's wife would accept Anita. Martha was an excellent judge of character and had exceptional insight. If his other friends ostracized him, so be it. It was the quality, not the quantity, of one's friends that counted.

"Anita is a strong woman," Adam informed Hays. "She has a way of overcoming obstacles. She'll break down those barriers of prejudice, and those friends of mine who persist in shunning us because of their bigotry would be no loss. They never deserved the title of friend in the first place."

Hays felt Adam's harsh words like a slap in the face. Adam had put the problem squarely on the line with his usage of the words "prejudice and bigotry," for they were attributes that no man wanted to be accused of, and yet Hays knew that he had been skirting the truth when he had evasively referred to the Texans' attitude as "feelings." He hoped that Adam didn't consider him one of those whose friendship would be no loss. He respected Adam, now even more so for the stand he was taking.

"Very well, Adam. I'm sure you know your own mind. I was only trying to point out something that I thought might not have occurred to you. Your request is granted."

"Thank you," Adam answered stiffly, then turned and walked toward the door.

"Adam?"

Adam pivoted and faced the colonel. "Yes?"

"I hope I'm not one of those who never deserved being called your friend."

"I hope so, too, Jack," Adam replied with all sincerity. "But I guess only time will answer that question."

Adam rode into Perote at dusk two days later. All through the trip, he had rehearsed his marriage proposal, painstakingly outlining all the reasons why he and Anita should be permanently united as if he was forming a battle plan, but he felt no more confident of her acceptance than he had in the beginning. The crux of the problem was that he wasn't sure of Anita's feelings for him. She hid everything behind that damned icy wall of hers. What if she scorned him? Adam didn't think he could bear that. He felt as vulnerable as a newborn lamb at the mercy of a fierce lionness.

After unsaddling his horse in the lean-to behind their small lodgings, Adam watered and fed the animal, taking more time than necessary, still struggling to get up the courage to face Anita. Finally admitting to himself that he was acting more like a timid schoolboy than a man who knew his own mind, he squared his shoulders and walked to the house, his nerves a tangled knot in the pit of his stomach.

Opening the door, Adam stepped into the dim room. Anita stood beside the cooking fire, stirring the contents of a pot hanging there, the firelight playing over her golden, exotic features. *She's even more beautiful than I remembered,* Adam thought, taking in the sight hungrily.

Finally realizing that Adam had entered the room, Anita turned and faced him. Adam had schooled himself to catch the fleeting looks that passed over Anita's face, lightning-quick expressions that betrayed her inner feeling before she could hide them behind her barrier of cool reserve. This time the fleeting look had been one of obvious pleasure, and Adam felt encouraged.

"The siege at Puebla has been lifted," Adam said. "I've come to move you there."

Anita peered around Adam. "Where's Buck?" Then as a sudden, horrible thought occurred to her, she paled. "He hasn't been wounded . . . or killed?"

"No, Buck's just fine. I came alone."

Anita thought it strange. As long as she had known them, the two men had been inseparable.

They ate in total silence, both uneasy, Adam still pondering over his task and Anita wondering how they would manage to get along without Buck to act as a buffer. Even more disturbing to Anita was her fear that she would be unable to hide her feelings for this half-savage, feelings that she constantly fought to suppress.

As soon as the dishes were washed and dried, Anita walked to their bedroom. Adam followed. When he saw her starting to remove her clothing, he knew the time had come. He had to ask now, before he got caught up in a whirlwind of passion and his senses were hopelessly dulled.

He reached up and stayed Anita's hand at the tie on her *camisa*. "No, don't undress yet. There's something I wanted to ask you."

Anita looked up in surprise, and Adam felt himself drowning in those velvety black eyes. He struggled against his rising passion, beating it back down with sheer will.

"What did you want to ask me?"

For a moment the words wouldn't come. Adam, the man who had faced hordes of Mexicans in battle, was frozen with fear before this small Mexican girl. When the words finally came, they came in a rush. "Will you marry me?"

Anita was stunned, speechless for the first time in her life.

Thinking that she hadn't heard him, Adam repeated, "Will you marry me?"

Anita's heart raced in her chest, and an immense happiness filled her. Then, remembering Adam's feelings for his wife, the feeling was replaced with hurt and anger. "Why do you ask me this, when you still love your wife?"

"Love my wife?" Adam asked in an incredulous voice. "What makes you think that?"

"You call for her in your sleep."

Adam flinched at Anita's words. The tone of her voice had been almost accusing, as if he had betrayed her by keeping his marriage a secret. He hadn't meant to deceive her by not mentioning his marriage. It was a part of his past, a past that was painful for him to talk about. Then, suddenly remembering something, he asked, "How did you know Beth was my wife, and not just some other woman?"

"Buck told me."

"Then you know how she died?"

"*Sí*, he told me everything. About your brother.

About your beloved wife."

Adam was relieved that his previous marriage was out in the open. Now, if he could admit to his true feelings for Beth just as openly. Taking Anita's hand, he led her to the bed. "Come over here. I want to tell you about my marriage."

When Anita was seated on the bed, Adam sat beside her. "Beth was my childhood sweetheart. I thought she was everything I wanted in a woman. She was beautiful, soft-spoken, and sweet-natured. But she hated Texas. She begged me to take her back to South Carolina, but I refused. Perhaps it was selfishness on my part, or just plain stupidity. I don't know which. But when she was killed, I was overwhelmed with guilt. That was my guilt crying out at night, not my love."

When Anita remained silent, Adam continued. "Beth was never the woman for me. I realize that now. She wasn't up to the hard life on the frontier. She had neither the physical strength nor the fortitude. She was nothing but a pretty bauble. She could have never been a true wife to me."

Anita sat bolt upright in the bed. "Ah! I see! You want me for your wife because I'm strong, because I have proven that I can survive under the harshest conditions. No! That's not enough. I'm a woman—not a workhorse!"

Adam had known it wasn't going to be easy, and now he knew that he had approached it all wrong. Carefully, he chose his words, "Anita, I don't want a workhorse. I want a woman. A real woman! A woman who's just as strong as she is beautiful. My love for Beth was immature, founded more on infatuation than anything else. I guess, in my own way, I was as much a child as she was. But I'm a grown man now. I'm ready for a mature love, a deep love, a lasting love. The kind of love I feel for you."

Ever since she had found her mother hanging from the rafters, Anita had been consumed with anger, not just anger at Santa Anna, who had betrayed her mother, but anger at her mother, who Anita felt had betrayed her. Anita had idolized her mother, giving all of the love in her little body to the woman who had given her birth. When her mother had committed suicide, Anita had felt the act as a rejection of her love. Her mother had abandoned her, weakly chosen the coward's way out, without once considering the terrible loss her death would be to her daughter. On that day, Anita had sworn never to give her love to another human being and never to be weak. She would offer compassion to others, but never her heart. Loving someone made you vulnerable to pain, to disappointment, to rejection. Carefully, over the years, she had built a protective shell around her, hardening herself to any deep emotions that might threaten her heart. Even when she had been forced to admit to her feelings for Adam, she had found refuge behind her wall, but now, hearing his unexpected, deeply moving vow of love, that shell cracked, the hard layers crumbling, then falling away as a tremendous torrent of deep emotion rushed to the surface and broke from her.

When Anita burst into sudden, violent tears, her small body shaking with soul-wrenching sobs, it had a devastating effect on Adam.

"Don't! Please don't cry!" he choked out, then crushed Anita to him, holding her tightly while she sobbed her anguished release from her self-imposed prison. Even after she had fallen into an exhausted sleep, Adam held her, afraid to let go or even loosen his grip. All along, he had wanted to break down her icy wall, had deliberately battered at it, but it had shattered so suddenly and so explosively that he feared it would destroy Anita. He held her to him fiercely, convinced that if he held her tightly enough, he could hold together the vestiges of her soul.

By morning, Anita had returned to her cool, reserved self, more from habit than from rebuilding any walls between them. Adam was relieved. This was the Anita he had come to love. If there was to be any warming, he preferred a gradual thawing, and not the flood of emotion that he had witnessed the night before. Her sudden outburst had shaken him to the depths of his soul.

At Adam's suggestion, they were married by

both a priest and the commanding officer at Perote, who served as the local magistrate for United States citizens, the former in respect for Anita's religious beliefs and the latter to assure himself that there would be no questions of legality when they returned to Texas. When Adam bent to sign the marriage certificate, he stared at the signature above his, surprised to learn that Anita's last name was de Vega. Strangely, he had never thought to ask. But then, not so strange, Adam thought with a smile. As Anita had so often said herself, she was "Anita," an identity so strong that she needed no supporting surname.

The two rode out of Perote an hour later, anxious to leave the grim, sandy town behind them. That evening, they made camp beneath a stand of fragrant pines, and as soon as they had finished eating, Anita washed the dishes while Adam spread the blanket that would serve as their bed on the ground.

Adam looked down at the worn blanket and wished he could offer Anita more. This was her wedding night. She deserved to sleep on a soft feather mattress with clean sheets in a real room and not in the open on the hard ground. Adam frowned, realizing that he had been much amiss in seeing to her comfort. He had dragged her back and forth across Mexico in his quest for revenge. No sooner had she set up living quarters for them than Adam had been on the move again, and she

426

had never complained. In truth, she had spent more time in the saddle than anywhere else. His eyes fell on the small wicket basket in which she kept her meager belongings, feeling yet another twinge of guilt. Not once had he thought to buy something personal for her, except for the plain gold wedding band, and that had been more of a necessity than any token of his love. Despite the fact that she seemed to prefer the peons' simple clothing, Adam knew she liked pretty things. That was evidenced in the attractive way she fixed up their lodgings. He could have at least bought her a pretty comb for her hair.

Adam was filled with self-disgust at the thoughtless way he had treated Anita. He fervently vowed that he would make it up to her when they got back to Texas. He'd surround her with pretty things, not necessarily costly, for Anita had shown him with her clever homemaking skills that things did not have to be expensive to be pleasing to the eye. But, by God, he'd see she had everything her heart desired.

He rose and gazed at her. Anita's back was turned to him as she dried the dishes. Adam walked up to her and slipped his arms around her waist, nuzzling her ear.

Anita jumped at his sudden appearance, almost dropping the tin plate in her hand.

"Leave the dishes for tonight," Adam whispered, kissing her throat just beneath her ear.

"But—"

"No," Adam interjected in a firm voice, "leave them. You shouldn't even be doing them. This is our wedding night."

A warmth suffused Anita at Adam's words, the feeling having nothing to do with passion. She could hardly believe that her dream had come true, that Adam loved her and she was actually his wife.

With his arms still around her, Adam took the plate and dishtowel from Anita's hand and tossed them down. Then he turned her in his arms and gazed down at her lovingly. "I love you," he said tenderly.

A lump came to Anita's throat and sudden tears came to her eyes. With a fierce will, she forced them back, afraid once they had started, she wouldn't be able to stop them, and she wanted nothing to ruin this very special night.

She slipped her arms around Adam's neck and said softly, "And I love you."

A tremendous feeling of happiness filled Adam. Although she had agreed to marry him, Anita had not told him she loved him. It seemed as if he had waited a lifetime for those words, and now, hearing them from her lips, he savored them, his joy so immense he feared he couldn't contain it. He wanted to shout his happiness to the world and jump up and down, clap and dance. Only with supreme will was he able to maintain his dignity. He bent his dark head.

His kiss was tender and so incredibly sweet that Anita feared the tears that were threatening would still spill over. When his tongue slid into her mouth, she leaned into him and kissed him back, their tongues touching, caressing, intertwining, speaking of love and not passion.

They undressed, their eyes locked as they stripped off their clothing and tossed it aside. Not even when they were completely bare, did either dare to look at the other's nakedness, for fear the sight would arouse their passion to a feverish pitch, and neither wanted that. By unspoken agreement, they wanted to savor their coming together, to draw it out and enjoy it to the fullest. This was their wedding night, and their joining would be more than a passionate coupling of their bodies. The act would be a beautiful expression of their love and the commitment for life that they had made each other.

Adam drew Anita to the blanket with him. They exchanged soft kisses, muttered love words, caressed, and fondled, each discovering the other's secrets as if it were the first time for them. And in essence, it was. With their mutual love out in the open, the act of loving had taken on a new, deeper meaning.

But despite their desire to keep their passion at bay, it was inevitable that with all of their intimate touching, their hunger for each other would come to the fore. Their passion was an integral part of their love, as impossible to separate from their deep feelings for each other as to sever their bodies from their souls. Adam's kisses became deeper, wilder, more demanding, his caresses more purposeful, and Anita felt her desire for him swell like a wave rushing to the shore.

She dropped her hand from where she had been stroking his shoulder and wrapped it around his hot arousal, glorying in Adam's hiss of pleasure as she sensually stroked his rigid length. Then she gasped as Adam slipped his hand between her thighs, his slender fingers gently delving into her warm moistness, while his thumb massaged the bud of her womanhood until he brought her to a shuddering release.

Not to be outdone in giving him pleasure, Anita relinquished her hold on him, slid down his body, and made love to him with her mouth, and Adam reveled in her erotic ministrations, his heart pounding, the blood racing through his veins like molten fire, his powerful muscles quivering, until he feared she would bring him to release.

He reached down and caught her head, pulling it up as he cried out in a hoarse, urgent voice, "No more!"

Seeing the distressed expression on her face, Adam knew that Anita thought he was scorning her boldness again. He smiled and said gently, "I love what you just did to me. I admit it excites me unbearably. But that's just it. It was exciting me too much. I want to be inside you."

Anita was vastly relieved. She wanted to be as free and open in her loving him as Adam was with her. And she, too, wanted him inside her. She wanted to feel his release deep within her, his life force spilling in her and scalding her as he filled her with his very essence. That was how it should be, how it was meant to be.

She smiled and went into his open arms. Adam kissed her long, deeply, and passionately, kissing her as if he were a part of her and seemingly branding her as his to the tips of her toes with his fierce possession. Then he rolled her to her back and positioned himself between her legs. Poised at the portal of her womanhood, so close that Anita could feel the hot, moist tip pressing against her softness, Adam bent and gazed deeply into her eyes. "Tell me you love me," he said in a voice thick with emotion, his warm breath fanning her face. "Say it again."

Anita felt as if she were being suffocated in that intense green gaze. *Dios,* how she loved him! Words could never express the deep emotions she felt, and yet that was what he had asked of her, just a simple affirmation of her love. She wrapped her arms around his neck, saying with a catch in her throat, "I love you. Words can't tell you how much. You are *mi amor,* my only love."

The pleased smile that came over Adam's face

431

tore at Anita's heart. He entered her then, with exquisite care and maddening slowness, savoring the feel of her soft, welcoming heat surrounding him, still staring deeply into her dark eyes. Then when he was buried deep inside her velvety sheath, he sighed deeply and folded his arms around her, relishing the feel of their union, their perfect oneness.

For a long while, they lay perfectly still, lost in the wonder of it, the beauty of it. Then Adam raised his head and dropped soft kisses over her face, down her throat, and across her collarbone. He began his slow, languid thrusts that were calculated to light a low, slumberous fire in Anita. Without breaking his sensual rhythm, he dropped his head to her breasts, ardently kissing and licking the soft, silky mounds before his lips closed over one throbbing nipple. At the feel of him tugging at her breast while he slid in and out of her, each stroke sending hot shivers of delight running through her, Anita's simmering passion broke through. Urgently, she locked her legs around his hips, drawing him deeper, glorying in his groan of pleasure. Then capturing his head in her small hands, she pulled it up, kissing him fiercely, telling him of her excruciating need.

Anita's urgency was infectious. The time for savoring their pleasure was past. Adam kissed her back, his tongue moving in and out in a sensual pattern that was in perfect unison with his plunges, harder, deeper, swifter. His sweet-savage assault on her senses drove Anita's passion to a feverish pitch. Her heels dug into the small of his back as she strained against him; her nails raked his shoulders. Hot waves of vibrant sensation flowed over her, filled her, became a living part of her. She was being consumed by fire. Her heart beat so rapidly and so hard she feared it would burst from her chest. She couldn't breathe and she couldn't think. The world spun dizzily on its axis, and a red haze fell over her eyes. An unbearable pressure was building in her, higher and higher as the time for release came closer and closer. Then the world ceased to exist and time stood still. There was only this breathtaking moment of intense anticipation.

Adam felt it coming, too. It swept through his body like wildfire, a tremendous, incredible surge of power that made him feel invincible, indestructible, immortal. For a split second, the top of his head felt as if it would be blown off before his release came in a shattering eruption, his cry of joyous exultation reverberating in the still night air as he poured himself into her.

They climaxed simultaneously, the convulsing of their sweat-slick bodies as one, heightening and prolonging their ecstasy as they were helplessly thrown into a burst of exploding stars where their souls melted and fused.

It took awhile for them to recover from the

experience. It seemed an eternity before the world stopped spinning around them, their hearts stopped racing, and their muscles stopped trembling. Then when Adam could find the strength and the breath, he tightened his embrace on Anita and whispered in her ear where his head lay in the dark cloud of her hair, "Oh, God, how I love you!"

For the life of her, Anita couldn't respond. She was too full of emotion. It rose to a hard lump in her throat, and she knew if she tried to force the words out, she would start crying again. And then, to her utter dismay, that's exactly what she did.

When Adam felt a teardrop on his shoulder, he raised his head, resting his weight on his forearms, and looked down at her in horror. "What's wrong? Why are you crying?"

"Because you love me," Anita sobbed. "Because I'm so happy I can't hold it in."

"Then it's not . . . not like last night?" Adam asked, a worried frown on his face.

"No, *mi amor*. These are simply a woman's tears of happiness."

Adam relaxed. Thank God. He didn't think he couldn't bear watching her go through another cataclysmic outburst like the one the night before. It had scared the hell out of him.

Knowing her tears were nothing but an expression of her happiness, a feeling of tenderness for her filled Adam. Lovingly, he kissed away Anita's tears and whispered soothing words while she quietly cried in his arms. When her tears were spent, he asked, "Are you through being happy now?"

Anita felt a little foolish. She was not one given to displays of emotions. Yet, two nights in a row, she had cried. She hoped she wasn't going to become one of those silly women who shed tears at the drop of a hat. "No, I'm still happy. I'm just more composed now. Why do you ask?"

Adam's eyes took on a smoldering quality as he gazed down at her. "Because I didn't want to interrupt your happiness with this."

Anita's eyes widened in surprise as she felt Adam move deep inside her. She hadn't even realized that he had not withdrawn. Now she could feel him, hot, immense and pulsating with the power of his desire. The second time Adam moved, her breath caught as an electric jolt danced up her spine, leaving her fingertips tingling. Her eyes darkened with passion, and she said in a husky voice, "I'm giving you fair warning, *mi amor*. If you make me too happy, I might cry again."

Adam smiled, a sensual smile that promised heaven and more. "I'll take that risk," he whispered against her lips just before his mouth closed over hers and he fulfilled his passionate promise.

* * *

It wasn't until the next day that Adam brought up the subject of the war, saying to Anita as she rode beside him, "I suppose you've heard that the new Mexican president has demanded that Santa Anna relinquish his position as commander-in-chief."

"*Sí,* I've heard. Presidente Pena has taken Santa Anna's power away from him and demanded that he prepare himself for an inquiry into his conduct in the war. I'm hoping the Pena government will find him guilty of treason and hang him."

"And if they don't?" Adam asked.

"Then it will be left up to you and your Rangers to bring him to justice."

Adam frowned. As far as the Mexican government and the United States were concerned, Santa Anna was out of the picture. But not the Rangers. They still sought revenge for the crimes he had committed against Texas. Anita understood the Texans' motives only too well. And so did Santa Anna.

"It may not be so easy to bring him to justice, Anita," Adam warned. "He's gone into hiding."

"I know. He's afraid of the Rangers' wrath. But you and your friends will find him. I have the utmost confidence in you."

When Anita and Adam reached Puebla, neither was surprised to find that Buck wholeheartedly

436

approved of their marriage. What did surprise them, however, was the giant's announcement that he would remain with the Rangers.

Anita looked around at the new quarters that she and Adam had just chosen, asking, "Why? Don't you like it here?"

"It ain't that," Buck answered. "You two are newlyweds. You need privacy to adjust to each other."

Adam almost laughed, thinking that he and Anita had been "adjusting" to each other for almost a year without any privacy. But the decision was Anita's.

As usual, Anita took the bull by the horns. "You're one of the family. You'll live with us."

The words were said with such decisiveness and authority that Buck didn't bother to voice an objection, and in truth, he was relieved. The Rangers' camp offered nothing in the way of comfort, and the food couldn't begin to compare with Anita's cooking. With a haste that brought a twinkle of amusement to Adam's eyes, Buck moved in.

Anita had hardly set up housekeeping when they were on the move again. But this time, the decision was not Adam's. It came from General Lane, who had been ordered to take his army to Mexico City.

Anita rode with Adam and Buck behind the

long column of Rangers. As they came into the capital city, the Mexicans crowded along the streets to get a look at the men whose reputations had preceded them, their eyes filled with fear and grim fascination. Over and over, Adam heard the muttered words, *"Los Diablos Tejanos,"* and *"Los Tejanos Sangrientes"*—the bloody Texans. He squirmed in his saddle, shame licking at his soul.

But the Mexicans weren't the only ones staring. The Americans did their share too. Seeing a group of soldiers looking at them with openmouthed wonder, Buck asked, "What in the hell are they gawking at?"

"I imagine that we Rangers look rather outlandish," Adam answered tersely. "Look around you. We wear no uniforms. Some of us wear long-tailed blue coats, some short, bobbed black coats, and some, like you and me, serapes. There's every imaginable kind of hat present—felt ones, dirty panamas, leather caps, sombreros, coonskins, and most of the Rangers have long bushy beards. Even our mounts are an odd assortment, all sizes and breeds, some mustangs, some thoroughbreds. Add all that to the arsenal we're carrying on our horses, and we look like a bunch of savages, or, at best, mountainmen."

"What's wrong with beards?" Buck asked defensively, stroking his bushy growth.

"Nothing, if they're well kept. But that's my point. The Rangers take no pride in their personal

438

appearance."

"I think you are being too hard on your friends," Anita said, surprising Adam with her defense. "It's not their fault that they have no uniforms and they have to suffice with whatever they can pick up. And no wonder their clothes are in filthy tatters, considering they have been camped in the open and fighting guerrillas almost nonstop."

Adam and Buck had seen no action since the siege at Puebla had been lifted. Adam assumed that Hays had felt they had done their share of fighting before the Rangers even arrived on the scene and had given them a brief respite. Secretly, Adam was glad. He dreaded going back to war, fearing the battles would be followed with a repeat of what happened at Huamantla. But he had volunteered his services freely, even enthusiastically, and Adam was not a man to go back on his word.

Buck had been pondering what both Adam and Anita had said. He sided with Anita. "Yeah, why are you being so hard on the boys?"

Adam didn't answer. How could he tell Buck that he was seeing the Rangers with new eyes, as others saw them—not just their sloppy appearance, but their savagery. A new guilt rose in Adam, feeling that he was betraying his own with his new insight. Many of these men were old friends, men he had ridden with, talked to for long hours into the night, men whose good shooting had even

439

saved his life a time or two. Surely, right or wrong, he owed them something.

The three settled down in their new quarters in Mexico City, and once more, Anita worked her magic, turning the hovel into a place with a cozy, homelike atmosphere. Watching the transformation, Adam wondered what she would do with his home back in Texas. He had certainly let it get run-down. But he had no doubts that Anita would set things to right there, with her amazing energy and determination. And probably the ranch, too, he thought wryly. Nothing was too big for her to tackle.

Weeks passed without the Rangers being called up, and Adam was glad. He still hadn't come to terms with his guilt. On the other hand, he grew restless, for he was a man accustomed to activity, and sitting around doing nothing wore on his nerves.

The inactivity wore on Buck's nerves, too. One day, his frustration came to the fore, and he spat, "If something doesn't happen soon, I'm gonna pull out—and Hays be damned! Hell, these peace talks ain't getting us anywhere. Let's either fight or go home. I can't even remember what Martha looks like, it's been so long since I've seen her."

"Well, thank God, Trist ignored Polk's recall," Adam commented. "Otherwise, we might be stuck down here forever."

"Yeah, if that don't beat all," Buck said in disgust. "First Polk sends Trist down here to negotiate peace, and then when the Meskins are finally on the verge of signing, Polk tells Trist to forget it and come home."

"Polk is under a lot of political pressure. Some Democrats are pressing for more than California and New Mexico. They've decided that they want all of Mexico."

Anita whirled around, dropping the broom she had been sweeping with. "All of Mexico?" she asked Adam in a shocked voice. "You aren't serious?"

"Yes, I am. And Polk is considering asking for more territory than he originally planned. He feels the Mexicans owe it to the United States as indemnity for the toll in blood and from the treasury the war has cost the Americans."

"Cost the Americans?" Anita shrieked, causing both men to jump at her sudden explosion. "What about the Mexicans? We've taken a toll in blood, too, much more than you gringos. It was the gringos who invaded us, who destroyed our property, who ravished our land. We've paid ten times the price you gringos have paid. Indemnity, bah! It is nothing but you gringos' greed for land."

Adam knew that everything Anita said was true. He could have ended her tirade by just agreeing with her. But, at that moment, Adam needed a good healthy argument. "Well, don't blame me!" he yelled back. "And don't call me a gringo. I'm a Texan! And the only territory I fought for was what already belonged to Texas."

"What territory?" Anita asked in a biting voice.

"You know damned right well what territory I'm talking about! The land between the Nueces and Rio Grande. It belongs to Texas, by right of the Treaty of Velasco."

"The piece of paper that coward, Santa Anna, signed?" Anita asked with a sneer. "That treaty was not made in the interest of Mexico. Santa Anna was only trying to save his own miserable neck. He would have signed away the moon, if the *Tejanos* had asked him to."

"Don't try and give me that hogwash that because Santa Anna was coerced into signing, the treaty was invalid. Santa Anna was the President of Mexico. He had the authority to sign. Mexico should have honored his word."

Buck had been watching the argument in dismay, his shaggy head bouncing back and forth between Adam and Anita like a tennis ball. He had thought that the couple's relationship would alter after their marriage, but nothing had changed. Anita was still as cool and reserved as ever in Adam's presence, and the two still seemed to go out of their way to pick fights with each other. It wasn't that he had expected them to become all lovey-dovey. That mushy stuff would have made him just as uncomfortable as their fighting. But there were other, more subtle ways of showing one's affection. He and Martha did it by teasing each other unmercifully.

Seeing Anita open her mouth to hurl back another retort, Buck decided that now was just as good a time as any to make his exit. He rose, cutting across Anita's, "Don't speak to me of honor!" by saying, "If you two don't mind, I think I'll go for a walk."

Buck's calm words had the effect of a dash of cold water on Adam and Anita's heated argument. They watched in silence as he ambled heavily to the door.

As the door closed softly behind him, Anita sighed deeply. "We should have never married. We fight too much."

"We don't fight. We just argue a lot."

"No. We fight!"

"All right, so we fight," Adam conceded. "But right now, I feel better than I have for days. Fighting relieves tension. Besides, I think what your grandfather said is true. He told me that a worthy adversary was as essential to a man as a trusted friend. At the time, I thought he was crazy, but now I see the truth of it. I'm a man who needs an adversary in my life, and I think you do, too. So you see, we're perfectly suited. We're both adversaries and lovers to each other."

"My grandfather is dead."

Adam wasn't surprised. He had known the proud old man was dying when they left Monterrey, and he didn't question how Anita knew he had died. She had an uncanny way of sensing things. But what did surprise Adam was how Anita could sound so sad and yet show no emotion on her face. He didn't understand her, and doubted if he ever would. She was a complex puzzle that fascinated him. Perhaps it was just as well that her essence eluded him. Adam had the lawyer's delving mind, if not their tastes in surroundings, and trying to figure out the mystery of Anita would be a lifetime challenge for him.

Anita turned to pick up her broom. Adam caught her hand as it descended and pulled her toward the bedroom.

Guessing his intent, Anita came to a halt. "No, Adam. Not in broad daylight. Buck might come back and guess what we're doing."

Adam could only stare at Anita. Once again, she had contradicted herself. Usually so straightforward and logical, her reasoning seemed ridiculous. Adam laughed. "And what do you think Buck has been thinking we've been doing all these nights? Playing tiddledywinks?"

Seeing her still hesitant, Adam dropped his voice and said softly, "Remember what I said? We're adversaries and lovers. We've had our fight, and now it's time for the loving."

Looking into the green eyes that shimmered with

promise of sensual delights, Anita couldn't deny him, any more than she could deny herself her own breath. Yes, he was her worthy adversary and her exciting lover, and much more. Adam was her very life.

Chapter 25

The next day, Buck rushed into the house, and breathlessly said to Adam, "Guess what I just heard over at the Ranger camp. Adam Allsens of Robert's company was murdered last night down at Cut-throat. Stabbed to death. When the boys found his slashed body, almost twenty-five of his company marched right into Cut-throat and avenged his death. Killed eighty of those sneaky, murdering greasers."

Adam felt sick. He had heard other reports of the Rangers' senseless killing since they had arrived in Mexico City. One had shot a sneak thief who had stolen his handkerchief and refused to stop when the Ranger yelled at him. Another had shot a Mexican who threw a stone at him. And now this.

"Where is Cut-throat?" Anita asked.

"That's that part of Mexico City where all those

446

young thieves and cutthroats hang out."

"The *leperos?*"

"Yeah. The boys figured the *leperos* were the ones who murdered Allsens, since they're so handy with those knives of theirs. They've been picking off American soldiers right and left for months now. Well, the boys showed them some of our Ranger justice. An eye for an eye and a tooth for a tooth. They won't mess with us Rangers no more."

Adam held his silence, deeply troubled.

Several days later, Hays came to call. Adam knew by the deep scowl on his boyish face that this was not a social visit.

As soon as he was seated, Hays said, "I've just come from General Scott. Actually, I've been to see him twice today. It's the first visit that I'm fuming over. I hope you don't mind if I blow off a little steam."

"No, of course not," Adam replied, curious to know what had upset Hays so badly. Usually, the colonel was as cool as a cucumber.

"Did you hear about that incident down in Cutthroat?"

Adam frowned, then answered, "Yes, I did."

"Well, Scott was already upset about that. A number of Mexican businessmen complained and demanded that he keep the Rangers off the streets.

Then there was another incident last night. Some of the boys shot some more Mexicans. Scott called me into his office, and he was livid. He told me he held me responsible for the actions of my men, that he wouldn't be disgraced, nor shall the Army for such outrages."

"And what did you say?" Adam asked.

"Well, I was hopping mad. He made it sound like the Rangers were the only ones having trouble getting along with the Mexicans. But you know yourself that the occupation here in Mexico City hasn't gone smoothly. At first, the sniper attacks were so bad that Scott had to order the streets swept with grape and canister and the big guns turned on the houses they were hiding in. And long before we showed up on the scene, there were some ugly incidents between the troops and the Mexicans. It's those thirty thousand convicts that Santa Anna turned loose when he pulled out who are causing all the trouble. Those who didn't run off to join the guerrillas crowded into Cut-throat, using it as a base for their operations. If Scott would just give us permission, we could clean that rat's nest in no time, but he won't. Those are civilians, he says. Why, they're nothing but criminals—common outlaws! Then, when some of the boys kill a few of them, the Mexicans get all hot and bothered. Hell, those scoundrels would have been hung by now if Santa Anna hadn't turned them loose on the Americans."

Hays took a deep breath, trying to calm himself, then continued. "So you see why I wasn't very receptive to Scott's criticism. I told him that the Rangers aren't in the habit of being insulted without resenting it, that in my opinion, the boys had done right, that I was willing to be held responsible for it."

"And what did Scott have to say to that?"

"He dismissed me with a firm warning to keep my men in line. But, Adam, there's no way I can control over four hundred men, not here in the city with all these saloons around, with those *leperos* baiting them at every turn. The boys are growing restless. They're just itching for a fight. What they need is action. So I turned right around and went back to Scott. I proposed an expedition against Padre Jaruata and his band. Scott was so anxious to see us out of Mexico City, he approved it on the spot."

Adam sucked in his breath. If Hays had gone looking for a worthy opponent for the Rangers to fight, he had certainly found one. Jaruata's infamous band of guerrillas was the toughest and meanest in all of Mexico. They had ravaged American supply trains coming from Veracruz, burned American outposts, murdered captured prisoners. They used their sabers, *escopetas*, even the lassos they slung over their shoulders, with deadly expertise. And they were all accomplished horsemen. Said to be four hundred fifty strong, Jaruata's

449

band were fierce fighters, so far unbeaten. The Rangers had their work cut out for them.

As Anita bent and poured Hays a cup of tea, the colonel looked up and asked her, "Is Jaruata really a priest?"

Adam smiled. Hays had made several visits since their arrival in Mexico City. Adam assumed that the colonel was trying to prove his friendship was genuine. On the first visit, Hays obviously had been uncomfortable. Then, as if she had sensed what was going on, Anita had set out to put the colonel at ease. Adam would never tell Anita to her face that she had a lot of her father in her, knowing that it would infuriate her, but she had inherited Santa Anna's determination, his indomitable will, and his ability to charm even the hardest and most suspicious critics—if it so suited her. Hays had fallen beneath her charm as if he had been smitten by a sword, so much so that he sought her counsel when it came to dealing with the Mexicans.

"No, Jaruata is not a priest," Anita answered, her voice dripping with scorn. "It's true he attended the seminary, but he was never ordained."

"Then why does he call himself a padre?" Hays asked.

"Because he knows the hold the Church has over the Mexican people, particularly the poor and illiterate. For centuries, they have been taught that a priest can do no wrong, to disobey one would

450

damn them to the fires of hell. And so Jaruata tells them he is a padre, to get them to do what he wants. He and his band live off the peons, as if the poor do not have enough of a struggle to feed and shelter themselves."

"I see," Hays said thoughtfully, then added, "Thank you, Anita. Perhaps that bit of information will come in handy."

After Hays had finished drinking his tea, he rose. "I hate to cut my visit short, but if we're going to pull out tomorrow, I'd better get busy."

"Tomorrow?" Adam asked in a shocked voice. "We're leaving tomorrow?"

"Yes, and would you pass along the word to Buck for me? We'll leave at dawn."

After Hays left, Adam fell to brooding. Anita had said the guerrillas lived with the peasants. It was inevitable that innocent bystanders would be killed. Besides, the guerrillas weren't trained soldiers, professionals. They were common men who were fighting for their country. Adam didn't want to go. Huamantla haunted him day and night. He didn't think he could survive another senseless rampage of murder and looting.

When Buck returned later that evening, Adam told him what Hays had said. He was excited at the prospect of a new campaign, so much so that he didn't notice Adam's glum expression or his virtual silence. But Anita did.

As soon as the bedroom door had closed behind

them that night, Anita turned to Adam, saying, "You are troubled."

"Yes," Adam admitted reluctantly. "I don't particularly want to go tomorrow."

"Why not?"

Dammit, why did she always have to have such a direct way about her? Adam thought in frustration. "For the same reasons no man likes to go to war," Adam lied smoothly. "Maybe I'm afraid I'll get killed. I don't want to leave you unprotected."

"You are afraid, but not for those reasons. You've been deeply troubled for some time."

Why did she have to persist? Didn't she realize that she was picking at his soul? Then Adam saw the compassion in Anita's dark eyes, and suddenly he wanted to relieve himself of the awesome burden he had been carrying.

The words came flooding from him in a torrent as he related the horrors that he had seen at Huamantla, admitted to the guilt and shame that his new insight had brought him, revealed his fear for his soul, his torn feelings about his fellow Rangers. Anita listened wordlessly, wisely knowing that Adam was purging his soul. When Adam finished, he felt weak, drained of all strength. He opened his eyes to find himself on his knees with his head in Anita's lap and wondered when she had sat on the bed and he had knelt before her like a supplicant confessing his sins. But then, isn't that what he had been doing? Confessing his sins?

Anita ran her fingers through Adam's dark hair, saying softly, "There is a beast in all men, not just you *Tejanos*. All human beings must work at keeping their individual demons at bay. You have finally recognized your beast and chained it."

Adam's head jerked up. "Dammit, it's not that simple! Do you expect my guilt just to vanish?"

"You have admitted your guilt to yourself, to God, and to me. You have shown your sorrow for your sins. Why must you punish yourself further? Have you not paid enough penance? God has forgiven you. I have forgiven you in the name of my people. Can you not forgive yourself?"

"Those were past sins. And I don't want to commit new ones. That's why I'm so worried about this new expedition. Those guerrillas aren't paid soldiers, trained in the art of fighting. They're peasants, patriots fighting for their country."

"Padre Jaruata and his band are patriots?" Anita asked in an incredulous voice. Then she scoffed. "No, Adam. That band didn't originate with the war. Jaruata's followers are a mangy assortment of common bandits and insurrectionists, making their own law of the land, and that law is the bullet. Now they call themselves guerrillas to hide their lawless acts behind a screen of false patriotism. They care nothing for Mexico or its people. They are nothing but leeches, as much, or more so, than Santa Anna. I told you that they

453

live off the poor, gorging themselves and dancing at fiestas that they demand the peons hold in their honor. And worse, the peon youths idolize them. They think they are gods, not men, and they lie and steal for them, dreaming of the day when they can be one of them. Jaruata's band are a scourge to Mexico. Your Rangers would be doing my country a favor by destroying them."

"And so you pit the Texas devils against your Mexican devils?" Adam asked bitterly.

"Sí. Sometimes it takes fire to fight fire. The Mexican government has not been able to bring them to justice. Perhaps your Rangers can."

"Haven't you forgotten something?" Adam asked in a hard voice. "What about your precious peons? Didn't you say the guerrillas lived with them? Innocent people are bound to get killed."

"It would not be the first time the innocent have been accidentally killed in this war," Anita pointed out.

"I'm not talking about accidental killing! I'm talking about deliberate killing! I'm talking about a repeat of Huamantla. Once the Rangers' blood lust is aroused, there's no telling what they will do."

"And you? When your blood lust is aroused, will you kill innocents, too?"

"My, God, no! Haven't you heard anything I've been telling you? I don't want to go tomorrow because I can't stomach another Huamantla. I

454

can't stand seeing innocent people murdered. It makes me furious. I want to kill them, my fellow Texans!"

"And now that you have judged yourself, you make yourself their judge and executioner?"

"No . . . no, I don't want to do that," Adam answered in an agonized voice. "That's the problem. My God, Anita, most of the Rangers are my friends. I can't turn my back on them, and I can't condone what they do, either."

Anita could see Adam's dilemma. He was torn between his loyalty to his friends and his newly awakened social conscience. Anita framed Adam's head in her small hands and pulled him to her breast. "No, no, *mi amor,* you must not take on the burden of their sins, too. No man can carry that burden. You are answerable only for your own. Each man must follow the dictates of his soul, for better or worse. Each man must fight his own battles against his beast. You cannot fight them for your friends. It's enough that you have conquered your own. Leave their souls to them, and to God, and do not judge them or make demands upon them. You cannot force them to change their ways or their feelings. No one can. That will have to come from within them, as it did with you."

Anita lay back on the bed, bringing Adam half over her, still holding his head against her breast in the age-old manner that women have comforted their loved ones since the beginning of time. Lying with his head nestled between her soft breasts and his arms around her, Adam felt at peace for the first time in years. His hate, his guilt, his fear, his doubts were all finally put to rest. And he felt closer to Anita than he ever had, even in their most intimate moments. Perhaps it was the very lack of that passion, with its dulling effect on the senses, that made him so acutely aware of this new oneness, which seemed to transcend the physical and reach into the spiritual plane. It was the ultimate fusing of two souls, one tortured and one soothing. The process of Adam's healing was completed that night.

Chapter 26

The next morning, the Rangers, with Adam and Buck amongst them, rode out of their camp at the southern edge of Mexico City in two columns, one with the Texas flag whipping over their heads, and the other with the Stars and Stripes snapping in the breeze.

They headed east into the Valley of Mexico, where it was said that Padre Jarauta and his band lived when they weren't marauding. For months, they searched the entire valley, passing through little villages where the peons stared at them with hostile eyes and insisted that they knew nothing of Padre Jarauta or his whereabouts, then, hearing a rumor, riding like mad to the place, only to find no enemy.

One night when Adam and Buck were bedding down, Buck said, "Damn, I'm tired of all these wild-goose chases. Chase here, chase there, and then when we get there, all we find is nothing!"

457

Buck gazed off into space. "I wonder how Martha and the boys are getting along?"

If Buck had asked that question once, he had asked it a hundred times in the last month. Adam knew the giant was homesick. So was he, for that matter. He was sick of the constant moving about, sick of the fighting, sick of the killing, sick of the abject misery he saw in every Mexican village he rode through, sick of Mexico. Recently, the seed that Anita's grandfather had planted in his mind about crossing longhorns with good breeds of cattle had taken root and grown. He was anxious to get back to his ranch and experiment. And his dream for a cattle empire had been resurrected, a dream he knew Anita, with her ranching blood, would share with him and work just as hard to attain. Yes, he wanted to go home to Texas, to resume his life, to put the past behind him and build for the future.

A flurry of sudden activity around him caught Adam's attention. "What's going on?" he asked.

"Mount up, boys!" Hays called out. "We finally got a clue where the padre's secret hideout is. Zacualtipan! Two days' ride from here."

"Did you hear that?" Buck asked, jumping to his feet. "We're finally gonna catch Jarauta. Hell, he's been as hard to track down as that sly old fox, Canales."

"We never did catch Canales," Adam reminded Buck as he came wearily to his feet. "This might be just another wild-goose chase."

458

For once it wasn't. The second morning out, just as the sun was rising, the combined column of dragoons and Rangers swooped down on Zacualtipan, catching the guerrillas completely by surprise. They stormed the plaza, where the half-dressed Mexicans had gathered for a hasty defense. The battle that followed was as fierce and savage as any Adam had seen. Six-shooters and *escopetas* roared at point-blank range, bullets tearing through heads and stomachs. Horses reared, wall-eyed and pawing the air, and lassos whizzed overhead. Americans and Mexicans wrestled on the ground, slashing with the long knives.

Adam fought with only one reason and one thought — to survive, and the long battle was an eternity of hell for him. Finally, in the middle of the afternoon, the padre and what was left of his band fled into the mountains.

The Texans and the dragoons in the plaza cheered and clapped each other on the back, proud of their victory. Even if the padre himself had managed to escape, they knew that his band had taken a beating they would never recover from. Adam staggered wearily to the fountain and sat down. He looked at the slashes on his shirt in stunned surprise, thinking it nothing short of a miracle that he had survived.

Buck lumbered over from the crush of men with whom he had celebrating to where Adam sat. "That was some fight, huh? Almost worth all that chasing around we did. And we'll get the padre the next time."

Seeing the fresh blood on Buck's sleeve, Adam asked in alarm, "What happened to your arm?"

"Oh, it ain't nothing. Bullet just grazed it. Kinda hope it was deep enough to leave a scar, though. I'd hate to go back to Texas with nothing to show Martha and the boys. Wouldn't want them to think I was making up tall tales when I tell them all that you and me have gone through down here." Buck swept his coonskin cap from his head and looked down at it sadly. "I sure wish that greaser hadn't shot the tail off my lucky hat, though. I was kinda attached to it. You know, it ain't often that you find a coon with a tail that long." Buck looked around the plaza that was strewn with both American and Mexican dead. "You suppose if I look around for it, I can find it?"

Adam could only stare at his friend, thinking that war was absolute insanity.

When the Rangers returned to their camp outside Mexico City, they were hardly out of their saddles when they heard the startling news. Over three weeks before, on February 2, in a small, insignificant Mexican town named Guadalupe Hidalgo, in utmost secrecy, the peace treaty had finally been signed. Except for ratification by Congress, the war was over.

Among the Rangers the reaction to the news was

460

mixed. Many, like Adam and Buck, were glad it was over and anxious to go back to their homes in Texas, but just as many were bitter, feeling they had not received their fill of revenge.

After getting permission from Hays to leave camp, Adam and Buck rode back to the little house in Mexico City where Anita was awaiting. This time she didn't hide her relief to see them, hugging both men fiercely. Then seeing the blood-stain on Buck's shirt, she demanded that he sit down and let her have a look at it.

Buck stripped off his shirt and proudly showed her the long scratch on his arm. To Anita's credit, she didn't demean it. Instead, she made a big show of cleaning and dressing it. Adam sat back and watched in amusement as Buck lapped up the attention.

Adam glanced up at Anita's face, noting that there was a certain radiant glow about her. "I take it you've heard the good news that the war is over," Adam said, assuming that the glow came from her happiness that Mexico's ordeal had finally ended.

Anita's expression darkened, blotting out the beautiful radiance. "*Sí,* I'm glad that it's over—at last." Tears shimmered in her eyes as she said, "But the terms for peace were so humiliating for Mexico. To lose half of our territory. *Madre de Dios!* Half! Mexico will never be able to hold her head up amongst the other nations again. We are shamed."

Adam didn't comment. The United States had gotten the territory it wanted, and the Mexican War had gone down in the annals of history. Adam wondered how future generations would judge it. It had marked the coming of the United States as a power to be contended with among other nations, but he feared it would leave a taint on his country's integrity.

The sad look on Anita's face was replaced with one of anger. Her dark eyes flashed. "And even worse, Santa Anna is still free. He drew the war out and caused Mexico's blood bath, and he walks away—free! The Pena government did nothing to punish him," she said bitterly. "And now he is leaving the country—at his request."

"When did this happen?" Adam asked.

"I heard the news after you and Buck had left. Santa Anna tried to go to Oaxaco to continue to war from the southern provinces, but its governor, Benito Juarez, refused him entrance. At least there is one man in Mexico who sees through Santa Anna and is not afraid to defy him. After Juarez turned him down, Santa Anna requested permission to leave Mexico."

"I can't say that I blame him," Adam commented. "After all the ruckus he's stirred up and its disastrous results, I imagine he's added even more to his ranks of enemies. Mexico isn't exactly a healthy place for him right now. He probably lives in constant fear of assassination."

"I only wish someone *had* assassinated him,"

Anita said fervently.

"Gosh, I'm sorry, Anita," Buck said, entering the conversation. "I guess we Rangers really let you down. But, believe me, we tried to catch him and bring him to justice."

"I know," Anita replied with a heavy sigh. "It's not your fault. Adam warned me in the beginning that I might have to settle just for Santa Anna's downfall . . . but I had hoped for more."

On March 18, 1848, the Rangers rode out of Mexico City, their part in the Mexican War finished. Anita rode with Adam and Buck at the back of the column. When they reached the pass in the mountains that overlooked the Valley of Mexico, they turned their horses and looked back. From that distance, Mexico City, with its domes and towers gleaming in the sunlight, looked as beautiful and peaceful as it had the first time they had seen it, revealing none of its battle scars. But Anita knew that they were there, marked for eternity in the walls of Molina del Rey, the castle at Chapultepec, the *garitas* at Belén and San Cosme. The heart of Mexico had taken a tremendous beating, and she wondered if the Mexican people would ever forgive their northern neighbors.

As they wheeled their horses back around to join the column of Rangers threading their way through the pass, Buck asked Adam, "Did you hear Hays's announcement before we pulled out?

He said we're going to Veracruz to be shipped out. Christ, after all this, I'm gonna get blown to pieces on one of those goddamned steamers!"

"You weren't paying very close attention," Adam answered. "Hays said we'd be mustered out first, then board the transports. Once we're mustered out, we can do as we please. Stay in Mexico, go back to Texas overland, or go home by transport. We're going back to Texas the same way we came—by horseback."

"I'm relieved to hear that," Anita admitted. "I, too, have been anxious. I can't swim."

"Well, there was no need for you to worry about that. If the ship were to sink, Buck and I would have saved you."

"Nope, not you and me. I can't swim, either," Buck confessed.

Adam stared at him in disbelief. "You never told me that."

"Well, hell! What grown man wants to admit he can't swim? Besides, I figured you'd guessed it. Didn't you ever notice how I clung to my horse for dear life when we were fording rivers, or how I hung back to see how deep the water was when we were crossing on foot?"

Adam grinned, his green eyes twinkling. "Well, I guess it's a good thing we're going back overland. I'd hate to have to tow you and Anita all the way back to Texas."

Anita smiled to herself. Since the night Adam had revealed his guilt and fears to her, he had

464

been a different man, and she liked this man, as well as loved him.

Taking the National Highway, they passed through Puebla, Perote, Cerra Gordo, all bringing back memories both good and bad.

Ten days after leaving Mexico City, they rode into the valley where Japala sat. Because they had tarried that day admiring the beautiful scenery around them, the trio reached the Rangers' camp later than the others that afternoon. The place was in a turmoil.

"What's going on?" Adam asked one Ranger as he dismounted.

"We heard Santa Anna is coming down that road on his way to exile," the Ranger answered, pointing to the National Highway a distance away. "Coming this afternoon! All the boys wanted to kill him, but Hays said we'd do no such thing, that Santa Anna was traveling under a safe-conduct pass signed by General Scott himself. Hays made us pitch camp here and told us to stay put."

Adam looked around the camp. "Where is Hays?"

"He and some of the other officers rode to Japala, where the Mexicans are planning on having a big celebration in honor of Santa Anna this evening. Hays told Adjutant Ford that he wanted to have a few words with his old enemy."

"Then Ford is in charge here now?" Adam asked.

"Yeah. Hays and the others left about an hour

465

ago. But the boys have been thinking over what he said, and we don't like it. A lot of us have old grudges against Santa Anna. Many of us had friends at the Alamo, and Goliad, and Mier. Dammit, Santa Anna ain't nothing but a murdering polecat, and we're gonna kill him when he passes by. By God, we're gonna kill him!"

Adam looked around him. The entire Ranger camp was in a white heat of fury. The Rangers wanted revenge, and Adam wished that Hays hadn't left. The Rangers respected him as they did no other. But then, maybe even Hays couldn't talk them out of it. Adam feared that no power on earth could stop them.

A rider shoved his way through the crush of angry men and stood in his stirrups. Adam recognized him as Rip Ford.

"Calm down, boys!" the adjutant called out. "I know how you feel. But stop to think of what the consequences will be. Santa Anna's traveling under a safe-conduct pass signed by General Scott himself! You all know what the penalty for violating a safe-conduct pass is. Death!"

"I ain't scared of Scott!" one Ranger called out.

"Me neither!" another yelled.

"Santa Anna waged an inhuman and unChristian war against us!" someone in the crowd shouted. "He should be punished!"

"He murdered prisoners of war in cold blood!"

"Yeah, I had a brother at Goliad!" Buck joined in. "Are you telling me to forget that?"

"What about the men who died at the Alamo?" a tall, lanky man at the back of the crowd yelled. "I'm from Gonzales. I had friends in those volunteers who slipped in right before the battle. We all know what Santa Anna did to them. Killing every single man wasn't enough. He had to strip and burn their bodies, too!"

"And look at the way he butchered those prisoners at Goliad!" another Texan yelled. "Cut them up into little pieces!"

Angry mutters came from all around him, and Adam could feel the Rangers' hate like a living, palpable thing. That old sick feeling rose in him. This is going to be another Huamantla, he thought in despair, except this time it was aimed at only one Mexican, the one who the Texans hated above all others — Santa Anna.

"Yes," Ford yelled above the angry murmurs, "I know what Santa Anna did at Goliad, but didn't the world condemn him for that? That was a stain on his reputation as a soldier. Will you dishonor Texas and yourselves by killing him?"

"Santa Anna isn't a prisoner of war!" someone shouted back.

"He's virtually a prisoner of war," Ford countered. "He's traveling under a safe-conduct pass granted by our own commanding general. To kill him under those circumstances would not be an act of war. It would be assassination. The whole world would condemn us for it. You would dishonor Texas!"

"Yes," another officer cried out, hoping to add his powers of persuasion to Ford's, "and wipe out all the good we've done in this war? Will you obliterate our good-service record, our good name as Texas Rangers by doing this? Shame Texas and yourselves?"

The Rangers glanced uneasily around at one another, and Adam knew that the moment of truth had come, just as it had come for him. Were they to act as beasts, or men of honor? True, there had been savage acts on their part, as on his own, some had even killed senselessly, but as a whole the Rangers had fought bravely and served with distinction, sincerely believing that their passion for revenge was a justified wrath, that they fought against political oppression and tyranny, that they fought for liberty and the rights of men. He held his breath, waiting for their decision, fervently praying that it would be the right one.

The long silence was finally broken as one man quietly said, "Then we won't kill him."

There was a murmur of agreement before one Ranger called out, "Can we at least see him when he passes?"

Ford knew that the men had given their word not to harm Santa Anna and gave his permission.

"Can we talk to him?" another asked.

Ford suggested that they hold their silence.

Grumbling beneath their breaths, the Rangers mounted and rode to the highway where Santa Anna would pass, forming a long line on both sides of the road. Adam, Buck, and Anita positioned their mounts a little farther down the road on a rise where they could see everything.

Adam glanced across at Anita. Her face was a thundercloud, her small body rigid with fury. He knew that she wasn't at all pleased with the Texans' decision. Adam had promised himself that he would give Anita anything her heart desired, but he couldn't give her Santa Anna's death. Not anymore. He was through with hate and senseless killing.

Seconds later, a rider tore down the road and reined in beside Ford, telling him that Santa Anna and his escort were just beyond the bend of the road. Every eye turned in that direction, everyone tense with anticipation.

The military escort appointed by General Scott came into view first, the American dragoons' saddles creaking as they trotted smartly down the dusty road. Behind them was an open carriage in which Santa Anna sat, the general dressed in one of his magnificent uniforms, the medals on his chest and the gold epaulets on his shoulders gleaming in the sun and the white plume on his tri-cornered hat fluttering in the breeze.

Adam glanced at the Rangers' weathered faces. One and all, they glared at their enemy with open hatred as the carriage passed, but not a curse or a single word passed their lips, nor was one fist raised. Adam was proud of them, knowing only too well what their self-discipline was costing them. At that moment, for the Texans who had come seeking revenge for the crimes perpetrated against them by this man, the price of honor was unbelievably high.

He looked back down at Santa Anna and knew that the general had recognized his old enemies from Texas. The color drained from his swarthy face. But to give the devil his due, Santa Anna faced the Texans bravely, sitting erect, not one facial muscle so much as twitching, as if he had decided if this was to be his final moment on earth, he would die as a true soldier should.

Adam turned his attention to the two women sitting opposite him in the carriage, both of a similar age to Anita. Santa Anna's wife was pretty in a childish sort of way, bowing and smiling at the Rangers, apparently totally oblivious to her husband's dangerous position. Turning his eyes to the second woman, Adam saw that Santa Anna's daughter sat as stiff and erect as the general himself. Adam stared at the woman who was Anita's half sister. She had her father's long nose, but otherwise her features were commonplace. She certainly didn't have Anita's exotic beauty, and Adam was left to conclude that Anita favored her mother.

As the carriage passed the rise where the trio sat on their horses, Santa Anna glanced up. For a split second, Adam saw the startled look in the general's eyes when he saw Anita, a lightning-quick expression that told Adam that Santa Anna knew who she was. Then the eyes swerved away to stare straight ahead, and Adam could have sworn that Santa Anna's face blanched even more.

As the carriage rolled away, the Mexican guard of honor passed, the cavalrymen's breast plates and long lances glittering in the sun. Behind him, Adam heard the jingling of reins and the squeaking of leather as the Rangers turned their horses and rode back to camp.

As Adam pulled on his reins to turn his mount, Anita cried out, "No!" and yanked the Colt from his saddle holster.

Buck stared in shock and disbelief as Anita raised the heavy gun with both hands and aimed it at Santa Anna's back. For a split second, Adam thought to stop her, knowing that to kill her enemy would be endangering her life. But he knew if he did, Anita would never forgive him. He remembered what she had said about every man having to chain his own demon. He had come to terms with his hatred and his thirst for revenge. Now it was Anita's moment of truth. He waited, tense and breathless.

Anita's arms trembled as she struggled to hold up the heavy gun, her face filled with rage, her finger twitching on the trigger. A minute passed, each second agonizingly slow. Then Anita's arms collapsed, and her shoulders slumped as the gun fell heavily to her lap. An immense wave of relief washed over Adam.

Tears streamed down Anita's face as she sobbed,

"I couldn't do it. I'm weak! I'm nothing but a coward."

Adam reached across and took the gun, slipping it back into its holster, then turned in his saddle to face Anita, saying in a firm voice, "No, you're not weak. And you're not a coward. You just have too much personal integrity to kill a man in cold blood. If you had, you would have been no better than he—a murderer."

"He'll come back. This is not the last Mexico has seen of that monster. Santa Anna will return and again bleed my country."

Adam didn't doubt Anita's words. From the very beginning, she had predicted what Santa Anna would do next. Adam thought that Anita knew the man better than he himself did.

"You can't change history, Anita. What's to be, is to be."

Anita remained grimly silent, staring off into space, and Adam knew that she was furious with herself for failing to attain her own personal revenge. He reached across the space that separated them and caught her arm, shaking it lightly and saying in a hard voice, "Give it up, Anita! It isn't worth it. I've had a taste of revenge. No!" Adam quickly corrected himself, "I've had a bellyful of it! It offers no satisfaction, and it leaves a bitter taste in your mouth."

Adam's voice softened. "Revenge can't bring back your mother or your family honor, no more than it could bring back my wife and brother and friends. It can't change the past. Nothing can! And we've both been living in the past too long. Put it behind you, Anita. Bury your hate, once and for all. Let's both stop being destroyers, and become what we were meant to be — builders. Look to the future. Our future." Adam exerted a gently pressure on Anita's arm. "Let's go home, Anita. To Texas and our future."

For a moment, Adam thought that Anita hadn't heard a word he said, but she had. Ever so slightly, her hands slipped to tenderly cradle her lower abdomen where deep inside her their tiny baby lay. She had not told Adam he was to be a father for fear he would insist the trip to Texas would be too hard on her and delay it until after the baby's birth. Anita would have none of that. If she could make it across the Sierras in dead winter, she could make it to Texas in the springtime, and she fervently wanted their child to be born in Texas, the land of its father, the land she had heard so much about but had yet to see. Yes, it was time to put the past behind them, to build for their future and that of their son, for Anita had already decided the baby would be a boy. And she knew in her heart that her grandfather would understand. She could almost feel him giving her his blessing.

She looked across at Adam and smiled. But it was not the smile that took Adam's breath away. His eyes were locked on her gaze. The warmth shimmered in her black, velvety eyes, passing over the distance between them, filling him with happiness and bringing a warm glow to his entire body. To Adam, it seemed as if he had waited an eon for this look of genuine warmth. He had never known such joy as he savored this long-awaited moment.

Suddenly, the smile was gone from Anita's face, and the warm look vanished. Her black eyes flashed as she said, "Perhaps I do not wish to live in Texas. Perhaps I wish to live in Mexico."

Adam knew exactly what Anita was up to and was in perfect accord. A little healthy argument would be stimulating right now. He turned his horse, snapping over his shoulder, "I don't give a damn what you wish. We'll live in Texas on my ranch."

Anita wheeled her horse, bringing it up beside Adam's. "No. We will live on *my* ranch, in Monterrey."

"The man chooses where a couple will live," Adam pointed out in a adamant tone of voice. "It's the wife's duty to follow her husband wherever he wants to go. Haven't you ever read the Bible? In the Book of Ruth, it clearly states, 'Whithersoever thou shall go, I will go: and where thou shall dwell, I will also dwell. Thy people shall be my—"

"I'm not Ruth. I am Anita! We'll compromise. We will live in Texas half of the year, and in Mexico the other half."

"Absolutely not! We'll . . ."

The voices faded away as Adam and Anita rode off. Buck stared at their backs and scratched his shaggy beard in puzzlement. Then he shook his head in exasperation, thinking that the two had to be the damndest pair of lovers on earth.

Epilogue

At the end of April, 1848, the Texas Rangers went home to resume their roles as guardians of the frontier.

The war changed nothing in Mexico. The poor and oppressed remained so, at the mercy of the aristocracy, the Church and the military and the Mexican government changed hands over and over in a never-ending struggle between those who lusted for power.

As Anita had predicted, Santa Anna returned to Mexico in 1853 and seized the reins of the government, declaring himself Supreme Dictator. In the two years that he held the country by the throat with his terrorism, he managed with his lavish living to drain the treasury so badly before he was overthrown and exiled to Cuba that his successor, Benito Juarez, was left with huge international debts which Mexico could not pay and which brought on another bloodbath for the country—the

476

French-Mexican War. Santa Anna tried to enter the country during this war, under his old guise as Mexico's guardian and defender, but Juarez, wise old Indian what he was, prevented his entry. Only after the death of Juarez did Santa Anna return for the last time. The opportunist extraordinaire, who had sought luxury and power his entire life, died in poverty and obscurity in the slums of Mexico City.

The war changed nothing in Texas, either. Stubbornly, the Mexican bandits refused to recognize the Rio Grande River as the international border and raided across it with more and more impunity. Doggedly, the Rangers chased them back over the river and administered their own brand of lethal justice. The cycle repeated itself over and over, keeping the hatred between the Texans and Mexicans alive. The hostilities on the bloody border between the two old enemies did not end until General John Pershing and his men crossed into Mexico and crushed Francisco Villa's army of bandits in 1916.

But in Texas, Anita and Adam put the old hatreds between their countrymen behind them. Using their considerable determination and energies, they built one of the largest and most successful ranches in the state to leave as legacy to their children and grandchildren, fighting like cats and dogs their entire lifetime together—and loving every minute of it.

ROMANTIC GEMS
BY F. ROSANNE BITTNER

HEART'S SURRENDER   (2945, $4.50)
Beautiful Andrea Sanders was frightened to be living so
close to the Cherokee — and terrified by turbulent passions
the handsome Indian warrior, Adam, aroused within her!

PRAIRIE EMBRACE   (2035, $3.95)
Katie Russell kept reminding herself that her savage Indian
captor was beneath her contempt — but deep inside she
longed to yield to his passionate caress!

ARIZONA ECSTASY   (2810, $4.50)
Lovely Lisa Powers hated the Indian who captured her, but
as time passed in the arid Southwest, she began to turn to
him first for survival, then for love!

FIERY ROMANCE

CALIFORNIA CARESS   (2771, $3.75)
by Rebecca Sinclair

Hope Bennett was determined to save her brother's life. And if that meant paying notorious gunslinger Drake Frazier to take his place in a fight, she'd barter her last gold nugget. But Hope soon discovered she'd have to give the handsome rattlesnake more than riches if she wanted his help. His improper demands infuriated her; even as she luxuriated in the tantalizing heat of his embrace, she refused to yield to her desires.

ARIZONA CAPTIVE   (2718, $3.75)
by Laree Bryant

Logan Powers had always taken his role as a lady-killer very seriously and no woman was going to change that. Not even the breathtakingly beautiful Callie Nolan with her luxuriant black hair and startling blue eyes. Logan might have considered a lusty romp with her but it was apparent she was a lady, through and through. Hard as he tried, Logan couldn't resist wanting to take her warm slender body in his arms and hold her close to his heart forever.

DECEPTION'S EMBRACE   (2720, $3.75)
by Jeanne Hansen

Terrified heiress Katrina Montgomery fled Memphis with what little she could carry and headed west, hiding in a freight car. By the time she reached Kansas City, she was feeling almost safe . . . until the handsomest man she'd ever seen entered the car and swept her into his embrace. She didn't know who he was or why he refused to let her go, but when she gazed into his eyes, she somehow knew she could trust him with her life . . . and her heart.